BLAINE L. PARDOE

TENURE

TENURE SERIES BOOK 1

FIND YOUR NEXT GREAT READ AT:

WarGatebooks.com

Blaine's Dedication:

Like many creators, I've been the target of woke activists. These online trolls smeared my name and reputation. They manufactured things I never said or did. They got me canceled from a franchise I had written in for thirty-six years. One stalker in particular threatened my life and is still barred from contacting me by a protective order. They tried to censor me, but failed miserably. You can't cancel someone who refuses to bend the knee to hate.

I learned a lot going through this experience. Chief among my lessons learned, no one is coming to help you. You have to rely on yourself.

Out of that came the impetus for the character Braxton Knox. He's a man who *will* come to help. While vigilantes are scorned, there are times when they are needed.

As such, I dedicate this book to anyone out there who has been wrongly targeted by self-proclaimed social justice warriors and/or the woke censorship crowd. Enjoy!

Mike's Dedication:

In the world of comics and graphic novels, we have a word for them. The Whisper Network.

I would dedicate this to my wonderful wife, Ann, who has been instrumental in my resurrection, but she can't read anything I write because it's too violent. Except for *Disco*. She loved *Disco*. So this is for Ann.

Acknowledgments:

Thank you to WarGate for publishing this book. Thanks as well to fellow author John Spears who helped me with some of the finer points of long-range marksmanship. Special thanks go out the team at Accuracy International of North America, Inc., and Vice President Scott Seigmund who hosted me for an orientation to their excellent weapon.

Thanks as well to films such as *D eath Wish* and *Falling Down* and the books about Max Bolan.

The age of men's adventure stories is back, with a vengeance!

Vigilante. noun. vig·i·lan·te, vij-ə-'lant-ē: An individual or member of a group who decides to stop crime, right wrongs, punish criminals, and administer justice (usually through violence). A righter of wrongs. Usually an anti-hero. The byproduct of when bad people push good people too far.

Chapter 1

The Worst Day Ever

It wasn't supposed to be one of the worst days of his life.

Professor Braxton Knox woke up that morning as he had hundreds of times. He kissed his wife and daughter goodbye on the way to his job at Eastern State University outside Portland. He had been raised in the Midwest. Oregon had never been on his list of places in which to live, but when the offer came through to teach at Eastern, he couldn't pass it up. Suzanna, his wife, had been supportive, despite being farther away from her family.

He always looked forward to Fridays. Grading papers, class prep, and one class in the morning. He would be home before traffic picked up. A quick stop off at Planet Fitness, then be in the driveway before his daughter, Angela, got off the bus. Easy peasy.

Fate had other plans.

As was his routine, he pulled into Wendy's for a breakfast sandwich. His wife had offered to cook him breakfast many times, but he enjoyed getting his sausage biscuit. The food wasn't good. No one bragged about the quality of Wendy's cuisine. It was consistent, and for Braxton, that counted. As he walked to the door, the short Hispanic manager tapped a sign. *Closed due to staffing*.

"Sorry, pal," the manager said.

"Hey," Braxton said. "What's the deal?"

The manager shrugged and spoke loudly to be heard through the door. "My whole team called out."

Braxton raised his voice. "How can your entire team call out?"

The manager cracked the door. "I'm sorry. I hired these kids, all college kids, and it turns out they're friends. They've got me over a barrel. When a party comes up, they call in at the last minute. There's just me and my drive-thru guy here, not enough to run the place."

"You should fire them," Braxton said.

"Then I'll be shut down completely. These kids know they're calling the shots. If I fire one, they'll all quit." His voice rang with desperation. It did nothing to assuage the wave of anger that washed over Braxton. Drawing a deep breath, he said, "I've been coming here for six years, like clockwork, every day at 0715. I need my breakfast biscuit."

"I'm sorry, sir. There's nothing I can do. There's a Wendy's off eighty-four in North Gresham."

Braxton spoke through a clenched jaw. "That's way out of my way."

"Sorry. There's nothing I can do."

Braxton knew the manager was sorry, but it didn't help. Sympathy for the man's plight nibbled at his attempts to keep his anger in check. He taught at Eastern State and knew the listless approach students took towards work. It wasn't that way when he was growing up. His father was a cop and an FBI agent the last fifteen years of his career. Braxton was expected to have a job after school. If he had skipped work to go to a party with friends, his father would have unleashed his belt to reinforce his work ethic.

"These damn kids…" he muttered.

"I agree," the manager said, closing the door.

Braxton drove through McDonald's down the block. As he glared at the menu, he saw all the prompts to download the app and order in advance. "Why should I do the work for you?" he muttered to himself as he finally pulled up. It was the same sort of logic as self-checkout lanes. They wanted him to do work the checkout staff should be doing. It bothered him that they had four people overseeing the self-checkouts, not to mention the security at the door to check his receipt when he left. All they had to do was put those people on registers and the problem would be solved. Instead, he felt as if they thought he was a thief, eyeing his receipt and what was in his cart.

Normally he went inside to place his order. Drive-up ordering was a source of frustration he strived to avoid. But time was short so he opted for the drive-thru, knowing he would likely regret it.

"Welcome to McDonalds," crackled the speaker.

"I'd like a sausage biscuit, please."

"Did you want that with egg?"

"Did I order the one with egg?"

"I'm sorry. What was that?"

He sighed, then continued, "No. Just a sausage biscuit."

"Two seventy-two. Please pull up."

It took a while to creep up to the payment window. He held out a five-dollar bill. The portly woman in the window seemed to wince upon seeing it. "Do you have any ones, sir?"

"No. Is there a problem?"

"We're out of ones. I'll have to give you the money in change, unless you want to put it on a card."

"How can you be out of ones? It's not even eight o'clock."

"We just are. Do you want to put it on a card instead?"

"No. Just give me the change."

It took her three minutes to calculate the amount. It wasn't even quarters. A half roll of dimes. She unceremoniously dumped them into his palm, almost spilling some of them. In disgust, he simply poured them out in the passenger seat. Pulling forward, he got his bag, and drove off.

Three blocks later, at a stoplight, he tore the wrapper open. "Damn it!" He pulled the slab of egg off, dropping it into the bag. It was too late. The aroma already tugged at his nostrils. Braxton tried to pretend that he couldn't taste the egg as he gulped down two bites before the light changed, but it was a lie.

Two blocks before he got to campus, his tire pressure warning light flickered, the product of a slow leak and procrastination. He pulled into a BP station, got out, and put in enough air to temporarily forestall the half-day he would need at the tire place. He didn't mind the waiting, but hated the upselling and shakedown they tried.

Maybe I can do it tomorrow.

After kneeling to pump in a few pounds, he rose. His pants knee hesitated, tugging downward. After recoiling the hose, he saw it, a pinkish smear on his knee. The gum had been camouflaged on the pavement with dirt and gravel, but now it clung to his knee. "Great," he muttered, "now I have to go to the dry cleaners tomorrow." He tried wiping it off, only to get gum on his hand. Despite being behind schedule, he paused to use the sanitizer.

Every time he used the bottle, it reminded him of the year-plus he'd spent virtually teaching his students. COVID had forced him to be not only an instructor, but tech support for students who couldn't care less about taking class online. He had given failing grades only to have the university override his decision. Braxton had been told that it would not be in the best interests of the students' academic career to penalize them. No one seemed to care that they had not done the work or even showed up.

He arrived at the campus and went to the commons building for coffee. It was the same barista that was always there. The order he placed was the same as every day. And, like every other day, the student employee mixed it and handed him the cup, having called his name. Braxton made sure the lid was on tight. She often didn't take the effort to do it right, resulting in a scalding hot splash on his hand. Glancing at the cup, he noticed his name was misspelled, as she did every day.

"You misspelled my name."

"What?"

"It's Braxton."

"That's what I wrote."

"No. There's no 'ck' in my name. It's written just like it sounds, with an x."

The barista glared at him. "So what? You understood me, didn't you?"

"I'd appreciate it if, in the future, you spelled my name correctly."

His words bounced off her armor of indifference. He glared. She glared. She didn't care. It mattered to him, though. He was proud of his name. It was a problem with the students. They didn't take pride in anything other than their emotions.

When he finally got to his office, he was fifteen minutes late. Braxton didn't have any appointments scheduled, but he always felt his day went better when he arrived on time, a byproduct of serving in the Army. His NCOs and officers had pummeled into him the gift of promptness, a lesson he had not shaken.

His military career was nothing special. No stories of glorious battles to tell his grandchildren. He'd been posted for three months overseas during the War on Terror, but had not seen any real action. He had been fired at, but it had been far from glorious. Other than deplorable living conditions and shitty food, it was like being anywhere else in the Army. Braxton had enlisted after high school for eight years. At one point, he had thought of making the Army a career. Braxton had even tried out for the Rangers, but had failed to make the cut. After that, he fell back on his original plan—leave the Army at the ignoble rank of Corporal and let the Army pay for his education.

But the Army had taught Braxton one skill: how to learn. He had gotten his bachelor's degree online, and his Master's and Doctorate on campus. That was where he had met his wife. She claimed she liked the fact that he was four years older than her, that he had a mature bearing about him. That was something else for which he thanked the military.

As he shuffled past his battered old desk, he noted how small his office was. That was going to change soon. He was on the short list for tenure. It hadn't been easy. All the diversity and inclusiveness initiatives on campus, and a highly agitated and liberal student community, made him uncomfortable. Gone were the days when you could have candid discussions with students. Braxton kept his comments to himself, sometimes walking away from people or situations he found infuriating. Once he had tenure, he promised himself he would relax.

He graded papers for American History 102 with a lack of enthusiasm. The students often wrote their tests as if they were texting, a jumble of incomplete sentences and half-thoughts. One even used acronyms that had nothing to do with the subject. Knox had a reputation as a strict grader. Students complained, but Dean Grooper had always backed him. Not that Grooper was a stalwart leader. Alistair Grooper usually took the path of least resistance in any decision. Despite Grooper's character weakness, Braxton considered him a friend.

Grades were always a point of friction—not just between him and the university, but between him and the students and their parents. The first time a parent called about his daughter's grade, he thought it was a prank call. It wasn't. Others did the same. He laid it out for one parent in plain English. "Look, this shit may have worked when they were in high school, but this is college. Your son didn't meet the academic requirements. No amount of nagging on your part is going to change that."

Halfway through his morning coffee, Braxton headed for the lecture hall. Today's topic was the US's role in the Great War, a talk he had given at least a dozen times. In the back of his mind he knew what the tiered lecture hall was going to be like. A minority of students would be listening intently. More would be on their phones, computers, and tablets—their minds far from the topic at hand. It was doubtful if any had read the material in advance. Some of the students took notes, assuming that what he said would be on the test. A few might try to derail the lecture, pushing some political agenda with meritless questions. A few would record his lecture on their phones, presumably to listen at their leisure. Those would be the inquiries that he would have to squash. There were always students out there that thought they knew more than he. Sometimes a good healthy debate led to actual learning.

Being a Friday morning, only around two-thirds of the students showed up for his class. He had been hired to teach Greek and Roman history, but the university had asked him to take on a one-hundred-level class on the twentieth century. The lecture started with the Wilson Administration's view towards neutrality. Shifting the talk, he mentioned the German sabotage of the armaments industry in the US, including the attack on Black Tom Island and the attempt to blow up the Capitol.

One of the more militant students, Debbie Driggs, raised her hand. He didn't dodge her questions, but she was always looking to frame history against the current political landscape. "Yes?" he asked, nodding.

"What you are saying is that the Germans were justified in attacking the western capitalist government that was selling arms that were being used to kill them back in Europe."

"No, that's not what I said. Germany was free to purchase arms as well. The US was still neutral in 1916. Germany was, in essence, waging a terroristic war against the American people at the time." Braxton had written the class textbook for the course, a brilliant moneymaking move if he ever saw one. Most professors and books overlooked what he was talking about. Braxton Knox made sure that history was not glossed over—that it was covered, warts and all.

"But the US was arming Britain and France in their illegal war."

"One could argue that all wars are illegal, if not immoral, Miss Driggs. That can't be used to justify blowing up factories and killing people."

"What did you just call me?" she said slowly, in a lower tone of voice. He saw other students lift their heads with her words.

For a moment, he was confused. "I didn't call you anything."

"You said, 'Miss Driggs.' My personal pronouns are they/them," she said boldly and proudly.

A flicker of anger burned in Knox's brain. "If you were offended by what I said, I'm sorry you feel that way."

"That wasn't an apology," she snapped. He saw several students holding up their phones, recording his reaction—which only made him angrier. "I want a full apology for your bigoted label."

"Bigoted? What did I do that was bigoted?"

"You didn't use my pronouns. That means you are homophobic."

Braxton rallied, if only for a moment. "I don't know anything about your sexual preferences. Nor do I care. They/them doesn't convey any of that either."

"You have to use my personal pronouns!"

Now all the students were paying attention, which only seemed to pour gasoline on his rage. For a moment, he tried to calm himself. His hands coiled into fists which he concealed behind the podium.

"No, I do not."

"Yes, you do!"

"While this isn't a civics class, let me give you a bit of education. Your desire to be called something does not override my First Amendment rights of free speech. I meant nothing by calling you 'Miss.' You, however, do not have the right to make me call you anything."

"I was right—you are a bigot."

"I advise you to be careful. What you are doing is slander and I will not tolerate it in my class."

Another student spoke up. "That's why I got a C on my last test. He's against gays."

"No," Braxton said. "That is incorrect. You got a C because you earned it. You missed a lot of questions on the last few assignments. I don't grade papers based on pronouns or anything else. You are all equal in my eyes."

"Then why not use her pronouns?" another student demanded.

The rage had reached its boiling point. "You think it's easy teaching you, having to watch what I say? I don't have a little chart up here with your name and photo and pronouns, nor will I teach my class that way. You are here at the university to learn. I am your instructor. Now, we are going to return to the topic of today's lecture."

The students stirred, then started to filter out. "We ain't staying with someone that doesn't respect us," another student stated. "You ain't going to be staying either once we show everyone who you *really* are."

Arms crossed, Braxton watched as they filtered out. In a matter of minutes, he was alone. "This day sucked," he growled to himself.

Chapter 2

The Spiral

The summons came at two, as Braxton ate his lunch. A ham and cheese sandwich from the student cafeteria. *At least there are no hairs in it this time.* Several times, Braxton had opened his sandwich to find facial hairs, although cafeteria workers were required to wear hair nets, both top and chin, if they had beards. He wondered why he continued to give them business.

Convenience and routine. Whereas his forefathers had fought every day just to survive—against bandits, tyranny, the plague, wolves—the modern American prized convenience above all. As long as there were no hairs, he considered himself victorious.

Braxton's office on the third floor of the Wyrick Building, named in honor of a generous alumnus, had a window overlooking the parking lot, rather than the sloping green commons with its statue of Abraham Lincoln at the top. Students had painted Abe red, black, and yellow, writing *Just Say No To Racist White Usurper, Dishonest Abe* and *Tool Of Oppression* on the curving concrete bench that circled Abe's back. Keeping the statue clean was a full-time job. And expensive. The Board of Regents was debating whether to replace Abe with a statue of Sojourner Truth or Nat Turner. Some students demanded Antonio Gramsci, Mao Tse Tung, or Karl Marx.

The parking lot was filled with Priuses, Teslas, and Fiats, rear bumpers festooned with bumper stickers. *Black Lives Matter. Women's Rights = Human Rights. Science is real. Love is love.* They were a reminder that he was a minority on campus.

The knock at the door.

"Come in," Braxton said, folding his sandwich in a napkin and putting it in a desk drawer. A young woman, half her head shaved, the other half blue, with a nose ring, wearing a rolled-up man's shirt and blue jeans with artfully ripped knees, entered with an envelope.

"What can I do for you, Magritte?"

"Professor Angesten asked me to deliver this letter."

"Thank you. How's your dissertation coming?"

Magritte's hands curled into claws. "It is just so infuriating to study that man, I only hope I can do the subject justice."

"What was it about again?"

"It's called Christopher Columbus: the Roots of Red Genocide."

"Ah. Good luck with that."

She let herself out. Braxton held the envelope, a corkscrew of anxiety drilling his heart. It wasn't sealed. He removed the crisp white linen letter folded in thirds and opened it, soaking in the emotionless Courier font:

Adjunct Professor Knox: You are summoned to appear before the Department of History Disciplinary Committee, ten a.m., March 12, Lumumba Hall, Room 336. Please come alone.

Yours,

Professor Emeritus Sylvia Baskin-Kulberg

Alone? Why alone?

A frisson of fear rippled Braxton's spine. He'd been at Eastern State seven years. For the first three years, students had provided overwhelmingly positive feedback. Then came the plague, the mandates, and two years of remote learning. Unlike many of his peers, Braxton did not enjoy teaching from home. He needed the human contact, that connection to ensure he was achieving his goals, and that the students were achieving theirs. Their papers, those that turned them in, took a turn for the worse, many of them filled with passionate screeds and appeals to the emotions, contrary to everything Braxton had learned. Especially in the Army.

Other students simply failed to deliver. When Braxton queried, through social media, many simply did not respond. When in-person classes finally resumed in Spring 2023, his class size had shrunk by thirty percent, and ninety percent of those attending wore masks. The lecture hall could accommodate three hundred. Prior to the plague, they filled most of the seats. Post-plague, some fifty returned, sitting as far as they could from their fellow students, spread out all over Ogden Luthor Lecture Hall.

Braxton carefully folded the letter, put it in the envelope, and tucked that in his jacket pocket.

Well, fuck. He'd hoped to avoid the culture wars. History was history. It was neither good nor bad. It was what happened, and he had tried to show that in every class. Some students liked to argue. Some students liked to posit. He'd had to deal with numerous challenges that the United States was irredeemably racist, that it had been founded by racists, that it was ruled by racists, that the president was a racist, and perhaps Braxton Knox was a racist. What business did a white man have explaining the Civil War to Students of Color? Or any student, for that matter? He prided himself on dealing with these provocations calmly and logically.

Since returning to in-person teaching, the challenges had increased in inverse proportion to dwindling attendance. He wondered what had set them off this time. Who was it? That smarmy little creep Elmer Kropotkin in the pea jacket and green beret with its red star? The corpulent hive-haired Eugenia Coleman who read Octavia Butler while Braxton spoke? Was it the Sandinista-boosting Geraldo de la Garza who only wanted to talk about the United Farm Workers?

Or was it Debbie Driggs?

He knew in his heart it was Driggs. The chip on her shoulder was huge and she practically dared people to knock it off. She was vegan. No need to ask; it was how she introduced herself. "Just so you know, I'm vegan. So please do not eat any meat or dairy products in my presence, as they can make me nauseous."

She was genderqueer. Whatever that was. It said so on her shirt. She had another shirt that said, "Neuroqueering is a rejection of able-hetero assimilation and counter-identification, in favor of disidentification." She was a walking billboard, a person broadcasting that she was looking for something to be offended by.

What did it have to do with American history?

"History deliberately obfuscates and hides the contributions of queer people of color!" So sayeth Debbie Driggs.

Braxton wanted a drink. He hadn't had a drink in twelve years, not since Suzanna read him the riot act. He was never a mean drunk. Just loud. How was he going to explain this to Suzanna? And Angela. She'd applied to Eastern State. She had a grade point average of four point four. They all assumed she was a shoo-in. Braxton envisioned the inevitable letter.

"We regret to inform you…"

He'd been counting on tenure. The dean had assured him he was on track and with all of the turnover of professors, it could happen soon. When he'd first mustered out of the Army, he'd lacked direction. He considered car salesman, real estate, advertising… Pursuing his childhood dream of writing novels. A military friend had set him straight. He'd known Rudy Petcock from his first day of enlistment. Rudy always had a plan. He'd entered the Army to gain invaluable life skills, not the least of which was breaking down and reassembling every weapon within reach. Rudy was a lifelong hunter and gun enthusiast. He was no extremist nut. You wouldn't know unless you asked him. Rudy deployed to Afghanistan and gained firsthand knowledge of military weapons while Braxton pulled security duty.

Braxton's curse was that he could type seventy words a minute. This made him invaluable to the Army. They always needed typists, and people who understood computers. He learned on the job, always pushing for the latest technology to "keep up with the bad guys."

Braxton felt sick to his stomach. He wanted a drink. One drink. What could it hurt? He had no more appointments for the rest of the afternoon. He eyed his bike in the corner. He could bike down the hill to Floyd's Tavern, chain his bike to a light pole. But he could read the future. One drink would turn into two, and then into four. When he finally headed for home, he'd wobble all over the street and get hit by a six-thousand-pound Rivian with a sticker that read, *You Can't Hold A Child With Nuclear Arms* on the bumper.

What were his options? He would ask Rudy. Rudy's Discount Shooter Supply had been growing like a fungus despite, or perhaps because of, the draconian measures the sneering oligarchs in Salem had imposed. Realistically speaking, Rudy was in no position to compete with his assistant professor's salary, a miserable eighty-seven thousand dollars a year, supplemented by Suzanna's shop profits. Suzanna rented a booth at Canning and Collectibles in Woodburn. People were crazy for Hawaiian shirts. She couldn't keep them in stock. She pulled in thirty grand a year. Together, they pulled the wagon.

Someone knocked. Braxton jumped. He got up and opened the door. Archie Silvano, a full professor specializing in Roman and Greek history, stood holding a sheet of red construction paper.

"This was taped to your door," he said.

Homophobe was written in heavy black marker.

Chapter 3

The Ambush

Braxton's weekend was normal. Grocery shopping, cleaning, reading, and unwinding. He spent an hour at a tire repair place getting the leak fixed. The Knoxes didn't watch television much on the weekend and when they did, they avoided local stations. They had rules. No checking of email, no sitting mindlessly on the internet looking at digital pablum. It was family time. When Monday came, Braxton went about his routine, pleased that the staff at Wendy's had showed up to work. For a few moments, he felt as if he had turned the corner.

As he approached Lumumba Hall, Room 336, he saw the gathered news crews outside the door to the lecture hall. The moment they saw him, cameras closed in and reporters thrust their microphones in his face. One woman barked louder than the others. "Would you care to comment about the controversy you've caused on campus because of your anti-LGBTQ stance?"

He used his shoulders to get to the door. Getting in was hard. The media pressed in tight. He understood why he was being asked to come alone. This was a trap and he was the intended victim. Something must have happened over the weekend.

Why is the media here? Debbie Driggs...it had to have been her. How could this have gotten out of hand so quickly?

Knox had been in the Army and knew there were several ways to deal with an ambush. One was to surrender. Another was to charge or punch through the trap. Another was evasion, attempt to circumvent the enemy. Braxton couldn't contemplate surrender and it was clear by the media circus, evasion was out of the question.

He jerked the door open, hitting a cameraman so hard that a plastic part of his camera flew off. He slid through the narrow gap and into the room.

Once inside he saw the six-member History Disciplinary Committee lined up at a long table. At the center sat Professor Sylvia Baskin-Kulberg, smiling smugly. A DEI hired to "expand the university's diversity." She had not published a paper in ten years nor had she written any books. She had been brought aboard because she was a woman of color.

"Professor Knox," she said, gesturing to the lone chair before the table, "please take a seat." He instantly loathed her haughty tone.

He sat down, looking at the five members of the committee, making slow eye contact with each.

"We have all seen the video taken in your class and, to be frank, we found it deeply disturbing."

"I haven't seen it."

She nodded. The projector shot an image onto the screen behind her. It was from a week ago, the minor rebuttal of **Debbie Driggs.** He watched it, then locked eyes with Baskin-Kulberg.

"Do you have anything to say in your defense?" she poked.

"Defense of what?"

"You failed to use the student's pronouns. You deliberately created a hostile learning environment for her," she snapped. "You trampled on her civil rights."

Braxton immediately understood that the disciplinary committee had already arrived at a verdict. Otherwise, why would they have tipped off the media? His anger was tempered by the absurdity of the situation. *They want me to overreact. It will give them justification for what they have done. I won't play their game.* He drew a long breath, knowing what was about to come. He smiled. "Three things come to mind. One is the first amendment. This pronoun crap is idiotic. How am I supposed to know what magical gender they think they are on a given day? What is she this week, a toaster? I have tolerated this BS about as long as I intend to. No one can tell me what words or phrases I have to use.

"Secondly, what Debbie Driggs has posted on the internet is an eighteen-second heavily edited clip off a much longer discussion. She deliberately posted this edited copy without context other than her own. As a leader in this institution, you of all people should know that without context, facts should be questioned and placed under scrutiny."

Professor Baskin-Kulberg opened her bass-like mouth, but Knox continued. "Furthermore, this concept of a hostile learning environment is ludicrous. We are supposed to be preparing these students for the real world. In the real world, not everyone is going to play their games of make-believe. They need to be able to function in reality, not this cushy little fantasy of safe-spaces and comfort zones you think is important."

Baskin-Kulberg grabbed her gavel and cracked it so hard on the tabletop that it shattered the head, sending a piece flying at his feet. "You will restrict your remarks to the matter at hand."

"Who called the media in, Sylvia? I didn't. You decided before I walked in here that you were going to terminate me. This 'committee' is a farce. No one will speak out against you because they are afraid you will label them the way you have done with me." He cast an icy glance at Dean Grooper who averted his eyes in shame.

"Now it is out for everyone to see."

"Professor Knox," Baskin-Kulberg snapped. "This is not a forum for you to expose your radical alt-right nonsense. We are here to discuss what should be done given the release of that video. There were protests today at the Student Union. This is a serious matter."

"Did you say radical alt-right? I'm not radical at all. I'm simply disagreeing with you. That's the problem with progressives like you, Sylvia. The moment that someone doesn't follow your doctrine *du jour*, you slap a nasty label on them. You stuff people like me into little deplorable buckets and assign negative traits to them. I'm frankly shocked that you haven't called me a Nazi—isn't that your next move?"

Her jaw fell open.

"As to what is to be done with me, let me ask you this—why are you not telling these students that my job is to instruct them, not pander to their fantasies? That is what we are here to do, educate them. I did that. If anything, Miss Driggs was a disruptive element in my classroom."

"You just did it again, you assigned a sex to her!" Professor Graham barked from the right end of the table.

"Oh please, Jamie," he replied. "She's female. If you don't believe me, call the Biology Department."

"You are out of line," Professor LaBolt said, using his deep voice to try and wrest control of the meeting from Knox.

"Harvey, this entire meeting is out of line. There are six of you. I have had no time or warning to prepare any defense. You're afraid, just like everyone else. You know that any student can make any allegation they desire, and you will be in this chair, just like me. Don't lie to yourself that being up there, behind your pseudo-bench, that you are somehow insulated from this. Sylvia would throw you under the bus the same way she has me."

For a moment, it felt as if the air was sucked out of the room. He had surprised his ambushers with logic and words, things they could not counter. Professor Baskin-Kulberg was beyond angry. He could see it in the way her face muscles tightened. It was pleasing, if not enjoyable.

Through gritted teeth she spoke slowly, enunciating each syllable with machine-like exactitude. "I don't think you understand the gravity of this situation. If the committee recommends you be terminated, that goes to HR. Your contract will be suspended. No university will hire you after this. Your books will be pulled from publication. You won't be able to work anywhere, not as a professor. I doubt you will be able to get a job as a substitute high school teacher." Satisfaction rang in her words. "Your mouth has put your shot at tenure on the line."

Knox pulled out his phone and held it up, tapping the video record button. "Would you mind repeating that for the record?"

"Put that away!" she snapped. "This meeting is confidential."

She was right about his career track, and hearing her words did hurt, though he thought he was doing a good job of hiding it. Tenure had been important to him, not for what it was, but as a goal. He hadn't killed that goal; she had.

This isn't just about me, it's about Suzanna and Angela.

Sylvia dangled the future in front of him as if there was still hope. He knew that had passed. "You've already made up your mind, Sylvia. Go ahead, make your recommendation to HR. I know my contract... the benefits of an eidetic memory. When I was hired, none of this idiocy existed. I haven't violated any of my obligations under the law or my contract. You fire me, I will sue your asses. In fact, I will go for all of you individually in civil court. You may drive me out of this college, but I will extract what is legally due me."

Dean Grooper stirred in his seat. "Sylvia, perhaps if he were to make a public apology of the matter... we could go with a two-year suspension."

Alistair Grooper was spineless. Braxton's expectations of him had always been low. *Even now he's attempting to weasel out of this public execution.* That line about suing them personally must have struck home. Given his disaster of a home life, he knew Grooper was afraid. Braxton decided to take away any hint of moral high ground that the dean was attempting to seize. "I will not apologize. I did nothing wrong. I certainly didn't do anything on purpose. You're just throwing that out there hoping I will latch onto it, maybe softening the blow that is going to come."

"That student's feelings have been hurt, perhaps irreparably," Baskin-Kulberg snarled. "She may very well sue the university. The very least you can do is to admit you were in the wrong."

Braxton laughed. "If I were to apologize, it would be an act of lunacy wrapped in guilt. I won't have any part in such idiocy. It also won't work. It won't satisfy this student or the others she has rallied to her cause célèbre. They won't stop. You've allowed them to believe that their feelings equate to facts. An apology will only fuel them to protest more because it will give them a false sense of victory—of validation. They will be relentless if I apologize."

As he spoke the words, he wrapped his head around the woke student body. *If I don't apologize, things will be the same. They will want blood, my blood. It's like the Reign of Terror all over again with these woke kids.* His mind danced into the future. *I will need to protect my family. Nothing is sacred to these students.*

"Very well. Do you have anything else to say in your defense?" Baskin-Kulberg pressed. Despite her rage, she was savoring the moment.

Knox knew his career was in jeopardy. "I'm American. I'm owed due process. You had plenty of time to prepare for this kangaroo court. I have a right to face my accuser. Have her come here and show you the full video of what I said in the classroom. I'm owed at least that much."

"There you go again," LaBolt said. "Assigning a gender to her. I think you've done enough damage to her without having her being further subjected to your bigotry."

The committee all nodded in unison.

"So, you are going to ignore my fundamental rights. If you think I'm going down without a fight, you're wrong." His words threw gasoline on Baskin-Kulberg's rage, but he wasn't done.

"No one in this country has the right to not be offended. This college is like so many others. You have created an environment to foster hate, and when anyone dares to stand up for what is right, you coddle the students. You gave them safe spaces when they needed critical thinking skills. Rather than prepare them for what the real world is like, you made them soft and weak. People like you have convinced them that anyone who doesn't agree with their way of thinking is an enemy. In short, you have created an army of monsters, miscreants that will tear this nation apart. This isn't a hearing about what I said or why I said it, it is you attempting to justify what you've done. I would blame the students, but soulless administrators like you are far worse than they are. They didn't know better. You did.

"Before I finish, answer me this: Who called in the media, Sylvia? The very least you can do is own up to that."

"I did," she replied with pride. "We need to provide the university with transparency."

"Why shut them out? Aren't you proud of what you're doing?"

Baskin-Kulberg smiled. "We afforded you the courtesy of a closed meeting. Based on what you've said here today, you don't deserve it."

The die was cast. He had known that the moment he had arrived. "Mark my words—what you are doing to me, what you have done to them, will come back and bite you. You're all allegedly historians, so consider this. After the French Revolution, the mob turned on its leaders and masters. That time is coming, and when it does, these students that you have so carefully groomed will turn on you. They will lie, distort the truth, put their delicate feelings ahead of reality, only it will all be aimed at you." He stabbed his finger at Baskin-Kulberg. "You'll be in exactly the place I am today, facing exactly what you are threatening me with.

"The best part is, you will wonder, 'How could this have happened to me?' And in that moment, I want you to remember me, remember this day, and what you did."

Chapter 4

Suzanna and Angela

Braxton drove to his modest tract house on Hanover Street where he lived with his wife Suzanna and their fifteen-year-old daughter Angela. He'd need to clear out his trunk and back seat to make room for his belongings. It was three thirty in the afternoon. Angela was still at Maulana Karenga High School, at soccer practice. The girls' soccer team was scheduled to play the George Floyd team that Saturday. The school board had voted unanimously to rename Martin Luther King High School after the dead junkie. His wife Suzanna was still at Nublenz and Myer, "Righteous lawyers for righteous causes," where she was a legal secretary.

How could he tell them that he lost his job?

Braxton popped the trunk, removed two lawn chairs, fly rod, tackle box, sleeping bags, pup tent, and golf clubs and stacked them neatly in a corner of the garage.

He went inside where their French bulldog Monsieur pogoed in excitement. Braxton stooped to pet him. "All right, all right." He went to the cupboard and removed a Whimzee dog chew from its bag. Monsieur capered happily.

"Sit."

Monsieur obeyed without a hint of hesitation. Braxton handed him the dog treat. A doggie door led from the kitchen to the fenced-in backyard so Monsieur could come and go as he pleased. Dogs didn't care about politics or jobs, they were just loyal… a quality he admired. Braxton stripped off his clothes and took a shower as hot as he could stand. He got out. The mirror over the sink had misted. He toweled off and went to his bedroom. As he put on fresh clothes, he heard someone banging around in the kitchen. He finished dressing, came out, and found Angela, tall, willowy, with her black hair down, rummaging through the cupboard.

"Angela. What are you doing home? I thought you had soccer practice."

"They kicked me off the team."

"What?"

"Yeah. Coach Rabeneck pulled me aside right after school and said I was a good player, but they had to make room for someone from a traditionally marginalized community. So I said, 'But coach, why not just add her and keep me on the team?' and she said they were afraid I might misgender the new player and couldn't take a chance that I might offend the new player, who apparently self-identifies as a differently abled quale of color."

"What's a quale?"

"It's complicated."

Sighing, Braxton hugged his daughter tight. "I'm so sorry. This is my fault."

"How is it your fault?"

"I was just dressed down by the committee to enforce group think for the same crime. I misgendered a student today. They fired me." He wasn't afraid of her not understanding the phrases he used.

Angela pulled away. "What?! They can't do that!"

"Apparently they can. I was six months shy of getting a full pension."

"What are you going to do?"

Braxton shrugged. "I don't know yet. One thing's for sure. I'm not going to wallow in self-pity. I'll get another job. I'm a not bad mechanic. I'll fix cars if I must. Maybe I can get a job as gunsmith." He had gotten himself certified as a Glock armorer a few years before.

"I've half a mind to drop out and get a job too. If all three of us are pulling, we should be able to make ends meet."

"This is not the future your mother and I had in mind for you."

"What future then? I know you wanted me to go to college. I wanted to study computer science at Eastern State. Now they won't let me in."

"Well, I don't see how my firing…"

"Oh come on, Dad! You know how they work. They don't just want to punish you, they want you and your whole family dead."

She pulled out her laptop, set it on the kitchen table, and sat down. "Look. Look. I want to show you something." Braxton watched over her shoulder as she went to Eastern State's home page, and went to the Sociology Department. She poked and stroked. "There is it is. A brand-new course."

The course "Queering the World" teaches "methods for… subverting heterosexist paradigms and binary assumptions that perpetuate oppression." Some of the key issues addressed include "What occurs when a congregation, community, or organization is queered?"

Angela looked clear-eyed up at her father. "Why would any rational person go there?"

Braxton stepped back, a burst of pride and love warming his heart. "Baby, I can't argue with that, and I can't help but feel proud of you. You're so mature for a girl of your age. I was never that smart."

"You were smart enough to go into the Army before it became rainbowed. You saw the world, learned some skills, and got out before the Secretary of the Army started wearing pink tutus and a feather boa."

"There are a handful of universities that still teach marketable skills. Hillsdale College, St. Mark's University…"

"Not sure I want to go to college."

"Oh come on."

"What happens if society collapses? What happens if all the mandated electric trucks can't get to market during a snowstorm? Or China just decides to poison us all with fentanyl?"

"Couple years ago I would have laughed, but I have to admit, there's some truth in what you say. Maybe we should go off-grid. Find someplace to live in the mountains, grow our own food, generate our own electricity. Your grandfather's got a big chunk of woodland with a cabin on it. We could get three stationary bicycles and hook them up to generators. Wood-burning stove. They're not going to come after us over that. The police will have their hands full with roaming thugs stealing everything they can get their hands on. No one goes to downtown Portland anymore. There's nothing left. The last retailer closed its doors in March."

He paused a mental beat, organizing his thoughts in terms of next actions.

"I have to go back to the university to clear out my desk. Will you stay here?"

"I might take Monsieur for a walk."

"I'd be happier if you stayed here."

Angela made a face. "This isn't Beirut yet, Dad. I think we'll be all right walking around the block. Besides. Monsieur's a killer. One word from me and he'll rip out their throats. Whoever they are."

Braxton was about to say something but the Common Sense Frog perched on his shoulder. *This is the United States of America. It's not Beirut yet. Let's be reasonable.*

"Okay, but be careful. Take the bear spray."

"If it makes you happy, I'll take the bear spray."

"Thank you."

Braxton plucked several cardboard boxes from a stack in the garage, got in his eight-year-old Toyota Rav4 with the banged-up tailgate he'd been meaning to fix, backed down the driveway, and headed back to campus.

It was five o'clock by the time he pulled into the faculty parking lot, easing into a spot between Chairperson Wilkins's massive Rivian and Professor Charlize Eberhard-Cumberford's Prius, the rear bumper and trunk lid festooned with stickers.

Healthcare For Profit Is A Crime Against Humanity
Capitalism Kills
Trump Done Says What I Be Thinkin' (cartoon of toothless redneck)
No One's Treading On You Sweetie
Record Profits Are Stolen Wages

Braxton took a couple of pictures, thinking it might help with a lawsuit. A grad student who had been cutting across the parking lot stopped.

"What are you doing?"

"I'm saving these precious memories."

"Aren't you the Associate History Professor who just got shitcanned for harassing a student?" There was an arrogance in her tone that grated on his nerves.

"Technically speaking, no. I was fired for referring to her as miss."

"You're doing it again. You called her her."

"You just called her her."

The grad student bit his, her, or its tongue. "You know what I meant. What are you going to do with those pics?"

"They're for my personal collection."

"How would you like it if I started recording you?"

"You're kinda late to the party, pal. That woman whom I quote unquote misgendered already did."

"You did it again. You called her a woman."

"You just called her a woman."

"No I didn't."

"You said, and I quote, you called *her* a woman. To what does the *her* refer, if not her gender?"

The grad student clenched up, ready to do battle. Braxton went into the building. At that hour, the floor was deserted except for old Professor Rasmussen, who had been there since the Pleistocene Era and taught Greek history. There had been much debate whether students needed or had any interest in Greek history, but in the end, a powerful alumnus had weighed in, insisting Rasmussen stayed.

Braxton loaded his books, papers, and files. They filled four boxes. Not much to show for years of work. Carrying two, he got on the ancient elevator and off on the ground floor, backing his way through the exit into the parking lot where his Toyota was where he had left it, only with four flat tires.

25

Chapter 5

Sins of the Father

Braxton called Gateway Towing.

"Gateway."

"Hello. This is Braxton Knox."

"Hey, Braxton. Ross here. I remember you. We swapped some war stories at the VFW."

"Yeah, thanks, Ross. I'm over at the university and someone slashed my tires. I have four flats. Any chance of you getting over here today and helping me out?"

"Jesus. Who would do such a thing?"

"I don't want to get into it, but I just got shit-canned because I misgendered a student. That makes me public enemy number one."

"Fucking hell, I'd like to turn a fire hose on those bastards."

"Tell me about it. It's actually kind of a relief. The atmosphere has been deteriorating for the last couple of years. I feel like I just got knocked into 1984."

"Yeah, okay. Let me check. I'm gonna put you on hold for a minute."

As Braxton waited, he noted the closed circuit cameras covering the parking lot. He'd love to put a name to whoever did it. It all depended on whether University Security was down with the program. A lot of ex-cops went into security. It was an easy way to get on the university's dime. The pay was better, the hours were better, and they no longer had to deal with crackheads.

Ross came back on the line. "I can be there in a half hour. Where exactly are you?"

"I'm in the history department parking lot. That's the Wyrick Building."

"Be right there."

"Thanks, Ross."

Braxton looked up and saw movement. Someone jerked back from a third-floor window where he/she/xe/it had been watching. Braxton knew which office. He went into the building, ran up three flights of stairs, burst from the stairwell and stood outside Room 312, Professor Ron Lauden, "American Colonization of Indigenous Peoples." The door was shut. Braxton knocked. Nada. He put his ear to the door and listened. Faint scuffing. Lauden was in there hiding. There was no point forcing a confrontation. Lauden was a far-left propagandist whose required reading included Howard Zinn and Ta-Nehisi Coates.

The security cameras all fed into Campus Security, housed in a one-story stucco building a quarter mile away. Braxton would not have time to go over there. It would have to wait until tomorrow, if it was even worth it. He returned to the deserted parking lot.

Eberhard-Cumberford's Prius was the only other vehicle. It was often there in the morning as the good professor spent most of her free time with her husband, Charlotte Naugahyde-Sanderson. Gateway's massive truck transport turned into the parking lot, Ross Hanson expertly maneuvering the vehicle so the back end was ten feet from Braxton's Toyota, which he had backed into the lot. Servo motors whined as two steel wheel ramps descended from the tail.

Ross got out. He was a big man with massive forearms wearing denim coveralls and a Gateway ball cap.

"Awright, let's get 'er hooked up. You want to drive forward real slow. I'll tell you when to stop."

"Won't rolling on the rims damage the tires?"

"Sometimes. Looks like they left a couple pounds in there. With any luck, the outers won't touch the rims."

Braxton started his vehicle and inched forward until Ross held up his hand. Ross fastened two chains to the chassis and slowly inched the vehicle onto the fifteen-foot bed. He unhooked canvas straps from both sides and the back of the cab and secured the vehicle to the platform.

"You need a ride home?"

"If you don't mind."

"Get in."

They drove for several minutes in silence past the red brick and white column antebellum fraternities, the boarding houses, and the Hillel Foundation where an armed guard was on duty since the student riot the year before when several hundred students carrying *Free Palestine* signs and cans of red paint had decorated the venerable building with slogans including defaced Stars of David and "From the river to the sea" spray painted in red. Hillel had removed the graffiti the next day, but it had reappeared in the night, and thus the security guard.

"They shit-can ya?" Ross said.

"Yup."

"Damn, that sucks. What are you going to do?"

"I don't know yet. I'm keeping my options open."

Ross laughed. "You can always come work for me. I don't pay as much, but you won't have to look those little shitheads in the eye."

"Thanks, Ross. Maybe I'll take the time to write that novel I've been talking about for fifteen years."

"What's that about?"

"*Barfalo*. It's about a bulimic buffalo terrorizing settlers in 1880s Nebraska."

"I'd read that. I love westerns. What do you want to do about the tires? They're shot. You want me to replace them with some nice all-weathers? I can do it for eight hundred bucks."

"Yeah, thanks, Ross."

"Where we headed?"

Braxton gave directions. Twenty minutes later, Ross dropped him off in front of his house. Suzanna's Hyundai sat in the driveway. Ross pulled away as Braxton went in through the unlocked front door. Suzanna was in the kitchen. The house smelled of beef stew. She came out and hugged him.

Some wives would have been upset when told their husband had been fired. That wasn't Suzanna. The level of understanding she had was why Braxton had married her. "Well, it's kind of a relief, isn't it? You weren't very happy there. You deserved better than they gave you."

"I was happy for about five years, until all this nonsense started." She walked over to him and gave him a hug, which he returned. He didn't want to let go, and he wondered at how lucky he was to have her in his corner. Slowly she returned to her cooking, her every movement gentle and efficient.

Her ability to comprehend a situation and demonstrate it with love is why I admire her so much, he thought.

"I mentioned what happened to Marv and asked him if you had a case," she said.

Marv Myer headed the firm where she worked.

"What did he say?"

"He said you had good standing legally, but trying it here would be problematic. You won't be able to find an impartial jury."

"I'm going to forget everything that happened today and not think about until Monday. I'm going to watch the Seahawks/Ravens game on Sunday. Where's Angela?"

"She went over to Tamara's house to write a song."

He wanted to brag about his daughter and how well she processed the news he had told her, but it wasn't necessary. Just thinking about her made him smile.

"Good. With any luck, she'll come up with a great song, it'll get a zillion hits over the weekend, and we won't ever have to work again."

Suzanna smiled at that, but her smile turned sad. "You love work. You'd be lost without it. You need a purpose in life."

He sighed. "I loved that job. Until I didn't. I don't know what's wrong with kids these days. They have no sense. They have no wisdom. Everything is political. You can't order a burger without some coed screaming that the cow that was butchered had a name. I saw one in the supermarket the other day, trying to chase people away from the butcher's counter. The owner started filming and threatened to send it to her parents if she didn't leave."

"Did she?"

"Well yeah, after screaming the 'F' word about a dozen times and flipping everyone the bird. Her outrage makes your famous beef stew taste all the better." Suzanna was the bedrock of the family and mentioning her cooking skills drove that point home.

Braxton took a seat in the breakfast nook which looked out on the backyard. Green grass and pine. Monsieur laid his muzzle on Braxton's thigh.

"Did you feed the dog?"

"Of course I fed the dog. It doesn't matter how much I feed him, he's going to act like he's starving. Our pooch is a consummate liar."

She plunked a bowl of steaming beef stew in front of him. The aroma made him salivate. He dove in. It was delicious. Braxton was famished. He hadn't realized how hungry he was until this morning.

After dinner, Braxton retired to his den, stretched out in a leather Barcalounger, and turned on the Fox evening news. *Watters' World.*

"Migrants" in New York had rioted at Penn Station, then spilled out onto 8th Avenue, smashing storefronts and grabbing everything they could carry. They then disappeared into the subway, jumping over the turnstiles, shoving commuters out of the way, and taking off for parts unknown. A sixty-five-year-old mother of four who'd been shoved onto the tracks had died, while a Democrat representative warned Americans not to jump to conclusions, and to try and understand what happened from the migrant point of view.

Bad news came in a steady stream. The Administration floated a fifty-cent national gasoline tax to fund a program giving sex-change operations to migrants, which only added fuel to his frustration. Braxton turned it off and picked up a book. *Finnegan's Week* by Wambaugh. He'd only got to Tuesday when Angela stormed in through the garage door, slammed it behind her, marched upstairs to her room, and slammed that door.

Suzanna stuck her head in. "What's wrong with her?"

Braxton shrugged. "Beats me. Give her a little time to cool down."

"Ix-nay, buster. She can't act that way around here without explaining herself."

Suzanna marched upstairs. Braxton heard yelling. Then silence. Suzanna descended, mouth a slit.

"What?"

"Someone called her a Nazi."

"What?!"

"Yes. They said she must have gotten it from her father."

Chapter 6

The Fight Comes Home

Braxton finally fell into an uneasy sleep at midnight. He'd lain in bed for two hours, tossing and turning, examining his life as if he could find the place he'd made a wrong turn. Oh sure, it was the misgendering, but that was such a tiny thing. What kind of person chose to go to battle over a verbal mistake? Braxton had sometimes mistaken mannish women for men and called them sir, and when he apologized, they just smiled. No biggie.

But when he called a hulking barista with eye makeup and a split tongue sir, the creature raised its voice and bellowed, "It's *ma'am*! I am not going to serve you! You're a homophobe! Leave or I'll call the police!"

He hadn't been to a Starbucks since. The incident had been a warning shot across the bow.

In the depths of his sleep, he dreamt he was in prison and a three-hundred-pound Samoan with a tarantula inked on his face wanted to fight. In his dream, Braxton kicked him in the groin. There was the sound of shattering glass. Braxton came wide awake, experiencing a flashback to the sandbox, when the Taliban launched a mortar attack and the klaxons went off. He heard people screaming, cars honking, and again, the sound of shattered glass.

Suzanna woke up in a fog. "What's going on?"

"Stay here."

Braxton pulled on pants, shoes, socks, a sweatshirt, grabbed an aluminum baseball bat from the hall closet, and opened the front door where several dozen young people, their faces all masked in black, were shaking aerosol cans and working on the front of the house. They froze as Braxton stepped out. He left the lights off. The living room window was shattered.

"Nazi!" screeched a person. *Man? Woman? Quagle? Who knew?* Braxton came down the steps, hefting the bat. The person ran back to the street and jumped into a beige Hyundai.

"I just called the police!" Braxton shouted. A brick flew by his head. He ran up to the Hyundai and laid into the rear window, taking three swings to shatter it. The car pealed out. The rest of the mob piled into a Kia and an old Dodge van and hit the gas, each vehicle flying the fuck you flag, middle fingers out the window. Braxton wheeled around as they left.

They'd painted red swastikas and *Nazi* on clapboard siding. Braxton shook with fury.

This isn't right. This is America. The Land of the Free. The days of the night riders were supposed to be over.

Suzanna appeared in the open front door. "I called the police," she said.

Braxton surveyed the street. Lights went on in two houses across the street. Old Mr. Gorelick appeared on his front step. Braxton waved.

"It's okay! They left! Sorry about the disruption!"

Gorelick, a Vietnam veteran, walked across the street wearing heavy boots and a terry cloth robe.

"What the fuck was that all about?"

Braxton sighed. "I accidentally misgendered a student. I called her Miss Driggs, instead of her preferred pronoun."

"Which is?"

"Fuck if I know. Probably changes every day."

"I'm glad to have grown up in a different America."

"I hear ya."

A squad car pulled up in front of the house and two officers got out, a tall black man and a short Hispanic woman. The tall one wore a nameplate that said Gunnison and sported a bodycam clipped to the shirt. They walked up the step.

"Who called it in?" Gunnison said.

"Me. Braxton Knox. I'm a professor of history at Eastern State. Or I was until yesterday."

The woman, whose badge said Flores, took pictures of the front of the house.

"Tell me what happened, Mr. Knox."

Braxton ran it down since the misgendering the previous Friday, the slashed tires, the midnight raid. "I haven't yet had a chance to review the security tapes from today. They might show whoever it was that slashed my tires."

"One thing at a time. Tell me about this demonstration."

"About a dozen. All dressed like ANTIFA. Black clothes, black masks, could be anybody. It started just after midnight when someone threw a brick through the window. That woke me up. I could hear them screaming from the bedroom, which is in the back of the house. Some shit about Nazis. They think I'm a Nazi because I used the wrong pronoun."

Gunnison pulled out a pen and pad. "Mind if we sit on the front porch?"

"We can go inside if you like. Would you like something to drink?"

"No, that's all right. My partner is Officer Flores."

They went up on the porch and sat in plastic lawn chairs while Gunnison took notes. "I don't suppose you have any pictures."

"I was too rattled to think about that. I'm thinking of putting up security cameras."

"That might not be a bad idea, if you plan to remain here."

"Huh?"

"I'll level with you, Mr. Knox. We are severely underfunded and understaffed. We have orders to respond to only to class one and two felonies. This is a class five felony, punishable by one to three years in prison and a thousand-dollar fine. This is first-degree trespass."

"Are you telling me there's nothing you can do?"

"I didn't say that. We're not happy about crowds of hooligans harassing honest people in their homes, and I can increase patrol of this neighborhood. Since these losers prefer to strike after midnight, we can do a drive-by every night. This isn't far off our usual beat so it would be no problem."

"Thanks, officer. What the hell. I'm up. I doubt I'll be able to get back to sleep. Would you like some coffee?"

Gunnison turned to Flores. "Hey, Anita. Want coffee?"

"Sure."

They went into the kitchen where Suzanna was grinding beans. She'd put on an athletic jump suit. Angela sat at the table in a blue terry cloth robe. She stood when the cops entered. Braxton introduced them.

"Angela, tell them what happened to you at school today."

"Out of nowhere, some fake account on Facebook starts calling me a Nazi."

"Hmmm," Gunnison said. "Would you care to forward a screen cap to the department?" He reached into a shirt pocket. "Here's my card."

"I will, but I heard what you told Dad. I know you've got more important things to do."

"I prefer too much information rather than too little."

"What history did you teach, Mr. Knox?" Anita asked.

"Introduction to Greek history with an emphasis on the growth of democracy under Athens."

"Not a lot of call for that kind of work I imagine."

"People are all too willing to repeat the mistakes of the past," he countered.

Gunnison stood. "I wouldn't know about that. We'll do what we can. Thank you for the coffee."

Braxton saw the cops out, watched them get in their cruiser and leave. He doubted there would be any more disturbances that night, but he didn't kid himself that it was over. Only yesterday he'd committed his cardinal sin and already he'd been fired, his daughter harassed, and nameless thugs had besieged him in the middle of the night. It made him want to do violence. He was no great martial artist, but he'd held his own among Army Rangers until he had been cut. Braxton knew that no ANTIFA, no tofu-sucking soy boy, was a match for him in a fair fight. He shook his head.

Don't be ridiculous.

Life was not a movie. Life was not *Death Wish*, *Dirty Harry*, or *Walking Tall*. Suzanna trailed her hand across his arm as she went upstairs.

"I'm going to try and get some sleep."

"You go ahead, babe. I doubt they'll be back tonight."

Angela sat in the kitchen, her head in her hands.

"What's the matter, baby?"

"I'm just so upset! It's just so unfair!"

"You know what? There's only one thing these creeps fear and that's bad publicity. I'm going to get you one of those tiny clip-on recorders to wear. If you wear a black sweater, no one will notice. You could put it on your belt and tell anybody who asks that it records your steps."

"What good will that do?"

"Take it from your old man. As a student of history, there's only one thing bullies fear, and that's being shown as what they truly are. In fact, I'm going to get one for each of you. Go to bed. Try to get some sleep. Tomorrow is another day."

Angela went upstairs. Braxton went into his office, went online, and ordered three HD Video & Audio Recording Camera Pens from Zetronix for $139.00 apiece. He went upstairs, crawled into bed, and fell into a fitful sleep.

Chapter 7

The Gut Punch

In the morning Braxton slept in, waking to the sound of Angela clattering around in the kitchen. He got up, took a shower, got dressed, and went downstairs. Angela looked up from the waffle iron.

"Waffles?"

"Sure. Where's your mom?"

"She went to work."

Anxiety insinuated itself into Braxton's heart. *Don't be silly.* She worked for a reputable law firm house in a suburban mall that also contained Lululemon, Verizon Wireless, Nordstrom, and Bath & Body Works. Not the type of place that attracted masked, screaming social justice warriors. They had their own security. Nublenz and Myer had their own building, a three-story brick structure which also housed two other legal firms and Northwest Taxworks.

"What are you doing home? Shouldn't you be at school?"

"I'm staying home today. I don't feel safe at school."

Braxton bit his lower lip. He couldn't blame her. But she had a four point four grade average. She could do what she wanted.

"You still got those guns, don't you?" she asked.

"Huh?"

She tonged a waffle onto a plate and handed it to him. "There's butter and syrup on the table."

"I got 'em. Why?"

"I want you to teach me how to shoot."

"Are you serious?"

She put her hands on her hips and looked at him.

"Okay. Okay. No problem. Just let me dig them out."

"Maybe we can set up a shooting range in the basement."

Braxton buttered, syruped, and forked the target waffles. He drank half a glass of orange juice.

"Nah. That'll attract unwanted attention. Not to mention the costs. The air purification and steel alone make it cost prohibitive." He knew that because he had priced it out when they had bought the house. "We don't need to shoot here. Once you get the basics down, I'll take you to a range."

"Why don't we just go to a range right away?"

"'Cause there's things you need to learn first. How to load, how to shoot, how to maintain weapons."

"What about those laser things that you fasten to your pistol and it tells you how you're doing?"

"Mantix X personal firearms training system. Yeah, we could get one of those."

She opened her notepad. "Great! I'll order it right away."

"You got that kind of money?"

"I have three thousand in my checking account."

"How'd you do that?"

"From Mom's booth at Canning & Collectibles. I've been buying Hawaiian shirts at thrift stores. I pay, like six to ten dollars a shirt and I sell them for twenty on up. I sold one with Rat Fink for a hundred. People go crazy for Hawaiian shirts. I think my stuff outsells Mom's."

"Does she know?"

Angela put a finger to her lips and looked around. "I think so. I'm waiting for her to say something."

"I had no idea! Way to go, little girl!"

"That's right, Daddy. Let me know if you need help with the bills."

"I will, but I don't think we're there yet. I'm going to line something up."

"Another teaching job?"

"Never again. I gotta talk to Rudy, bounce some ideas off him. Do me a favor. Don't order the Mantix over the internet. I'll get one from Rudy."

"Who's Rudy?"

"Rudy Petcock. Army buddy who has a gun shop."

"Would you sell guns?"

"I don't know yet. I have to talk to him. I don't want a retail job. I'm a qualified marksman. I could always teach at a shooting range."

"Daddy, can we get the guns out, puleeeeeze?"

"Just let me finish my breakfast."

Angela clapped her hands and squealed.

They went down the wooden steps to the unfinished concrete basement with a two-year-old furnace, a one-year-old water heater, and a washer and dryer that were as old as the house itself. Braxton had built bookshelves using cinderblocks and two-by-eights. His gun safe sat in a corner. He entered the digital code and it clicked. He swung it open revealing a Mossberg twelve-gauge, a lever action Henry 30-30, and an AR-15.

Angela pointed at the AR-15. "What's that for?"

"Just in case."

"In case of what?"

"The breakdown of the rule of law. Hordes of criminals roaming through the neighborhood taking whatever they want and raping the women. Kind of like last night."

"Oh Dad!"

"Don't kid yourself. You saw what they did during COVID. We'll get to the rifles later. Let's start with the handguns."

He opened a drawer at the bottom and removed a Taurus .38 revolver. He shut the door and locked it.

"Pull up a chair."

Angela hooked an old wooden kitchen chair from the wall and dragged it over. Braxton sat in a folding chair. He released the cylinder and rolled it out. "Takes five cartridges. The first rule of gun safety is always assume the gun is loaded. Got it?"

"Yeah."

"What did I just say?"

"Always assume the gun is loaded."

He handed her the gun. "Push the cylinder back into place."

She did so, pointing the barrel between her legs at the floor.

"The second rule is to never point it anybody you don't intend to shoot."

"Got it."

"What did I just say?"

"One. Always assume the gun is loaded. Two. Never point it at anybody I don't intend to shoot."

"Very good. Now you see these gangbangers and whatnot holding their guns sideways. Those are photo ops. It's not how we hold a gun we intend to use."

"What if I order a BB pistol and practice down here?"

"You can get a BB pistol, but please don't order one over the internet. You never know who might be listening."

"Oh Dad! A BB gun? Really?"

"I'll get you one. I'll ask Rudy."

They worked stances, grips, trigger pull for forty-five minutes. Angela dragged a hand across her face.

"All right! I'd better get to work. That term paper isn't going to write itself."

"What's this about?"

"How artificial intelligence will impact the media."

"That sounds kind of challenging. Are you sure you're at the right school?"

Angela laughed. "I know! Mr. Henninger is old school; he insists on letter grades. I don't know how long he's going to last."

They went upstairs. Braxton sat at his desk and checked his email. Twelve messages from addresses he didn't recognize. He clicked one on.

I hope you rot in hell, you piece of shit racist.

He blocked it. He clicked on another.

How does a worthless piece of shit CIS-gendered white man get a cushy college job?

He blocked it. Braxton actually had to Google what CIS-gendered was and immediately resented the definition he found. It was embarrassing that he had to look up what the intended insult was. *They play games with the English language, crafting nasty little acronyms and definitions to mask their hate.*

Returning to his email, he blocked all the letters he didn't recognize. It was no mystery how they got his email address. He'd encouraged his students to write. Now he would have to change his address, get new passwords, rethink all his online activity. There seemed to be no end to the harassment. He sat back and tried to clear his mind.

That novel isn't going to write itself.

And just like that, he found the silver lining. He'd always wanted to be a novelist. He just never got around to it. Now, with enforced inactivity, was the time. Braxton started to look for his original notes on his PC, but after several searches, Braxton couldn't find the files.

Maybe this is a blessing in disguise. He wanted to write an historical novel about the Peloponnesian War from the point of view of a young warrior named Lacedaemon. The first sentence lurked in his skull like a crouching bobcat, but Braxton believed in preparation. First he had to write an outline. Mulling over the words and shifting it around on the screen, he finally opted to dig into the actual start of the book.

He wrote five hundred words when there was a knock at the door. He looked up. It was already past six o'clock in the evening. Where had the day gone? Another feeling swept over him. Suzanna should have been home by now. As he rose to answer the door, each footfall made him wonder if something was wrong. It wasn't like her to be late. She was usually home by five. If she were working late, she would have called. In an instant it felt as if the room was shrinking in around him.

As Braxton entered the front hall, his heart sank. Through the narrow windows that framed the door he saw police uniforms, blurred by the white curtains. He paused at the door, fearing opening it. He rallied his courage and grasped the doorknob. Officers Gunnison and Flores stood on the porch with blank faces.

"Can I help you, officers?" he managed to meekly ask.

"May we come in, Mr. Knox?"

Braxton held the door. *If they want to come in, it is bad news.* Angela came halfway down the stairs.

"What's going on?"

"It might be better if you sat down," Gunnison said.

They went into the living room. His feet felt like lead, fighting each step. *Something has happened to Suzanna.*

"There's no way to sugarcoat this. Someone ran your wife off the road. Her car plunged into a ravine in Emeryville. She's at Cedars Sinai Hospital in intensive care."

Angela cried. Braxton held her in his arms.

"If you like, I can give you a ride to the hospital."

"I can drive. We'll follow you. Did anyone see who did it?"

"We have a couple of eyewitness reports. All of them said it was deliberate. One said it was a white Honda SUV. Another said it was a beige Hyundai SUV. We have a partial plate number, but chances are the vehicle was stolen. We have an APB out. Can you drive?"

"Let's roll."

Angela grabbed her backpack and got in the car. Braxton followed the cruiser through Holmby Hills, a leafy Portland suburb, until they hit Maynard Boulevard. Gunnison turned on the lights and siren and they followed him at seventy as the suburbs gave way to urban sprawl. McDonald's, Hardees, Wendy's, Arby's, Taco Bell, Taco John, Checks Cashed, Discount Furniture. Traffic pulled aside to let them pass. It took twenty minutes to reach the hospital. Braxton followed Gunnison around to the emergency exit and parked next to him in the lot.

They went in together. The orderly looked up from his desk.

"We're here to see Suzanna Knox. We know where to find her."

The orderly fished beneath the desk and handed Braxton and Angela two lanyards with laminated plates. "Wear these."

They took an elevator to the third floor and stepped into an antiseptic corridor smelling faintly of pine cleaner, past physicians in green garb and hats, past nurses wearing masks, to Room 353. The door was open and a doctor and nurse stood in the hall talking quietly to each other. The doctor looked up and intercepted them.

"This is Mrs. Knox's husband and daughter," Gunnison said.

The physician put a hand to Braxton's arm. "I'm so sorry."

Angela wailed. A few moments later, he joined her.

Chapter 8

The Good Guys

The next two weeks were a blur. Angela kept him centered. He had to be strong for her because he was all she had left in life. They spent hours holding each other tight as he struggled through the funeral process.

He had tried to work on his novel, hoping that it would prove therapeutic. It was a struggle to put together sentences and thoughts. Each day, he made a little progress, but it was far from what he had hoped. It was hard to breathe life into characters when so much had been ripped away from him.

Suzanna didn't want to be buried. They had talked about it years earlier. She wanted to be cremated and as her dutiful husband, he honored her wishes. Braxton held a private ceremony for close friends and family. Even so, someone slashed one of his car tires while parked at the funeral home to make plans for Suzanna. His self-proclaimed enemies had no boundaries, no sense of decorum. As a light rain fell, he changed the tire for the donut spare while Angela stood by.

His father was former law enforcement—FBI, back when they stood for law, order, and justice. Grayson Knox used his former position to dig into what the police were doing to find who had run Suzanna off the road. The sheriff's department had some grainy photos of the suspected cars, and a license plate that was registered to another car. Suzanna's death was already being fast-tracked to the cold case pile. Law enforcement's official stance was that the car was stolen and they still didn't have evidence that it had been directly involved with his wife's accident beyond the witness accounts. It was no accident to Braxton. Suzanna was a great driver, better than him. Their use of the word "accident" seemed to be a way to justify no further investigation.

In a matter of days, he'd had his career ripped from him, his wife killed, and had become a pariah. There had been no court, no chance for him to prove who he really was. Due process didn't exist as the woke tore him apart online. Deep down in his soul, he raged, his anger only held in check by his daughter and her need for his attention.

His wife's law firm agreed to take up his case against the university. That had only drawn more unwanted media coverage. It was bad enough that the school and student bodies were painting him as some alt-right crazy, but the media made matters worse. They highlighted his years in the military. The phrase that tore at him was, "He was a failed Ranger candidate. Oftentimes such men prove to be a risk to the community." One report referenced George Zimmerman and the death of Trayvon Martin, comparing their photos. His lawyer, Donna Craig, filed defamation and libel suits against the media outlets.

Braxton knew he wasn't a threat, as did the people that knew him. None of them stepped forward though, most likely out of fear of becoming targets themselves. His father gave two interviews, but having an older white man talking about how his son wasn't racist simply played into the hands of the media. Braxton was being tried in the court of public opinion.

The house would have been empty, if not for Angela's presence. Braxton tried to keep her in sight. She was one of the few things that still connected him to life before the chaos. They ate, studied, and cried together. He understood what she was feeling, the deep sense of loss. They read together, from two books he thought would help. One was the Bible, the other was *The Lord of the Rings*.

As the days passed, Braxton felt more human, despite his follow-up calls with the police which proved frustrating. Nothing was being done to find the cars that drove Suzanna off the road. The police voiced sympathy, and told him about their backlog of similar cases as if that would somehow lessen his anguish. He talked to a supervisor, a lieutenant who was ten years his junior. It was pointless. No one cared about what happened to his wife other than Braxton.

One morning he awoke to find his mailbox destroyed, caved in with a club or bat. The police told him there was nothing they could do and didn't bother to come out. After a trip to Lowes, he replaced it.

Two more days passed. After reading aloud from *The Fellowship of the Ring*, he made sure his daughter was in bed. Turning on the television, he watched a late-night rerun of *Star Trek—the Original Series*. Mindless entertainment, something that harkened to his youth when he could come home from school and the show played on his family's black-and-white TV. Times were so much simpler then. The differences between the good and bad guys were clearer, more defined.

At one in the morning, he turned off the television and started down the hall to the guest room. He couldn't sleep in the bed he and his wife shared, not yet. As he entered the room, he heard a loud booming sound from the front door. A battering ram!

He wheeled, thinking about the guns he had placed in the house. The closest one was on the nightstand, an old-school .357 revolver. Braxton darted for it as he heard the thunder of numerous boots cascade into his house. Someone yelled "Police!" but Braxton ignored that, grabbing the gun from the nightstand drawer.

Two officers in full tactical gear, weapons aimed, filled the doorway to the bedroom. Others rushed through the hallway towards Angela's room.

"Drop the weapon, now!" a man's voice commanded.

These were real police. He'd done nothing wrong. Carefully, he held the gun by the grips and his thumb and forefinger, moved it to the bed, and set it down. His gaze focused on the name tag on the leader's vest, Kreiger.

They were on him in an instant, whipping him around, cuffing him and securing his pistol. Voices called out throughout the house and he heard Angela cry out, more from fear than pain. "What is going on here?" he demanded, but was ignored.

They shoved him to his living room. Relief hit when he saw officers leading Angela out of the hallway, taking her to the front door. At least eight policemen in full SWAT gear, moving through the house, opening every cabinet door in the kitchen, checking furniture. He asked again what was happening, but none responded. Someone found his wallet and radioed in his name and address to a dispatcher.

Someone called out, "Gun!" It ratcheted the tension of the officers—he saw it in their body language. Others barked, "Clear," as they moved through the house. Two officers bent down and were talking to Angela. One finally came over and talked to the officer standing guard over him, whispering something in his ear.

The officer watching him turned him around, far more gentle than Kreiger. "Sorry about this, Mr. Knox. We got a 9-1-1 call that you were holding a gun on your daughter." He removed the handcuffs and Braxton turned around. He memorized that officer's name tag. Grace.

"That's ridiculous, Officer Grace."

The officer seemed far more relaxed. "We get them from time to time, swatting calls."

He had heard of the calls. They went beyond mere harassment. He or Angela could have been killed by an officer that overreacted. Suppressed anger rose. Slashing tires was annoying. This was an invasion of his home that had put both him and his daughter at risk. They released Angela who came up and hugged him tightly. Braxton rose, rubbing his wrists from the too tight handcuffs. "Who made the call?"

"Sir, we will look into that. The kind of people that do this often use burner phones though... sometimes old payphones."

"You're saying they are going to get away with this? You broke down my front door and tossed my house. Someone can make that happen and not go to jail?"

The officer held his hand out as if to pat down Braxton's rage. "Sir, we will do everything possible to find the people behind his. You have my word on that."

His word meant nothing.

"Look, someone killed my wife. I'm willing to bet it's the same people behind this and the vandalism to my car and my mailbox. You have got to do something other than make promises."

"I assure you, Mr. Braxton, we take this seriously. You think we like being rolled out on a possible hostage situation in the middle of the morning? Trust me, we don't."

Braxton set his jaw set and gathered his thoughts. "Everyone keeps telling me what they can and can't do. When is someone going to take this seriously? These people keep screwing with my life. They are putting my child in danger."

Officer Kreiger strolled into the conversation. "You have a lot of guns here. More guns than people, in fact."

"What does that have to do with anything? I purchased them legally."

Kreiger planted his fists on his hips. "Nothing. I was just making an observation. It makes me wonder if you are one of those alt-right crazies too."

"Too?"

"I saw the news about you. You got fired for being a radical conservative. What did you think was going to happen?"

Braxton took a half-step forward to the officer, forcing the first cop to intercede. "Back off, Tony." The second cop stepped away, but his face told Braxton he wanted to have a reason to beat him up.

"I have a right to protect myself and my daughter," Braxton growled.

Officer Grace nodded. "Yes sir, you do. What my colleague was pointing out was that you got on the radar of some bad people—folks that don't play by the rules. He's trying to figure out if you are somehow deliberately punching their buttons."

"I'm the target here," he snapped back. He refused to use the word "victim." He didn't want sympathy or pity; he wanted action. "I legally own those guns to protect myself and my daughter. I haven't done anything to antagonize these people. What I need is for you people to do your jobs."

His words made Officer Grace bristle. "We are doing all we can do. We will open an investigation for filing a false police report on this perp. We'll try to find out who called it in. I'm merely trying to set your expectations."

"Oh, my expectations are set. You'll go through the motions, but as soon as you hit a dead end, you'll stop and move on to the next case. In the meantime, I have to worry about how these hoods are going to come at me next."

"Have you considered moving?" the officer suggested.

Braxton's eyes narrowed. "Are you suggesting I should run? I haven't done anything wrong."

The police officer nodded once. "I know. Your safety is important and this place may not be it."

Deep down, Braxton knew the officer was right. At the same time, he refused to concede.

They keep taking from me, and I will not let them do it anymore. This is our home.

Taking Angela someplace different would be another mental hit on his daughter, one that he could not tolerate.

One of the officers tossed his wallet onto the couch and the members of the SWAT team left the house, closing the door behind them. His eyes swept the room. He saw every drawer open, every cabinet exposed. A sense of violation gripped him. Moving next to his daughter, he held Angela tight.

"Why did they do this?" she sobbed.

"All they have is hate, honey," he tried to assure her.

"They took Mom from us. These people took your job. What else do they want?"

"When all you have is hate, there is no end. They operate outside the law and know it. They don't care about what they've done. In their eyes, they only see targets. They will keep coming until they find new ones."

"What can we do?"

"Be vigilant, be smart. We are the good guys, remember?"

Chapter 9

The Hammer Shot

Braxton felt as if his entire world was under assault after the swatting. What he had left of his former life was Angela. A primal urge came over him to make sure she was safe. He started with showing her how to break down and reassemble one of his guns, a Ruger. She absorbed the information, almost as if she could read his mind and felt the same fears he did.

Then came weapons handling training for two hours.

"So why do the gang members in the movies always hold their guns sideways when they fire?" she asked.

"Because, Hollywood is full of morons."

She actually cracked a thin smile which he burned in his mind.

They went to Rudy's range and he taught her to discharge the weapon, drilling in safety the way the Army had done with him. Angela was a quick learner. Her grouping got better each time. When they finished, he drove back home.

"You did really good," he assured her. She smiled, but not like she used to, when he praised her *before*. This smile was sad.

"I had to, Dad."

"Why do you say that?"

"It's just us now. You and me."

She does understand. "I don't think these people are going to let up. Whoever called in that swatting on us did it out of spite."

His daughter glared, looking older than her years. "You lost your job. What else do they want?"

My life? he thought, but said instead, "I taught at the university for years. I understand these kids. It's not enough for them, nothing ever is. They want to destroy people's lives. They don't see it as harassment. They see it as justice."

"They picked the wrong people to pick on," she assured him.

"It's us against the world," he assured her. "In a few days, we will go up to Grandpa's cabin. I think we'll both feel better being there. If nothing else, they won't know where we are to harass us."

Angela walked over to him and gave him a hug. "Don't worry, Dad. I've got your back."

* * *

Braxton's lawyer, Donna Craig, commanded his respect. She had demanded the police reports on the swatting call, and had followed up for him. Her legal war against the media outlets was unrelenting. Channel 3 had succumbed with a retraction to their characterization of Braxton. From what Donna told him, they were negotiating damages.

Donna talked to him every day, if only to assure him she was still working the case. It had been two weeks since the swatting call and a part of him wondered if things might be calming down finally. There was a tension in her voice that told him something was different, and it might not be good.

She cut to the chase. "Mr. Knox, the university has told me they joined with that student, Debbie Driggs, in pushing the DoJ to look into your utterance in class as a civil rights matter."

"You're kidding, right?"

"I wish I was. They probably hope that you'll be charged with violating Ms. Driggs's civil rights with an aim at reducing what they have to pay you for wrongful discharge."

"I can't believe this is happening," he said.

"I'm going to reach out to the Bureau. I know some people there. I'm going to try and get in front of this, find out what their intentions are."

"Thank you," was all he could muster. There was a feeling that washed over him, a feeling that the rest of the world was conspiring against him.

"You will get through this," she affirmed. Donna had already done a great job in handling the insurance company in terms of his wife's death. Per his contract, the school owed him for the rest of his time. This latest dirty trick was irritating, as if they were rubbing salt in an already open wound. It amazed him how Driggs's one loud voice was capable of inflicting such carnage on his life.

He went to Planet Fitness, leaving Angela to study. The workout took his mind off the news that Donna had laid on him. His muscles ached, but it was a good pain. It reminded him of being in the Army. Back then, he didn't have to worry about pronouns or people's little sensitivities. In the Army he did what he was told to do, and enjoyed it. His NCOs pushed him hard and the reward was a physique that he still maintained.

Stopping at the library, he printed off articles on when the Department of Justice had recently used the Civil Rights law. While he trusted Donna, he wanted to understand the law as much as he could. From what he saw, the application of the law had morphed over time. What had begun as a law to prevent denying someone their civil rights had turned into a cudgel that the federal government applied when other legal actions had failed.

Braxton stopped at Chipotle and got two meals. When he got home, she was still reading her textbooks. She stopped when he came in, quickly grabbing the bag. "No queso, right? Their queso has a weird texture."

"No queso."

They sat and ate, and for a few minutes, life seemed normal. He didn't want to burden her with the call he had taken from Donna. There was no need to spoil the moment. That was what he missed, being able to share the minute details of life with Suzanna. There were times that Braxton had to remind himself that he couldn't open up with Angela the way he had with his wife.

They watched television for an hour, their nightly ritual, then he sat in the chair next to her bed and started reading her *The Return of the King*. After white-knuckling her way through the Battle of Helm's Deep in the previous book, Angela was excited to be nearing the end of the saga. Braxton made it through two chapters, savoring the flow of Tolkien's prose. As they finished, he bent down and kissed his daughter on the forehead.

His normal sleep pattern was slowly returning. At around eleven o'clock, he shut off the lights and slid onto his side of the bed. He could feel the void still, the spot where his wife would have laid next to him. Sometimes in the night he reached over and felt for her, more out of instinct than anything else. Finding nothing in the space, he rolled over and let sleep take him.

He jerked awake to a series of bangs in the living room. Voices barking orders. He knew the sound; he had heard it just two days previously. A battering ram hitting the front door. He thought first of Angela as footsteps thundered through the house. He sat up, making sure his hands were visible.

His bedroom door flew open. Flashlights stabbed his eyes.

"Police! Don't move. Put your hands on your head."

Voices boomed from the hallway. It was just him and Angela in the house. Why were they so nervous?

A gunshot pierced the air. Not like television. Loud enough to make his ears ache. He jerked upright. Black-gloved hands grabbed him, throwing him face down on the bed.

They roughly handcuffed him.

"Where is my daughter?" he cried.

Chaos roared as he struggled, trying to roll over, only to be held down.

"What was that shot? Where's my daughter?"

He heard Monsieur barking upstairs, then Monsieur whined.

A voice came from down the hall. "Ambulance is on the way."

"I want to see my daughter!"

"Relax, Mr. Knox. I'm Agent Lawson of the FBI. You are under arrest."

"Why is an ambulance coming?" Craning his head, he called out "Angela!" but her voice didn't respond. He tried to rein in his panic, but couldn't. Agent Lawson read him his rights as if the shot hadn't happened. They asked if he understood the words, and he grunted a yes. Hands grabbed him once more, turning him over. Braxton rose to his feet, only to have more hands grapple with him. "Is my daughter alright?"

"Paramedics are on the way," another agent said.

"I want to see her!"

"Mr. Knox, you need to calm down," Agent Lawson said.

"Screw you! That's my daughter. I want to see her—now!"

"You need to calm down," an officer said.

Time stretched to infinity with nothing but the voices of the agents as they tromped through his home. The less he said, the better. A part of his brain wanted to know what he was being charged with, but everything depended on the status of his daughter.

The paramedics arrived, and he saw the gurney go down the hall. A few minutes later, he saw it come out with Angela on it. A sheet was placed over her body and when he saw her face, it was ashen.

"What have you done? What happened to my daughter?" he cried.

Brutish hands grabbed him, forcing him to stand. "We're taking you in now." An officer came down the hall holding his guns, all tagged. They pushed him out through the family room, grabbed him by the cuffs to guide him out of his house. The doorframe was shattered, as it had been from the swatting incident. His house was in shambles once more. It was different this time. They had hurt his little girl. The swatting incident had been a vicious prank. This time it was his own government acting with intent.

Angela was all he could think about on the ride to the county sheriff's office. He asked three times for updates, but the officers remained mute. As the black SUV wheeled up to the sheriff's office, he saw the reporters assembled. Someone had tipped them off.

Braxton was led out of the car and bombarded with lights and questions. Still in his pajama bottoms and T-shirt, he was forced to make the perp walk. They fingerprinted him, lined him up for a mugshot, and refused to talk to him about Angela. When he was placed in a holding cell, he asked once more.

"I'm sorry, Mr. Knox," the sheriff's deputy replied. "The FBI agents said they thought your daughter was reaching for a weapon. She was shot."

A drain opened beneath him, sucking the life from his body. Angela didn't have a weapon. A numbness washed his mind.

"How is she?" was all he could get out.

The deputy shook his head. "I'm very sorry, sir. She was dead by the time she got to the hospital."

He opened his mouth but no words came. His child was gone. Tears formed in the corners of his eyes. Angela was not just dead; she had been murdered. The government that he had fought for and supported had killed her in her bed.

His entire world crumbled. Memories of Suzanna resurfaced, fanning the flames of grief. How could they have done this? They had told him the charges against him, but he couldn't remember. All he knew was the soul-wrenching pain that held him in its grasp.

"Is there anything I can get you?" the deputy queried.

"I want my lawyer," he said through clenched teeth.

Chapter 10

Alone

They took him to a meeting room, uncuffed him and told him to sit. He hated the orange jumpsuit they had put him in, almost as much an indignity as the cavity search. Orange prison crocs were the crowning touch, making his feet sweaty and cold. The door to the outside hallway opened. Donna Craig and her senior partner Marv Myer entered the room. Meyer's presence gave Braxton a sense of the meeting's importance.

"How are you?" Donna said, her metal chair scraping on the floor.

"They killed my daughter."

Myer nodded. "I'm sorry for your loss. We got a short briefing with the Bureau. Two of their agents were convinced that Angela was reaching for a weapon."

"A fifteen-year-old girl? That's ludicrous and you know it."

"So does the FBI," Donna says. "The media highlighted that aspect of the incident. It's been a PR nightmare for them. But, it's the FBI. They are more interested in protecting their reputation than the actual pursuit of justice. Their press announcement highlighted the number of guns you owned and that one was, and I quote here, 'near,' the room your daughter was in."

Braxton knew he should ask about his own legal woes, but the death of his daughter tore at him in ways he could not comprehend. "They can't get away with this."

"They won't," Myer assured him. "But right now, we need to deal with these charges against you. The good news is that half of the country thinks that the FBI is corrupt. This is going to play well with them. Fox News has reached out to discuss this. I can get your story and that of your daughter out there. This is our shot at controlling the narrative. I didn't want to do that without a green light from you."

"I don't want to talk to the media."

"You don't have to. Donna and I will handle it."

He nodded.

Donna spoke in a soothing tone. "We posted your bond. Marv has arranged to get you out a side door. I don't think you should go home. The media have it staked out and there are a lot of crazies coming out of the woodwork."

The house no longer had meaning for him. What made it a home were his wife and daughter. They were gone, dead. Now it was just a building where he kept his things. If anything, it was a material reminder of his life that no longer existed. "I have a place I can go. My dad has a cabin. Pretty much off the grid."

"Good."

"What about my guns? I need the means to defend myself."

Marv nodded. "I pushed the US attorney on that. None of your charges were violent. She assured me they confiscated your weapons for the protection of the agents. They are going to release them to you."

"Their protection? They broke in my door unannounced and shot an unarmed girl. Where exactly was the threat?"

Donna put her hands on his in the center of the table. "Braxton, they are hitting you with denying civil rights charges. If they had said they were going to arrest you, I would have arranged to have you come in and surrender. This is not about the law. This is about politics and posturing. I think the university is working behind the scenes in all of this. Everything they did, they did for show. In terms of substance, their case is thin."

"None of that brings back my family."

"You're right. I'm sorry." She squeezed his hands. "But right now, we need to focus on you. In the next few days, I expect them to float a plea deal. The press they got from Angela's death makes them look like gun-toting tyrants and that is an image the FBI doesn't like. They will move to try and wrap this up as quickly as possible."

"I want the person who killed Angela brought to justice." The last word he spoke was bitter in his mouth. Justice no longer had the same definition it did through most of his life.

"There will be an investigation," Meyer stated.

"You mean there will be a cover-up."

"They'll try," Donna said. "We need to go after them all."

"For what? None of this brings back Suzanna or Angela." Futility's icy grasp held him for a moment.

"No," Meyer cut in. "Sometimes making them pay is the only way to extract vengeance. They will pay. The Bureau didn't follow their own procedures. They knew Donna was your attorney but never reached out to her. Despite that, they went in with excessive force. We will make them pay, Braxton. You have my word on that."

"I can't even live in my house. They are making me a fugitive from their *social justice*." He spat the last two words with venom. "Every aspect of my life has been taken from me. Money won't fill that void."

Donna nodded. "I get it—I understand fully. This is a very emotional time for you. When the dust settles, you will feel differently. These people are relentless. You told me about your novel; they will make sure no publisher picks it up. They will bomb you with bad reviews. They won't stop, not until it costs them dearly. Let me handle that. I will extract blood from them in the form of dollars. I'm going to go after the FBI and the university."

"That's not enough." He thought about Debra Driggs, the people that sabotaged his car and called in the SWAT. "You are going to where the money is, but there are a lot of guilty people out there that you are not going to change with lawsuits."

"It will be harder, especially in this state, to get to the instigators of this. They will wail about their freedom of speech, regardless of the carnage they cause. And the judges will side with them in the end."

"They leaked this to the press. The media was all lined up for my perp walk. They can't do that, can they?"

"The FBI is not supposed to do that, no," Donna replied, glancing at Meyers. "But they do it all of the time. Look at what they did down at Mar-a-Lago with the former president when they raided him. The FBI has a lot of good people working there, but it is a political organization at its heart. You can thank Hoover for that. They are masters at manipulating the media to taint public opinion."

"Or future jury pools," Meyer added.

Braxton remembered the raid. He found himself facing the same indignity as the president. "Can we learn who did that? There has to be a way."

"The only way we learn that is if someone in the media spills the beans. They are highly motivated to not burn their sources in the Bureau. We will use it as one of our talking points when we go after the FBI for what they did to Angela."

"Talking points won't bring her back."

She nodded, then wiped a tear from her eye. "I know. It's impossible for us to roll the clock back. The war against the establishment that has come after you has already started. Once we walk out of here, we will escalate this war they've started. Suzanna wasn't a coworker for us, she was a dear member of our family. We will find a way to get you and your family justice."

Braxton believed Donna, but he also lived in the real world. He knew that the people that ran Suzanna off the road would never be found, not by the police. The woke were a plague of locusts, devouring their targets, moving on to the next field to wreak havoc. The legal system took too long and had too many variables. Braxton knew he couldn't rely on it. In the pit of his stomach, he knew that most of the people who had destroyed his life would never face justice.

Unless he delivered it.

It wasn't a comforting thought. Suzanna and Angela deserved better than what the legal system could provide. How he would do that was something for another day. His immediate concern was getting out of jail. "When can I leave?"

Meyer responded. "They are processing the paperwork and will bring you your possessions. We have a car outside at the side door to get you out of here. Tomorrow the counterattack starts. We go after these people hard and fast. We get the media to see what the FBI has done."

"You've already got many people riled up online," Meyer added. "A lot of folks are sick and tired of this woke cancel-culture crowd shit. Someone started a GoFundMe for your legal defense. Of course, a handful of crazies have come out of the woodwork. The usual militia types. We have someone in our office handling the social media spin, blocking the dangerous ones."

"I can pay my own way. People don't need to donate money to me."

"We're doing this pro bono, but don't be so fast at shutting down the GoFundMe. There's going to be expenses that none of us can anticipate. What's important now is to get you someplace safe and solidify our strategy."

"I want my guns back. I have to be able to defend myself."

"I assumed as much. We spoke to them and they have agreed to return them as soon as they are done validating they were purchased legally."

"They had no reason to take them."

"That's what I told them. We will make sure that happens today... tomorrow at the latest."

Braxton nodded. He admired his wife even more given the people she had worked with. Suzanna had always been strong, always been his rock in life. She would not want him to roll over given the events that had hit him. She would want him to fight back, fast and hard. He knew he needed to resolve his legal problems first, then find a way forward.

Suzanna and Angela deserved that much from him.

Chapter 11

Bugout Bag

It was two thirty when they left the police station through the underground garage. They exited via a back entrance, turned onto Parsons Street, and drove toward the city, leaving a gaggle of confused media parasites milling around the front entrance.

"Braxton," Donna said, "are you sure you want to go home?"

"Why wouldn't I?"

"They know where you live now. It may not be the most secure location."

Braxton buried his face in his hands. "Where am I supposed to go?"

"You mentioned your grandfather had a cabin in the woods."

"Let me think about that." He pulled out his phone. He dialed Rudy Petcock.

"Discount Shooter Supply," a cheery woman answered.

"Is Rudy in?"

"Who shall I say is asking?"

"Braxton Knox." He leaned in as the car made a tight turn.

"One moment."

"Braxton! How the hell are ya?"

"Hey, Rudy. I hate to bother you, but I wonder if you have time to get together?"

"Sure. What can I do for you?"

"You hear that my house got swatted?"

"No. Are you kidding? What happened?"

"Rudy, it's a long story and I'd rather tell you in person. Do you have any time tomorrow?"

"Sure. Want to meet me for lunch? Say two o'clock at Smoky's BBQ in Stevenson? I'm going to need a consult on some weapons purchases."

Stevenson was sixty miles away.

"Yeah, I can do that. See you tomorrow."

"Looking forward to it."

Braxton put the phone away.

"Who was that?" Donna said.

"An old friend."

"You want to tell me any more?"

"I'd rather not. The less you know, the better."

"You're not planning something illegal, are you?"

"Of course not. Let's just say he's an old friend who can help me. There's no illegality involved."

"Braxton, believe me, I understand how the events of the last couple of weeks have upended your life in ways you could never anticipate."

"That's the thing. I could anticipate them. I should have seen this coming."

They turned on to his street. His house still stood, the smashed door shut, lawn trampled. The flowers that Suzanna had put in decorative pots were there, but the pots themselves were moved out of their usual place. He vaguely remembered thanking Donna as he got out of the car, moving almost zombie-like towards his house.

Our house. Now just my house.

Across the street, Albert Gorelick sat in a folding lawn chair on his front porch. He waited until Braxton got out and Donna drove off before walking across the street. Gorelick was a retired pharmacist with a white beard, wearing blue jeans and a plaid shirt. Braxton stood at the bottom of his steps, dreading going inside.

He saw Albert and nodded.

"Heard about what happened. I am so sorry, Braxton. Let me know if there's anything I can do."

"I don't think there's anything anybody can do."

"I been watching your place since the Gestapo came by. Car came by filled with those ANTIFA types. You know what I mean.

All masked up. They slowed down so I took a picture with my phone and wrote down their license plate number. They saw me and thought better of it, whatever shit they were plannin', and took off. I called the police but they said they wouldn't come out unless there were guns involved. Damned cops. Thought you'd like to know."

"Thanks, Albert."

"Way I understand it, all this shit you been through, is just because you called a woman a woman, is that it?"

"Pretty much."

"Yeah. Well, I keep to myself. I'm not interested in fighting with these lunatics, but this is our neighborhood. We got to stick together."

"I appreciate it."

Gorelick shook his head. "I just don't understand what happened to this country. I'm glad my parents didn't live to see what the world is turning into."

"Amen, brother. I may be going off grid for a while."

"I don't blame you. Want me to keep an eye on your place?"

"Thank you. But don't get involved. These people will stop at nothing."

"I'll just sit on my porch and take pictures. Want me to collect your mail?"

"Yeah, thanks."

Braxton paused to adjust the potted flowers, then pushed open his unlocked front door. Monsieur was excited to see him. Braxton let him out in the fenced-in backyard. The dog was one thing that hadn't changed.

He had to arrange the funerals. Suzanna's parents had called while he'd been in police custody. Desperate. Inconsolable. He called back. Suzanna's mother Martha answered the phone.

"Oh Braxton!" she wailed. "What has happened to our girls?"

"Martha, I am so sorry. I'm sorry you had to hear this secondhand. Ever since she was run off the road, I've been dealing with the police. All they have is a description of the vehicle and a partial plate number. They'll find them. This won't bring Suzanna back, but they will find them."

His father-in-law Patrick took the phone.

"Braxton, it's Patrick. Would you like us to come out there?"

The Boyettes lived in Maryland. It seemed unnecessary.

"There's nothing you can do right now. Let me make the arrangements. I'll do it for next week. You know that Suzanna wished to be cremated. I'll do the same with Angela."

"We would like to bring our little girl back to Maryland. We have a family plot nearby. My parents are in it. It would give us some small measure of solace."

"She was very specific about this, Patrick."

"I understand. Let me talk it over with Martha and get back to you. I think we can accede to her wishes and still bring the ashes back home with us."

"Of course."

"Are you taking any action against these cancel pigs?"

"There's nothing I can do. You know what it's like out here."

"We feel so hopeless. People like us never go into DC anymore. We used to love to take visitors, show them the memorials. Even here, in Ellicott City we have homeless encampments, people shooting up in the street..."

"Patrick, we'll talk about this when you come out for the funeral. We are going to say goodbye to Suzanna and Angela together. That's the way they would have wanted it."

"Will you call me as soon as you know?"

"I promise."

Braxton sat in his empty house staring at the walls. The police had not yet released his guns. They were in a frenzy trying to connect him to some illegality. But they hadn't got all his guns. He'd kept a nine-millimeter Ruger hidden behind a rafter in the basement. He thought about getting it. There was an excellent chance that the hoodlums would return and try to set fire to his house. He knew how they thought. As a teenager, he had come perilously close to becoming a sociopath. He was a junior at Jefferson High School in Midlothian, Illinois, when Roger Vandergraff, the guidance counselor, called him into his office one day.

"Braxton, I like you. I saw you stand up for that Bradford kid when Max Haley was pushing him around."

Braxton shrugged. A command appearance before the guidance counselor was never a good thing.

"You have character. You also have flaws. I know you stole those tools from shop class, and I'd like you to return them."

"What   tools?"

"The ones you put in your locker when you thought nobody was watching. I have also spoken with the man who manages B-Side records on State Street, who suspects you of shoplifting CDs."

"Shit."

"When I was your age, I did a lot of dumb shit too. I had a Scout leader who kicked my butt. I'm here to kick yours. I see your potential. I don't want you wasting it on stupid adolescent activities like shoplifting and stealing from the school. What is it you want to do with your life, son?"

Braxton went blank. "That's a good question."

"It's a very good question."

He thought about the prayer of gratitude he had uttered that night years ago. How it turned his life around. Yet here he was, sitting in an empty house with the walls closing in. Everything he had achieved, everything for which he'd worked, turned to ashes. Regret. Bitterness. He knew what they wanted. They wanted him to kill himself. He'd known such people all his life. They had been the bullies and mean girls in high school. Most of them grew up, wised up, and became better persons. But recently, it seemed that society— education, parenting, whatever you wanted to call it—was turning out a new species devoid of empathy, understanding, or the ability to love.

Downtown Portland was a ghost town. Even Nike had closed their signature store because of crime. Homeless camps everywhere. Every park, every commercial district, was covered with discarded needles, bongs, human feces, insane people staggering through traffic. He'd hoped to move his family east, to a more rural and civilized life, but that had depended on his job. And having a family.

He heaved himself out of the chair, went down to the basement, dragged a footstool out, and reached behind the rafter for his pistol, still in its carbon fiber box along with two magazines. He grabbed two boxes of ammo and stuck them in a rucksack. A bugout bag. If someone had suggested twenty years ago, or even ten, that the country was on the verge of collapse, he would have laughed.

He wasn't hungry. He took the bugout bag upstairs with him and tried to sleep. Every minute sound in the house stirred him, made him wonder if someone was there with him.

Chapter 12

"Rudy"

In the morning Braxton forced himself to eat a banana and an English muffin with cream cheese, then rode his bicycle to Gateway Towing, located in an industrial strip that included some auto body shops, Discount Tires, and a pawn shop. He set his bike on the pavement next to the office entrance. A picture window framed a neon sign. Gateway Towing. On the other side of the window was a three-car service bay where Ross tinkered with his cars and did some custom work for pals. Ross was in the service bay wearing a gray coverall with his name stitched on the breast in red, bent over the engine bay of a recent Mustang pointing. On the other side of the hood stood a big guy with a beard, pumped to the max, wearing a Hawaiian shirt covered with Rat Finks.

Ross looked up. "There he is. I had to replace those tires. Gave you a deal."

"That's fine, Ross. What do I owe you?"

"Come into my office."

Braxton followed Ross into his office, the one with the window, where Ross was behind a gunmetal gray desk and Braxton sat on a red vinyl kitchen chair. A table held copies of automotive magazines.

"You want a Pepsi?"

"Sure."

Ross swiveled to a cube fridge on the floor and pulled out two cans, slid one across the desk. They popped their cans. Ross looked at a sheet of paper. "I put on Goodyear Wranglers, balanced the wheels, filled them to thirty-five. Four hundred and fifty-six dollars."

He slid the receipt across the desk. Braxton folded it and put it in his hip pocket, pulled out his wallet and slid the credit card across.

"I appreciate this, Ross."

"This shit they pulled with you, it pisses me off."

"I know."

"And they pull this shit every chance they get. I don't know what to say. Deepest condolences doesn't really cut it. If it were my family…"

He shook his head and took the card.

"I'm not going to take this lying down."

"What are you going to do?"

"I don't know yet. I don't want to break the law. I don't want to become a fugitive. They'd love that. I'm thinking of going to the press. Dan Bongino maybe. Somebody at Fox contacted my lawyer this morning. They wanted to know if I'd appear on his show."

"You gonna do it?"

"I'm thinking about it. If there's one thing I've learned out here, it's that these scumbags only fear one thing: bad publicity. They can't handle it. They're like shrieky high school girls."

"Yeah, but what about these fuckers that swatted your house?"

"I don't know how to find them. I may know some people that do. And the people that drove Suzanna off the road wore masks. It was a stolen vehicle."

"Did they find it?"

"Don't know."

"Let me know if there's anything I can do."

Braxton's bike just fit in the rear seat after he removed its front wheel. He headed for Stevenson, a town of thirty thousand at the foot of the Cascades in Clackamas County. Smoky's was right on the main drag, sandwiched between a big box store and a Ford dealership. A sign at the dealership advertised, *Fully Electric F-150s —30% Off.*

He drove past the restaurant. It was one o'clock when he parked in front of the Stevenson Public Library on Brand Street, a tree-lined semi-residential area. He went inside, smiled at the librarian, and took a seat at one of the three computer stations. Using his daughter's email, he created an account, came up with a password, and went to the satellite phone store. Satellitephonestore.com. He ordered the Inmarsat IsatPhone 2, entered Angela's credit card number, and had them ship the phone to Albert. He sent the receipt to his phone, stopped at a FedEx Kinko's on the way out of town, and printed it out.

Smoky's parking lot was about half full, and half of those were pickup trucks. Braxton parked next to a Prius with a *Meat Is Murder* on the bumper. The smell of burnt ends and hickory hit him before he reached the door. That barbecue aroma. He was already salivating. Inside, a pert hostess behind a wooden desk looked up.

"Hello! Would you like to be seated?"

"I'm looking for a friend of mine."

"Ah. You would be the gentleman. Follow me please."

Holding two laminated menus like Moses descending the mountain, she led him to a booth in the back where Rudy Petcock sat staring at his phone. Rudy looked up, smiled, and took off his glasses. He stepped out of the booth to hug Braxton.

"Good to see you, bro."

"Thanks, man."

They slid in the booth opposite each other.

"I cannot believe the shit storm you've been through. Tell me how I can help."

Braxton looked around. No one near. No cameras. "I'd tell you what I'd like to do, but you never know who's listening."

"I hear that. Anything you need, as long as it's legal."

"I need time to process this. I'm going up in the mountains. My grandfather has a cabin there, if it hasn't been broken into by the homeless."

Rudy held up a hand. "I didn't hear that. Don't tell me anything you wouldn't want the cops to know."

They looked at the menus.

"I'm getting the brisket sandwich," Rudy said.

The waitress returned and they ordered.

"I need five hundred rounds of nine millimeter," Braxton said.

"I can do that. Let me check my inventory. That's a lot of ammo. I trust this is just for target practice."

"Correct. I also need an Accuracy International in .308 with six hundred rounds of ammo. Oh and a few spare barrels of varying lengths and some spare bolts. And some Tannerite too. A case of that should do."

"What the fuck, man? I'd ask you what you're planning, but you might tell me."

"The NRA's holding a shooting contest in a couple months. There's a five-thousand-dollar prize." The lie came easy to him. Rudy knew he was lying.

"The rifle you want costs a pretty penny. Brand-new, a full setup can bump you up into the thirty-thousand-dollar range."

Braxton had done his research and knew that the Accuracy International was what he wanted. It was used around the world by snipers. "Shit. I had my heart set on that baby."

"I think I can get you used for about ten grand. Let me look into it."

"All right."

"I can have it shipped to my sister's place in Idaho. You'll have to drive to pick it up."

"I can do that. Why would your sister agree?"

"Stella and I see eye to eye. She's a competitive shooter, lives on a ranch in Homedale. I'll phone her today. She was a helicopter pilot in Afghanistan. She used to live in Portland. When she returned four years ago, she couldn't believe the changes. They sold their place and moved to Idaho. Her and her husband, they raise horses, and they have a shooting range on their property."

"All right."

"I'll make a few phone calls and let you know. You still using that phone?"

"Today's the last day. I'm getting some burner phones. I'll phone you."

"Forgive me for asking, Brax, but..."

Braxton shrugged. "Just preparing for the apocalypse, Rudy. Nothing a million other veterans haven't done. Going off-grid. I've lost my family—I've lost everything. My academic career is finished. Suzanna was my rudder and I feel like I'm adrift right now. I need to get away from society for a while, sort things out."

"You sure about that? There are colleges that would hire you. You know who they are."

"Maybe. Like I said, I need some time by myself to figure out what's going on."

"All right. Here's my sister's address. Write it down."

Braxton pulled a pen and pad from his jacket pocket. Rudy gave him the address.

The waitress brought their orders. Rudy insisted on picking up the tab. Braxton stopped at the bank and withdrew five thousand in cash. The teller didn't blink an eye. For all she knew, Braxton wanted to buy drugs, a perfectly legitimate exercise in Portland.

He returned to his house. Across the street, Albert Gorelick gave him the thumbs up. Braxton waved, went inside, and started packing. Cold weather gear, canned goods, a hand-cranked radio/flashlight, the Ruger, all his remaining ammo, and his camo uniform from the Gulf. After he loaded the car, he went across the street.

"What's your phone number, Albert?"

Albert told him. Braxton wrote it down in a small spiral notebook.

"I'm going away for a few days. I'll call you when I get to where I'm going. You won't recognize the number, but it will be me."

"No prob."

"Albert, I'm ordering a few things. Would you keep an eye on my doorstep, and take them into your house?"

"No prob."

With Monsieur sitting in the passenger seat, Braxton headed east. On the way out of town, he passed a homeless camp that had taken over a roadside stop. The cabin was in the Mt. Hood National Forest, grandfathered in before the park service began restricting construction. It lay at the end of a six-mile dirt trail south of Breitenbush that defied most vehicles.

The last few miles were like riding a bucking bronco as the RAV4 negotiated ravines, rocks, and massive roots. Finally Braxton pulled into the clearing in front of the cabin. It looked like it could have been built in the nineteenth century with layered logs, a stone foundation, and a chimney. The metal roof had been designed to look like shingles. A sheltered wood porch encompassed the front expanse, two steps up from the yard, covered in pine needles. The shutters were closed. It was so far off the beaten path that few knew it existed.

Braxton retrieved the key from beneath a hollow rock in the backyard and entered through the back door. The interior smelled of musty pine. A fine patina of dust covered the hardwood floor and countertops. It was basically three rooms plus a loft and a basement, two bedrooms and a big kitchen/living/recreation room looking out the front. One bathroom. The electricity had been turned off long ago so he would have to pump his own water. The living room contained a massive stone fireplace. A cast-iron stove sat in a corner of the bedroom.

A tarp in the backyard covered a hefty stack of firewood. Years before, his grandfather had brought up an EcoFlow portable power generator hooked up to an exercycle. It could also draw power from solar panels. Braxton didn't know how long he could stay there off-grid, but if it turned into an extended stay, he might have to look into that. In the meantime, he needed solitude to figure out what had happened and what he intended to do about it. He opened the trap door to the basement and descended the rickety ladder holding a flashlight. Braxton opened an ancient sea chest in the corner and took out an untapped bottle of Cutty Sark. Going back to the living room, he sat on the worn leather sofa and opened the bottle. Monsieur jumped up and rested his head on Braxton's lap. He let the alcohol burn in his throat as he enjoyed the physical contact of his pet.

It's you and me, Monsieur… we're all that is left.

Chapter 13

Prepped

It took two days for Braxton to hook up a solar power system. He installed a water filtration system for the well and hooked up three cameras outside. It wasn't a comprehensive security plan. That would take more research. But he wasn't taking any chances. Besides, doing the research filled his days, gave him a temporary sense of purpose.

Figuring out internet connectivity took another two days. He arranged for a satellite provider, Iridium, for his communications. He set up a VPN to mask his IP and made sure that all his connections were secure. For the first time since his nightmare began, he felt a sense of pride and accomplishment. Less glamorous tasks had been setting up a pump for the wellhead and using three cans of insecticide to devastate the spider population.

The funeral arrangements were complicated. It was a double ceremony. Communicating with Suzanna's parents was as pleasant as a root canal. Not that he didn't like them. It was the feeling they imparted he wasn't doing enough. They peppered him with questions that he couldn't answer. Why had this happened? Who was responsible? Why weren't the police doing more? Were there any leads? He wrestled with the pain daily and talking to them only amplified it.

Grayson Knox, Braxton's father, had been an old-school FBI agent. The thought that his beloved agency had killed his granddaughter hit him hard. "This wasn't the work of the Bureau I was an agent in," he assured his son over the phone. "I will get some answers. The people that did this need to be held accountable."

"It won't bring Angela back, Dad."

"I know. I spent my entire career working for the Bureau. The long nights, weekends, hell—vacations that got ruined. I gave it my all. Now they do this, murder my unarmed granddaughter in cold blood. I will get answers, boy, you can depend on that." As much as Braxton wanted to tell him to not waste his time, he couldn't form the words. Grayson was hurting almost as much as he was.

The insurance money for his wife and daughter came in. Tapping those funds, he returned to the house to pack up. His neighbor, Albert Gorelick, told him that there had been nightly cruises by masked men in front of his home. Slow drive-bys in the middle of the night. He thanked Gorelick for his assistance, then went about packing.

He stopped at Planet Fitness every day, worked out, and took a shower. The cabin had a bathroom, but it needed work. It was part of a long list of improvements he planned on making. Until it was done, he would avail himself of the gym's facilities.

He had taken his tools to the cabin, leaving little of worth in his garage. After that he turned his focus to the house. As he worked, he organized things into two piles. Things he was going to take to the cabin and things he wanted to go into a storage unit. The rest was just stuff, furniture and other items that no longer had meaning. Going through Suzanna's closet he had smelled her clothing, catching just a hint of her perfume. Memories tore at him. Tears formed in the corners of his eyes, but he held them at bay. Suzanna would not want him to cry. She would want him to find the people who killed her.

In Angela's room, the bloodstains on the bed and carpet remained, along with the chaos that the FBI had left. Fingerprint residue marred the door and nightstand. The dark maroon of the blood made his stomach knot as he gathered the few things he wanted to preserve.

Braxton found the yellow paged dog-eared copies of *The Lord of the Rings* that they read together. *The Return of the King* had a small blood stain on it. He took it into the bathroom, wetted a piece of tissue, and scrubbed it off so hard that his rubbing damaged the paperback. Drying it off, he held the books close for a moment, remembering when he read to Angela last. He took them to the car and put them in a box in the back seat.

The house was a disaster. In the basement they had emptied drawers, and thrown everything back when they were done. They had tossed his reloading equipment around but none of it seemed damaged. All of that gear went into a Rubbermaid bin to go to the mountains.

He debated taking a television. Everything he watched only seemed to add fuel to his depression. Most shows were propaganda. The news was all slanted, regardless of the channel.

His military training kicked in, especially the need for situational awareness. He needed to know what was going on, if only to avoid trouble. Television was a tainted necessity. He brought two, the small one he could hook up to his computer if need be, the large one for the news.

Standing in his tiny home office, he saw his diplomas on the wall. He hadn't wanted them hung there; that was Suzanna's handiwork. She was prouder of his academic accomplishments than he. To Braxton it felt like bragging, flaunting his degrees and published papers. Suzanna always saw the best in him. Now that she was gone, so was that aspect of who he was, or at least that was how he felt. Taking the framed documents down, he put them in a pile to go to storage. During the day he made two trips to the cabin, and several to the storage unit. Each trip tore at him, as if he were packing away a part of his life, not by choice but by necessity.

Braxton had arranged for the rest of the house's content, furniture and clothing, etc., to go to a group for which Suzanna had volunteered, Young Lives. They helped pregnant girls whose families had turned their backs on them. They provided housing, parental training, and support so the young women could get on their feet. Braxton told them to take what they could use and sell the rest. The church leaders in charge of Young Lives were so thankful, they arranged to have his house professionally cleaned and repainted.

By the time he finished, darkness had come. He attached a padlock to the doorframe and walked to his RAV. He looked back, knowing it was no longer his home. His home had perished with his wife and daughter. It was a structure. The home was in his memories.

As he got in his car, he saw headlights in the distance, slowly creeping down the street. A corkscrew of anxiety inserted itself in his spine. Were these the people who had been stalking him?

His Glock was in a back holster and for a few moments, he could feel its heat, as if the weapon were beckoning him. His mind shifted to tactical. The car would provide some concealment, but not much in the way of cover. Still, it would be enough to block him reaching for the weapon. Braxton sidestepped, putting the vehicle between him and the approaching car, and pulled his gun, chambering a round as he brought it out. He held the pistol at his side.

The car's brakes squealed slightly as the vehicle came to a stop. The tinted driver's window came down and he saw a black gaiter masked face glaring at him. His mind drank in the details. White male, in his twenties. From what he saw, he was a ginger with bright red hair. The two of them locked gazes.

"Can I help you?" Braxton asked, itching to point the Glock.

"You live here, right?"

He stepped toward the car. "Who wants to know?"

"You know," the kid replied. "This isn't a safe neighborhood with you in it." There it was, the arrogance in his voice. He thought he had the upper hand.

"Last I checked, it was a free country."

"Well, it should be, once people like you are gone."

Braxton had his threat. With a fluid motion, he pulled his weapon and leveled it at the young man. "I think you should be moving along." He saw a passenger in the car but no one in the back seat. Nissan Sentra. Probably stolen.

The young man forced a feeble smile. He was nervous. Before he could respond, Albert Gorelick came out of his door with a double-barreled shotgun. Braxton shifted position in case Albert fired.

"I think you boys should move on before the police show up," the older man said.

Braxton hoped the punks would do something that would give him the opportunity. Rage surged. His finger wanted to squeeze the trigger. The driver's eyes went wide. A flicker of terror. His cocky grin eroded.

"We'll be back." The Nissan accelerated.

Braxton kept his aim on the vehicle. Gorelick came over and put his hand on his extended arm. "Relax, Braxton, they're gone."

He lowered his weapon, put it in his holster. "Thanks, Al."

"Those kids were up to no good."

"They weren't kids. When they decided to kill people, to destroy property, they forfeited their childhood. Now they're just thugs… criminals… murderers."

"You okay?" Al asked.

Braxton nodded as adrenaline waned. "I'm fine. I appreciate the assist. Would you do me a favor?"

"What can I do for you?"

"Pick up my mail. Hold it for me. Keep an eye out."

"You already asked me."

"That's right."

Braxton drove up the mountain in silence. He jounced up the dirt road, parked in the yard and emptied the car, putting things in the loft and in the main room. He unpacked the fresh sheets, putting them on the bed. He stored the cooking gear and food. While he was physically and mentally exhausted, he couldn't sleep. Images flashed in his mind of him holding a gun on the car in front of his house. He drifted off, only to jerk awake at the memory.

Braxton got up before dawn and made coffee, embracing the mug like a child clinging to its favorite blanket. Tomorrow was going to be rough. The funerals loomed. Braxton knew he needed sleep. To do that, he had to push himself. Exhaustion was bound to win over his mental turmoil.

He went outside as the sun rose and toured the grounds. Dense forest reached to within ten feet of the rear deck, mostly Douglas fir, red alder, and Sitka spruce. Plenty of cover for someone coming up from behind. He didn't have the time or wherewithal to expand the clearing, but he could get the means to alert him to any approach. They'd used everything from cameras to silk threads in Afghanistan. The threads were attached to bells or empty cans filled with rocks. Of course, the winds could be ferocious. He'd have to find a way to eliminate false alarms. Electronics were the surest way, but then he faced the power problem. The humidity eroded battery life. The average lifespan of a car battery was three to four years. AAs lasted five to ten years. He'd brought twenty pounds of AA and AAA. It would be a simple matter to link them to a flashing light or low buzzer in the cabin.

He needed clean fields of fire. Using a battered Homelite chainsaw, he cut down trees to improve his line of sight from the windows and porch. Every muscle ached as he pulled the cut logs over to his wood pile. Using a shovel, he took out brush. Some thorny bushes he dug up and replanted at the far perimeter, to act as a deterrent for anyone attempting to sneak up on the cabin. The work was hard, exhausting. He welcomed it.

When finished, Braxton surveyed the work both from the cabin and from various approaches. There was one flaw, a boulder jutting up that provided some cover. A few well-placed pipe bombs with remote detonators put behind the boulder and along the driveway would augment his defenses.

In the log storage shed at the rear of the cabin, he found three rusty bear traps. They would still function. He set all three, hiding them on paths of approach, buried just under the dirt with a sprinkle of dead pine needles. The rest of the approaches he planned to address with small pits where he would place boards with nails poking up. Braxton had always believed that low-tech solutions were as effective as high-tech ones.

He took a sink shower and prepared his lone meal for the day. Braxton had enjoyed cooking for his wife and daughter. They always jerked his chain about what he prepared. Now his meals were lonely, pathetic. He packed on protein, hoping to build up his muscles. As a professor, his build and strength didn't matter. Things were different now. There were people out there who wanted him dead.

After dinner, he researched what he needed to remake the bathroom. It was tempting to research how to build a pipe bomb, but that would only invite scrutiny. He had no doubt he was on a watch list. He'd look it up at the public library. After setting up the television, he watched the news. An incoherent president shrieked about MAGA Republicans. A Democrat senator said the safety and welfare of undocumented immigrants was his number-one priority. A Congressional committee warned of the dangers of natural gas ovens.

Shutting it off, he pulled out *The Two Towers*. Tolkien's prose was the best prelude to sleep.

Chapter 14

Last Sorrow

A light drizzle fell as if God felt his pain and was shedding tears for him. Putting on his suit he remembered the last time he wore it. A dinner cruise with Suzanna. She had adjusted his tie no less than five times that night. As he wrapped the blue silk tie around his shirt, he made sure he got it right. Thinking of her.

The crowd was larger than expected. Angela's former classmates, from before her homeschooling, showed up. Suzanna's coworkers. Donna hugged him, sobbing and sniffling as she did so. His in-laws, including his sister-in-law Sally, arrived along with his father Grayson. No one from the university came. Anyone coming to support him might find themselves a target. A small neighborhood contingent led by Albert showed up. There were a few people in attendance that he didn't know; presumably friends of his wife. The small gathering comforted him.

Braxton sat in the front row with Grayson. His shoulders slumped and his face sagged. He struggled to hold back tears. There was a part of him that felt like he had failed his family. In his view, part of his role was to protect them. Instead, his actions had attracted evil people, resulting in their deaths.

There were no bodies on display, only two matching urns placed under a pair of lights on a table covered with a black cloth. There were flowers, despite his request that none be sent. He had asked that donations be made to Young Lives. Reverend McDonald stood at the podium.

"But our commonwealth is in heaven, and from it we await a Savior, the Lord Jesus Christ, who will change our lowly body to be like his glorious body, by the power which enables him even to subject all things to himself."

When he finished, the reverend motioned to Braxton. He stood and joined the pastor, facing the mourners.

Braxton felt the heat from the lights and sweat formed on his brow and his palms, adding to his discomfort. He caught a whiff of the flowers. Looking out at the sad faces, he wished he could pass on saying anything. The urns reminded him of his responsibility. He had to be brave for them.

"I met Suzanna after I was out of the Army, when we were both in school. Our first date was a disaster. I was nervous and spilled iced tea all over both of us. When we were done, I was pretty sure she would never call me back for another date. I was wrong, and have never been happier at being wrong in my entire life.

"We got married in May because she loved the spring. Those first years, we lived paycheck to paycheck, and we couldn't have been happier—or so we thought. When we found out she was pregnant, our love only got stronger." Braxton paused as a lone tear streamed down his cheek onto the podium. There was no thought of wiping it from his cheek, nor was there the energy. Even to him, he sounded as if he were rambling, but he didn't care. This was not a class where his wording mattered. This was a deeply personal talk with family and friends.

"I loved my wife and daughter more than anything. Angela got her looks from her mom, thankfully. Every night we read together, it was our thing." Once more, he paused, struggling to continue.

"None of this should have happened," he croaked. "The people responsible for this need to face justice… the FBI needs to own up to murdering our little girl." Braxton wanted to say more. There were harsh words, angry phrases, that were on the tip of his tongue. Looking out at the faces, he knew that this wasn't the place for such an outburst.

The chaplain stepped forward and put a hand on his shoulder.

He knew in that instant that he was going to act.

Slowly, he took his seat in the front row. His father put a hand on his arm. The funeral director got up and thanked everyone for coming. People came up and shook his hand as the small ceremony ended. Rudy patted him on the shoulder and Donna came in close, giving him a bent over hug. It was a blur to Braxton, the faces and kind words people offered. Eventually, he rose to his feet and watched as people slowly filtered out of the room. A half hour later, a few relatives remained.

The funeral director came up, speaking in a soothing tone. "Their remains are in the urns. If you like, I can have them delivered to you."

He glanced over at his in-laws. "Suzanna's parents want them."

The director handed him two small glass bottles, each the diameter of an ink pen, and half that length. One was marked *Suzanne* and the other *Angela*. "These are some of their ashes. Some people have them made into necklaces or rings. We provide them this way so that you don't have to open the urns."

Braxton put them in his jacket pocket. "Thank you."

His in-laws came up. "We were thinking that we should go to dinner, you know, as a family—so we can talk."

Food was the last thing on his mind, but Braxton agreed with a nod.

"We'll go to RingSide Steakhouse. I will get us a private table," Patrick said.

"You and Martha wanted their ashes. I think that is something that Suzanna would approve of."

Patrick nodded and went to talk to the funeral director, no doubt making arrangements regarding their remains. Braxton's father came over, his eyes red from his own tears. "You okay, son?"

"No. I'm not."

"It was hard on me when your mother died. In time, things will be easier."

For a moment, he looked into his father's eyes, saying nothing. "It was different with Mom. That was cancer. No one was at fault. There are people that are to blame for what happened with Suzanna and Angela. People that have not been held accountable." Turning, he walked towards the door.

* * *

RingSide was a posh restaurant, the kind of place that Braxton had taken Suzanna to only twice. Patrick got them a private room. Braxton took a seat at the table, opposite his sister-in-law, Sally, who stared icily. Grayson sat next to him. The waiter took their drink orders.

"What have the police told you, Brax?" Patrick said. "Have they got any leads?"

"No. They claim the car was stolen, but they haven't located it. They're shuffling this off as a traffic accident gone bad—a hit-and-run."

"Was it more?" Martha said.

"It was murder. The people behind me getting fired have been driving by the house. Suzanna was a great driver. Someone ran her off the road." His words sucked the air out of the room.

"They've got to be looking into it then," Patrick said.

"What about the FBI?" Martha asked, looking at Grayson. "They killed Angela."

Grayson Knox shifted in his seat uncomfortably. "I spoke with an agent there, Sonya Turner. She assured me that they are undergoing an internal investigation into what happened."

"Internal investigation?" Patrick said. "Who pulled the trigger? I want him or her to issue an apology. We deserve that much at the very least! What they did was wrong, thinking she had a gun. For God's sake, she was a kid in bed."

"The Bureau rarely releases the names of its agents in such instances," Grayson said. "Make no mistake, this is an enormous embarrassment for them, Agent Turner admitted that to me. There was no reason to round up the guns in the house, or to come in with that much force. They have procedures, and they weren't followed. They need to investigate that first."

"This is bullshit," Sally spat. "You're defending them. They killed my niece. I want answers."

"I'm not defending them at all," Grayson said. "This pisses me off. She was my granddaughter too for Christ's sake! I'm just telling you what they said."

"What can we do?" Martha asked.

Braxton set his jaw. "I don't think the police will do shit. I'm going to start with Suzanna. I'm going to see if I can find out who ran her off the road."

Patrick nodded. "You need to be careful, son. Your legal trouble is already looming with these civil rights charges. You don't want to get in the middle of meddling with an active police investigation."

"The hell I don't. Someone killed my wife and daughter. They did it because of me. I intend to get resolution, one way or another."

"Damn right, it's your fault," Sally said from across the table.

His relationship with his sister-in-law had always been tumultuous. "Your sister, my wife, encouraged me to take a stand."

"And now she's dead. All because you couldn't use a damned pronoun."

A spark of anger glowed in his heart. "You're right, Sally. Maybe I should have. Maybe I should have tried to apologize. Maybe I should have bent my damned knee to these spoiled-ass kids and pled for their mercy. The cost would have been my soul. You *do* understand that, don't you?"

"If you had, maybe Suzanna and Angela would still be alive."

Her words were not devastating as Sally hoped. "My wife stood by me. So did Angela. I'm not asking for your blessing. You weren't there. You have the advantage of hindsight. No one could have seen this coming, not like this. I get it. You're bitter and pissed off. Join the club. Leveling your anger at me won't help get them justice. I will. What are you going to do, criticize me for it?"

Sally wasn't used to anyone pouncing back. Before she could counterattack, Patrick cut in. "None of this is going to help. We're all hurting here. The last thing that Suzanna would want is us sitting here fighting. Sally, Brax has been through a lot; so have you. We're all tired and spent emotionally."

Sally shifted her gaze to her father.

Patrick turned to Braxton. "What do you need, Brax?"

For a few moments, he was silent. The server arrived and distributed their drinks. "My lawyer is pressing the DoJ on the charges against me and to get some sort of action on the FBI. My dad is pushing the Bureau as well. Local law enforcement is in charge of Suzanna's case. I'm going to track down these ANTIFA goons and find out who was responsible for her accident."

"What makes you think they're going to cooperate?" Sally asked, crossing her arms.

"I will... *persuade* them."

"Son," his father said in a low whisper.

"If the legal system isn't going to do anything, then I will."

Chapter 15

Bumps in the Night

Joel Schumer, Ajax, sat on his cot in his basement apartment and pulled on his Red Wings. Normally one hundred and twenty-five dollars, these were free. Five weeks ago, he and his cell had stormed into the Red Wing store in the Newbury Mall shouting, "Justice Now!" and grabbed everything in sight while the lone female employee cowered behind the counter.

There was no point in the store calling the pigs. Stealing up to nine hundred and fifty dollars' worth of merchandise was no longer a felony. It wasn't even a misdemeanor.

Joel pulled his watch cap low on his face and adjusted the black bandanna that concealed his mouth and chin. He pulled on the Steel Outdoor Motorcycle Safety Gloves he'd purchased from Temu for twenty-two dollars. They could punch through a cinder block. Joel couldn't. But someone bigger could. He slipped into his black leather jacket, also from Temu, and put the telescoping ballistic wand through a pant loop. Now he was ready. He paused at the basement door and looked back at his three-room apartment with its filthy carpet, kitchenette, and bathroom that had never been cleaned.

Someday, he thought. *Someday I'll have my own home with a pool.*

In the meantime, the price was right. ANTIFA had liberated the six-unit apartment building several years ago during the Autonomous Zone protests. The landlord had sought help, but the law was on ANTIFA's side as the occupiers. You couldn't just kick a person out on the street. No sir. Every person had rights. A right to three square meals a day. A right to lodging. A right to free health care. The list was long and growing.

Tonight's target was Abe's Jewish Deli in Lake Oswego. They had refused to place a *From The River To The Sea* sign in their window and now they must pay. Joel picked up the Samsung Galaxy he'd taken from the car they'd stolen and used to run that Nazi bitch off the road. He was pretty sure they'd never find the Subaru, which they'd plunged into a gorge in Hood River. The registration in the glove compartment revealed that the owner, Ethel Rubinstein, was a fifty-five-year-old woman who lived in Portland. Joel was pretty sure she wasn't hip enough to try to trace her own phone, so he felt free to use it for a week before he sold it to Hip Billy. He put it in his inside jacket pocket. He might use it to order more shit from Temu. Then he would pass it off to Tyler. Passing it around created some plausible deniability.

Joel emerged as Stormbringer, Storm for short, pulled to the curb in a new Jeep Cherokee. Joel slid into the passenger seat. Stormbringer was a short excitable college dropout who didn't care much for ANTIFA's ideals. He joined for the violence.

"Nice wheels!"

"Yeah. Dude had a couple hundred in groceries too. You want some ground bison?"

"I'm not much of a meat eater. You get any bourbon?"

"Oh yeah! Take a look back there. There's a box from King's Liquors. Take what you want."

Joel leaned over the back seat and rummaged around. The bottles clanked while they drove. He pulled a bottle of Buffalo Run and put it in the footwell.

"We pickin' anyone up?"

"Nah. They're gonna meet us there. We got a good crowd tonight. Sidney's bringing her girlfriend Connie. That bitch could crush you like an eggshell. They're bringing the cocktails."

"Man, I don't know. We start a fire and the pigs'll be all over the place."

"Let's see how it plays out."

Stormbringer drove the Jeep with abandon, cutting off a suburban hausfrau as he veered onto 99. He could see that she wanted to flip him off, but when she saw his masked face, she simply applied her brakes. It was a typical Portland night, overcast, temp in the fifties. He pulled off on Wilbur Street and headed for Old Town, into

George Rogers Park, next to a couple of hot hatches and an old pickup. A group of ANTIFA gathered around a fifty-gallon drum that spewed flames and sparks into the night air.

"Where'd that barrel come from?" Joel said.

"Morris brought it. We're done freezing our asses off."

"So are we gonna drive to the kike's place?"

"Might as well. We can close off the street."

Storm and Joel joined a dozen ANTIFA gathered around the barrel. Lord Sumbitch, who was six foot two and weighed a hundred and thirty pounds, grinned, exposing teeth like an abandoned cemetery. "Hey there, amigos! You want a toot?"

"Wouldn't mind," Joel said.

Lord motioned them over to a four-door Civic with oversized wheels and a huge spoiler on the trunk. "Slide in."

Lord Sumbitch got in the driver's seat, Joel in shotgun, Storm in the rear. Lord pulled a round vanity mirror from the console, set it in his lap and wrangled three lines of white powder from a small amber vial. He snorted with a plastic straw, passed it to Joel.

"Where'd you get that straw, man?" Joel said, leaning forward and hoovering the line.

"I got a secret source. Why? You want some?"

"Nahh, I'm good." Joel ran a finger under his nose, felt the rush hit his brain. "Wow. Good shit."

Lord passed the mirror to Storm in the back seat. Storm snorted.

"Awright! Let's get ready to rumble!"

It was nine o'clock. They'd decided to strike late, to take the deli by surprise, and minimize civilian casualties. When they got out of the car, another dozen had joined, all dressed in black, some wearing helmets, all with bandannas or clothes to pull up over their faces. Stormbringer blew a whistle on a lanyard.

"Listen up! Who's driving? Raise your hands."

A half dozen hands went up.

"Okay. I trust nobody is stupid enough to bring their own cars, amiright? Huh?" He looked around.

"You're right!" someone yelled. "Let's roll!"

"Okay. When we get there, we're gonna gather out front and give them one last chance to put up the sign. If they refuse, wait for my signal. Do not start breaking things until you hear me blow the whistle. We're not a bunch of stupid assholes! Discipline! Where's Connie?"

A big mama dressed in sweats and a hoodie rolled to the front. "Yo!"

"What's the chant, Con?"

Connie raised her fist. "From The River to The Sea!"

"Let's hear it!" Storm demanded.

Two dozen people threw their fists in the air and chanted, "From the river to the sea!"

"Awright! Let's roll. Follow me."

Storm and Joel got back into the Jeep. The rest loaded into cars. A half dozen followed on foot as Stormbringer pulled out of the parking lot and headed west toward the strip mall. At this hour, there was little foot traffic. This part of Lake Oswego had once been popular for its upscale boutiques, cafes, and taverns, but years of rioting had hollowed it out, leaving only those who were too poor, stubborn, or desperate to leave.

Abe's had always been a popular café with the locals, as was Korean Barbecue across the street. They turned onto Haskell Street, Morry's Liquors on the left, still open, its windows covered with a steel gate. Sing's Karate on the right, lights off, door locked. A few late-night shoppers saw them coming and hurried to their vehicles.

Stormbringer parked in a red zone directly across from the deli. Other vehicles double-parked up and down the street until it was impossible for traffic to proceed. They piled out of their vehicles and gathered in front of the deli, which was still open. A boy at a table with brillo hair looked up, startled. An old woman pulled out her cell phone and called the police. It didn't matter. The police were understaffed. Their ability to respond only encouraged the night's activities.

Stormbringer waited until two dozen people crowded the sidewalk, preventing anyone from entering or leaving. He blew a shrill blast on his whistle. He raised a bullhorn.

"Hey hey, ho ho! Jewish racists have to go!"

They all chimed in. "Hey hey, ho ho! Jewish racists have to go!"

Someone produced the hand-lettered sign on sturdy baseboard: *From The River To The Sea*. Two men held it up so that it faced the deli.

Stormbringer spoke through the bullhorn. "Jewish racists! This is your last chance! Display the sign or we will shut you down!"

A powerful spotlight momentarily blinded him. Covering his eyes with his hands, he tried to find the source. It was coming from the roof of the deli. Three men stood on the roof looking down. Holding AR-15s, ready to shoot. A blanket of silence fell over Schumer's ANTIFA chapter.

"You leave now," said a man on the roof, holding his weapon at port arms. The other two each put one foot on the parapet and looked down. Someone pulled out a flashlight and shined it up at them. Three stolid men, wearing camo combat fatigues, the kind you purchase at any military surplus shop, and black watch caps. They did not conceal their faces. They were Korean and it was clear they would not put up with a protest or the violence.

Joel grinned under his mask. Showing fear wasn't in his nature. He knew that his own people were filming the Koreans. But now wasn't the time to fight, not when someone was going to fight back. "Alright, folks—let's roll."

Next time, the Koreans would pay for daring to resist.

Chapter 16

Snail Mail

Braxton walked the perimeter, Ruger on his hip. It was twilight the day after the funeral, and he'd returned to the cabin that afternoon and hooked up his satellite phone. Much of the morning had been spent digging holes, putting nails in wood, and concealing the holes. Anyone falling into them would have their foot skewered. He concealed the three bear traps under heaps of pine needles.

He installed a large plastic rain barrel. With the internet running, he'd read two books on security systems and set up the first batch of cameras. The other cameras and sensors were on order.

Donna had filed lawsuits against the university and the FBI. She had set his expectations clearly about suing the federal government, but he didn't care. They had killed his little girl and they were going to have to pay for that.

As soon as he finished setting up the phone, it rang. He picked it up but remained silent.

"Brax?" Rudy said. "You there?"

"I'm here, Rudy. What's up?"

"That item you requested has been delivered, but you'll have to drive to my sister's place in Idaho to pick it up. And she wants cash."

"How much?"

"Twenty-five hundred."

"I thought you said two gees."

"She's taking a risk."

"All right. All right. Let's see. It's Saturday. I can head out tomorrow, be at her place Sunday evening. Are there any motels in that town?"

"You can stay at her place. I already cleared it."

"What's the address?"

"I gave it to you last week. You wrote it down."

"That's right. That's right. Sorry. I'm a little distracted."

"Don't worry about it."

Braxton hung up. The temperature began to drop. A light rain fell. Braxton put on long johns, wool socks, and pulled his watch cap down over his ears. He started a fire in the fireplace and soon the cabin was toasty. It was March. By seven, it was dark outside. Braxton hauled out a cardboard box filled with paperback thrillers his grandfather had collected. Herbert Lieberman. William H. Hallahan. Brian Garfield. John D. MacDonald. All pulp writers of the sixties and seventies. Braxton took off his cap and put on a headband light. The full set of Foxfire books was there as well, his father's contribution to the library.

He picked up Garfield's *Death Wish*. He'd enjoyed the movie with Charles Bronson. Not until the movie began did he realize its significance.

Am I that spacey? Am I really going gunning for these creeps? You bet your ass, I will. You bet your ass. Just thinking about it gave him a boost of energy he hadn't felt in a long time. A sense of purpose.

He opened the book and began reading. The satellite phone lit up. He didn't recognize the number.

"Yes?"

"Braxton, it's Albert from across the street. I hope this isn't too late."

"No, it's fine. What's up?"

"I've been collecting your mail. Some of it looks like harassment, but that's up to you. I was sitting on my front porch yesterday when a man in a Buick stopped at your house and an older woman got out and put something in your mailbox. I was curious, so I walked down there. They didn't look like revolutionaries or anything. Just a typical middle-aged couple, and I asked if I could help. The woman asked if we were on good terms. I told her yes, and she said she had something for you and if I would be kind enough to give it to you personally. She said she was afraid if she just left it in the mailbox, some of these ANTIFA or something would come by and take it."

"What is it?"

"It's a letter addressed to you. No return address. Would you like me to read it to you?"

"No. I'm not sure this line is secure. Hang on to it. I'll come by in the morning and pick it up. Thank you for telling me, Albert."

"No problem."

"Any suspicious activity?"

"It's been pretty quiet around here for the past week. I think they've moved on to other targets. There was a crazy incident in Lake Oswego last night where a mob of shitheads went to trash a Jewish deli. Get this. The deli refused to put an anti-Semitic sign in their window, so they were going to destroy the place, but when they got there, the Koreans who owned the restaurant across the street were on the roof. With guns. They cleared that street in five minutes. Someone posted a video to YouTube. It was a thing of beauty."

"You gonna be home tomorrow around ten?"

"Where else?"

"Okay, thanks, Albert. I'll come by."

"I'll make some coffee."

Braxton couldn't sleep. His thoughts leaped around like gaffed fish. He'd qualified as a marksman, but when the brass learned he could type seventy words a minute, he dodged that bullet. He hadn't fired a rifle in years. He'd shot with Rudy in the range, and sometimes up the mountains when no one was around, but it was all pistol.

So what are you going to do, Brax? Find the perps and shoot them?

Well yes. That's what I had in mind.

What are the repercussions of that, Brax? What if they catch you?

He tossed and turned. He forced himself to think about the good times. With Suzanna in Hawaii. Angela's first concert. She played viola. She wanted to join a rock and roll band. That time he took her to Cheap Trick. He eventually fell into a shallow sleep, woke up at five in the morning, Monsieur snoring on the bed, got up and headed west toward the city, Monsieur riding shotgun.

It was seven by the time he pulled onto his street, parking in Albert's driveway. He planned to wait until Albert woke, but Albert surprised him by coming out on the front porch fully dressed, holding a mug. "Come on in."

Braxton and Monsieur followed Albert into his house, a typical Portland bungalow set up and back from the sidewalk. He'd been in there a couple times when he'd helped Albert find a leak in the kitchen, and once to help move a desk. The kitchen looked out on a small fenced-in yard. Braxton sat at a Formica-topped table while Albert poured him a cup, set it on the table with a pint of half-and-half and a bowl of sugar.

Braxton added half-and-half and sugar to his mug, stirred it with a spoon. Albert sat opposite and handed Braxton a white nine-and-a-half-inch envelope addressed in elegant cursive to Braxton Knox. The return address read Ethel Rubinstein, 494 East Rutherford Street, Portland. Braxton pulled his pocketknife and slit it open.

Dear Mr. Knox:

First of all, please accept my deepest condolences for the terrible loss of both your wife and your daughter. I don't understand how these things happen. It almost seems as if there's a tragedy every day now, and no one is ever held accountable.

My Subaru Outback was stolen from the State Street Parking Garage in downtown Portland on September 20. We reported the theft to the police. They told us they would add it to the list of stolen vehicles and explained that they were more concerned with violent crime, and that they were seriously understaffed, and could not launch an active investigation, but the list would go out to every patrol vehicle.

I foolishly left my phone in the car. It was a Samsung Galaxy. Whoever stole my car probably sold it, but there is a chance the thief still has it. I have since acquired a new phone. The telephone number on the old phone is 503-271-2771. I gave this information to the police, but they did not seem very interested. I asked if it was possible for them to track the number, and they said it was, but they were simply overwhelmed with more serious crimes.

On Wednesday, hikers in Mount Hogg National Forest found my Subaru at the bottom of a steep ravine and reported it to the police, who were unable to retrieve it until Thursday. They told me that it had been totaled. They also told me that the right front bumper had been impacted as if by collision, and paint residue from the other vehicle led them to believe it had been used in a felony. They said the paint was blue. The news reports referenced a Subaru Outback being involved with your wife's death. I believe that was the color of the vehicle your wife was driving.

I understand you are a veteran. Thank you for your service. Perhaps you know someone who could track the phone, thereby leading you to whoever stole the car. If you would like any more information, please feel free to call me at 503-691-2985.

Yours sincerely,

Mrs. Ethel Rubinstein

Braxton folded the letter, returned it to the envelope, and put it in his inside jacket pocket.

"What did she want?"

"She has some information for me."

Albert nodded. "Whoops. Almost forgot. Let me get you the rest of your mail."

He walked out of the kitchen and returned a minute later with a cardboard box half filled with mail. Braxton flipped through it. AAA, magazines filled with coupons, the Eastern State Alumni magazine, three dozen letters. Some he recognized, shaped like sympathy cards. Several were suspicious, addressed in block letters with bulging interiors. He doubted it was Anthrax; getting that through the mail system after 9-11 was nearly impossible. Powdered fentanyl was always a possibility. "Off the pig," adorned one of the envelopes. There was no point giving them to the police.

95

"Got a garbage bag I can have?"

"How big?"

"Three or four gallons."

Albert looked beneath the sink, handed him a gray garbage disposal bag. Braxton put the suspicious letters in the bag and pulled it tight. He would drop them in a dumpster on the way out of town. The rest of the letters he set aside to read later.

"Thank you, sir. I have to leave town for a few days. When I get back, I'm going to need a realtor. If you have any suggestions, it would be appreciated."

"I know a good realtor. She's also very conservative."

"Gimme."

Albert rose again, went into his study and returned with a fat loose leaf binder filled with business cards. He flipped through, found what he needed, and slid the card across the desk. Braxton copied the info. *Jade Hopkins*. He rose slowly when finished, tucking the card in his pants pocket.

"Thanks for everything, Albert. I'll be in touch."

"Good luck, Braxton."

Chapter 17

The Federal Bureau of Traitors

Special Agent Sonya Turner waited in the Special Agent in Charge's office. Robert Durston, the SAIC, entered red-faced. He sat behind the desk and ran his hand through his salt-and-pepper hair. He was older than Turner, more rigid, old-school FBI. She was young, four years out of the Academy. Where her boss fought a losing battle with gray hair, hers was naturally blonde and worn short. Durston focused on looking the part of an FBI agent. Sonya went with whatever was easy. Where he wore tailored suits, hers were off the rack, mostly because when investigating, they often got stained and damaged.

"Thanks for responding so fast, Sonya."

"Is there a problem?"

"That would be an understatement," he sighed, leaning back in the Aeron chair. "I just got my ass handed to me on a silver platter by the US attorney."

Turner knew the US attorney, Aurora Rainsong. On her best day, she was a four-star bitch. Birdsong forged her career on her heritage. She was a member of the Coquille Tribe. As US attorney, her focus was almost entirely on cases tied to social justice as opposed to regular crimes. The inside joke among Sonya's small circle of work-friends was that her record was that she only prosecuted white men, especially conservatives. She referred to Turner's boss as "Pale, male, and stale," which Durston took personally.

Rainsong was always in front of the cameras, setting herself up for a judicial appointment. Sonya hated people who were more focused on their next job than the one they had. It clouded their thinking.

When angered, Rainsong became a verbal and physical tiger, renowned for throwing a stapler through her office glass door when a judge ruled against her. Sonya almost felt sorry for Durston, but he was the SAIC. Managing the relationship with the US attorney was part of his job. "Why is she upset this time?"

"A producer from KGW called her. They have bodycam footage from the shooting of that Braxton girl. They wanted to know if she had a comment."

"I was there the night that went down. I was in the room in fact. If they have footage, it's pretty damning."

"You don't have to tell me. I have two agents on administrative leave because of the shooting. Now that footage is going to be on the evening news. Their names are going to be out in the open. You can be sure this is going to go national. Those pricks at Fox News would love to get their hands on video of FBI agents killing a young unarmed girl. Needless to say, this is a PR and legal nightmare. Especially with this Knox's attorney filing a wrongful death lawsuit against the Bureau."

"Has she tried to get them to hold off running it?"

Durston frowned. "Yes, and it was a total waste of effort. NBC Nightly News is already chomping at the bit. This is going to devour our weekend."

"Our?"

"That footage should have been secure."

"So someone leaked it," she said slowly.

"Damn right! I don't need to tell you that the FBI's reputation is everything. We've taken a lot of hits in the last seven years or so, and this is only going to make matters worse."

Turner knew all too well the value the leadership placed on maintaining their reputation. She had attended classes on the subject. For her, it was a bit of a paradox. In the Knox case, many mistakes were made. The Bureau should have negotiated with the father to come in and surrender. Rainsong wanted the perp walk; she wanted to plant the image in the potential jury pool that Braxton Knox was a dangerous criminal.

Then came the two agents shooting the young girl. Turner had been in the room. Yes, Ms. Knox reached for her nightstand, but there was nothing there that could have been confused with a weapon. Agent Forsyth fired first, and Agent Hayden panic-fired as well. They knew they'd fucked up instantly, Forsyth said so out loud. When that footage played on TV, it was going to scuttle their careers, maybe Durston's as well.

Turner had raised concerns from the start. "It's like we are using a nuclear weapon to kill a mosquito," she'd said. Rainsong had dressed her down, rambling on about the "bigger issues at stake." The footage being released to the public was karma in action.

"Look, Sonya, IA is going to be all over this like white on rice. It will take them a day or two to get the tasking. In the meantime, we have a traitor in our ranks, that's the only logical explanation. This is the kind of crap that could torpedo my career. I need someone I trust to look into this. Sideline everything else you have on your plate. Pull whatever records you need. Find out how this footage ended up in KGW's newsroom. I want to be a few steps ahead of Internal Affairs. Once they get tagged to this, everything will lock down. I know you met with Knox's father. You were there that night. You are one of my top assets. If anyone can figure this out, it will be you."

She remembered meeting with Grayson Knox. He was old-school and gentlemanly. The Bureau he had served had killed his granddaughter and arrested his son. He wanted answers to the first part. How could they have thought she had a weapon? Why did the two of them fire? Why had the Bureau come in with so much force in the first place? Legitimate questions. Sonya had done what good agents do, she listened, kept her answers short and to the point, and promised to dig deeper.

Protocol was to withhold information. If that meant lying, then so be it. The part that ate at her was that the elder Knox had been a special agent just like her. His years of service should have mattered. When she had taken the inquiries to Durston, he had shut her down.

"That old fart was in the Bureau back when Clinton was president. We don't owe him anything. Don't share a damn thing with him."

Sonya felt differently. If the Bureau were interested in doing their job, they would ditch the manhunt for whoever was responsible for leaking the video and focus on reform. But the Bureau had not been interested in doing their job for a long time. Individual agents were. But not the top brass.

The Bureau demanded loyalty, so Durston's rage was justified. For her, the door of loyalty swung both ways. It tore at her to turn her back on Grayson Knox. In her mind, he deserved special consideration. What she was being told to do with him, or not do, gave her a good indication of what the Bureau thought of her when things mattered.

If we turn our back on men like Grayson Knox, what will they do with someone like me if I ever face a similar situation? Turner already knew the answer.

She cleared her calendar for the next two days. In many respects, her digging into how the data got out was a pointless exercise, but one she undertook for both professional and personal reasons.

Bodycams didn't transmit. The Bureau's policy was, after they were worn, agents took them to a small room attached to the locker room. There they were plugged in to sync up, a process that transferred the data along with metadata on the agent, and transferred them to a closed cloud storage system. Given that there had been a shooting in the Knox case, that would have been done immediately.

From experience, she knew that the syncing process only made a copy of the data. The original footage remained in the memory of the bodycam worn by the agent. It stayed there until the bodycam ran out of space, then it was written over by more current data. It was a redundancy that ensured that if anything went wrong with the syncing, a copy might still exist.

Sonya started with the IT team. They were contractors, put in place by some beltway bandit whose expertise was limited to being the lowest bidder. The IT team rarely interacted with agents, and with good reason. There was a reason they were computer geeks.

They didn't work and play well with law enforcement professionals. They were socially awkward.

For two hours she grilled them. Was there any sign of anyone accessing the bodycam footage? No. Was there any sign of the files being copied to a computer, either external or internal? No. Who had access to the server who could have pulled the files? Over forty individuals. Was it possible that someone used the syncing software to abscond with a copy of the files? No. Each inquiry required a boring technical conversation and debate, along with checking files on the computers. She came to the conclusion that the files hadn't been accessed from the cloud storage, though she was fairly sure that was the case to begin with.

That left the copies in the bodycam. She asked the techs if it was possible to use an external storage device or a flash drive to connect to the bodycam itself and pull down the files. One of the IT team, Francis Kurland, who stank like a coyote, got excited. "It's super simple. That is how we sync them, with a USB port. When you plug in, it automatically kicks off a download. If you look on the back of the bodycam, there is a small LED screen. If you use the little buttons to download, it will kick off. Super simple."

"Does the bodycam keep a log of external access?"

"No. There's no reason for that."

She asked for email logs for the field office, specifically any that were sent to a KGW email address or any of the reporters or producers at the station. They were excited by the prospects, most likely because they rarely were engaged by agents on an investigation. The supervisor, a young man in his 30s with a plastic pocket protector, assured her she'd have it by the end of the day.

Turner thanked them and went to the locker room. She found the lockers for Rocky Forsyth and Frank Hayden, the two agents who had shot Angela Knox. Their lockers weren't locked. This was an FBI locker room. If you couldn't trust your fellow agents, you didn't belong there. Opening both, she checked their bodycams and made sure they were still in place. Sonya didn't think she'd see anything helpful, but she went through the motions.

Her next stop was security, managed by an external contractor. Two of their people sat in on the discussion. She asked if there were cameras in the locker room, knowing the answer. No. Filming agents in various stages of undress made no sense. The security of the field office was almost all external, to deal with threats coming at the building. Inside there were cameras operating in some corridors and stairwells, but never in office areas because there was a risk of filming classified materials. She drilled in further—were there cameras in the hallways? No.

At her desk, she leaned back. Next would be phone contacts. All agents' cell phones were owned by the government, so pulling data was easy. She accessed the last few days of data for the entire field office, cross-referencing the phone number prefix for the NBC affiliate. Another dead end. No one had called KGW, not on their government phones. It would take warrants to get access to their private phones, and for the time being, she didn't have probable cause.

Her email alerted her that the security team had sent their report. No one had used an FBI account to contact anyone associated with station KGW or anyone on the staff there. Sonya typed in a thank you, and filed the report in her email account. It wasn't a surprise. Anyone smart enough to be in the FBI and betray the Bureau would not be sloppy enough to leave a digital trail.

Dead ends across the board. It was not what Durston wanted to hear. That didn't bother her. Her task was to investigate, and she had done that. She opened an internal report template and logged her findings. The only weak link in the handling of the bodycam footage was the locker room. Chances were good that whoever had copied the material had done so with a low-tech, non-traceable means, like a flash drive, and had delivered it to KGW to avoid detection.

She added a few recommendations, such as adding cameras to locker rooms, requiring bodycams to be locked up after use, etc. The recommendations were window dressing and she knew it. Durston would blow past them. Instead he would be enraged that she didn't find out who had given the media the footage. If he was going to be pissed, US attorney, Rainsong, would be livid. They might as well order her replacement glass for her door when the news ran the footage that night, if she hadn't shattered it already.

None of that bothered Turner. She had been true to her oath. "I do solemnly swear that I will support and defend the Constitution of the United States against all enemies, foreign and domestic; that I will bear true faith and allegiance to the same..." Justice, for her, was more than written law. It was the razor-thin cutting edge between right and wrong.

And Sonya Turner always did what was right.

Chapter 18

Images of Death

Braxton was exhausted. He had gone to pick up his shipment from Rudy's sister, a delightful woman who'd prepared a fried chicken dinner. He'd stopped at the UPS store on the way back up to the cabin and got a few other packages, including one from Gore and Raven Aerostar containing a Nemesis ghillie suit and hood that suppressed heat and IR signatures.

He got bulletproof plates for his RAV custom designed to fit in the doors and seats. The boxes were heavy and they were expensive, but he was cash rich thanks to Suzanna's and Angela's insurance policies. He wasn't the kind of person to buy a boat or go on a cruise.

Returning to the cabin, he resumed fortifying and securing. The installation of a shower with hot water was his last bit of work. He had studied YouTube videos on setting up the system and plumbing, then went to work.

Braxton hadn't shaved in three days. While his hair was brown with a few streaks of gray, his beard had come in reddish. Suzanna had always scoffed when he tried to grow facial hair. Now it seemed to fit. A beard and mustache served as a natural disguise. His loss of weight and added back muscles were starting to show. Looking in the mirror, he realized just how much he'd changed. While it was only two days' growth, he thought the beard a good thing.

He dropped into the old leather couch. His satellite phone rang. It was Donna. She'd been gracious about limiting her calls. They stirred up memories of everything he'd been through.

"Braxton," she said. "Please tell me you're not watching television."

104

"I'm not. Why?"

"It's all over the news. The NBC station in Portland got a copy of the bodycam from one of the FBI agents. It shows the shooting of Angela."

His jaw muscles tensed. "Damn it! How did they get it?"

"I don't know. I didn't want you to stumble onto it. Fox News is likely to pick this up. There's going to be calls for you to comment."

He didn't want to respond. He suddenly felt hot and uncomfortable. "You're my lawyer, what do you recommend?"

"Your case isn't just about the law. It's also about swaying public opinion. This is going to put a lot of pressure on the Bureau and the US attorney's office. The last thing they will want is for people to see you as sympathetic or as a victim. This can be a game changer for us. But that means you will need to do some interviews."

"It means I will need to see the video, doesn't it?"

"They will want your reaction, yes."

"How bad is it?"

"It's bad. They blurred out Angela for the most part, but the blood—" She stopped speaking for a moment. "It's hard to watch."

Braxton went blank. At first, his thoughts were about himself and how he felt. How the images would summon the demons in his soul to torture him.

Then he thought of Suzanna. *Babe—tell me what you'd want me to do?*

The answer he got was simple. *Make them pay for what they did to our little girl. Cowboy up, Brax!* He heard it in her voice. It allowed him to forge a thin smile. Suzanna always knew right and wrong, even when he didn't. This is what she would want him to do.

"Will this make them drop these idiotic civil rights charges?"

"That's hard to say. My instinct tells me it might. If you opt to keep quiet and this dies down, the US attorney might feel emboldened to press on. I think their case is pretty thin as it is. If you do the full media circuit, that's going to put some real pressure on them. It's hard for the DoJ to claim they're doing the right thing when there's video of them killing an innocent kid."

Donna's logic was inescapable. That didn't make it any more palatable. He didn't fear public speaking, a byproduct of being a professor for years. What propelled him beyond his thoughts of what Suzanna would want him to do, was that his interviews would cause those that had come for him and his family angst. They deserved it after what they had done.

"This will hurt them, won't it?"

"I think it will be devastating. Unfortunately it comes at the expense of having those images of Angela being shot out there. The media gave us no opportunity to stop them, they just broadcast them."

Braxton knew he would have to watch the video. He had been in Angela's room, seen the blood. In many ways the damage had already been done. This was the last step, facing the events that had unfolded as the FBI held him down. "If you'll prep me some bullet points and arrange the interviews, I'll do them."

"Alright. I recommend a sport coat and tie. Some of the media have already tried to portray you as some sort of extremist. This is your chance to erase the images they got of you during that perp walk."

"In other words, I can want retribution without looking like I'm out after it…"

"I agree. I want to set your expectations, though. This is the first step on what is going to be a journey."

"Can you email me a link to the video?"

"I will. I'm so sorry."

"You have nothing to be sorry for."

"It doesn't feel that way to me. I chose a career in the law. Seeing what the sheriff and FBI have done makes me feel tainted."

"You were a good friend of my wife and of me. Let's take the fight to them." He hung up, pulled out his personal cell, and waited for the video.

When he opened it, he stared at the link, mesmerized. Memories of Suzanna and what she would want made him press the link. The images played out as he expected. The voices of the FBI agents were crisp, yet fearful. Flashlights splashed Angela as she awoke. She reached up, as if to block the flashlight beams, then the first shot came, followed by two more, the flashes flickering on the video as her blood splattered the wall behind her.

Braxton didn't cry. In his mind, he had imagined what had happened to his little girl many times. Seeing the actual footage didn't startle him as much as he thought it would. Instead, an inner rage burned. The students at his school, ANTIFA, the FBI, the US attorney, the sheriff's office, the university, the media—they all had roles in what had been done to his family. They didn't give a second thought to the harm they had inflicted. Some even enjoyed their part in his tragedy.

The Bible told him to turn the other cheek. That wasn't who he was now. The events that had destroyed his existence were intense, made more intense by the media. They had forged him into something new. A weapon. No one dared stand up to them all. They ruled by intimidation and twisting the truth. Braxton was immune to that now.

He had nothing to lose. They had taken everything from him. In doing so, they had created something new, something dangerous to those who stalked and harassed innocent people for merely having a differing perspective.

The Fox News interview was done at local affiliate KPTV studios the next morning. They talked to him for almost four minutes, opening with the image of Angela being shot. He avoided looking at the screen. The hosts were outraged, but at the advice of Donna, who had accompanied him, he spoke calmly. Braxton brought up the non-investigation of his wife's death by the sheriff's department and how the university had pushed for the civil rights charge to try to mitigate the damages of his lawsuit. He called the FBI incompetent and asked viewers to reach out to their elected officials about the US attorney. It was exactly as Donna had outlined for him, and he played his role perfectly.

There were five other interviews that day, all following a similar format. It was emotionally draining for Braxton, but he prevailed. The Army had taught him long ago that mental toughness was as important to a warrior as physical toughness. He fell back on that knowledge as the day progressed. The last two were radio interviews, which he appreciated since he didn't have to think about how he looked on camera. One of the TV commentators shed tears at the footage on the air, and he thanked her for that. Braxton's time of weeping had passed. It was time for the forces working against him to play defense. He was through taking blows. Now came retribution.

When they were done, they stopped at Burgerville. After they ordered, Donna looked at him. "You did good. Suzanna was right about you. You are a strong man with a good soul. Most people would have struggled with those people asking you questions like that."

"I did it for her, and for Angela."

"They would be proud."

"I like to think so. I hope that this wasn't a waste. I want justice."

"So do I," she assured him. "Tomorrow I'll schedule some time with the US attorney. The fact that she and the FBI both declined to comment about the video tells me they're reeling. That makes this the right time to strike back. I'm going to convince her that in light of that footage being out there, there's no way she can hope to take her charges of a civil rights violation to a jury and hope to win. Someone is bound to be sympathetic. If she wants a hung jury, that's fine. Me, I want the charges dismissed."

The waitress brought their drinks.

"That's a start," Braxton said. "But that's all it is, a start."

"We still have our civil suits against the FBI and the university."

Braxton shook his head. "Courts and laws—I know you think that's a solution. I've come to think of them as part of the problem. Justice isn't won in court. All I can hope for is some sense of validation." He nodded toward the window. "Real justice is out here, where it's made."

Donna's voice lowered as she spoke, "I think I understand what you are saying. That being the case, you know what my response has to be."

"I know. You have your arena, I have mine."

"Don't do something I can't undo."

Before he could respond, a hefty man brought their food to them. He set the plates down. "You're that guy I saw on the news this morning."

"Yes."

"Dinner is on me. Fletcher Morris." The man looked more like a lumberjack than a server, right down to his red-and-black plaid flannel shirt and long dark beard. "I just bought this place a few months ago. I'm really sorry about what happened to you and your family. I can't believe the FBI would be so incompetent. Then again, after January 6th, I shouldn't be surprised."

"Thank you. It's really not necessary."

"I insist. My kid started getting harassed when she went to college. She was a conservative and those students picked on her, got onto her social media, made her out to be a monster. She tried to kill herself, and thank God she failed. Someone has to take a stand against all of this woke bullshit out there."

"We were just talking about that," Braxton replied, casting a slow glance over at Donna.

"I hope you take those bastards to the cleaners," Fletcher said.

"Thank you. I will do what I can."

Fletcher walked away, and Braxton looked at his burger. He remembered the letter he had received from Ethel Rubinstein. Donna had her battles to wage, and he had his.

Tomorrow was going to be a very busy day.

Chapter 19

The Law Library

The Oregon State Bar's law library was located in Woodburn, a town of some twenty thousand located at the head of the Willamette Valley. It was a rainy, overcast day as Braxton parked on the street in front and approached the Greco-Roman building with its Ionic pillars. Across the street, a dozen tents covered what had once been a community park. The homeless sat around portable Webers, grilling squirrel, shooting up, and muttering incoherently.

Braxton had visited the library several times over the years. It had an excellent history section including many hard-to-find books about ancient Greece and Sparta. Inside the foyer, a homeless man slept against the wall, covered in rags and snoring loudly.

He entered the main library. It had been built in 1939 and smelled of dust, books, and history, with a hardwood floor, reading nooks surrounding the main stacks, and a vaulted ceiling. A sign just inside the front door said, "You belong here. Hate doesn't. Choose action to stop hate." A homeless man sat at a wooden table at one of the four computers. John Baumgartner looked up from behind the desk.

"Hello, Professor," he said softly.

John had been born in Korea. He never knew his parents. They left him at an orphanage and he had been adopted by a German couple in Salem, along with two others, a boy and a girl. The Baumgartners' also had a son of their own blood, who was a schoolteacher. John barely weighed a hundred pounds. In his outsized gray jacket, white shirt, and blue tie, he looked like David Byrne from the Talking Heads. He was mildly autistic which made him a great librarian, and he was active in his Lutheran church where he sang in the choir.

"Hi, John," Braxton said. "I need to use the computer."

John gestured toward the table. "You know where it is."

Braxton sat as far as he could from the homeless man, who had a stubble like Bluto and pulled a watch cap low over his eyes. He smelled. Braxton brought up DuckDuckGo. He had stopped using Google years before when he realized that they tracked his every move. If he ordered a pair of snowshoes, he was inundated with snowshoe and skiing ads. As a professor, he had maintained a low-level Facebook page to interact with his students, but he'd eventually nuked it due to unrelenting anonymous attacks, mostly based on his modestly conservative views. What was so controversial about the Constitution? It was his impression that most young people had never read it, indeed, didn't even know what it was. He had made it part of his assigned reading list in Overview of Western Civilization, until the university asked that he concentrate on ancient Greece, Sparta, and Rome.

That left the Greek philosophers. Administration didn't like them much either, but there was little they could do about it.

Duckduckgo. *How can I track a stolen cell phone?*

TRACK ANY STOLEN PHONE. ENTER NUMBER TO TRACK NOW

PHONE TRACKING SOFTWARE—NO NEED TO ROOT THE DEVICE

FIND, LOCK, OR ERASE YOUR ANDROID DEVICE— GOOGLE HELP

A quick perusal of any of the suggested sites set off warning bells. Why use DuckDuckGo if it was going to send him to Google? The homeless man at the other end snorted, wound up, and sneezed, blowing snot all over the screen. Braxton's stomach lurched. He looked at his hands. He wasn't a germaphobe, but incidents like that made him think about washing more frequently.

Like several years before during the pandemic when the authorities insisted he wear a mask and stand six feet from everyone, while they roped off picnic tables in the parks. The university had insisted he get the vax, and he had obediently stood in line to receive the Moderna vaccine. It required two shots, and he counted himself lucky there were no aftereffects. He refused the boosters. He survived but came to resent having his freedom of choice taken from him.

Braxton went into the men's room, which was off the foyer, and washed his hands in the sink. The room smelled of feces. The bathroom stall door was open just wide enough to show a pile of human shit on the seat. Using a paper towel to open the door, Braxton returned to the front desk where John sat at his computer, absorbed in some task. Braxton waited.

John looked up. "What can I do for you?"

"Someone shit on the toilet seat."

"Oh dear. I'll call the janitor. He only comes in during the morning, then he works the City County Building in Oregon City."

"What if he can't make it?"

"I'll do it myself. I have nitrile gloves."

"You shouldn't have to do it."

"I don't mind. I consider myself a custodian not only of the books, but the physical building. Did you find what you needed?"

"No, I fell into a hole of insincere pitches by malignant entities eager to get their hands on my wallet."

"Oh dear."

"You know about what happened to my wife and daughter?"

John looked up, sunken eyes in olive skin. "No. Did something happen?"

"I was fired from the university for using the wrong pronoun. I started getting hate mail from all over the world. ANTIFA ran my wife's car off the road and she died. Someone swatted my house, and the FBI shot my daughter to death during a raid." Just rattling it off made him realize once more how screwed up his existence had become.

John stared, unblinking. "No."

"Yes."

"That's terrible. I don't know what to say. I will pray for you."

"Thank you."

"In fact, let's pray now. Come back here and we'll retreat into the stacks. They don't like it when I pray up front. They've had complaints."

Braxton walked around the end of the desk and John led him down a dark corridor that was exclusive to the administrator, holding rare and valuable books. John took Braxton's hands in his and closed his eyes.

"Dear Lord, please take pity on this good man Braxton Knox and let him know peace in this hour of need."

"And Lord, please help guide his hand as he deals out justice to whoever destroyed his life."

Eyes closed, John added, "That's not from me, Lord. That's from Braxton. In Jesus' name, amen."

"John, can you help me access the dark web?"

"Why would you want to do that?"

"I need someone outside the system. I have the number of a phone that was in the stolen vehicle they used to kill my wife. If the thief still has it, I can find him."

"Why would he keep such a thing?"

"These people aren't too bright. He might want to resell it."

"Well, the dark web is not very safe. You don't want to give them your contact info."

"That's why I'm here, John."

"Excuse me," someone said from the desk. They emerged from the stacks to find a middle-aged woman in a pixie cut and a gray houndstooth business suit, leather briefcase flat on the counter.

"Can I help you?"

"Yes. Can you point me to the books on tortious interference?"

"Yes, ma'am. We house those books in the tort stacks, which have a label on them. Is there any particular book you'd like?"

"Well, I don't know. I'm kind of new to this."

"Why don't you use a computer to bring up the list of books on tortious interference?"

"Thank you. I'll do that."

Braxton watched her walk to the table, sniff, grimace, and sit at the computer he had used. The one furthest from the homeless man.

"Can you access the dark web?" Braxton asked.

"I can, but I think I can help you another way."

"How is that?"

"This fellow who comes in here sometimes. He's a private investigator. He told me once that he had found a runaway child by tracking her cell phone."

"Really. He's not ANTIFA, is he?"

"Oh no. Quite the opposite. He once wore a T-shirt saying that he supported the Second Amendment and several people complained. He used to work remotely for one of those Big Tech companies but is a real straight shooter."

"How do I find him?"

"I think I have his card." John opened a desk drawer and rummaged around, plucking a card and sliding it across the top. "Here it is. You may take that if you wish."

Braxton picked it up. Ronin Kropenski, with an email and a phone number.

Chapter 20

The Shadow Cyber-Samurai

Ronin sat in the small diner, warming his hands on a black coffee that was strong enough to peel paint. Just as he liked it. He had come early to Grits N' Gravy for the meeting with Braxton Knox, mostly to relax.

When the former professor had called him, he knew instantly who he was. Ronin had seen the footage of Knox's daughter getting shot and the snippet from his class. Kropenski considered himself a patriot and what the FBI had done was horrific. Researching Knox, he got the full story, unfiltered by the mainstream media. All he did was not use a pronoun and now the guy faced the full weight and fury of the federal government. That alone made Ronin want to help him.

Once Knox had told him his story over the phone, Ronin had gone to work. Knox entered the busy diner and looked around. Ronin waved his hand and Knox slid into the seat opposite him.

"Ronin, I presume. I take it that's not your real name."

"A pleasure to meet you," he said, shaking the calloused hand. This was not the hand of a college instructor. This was someone that had been doing real labor.

"I thought you'd be older," Knox said.

"Is that a problem?"

"No, just surprising that's all. I just assumed you were a seasoned hacker."

"We don't use that word, hacker. I'm more of a cybersecurity specialist."

"Apologies."

"None are required. I started out at one of the largest social media companies. I moved on to freelance work. I still have connections in Big Tech. Friends in high places. Our mutual acquaintance John told me you were on the up-and-up. I looked at what they put you through. I never thought I'd see my government turn on a citizen the way they have on you."

"Will you be able to help me?"

Ronin sipped his coffee as the waitress sauntered over and took Braxton's order. Ronin waited for her to leave before he replied. "I've already started. I have a friend at T-Mobile who was the service provider for Ethel Rubinstein. He confirmed that her phone is still in use. Those Android phones are pretty easy to do tower tracking and movement. He was able to narrow it to three possible addresses."

Taking a deep breath, he continued. "Using some of my own tools, I ruled out one of them right off. It was some old guy, seventy years old, not exactly the car-and-phone-thief type. It took a little digging, but I learned who it was you wanted."

"And that is?"

"Tyler Thompson," he said, sliding Thompson's Facebook photo along with three other images across the sticky table to Knox. "He's ANTIFA."

"Are you sure?"

"I ran facial recognition of their recent rallies. I got three hits on this guy, despite the mask. He's a four-star douchebag. He runs with a guy named Joel Schumer who runs the second largest ANTIFA chapter in Portland. Cute man bun, not so much on a man, but still, cute.

"Your guy, Tyler Thompson, he's the one with the phone which puts him in the car that was used to run your wife off the road. It's important to note, this guy isn't the kind of person that does these sorts of things on his own."

"A follower."

"At best. I've been monitoring these ANTIFA cells for some time. They tend to work in groups, rarely alone."

"I caught a pair of them cruising by my house."

"There you go. They get their bravery from numbers. I got some pics of Schumer here too."

Knox studied the photos. "Look at this. Schumer's wearing this sweatshirt." Braxton expanded the picture so they could read the slogan. *If It Costs You Your Peace It Is Too Expensive.* "And here it is again at a different rally."

"Good eye. If you don't mind me asking, what are you going to do?"

Knox locked eyes with Ronin and spoke softly. "I am going to kill them."

Ronin responded with a single nod. He was fairly sure he knew the answer before he had asked the question.

"Does that response bother you?"

"No. I was in a bad situation once with these fuckers. If my boss hadn't been who he was, I would have lost my job simply because of something I clicked. They hounded me for two years. Hell, they harassed my parents and my little brother too." Mentioning his brother made him wince. "So no, dog, your response changes nothing between us. In fact, it makes me appreciate you more."

"Thank you."

Ronin could see the weight on the man's shoulders. "I'm monitoring the members of this cell's activities. They use an encrypted chat app. I've been able to get bits and pieces from that. These punks are pretty brazen. The members of the chapter post a lot of shit online. They brag about what they're doing."

"They have nothing to fear from the authorities, that much is sure."

"It wasn't helped by members of Congress claiming that ANTIFA doesn't exist, that it was, 'an idea.' I wouldn't be surprised to find out that they and their staffs helped fund some of the ANTIFA cells."

"I've been doing my own research. They're anarchists—domestic terrorists of the highest order."

"And the Department of Justice is tracking parents at school board meetings…"

Knox nodded.

117

"I feel the need to say this out loud. If you kill Thompson, Schumer, and whoever else might be involved, it won't bring your family back."

Knox understood. Ronin saw it in his eyes.

"Justice is an ancient concept that crosses all cultures. Law enforcement killed my daughter and refuses to help me find my wife's killers. I know it's impossible to bring them back. What I can do is make sure this never happens again, not from these people."

"The law is so twisted now; they will be coming for you when this is over. They'll call you a serial killer, or worse, some sort of alt-right nutjob—a threat to society."

"*Their* society. Throughout history, some of the greatest stories are those of vigilante justice. It goes way past our westerns. In Greek mythology, Nemesis was the goddess of retribution and justice. The word 'vigilante' comes from the Romans, the night watchmen that protected the civilians. I like to think I'm joining a long line of those that take justice into their own hands."

"That all sounds cool, doc. But they will come at you with everything they have. The last thing that the establishment can tolerate is something that bucks the system. They will come at you hard and fast." Ronin appreciated the fact that Knox was unlike others he had engaged with on similar topics. They tend to be fanatics. *This guy is well-learned. He's a thinker before being a doer.*

"They might try." There was determination in his tone, as if he were challenging law enforcement to come at him.

"You're going to need help. Just before you showed up, I emailed you everything I have that you might be able to use. It's encrypted. The password is FTFBI911, no spaces."

"What does that stand for?"

"Fuck the FBI," he grinned as he said it out loud. "Something I thought you'd be able to remember."

Braxton smiled. "Thank you. You've done more than enough."

"I don't think so. Let me come out to your place, make sure you're invisible to these people. I have friends who can help."

The waitress brought Knox's grits and cheese and refreshed their coffee. As Ronin stirred, Knox shook his head. "You've done more than enough. How much do I owe you?"

Ronin waved his hand. "Nothing. I don't take money from victims. And in terms of making sure you are cyber secure, that's also pro bono."

"Nonsense. You're a professional. You should be paid for what you do."

"My payment is you not getting caught."

* * *

Four hours later, Ronin powered up his network. Three curving screens came to life, surrounding his world. A row of action figures stood along the top of the curved monitors looking down at him. He had an Ironman mouse pad and a Punisher thermal mug with yesterday's coffee in it. This was his world, where he ruled supreme.

He opened a secured line to his former boss. The familiar face came on video. "Well, this is an unexpected surprise. How are you doing, Seymour?" His boss was the only person that ever referred to him by his real name. He allowed it out of deep respect for the man who had reshaped social media in the last two years.

"I'm good. You know me, fighting the good fight. Looking for trouble in all the wrong places."

"I take it this is not a social call?"

"You told me to keep my eyes peeled for a certain kind of profile... the kind of person who might take matters into his own hands for all the right reasons. Most of them don't pan out. They usually get hijacked by radicals or respond in ways that are overkill. I have one that fell into my lap though."

"Talk to me."

"His name is Braxton Knox."

"That professor whose daughter was killed by the FBI?"

"That's the one."

His former employer said nothing for a minute. "The media moved on with his story. Always chasing the next shiny thing. So he fits the profile I gave you?"

"He does."

The man in the video window grinned. "Tell me more..."

Chapter 21

Into the Den of Evil

Ronin had come out to the cabin two days later, bringing a trunk's worth of hardware. The man was a genius when it came to securing his cyber connection. He explained everything as he went. Far too many IT people liked to obfuscate what they did. Ronin knew how to speak plain English and make Braxton self-sufficient.

At night, Braxton devoured the stockpile of intelligence Ronin had assembled on Tyler Thompson and his cohorts. As Braxton read, he planned an infiltration of their upcoming meeting. Braxton had watched a number of videos and read Andy Ngo's book, committing pages to memory. He studied them intensely, drinking in every detail. Infiltrating them was risky, but he needed to know whom he targeted. From reading their local website, he knew they were anarchists. They wanted to overthrow the government and topple capitalism. While those goals alone made them an organization that he loathed, he wasn't going to kill them for that alone. There was a line he didn't want to cross, which was just being a mass murderer. Braxton intended to kill the right people.

They had posted videos of previous meetings, so he knew how to dress. Donning a tactical vest over his hoodie, he wore black pants, combat boots, and a knit hat, his lower face obscured by a black gaiter. Combined with the hood from the hoodie and a pair of sunglasses, it was hard for anyone to know who he was.

There was no misconception of the risk he was taking. He was tempted to strap on his Glock 19. He loved that weapon; it was his go-to Glock. It was compact, but anyone patting him down might find it. While he was a Glock Armorer, he was not a purist that only had guns from one manufacturer. Going through his arsenal, he opted for a smaller pistol, a pink Ruger LCP Max .380. When Rudy had sold it to him, he had said, "LCP doesn't stand for Little Crappy

Pistol with this one," and he was right. Loaded with hollow points, it was a great gun at close range. Suzanna had a concealed carry permit and often took her Ruger. It was very compact with a ten-round magazine. Unlacing his right boot, he put the weapon in the boot, re-laced it, then covered it with his pants leg. Checking it in the mirror, he couldn't see the pistol. While it was going to be nearly impossible to pull quickly, knowing it was there made him feel safe. If nothing else, if he pulled a tiny hot-pink gun out, his enemies might double over in laughter while he shot them.

The Ruger helped bolster his confidence. He wanted to take his Pro-Tech TR-3 X1M automatic knife as well. His knife fighting skills were not great, but he knew his had to be better than the average ANTIFA thug. If they did pat him down, he didn't want them finding the blade. Most amateur pat downs were sloppy; they worked the flanks of a human's limbs. As such, he taped the knife to his chest with some duct tape, making sure that if it did accidentally spring the blade, it wouldn't cut him. He was counting on if they find the gun, they might very well miss the knife.

The local ANTIFA chapter was brazen in their meetings and planning. Congress declaring them to be an idea, not an organization, which emboldened them. New members were encouraged to join in their "protests." He parked several blocks away so that his vehicle wouldn't be recognized, then made his way to the recreation center that was being used for the meeting.

His palms were sweating as he entered. There was no asking for names or producing of IDs. ANTIFA didn't care who you were as long as you were committed to their cause. They asked him to pull down his mask, which he did. They took photos of his face. The hefty girl doing it assured him it was to record what he looked like before their upcoming protests, in case he was beaten up. For Braxton, it was a moment of dangerous exposure. If anyone recognized him, even with his new beard, things could go badly.

There was a lot of stupid rhetoric from people at the podium. Capitalism was evil. White men were the root cause of systemic racism. One fat fuck with pink hair got up and railed about how American history was all a lie, that it glorified the theft of land and the subjugation of women and minorities. A local statue commemorating the Spanish American War was her target.

"We need to tear that mother down!" she declared to whooping and applause.

She claimed to teach high school history. Only she called it "herstory." Her speech was the dumbest thing he'd heard all night.

He focused on her horrible dye job and nose ring. Suzanna had always said, "If you are going to dye your hair, spend the money and do it right." Braxton chuckled. It was clear she had gotten her hair color from a box in the discount aisle at Dollar General. Her long, dishwater blonde roots were far too visible. And the nose ring. Why did girls think that was attractive?

The people smelled like a strange mix of Axe body spray and unchecked perspiration. One morbidly obese man waddled past, his BO so strong Braxton recoiled a step. It struck him as strange that so many of them smelled so badly.

It must be something with the environment... some sort of Green thing, he thought.

As he mingled with the crowd, he experienced two feelings. The first was a sense of paranoia. Each casual glance in his direction seemed to scrutinize him. While he knew he wore the same garb as everyone in the room, he felt he stood out. Braxton went out of his way to limit eye contact.

He felt old. Braxton was thirty-nine, but he felt ancient in the room. There were a few other older people but they were the minority in the room. How could so many people with so little life experience be so angry with their lives and society? It made no sense.

Their leader, Joel Schumer, an unimposing figure who went by the nickname of Ajax, rattled off a list of targets. By targets, he meant people. Two were some Korean business owners that had threatened them, and an owner of a Jewish deli. Teams were assigned to prep Molotov cocktails. A PowerPoint slide showed the streets and where Schumer wanted his diversion teams placed. In order to lure away law enforcement, one group was going to commit an armed robbery some ten blocks away, complete with random gunfire. Once the police were en route, they would firebomb the two businesses.

In just a few days, these cockroaches planned on attacking unknowing innocent people and destroying their businesses. He had not wanted their plight to be his problem. He had come for his own reasons. Suzanna's voice spoke in his head. "You protect the innocent, babe." That's what she would want him to do.

Young people, weirdly excited about destroying lives and businesses. None looked poor to him. The one next to him wore Air Jordans. All had iPhones. From some of their gear, it was clear they had access to money. Braxton was willing to bet that all of them came from good families, with parents who probably had no idea that their kids were out plotting murder and arson.

The only mention of him was when Ajax declared victory over "The Transphobe Knox." Their version of events is that he had been forced to leave town and put his house on the market—bragging that the FBI had gone in and done what they had planned, killed his daughter. "We showed Knox and people like him what will happen if you don't accept our new norm. You will lose your families, your precious possessions, everything."

He kept his rage in check.

As the meeting broke up, he spotted Tyler Thompson and his man bun. He'd let his hood down. Braxton thought about shooting him. There were too many witnesses, but that didn't matter. Everyone looked the same. No one would stop him. They would reel back in terror. Braxton's plan was simple. Follow him when the meeting broke up, then kill him. The thought of hollow point bullets tearing his internal organs to shreds was oddly soothing.

His mind went to the intended targets that the ANTIFA thugs were going after. Innocent people who had no idea of the hell about to be unleashed on them. Who protects them? Would they suffer the way that he had? What about their families? They would lose their livelihoods simply because they were made targets of hate.

Braxton didn't engage with the others. He felt older than most of them and he didn't want to risk revealing who he was. His movement was casual; his eyes and ears soaking in every face, every detail he could. These people had taken from him what he held most dear. Not all of them, but enough to make him loathe them all.

Thirty minutes later, he saw Thompson slide out the door. Braxton followed, as casually as possible. Once outside, the dim streetlight showed Thompson walking away. Braxton followed, closing the gap.

Someone tapped him on the shoulder. Wheeling about, he saw four of the black clad youths, fists already streaking in the darkness at him. In that instant, he knew he'd been made. Two punches hit his ribs, another hit his face. His tactical vest lessened the blows to his rib cage. His face squirted blood, which he ignored.

Raising his arms, he blocked another pair of blows to his face, but they were already moving to his sides. Braxton backed up, throwing a jab at one, connecting with his nose. He felt the crunch in his knuckles. The slickness of blood on his skin was warm as all of his senses seemed heightened. He had been in fights in the Army, but this was different. These people were intent on killing him.

A punch collided with the side of his face, popping his ear. Braxton continued to back up, then saw a short baton drawn. He missed blocking it and it slammed into his left thigh. As one of his assailants closed in, he threw a haymaker, catching him in the stomach and knocking the air out of him, sending him staggering backwards. That move cost him distance, something he instantly regretted. Two more fists slammed into his upper body, and a fist with brass knuckles hit the side of his jaw, forcing his head to twist.

His knees buckled. He dropped to the sidewalk. For a few moments, he struggled to stay conscious, breathing hard, fighting to ignore myriad painful strikes. This had happened to him once before, in boot camp. This time he staved off unconsciousness. But it cost him a precious few moments. His attackers pounced.

Boots, propelled by the vigor of youth, kicked at him, hitting his arms, body, and legs. Braxton eyed a kneecap and landed his bootheel on it with a violent kick, forcing it to hyperextend. The young man howled, falling over backwards grasping the knee. His payment was another brutal kick to his stomach, knocking the wind from his lungs.

He had the gun in his boot. Bending his leg, he reached for it. The baton coming at the side of his head was faster. His vision tunneled and darkness closed in. Ajax loomed, a feral grin on his face. "Pretty brave of you to come here, Professor."

Braxton's mouth was dry. He couldn't speak.

"You fucked up, old man. Zip-tie him, Sledge. Drive him up in the woods where they won't find him."

Joel Schumer got right into his face. "If it makes you feel any better, Professor, you'll be with your wife and daughter soon."

Schumer rose. "Don't burn the body. Just put it somewhere where it's hard to find. I want some hunter to stumble across it. It'll send a message to anyone that dares to stand against us."

With that, darkness overtook Braxton. His last thought before he lost consciousness was of Suzanna and Angela and how he had failed them.

Chapter 22

In a Ball of Flames

Braxton was with his daughter on the bed. A lifetime ago. The events of the last two weeks were a fading memory. He looked at his daughter.

"What is your favorite part of the trilogy?" she asked him.

He smiled. "We haven't gotten there yet. I don't want to ruin it for you."

"Come on, Dad, you won't ruin anything." Her smile was contagious. He grinned.

"My two favorite parts are the Battle of Helm's Deep and the Scourging of the Shire."

"What's the scourging?"

"It involves the Sackville Bagginses."

She always wanted to know what would happen before they got to that part.

"Oh!" Her eyes lit up. "I remember them from the party."

Braxton reached out to Angela, to hold her one more time. There was a jarring bump shattering the dream-like memory. Angela and the bedroom flickered out of existence as he bumped back to reality.

When he opened his eyes, he was in the dark, being jostled side to side. His wrists were zip-tied. His left hand was numb. Flexing his legs brought pain. Something blocked his feet. He was surrounded by a low rumble and vibration. The sound of a car on rough road.

I'm in the trunk of a car.

His head hurt, as did every joint and limb on his body. Pushing past the pain, he reached deep into his mental stamina and gathered his thoughts. The first priority was to get his hands free. Drawing up his knees, he worked his hands from back to front, every joint screaming. Reaching to his chest, he found the knife. The duct tape had come free, taking some chest hair with it. He sprang the blade in darkness. Gripping it blade down, he sawed on the zip tie.

His hands burst free. His left hand tingled as blood flowed once more. Had they found his gun? Bending his right leg, he felt bruises that he didn't know existed. The gun was still in his boot. Yes! The ANTIFA thugs liked to pretend they were professionals, but they had overlooked his knife and gun. They probably thought he didn't have a weapon because he hadn't drawn one when they'd ambushed him.

Unlacing the boot was hard with one hand still numb. He'd been tempted to just pull it out, but he wanted to be quiet. After a minute of struggle, he freed the gun. Holding it gave him a sense of power and hope. The fight wasn't over, not by a long shot. Braxton was ready for round two.

Laying down the pistol, he felt the back of the seat that formed a quarter of the trunk. It was a cardboard-like material, carpeted, designed to be folded into the rear seat. He needed a view of who was in the car. He carefully sawed with the Pro-Tech, cutting through the cardboard backing, opening a six-inch hole. He felt through, past the springs, to make sure no one was seated in the back. There was no resistance.

The car made a sharp turn and the gun slid to his knee. As he pulled it back, he cut a vertical slit in the seat material, then made a pair of horizontal cuts. Pulling the material back, he saw a driver and a passenger. It was still dark outside. There were no streetlights, so he guessed they were out in the country.

Memories of Schumer speaking as he lay in agony on the sidewalk slowly came back. *"Drive him up somewhere in the woods and get rid of him."* That meant either Mt. Hood or Forest Park. Lowering the knife, he gripped the pistol with his right hand. Firing in the trunk would be loud but necessary.

"Why didn't you tie up his feet?" the young man in the passenger seat asked. He was smoking and Braxton caught a whiff of marijuana.

"Think about it. If we tied up his feet, then we'd have to drag him out of the car. This way we can make him walk to where we want to do it," the man behind the wheel said with a sense of pride.

"Ah. Smart."

There were two potential courses of action. First, wait until they opened the trunk, then shoot them. Chances were they would be armed when they opened the trunk. They needed weapons to force his compliance.

The second option was more dangerous. Shoot them from the trunk, from behind. He estimated their speed between forty-five and sixty. Killing the driver would likely crash the vehicle.

The decision was easier than he would have expected. Holding the Ruger LCP Max with both hands, he took careful aim at the back of the driver's seat, doing his best to estimate where the man's body was. His extended trigger finger slid off the slide and caressed the trigger. For a moment, he wondered if this was the dumbest move he'd ever made.

He squeezed the trigger twice.

His ears popped with the first round going off. He only heard the muffled bang of the second. A crimson mist hit the windshield and the driver lurched forward.

The car jerked as Braxton shifted to the passenger, throwing off his aim. His first shot missed, hitting the windshield as the man squealed like a teenage girl. Craning his head around, the ANTIFA goon looked for the source of the shot. Braxton fired two rounds. The man howled. The car pitched forward and rolled over three times. Braxton's battered body slammed into the trunk lid, the floor, and the back of the rear seats. Metal groaned. Plastic cracked and popped. Pain tore at his left shoulder and his headache doubled in intensity. The car stopped, rocking at an awkward angle. He looked through the hole. The headlights reflected off of the trees. The dashboard lights revealed the limp driver slumped in his seat. The passenger moaned, clinging to life.

Braxton felt around the rear of the trunk for a grip to the emergency trunk release. He grabbed the handle and pulled. The trunk sprung open with a *thunk*. Night air chilled his sweaty body.

The car had gone over an embankment and rolled down into a thick copse of pines. It had rolled through thick brush, blocking the view from the road. Despite the pain from his beating and the crash, Braxton climbed out and got his footing on the soft ground. One ear popped. He heard the whine of the engine, somehow still engaged and spinning the front tires.

Holding the gun, he went to the driver's side. The dead man behind the wheel was hard to see. The other one's head slumped forward. He looked up. His eyes flared in terror. "Get out," Braxton commanded. The punk's left black sleeved arm was limp, wet with blood. The man struggled with the door in agony. Braxton moved around the tree that had stopped the car, keeping the gun on the punk.

The punk fell out. Braxton stood above him as he lay in mud and pine. "Where's your weapon?"

"I—I don't know." He glanced back at the car. Braxton found the gun on the floor, cleared the chamber, then put it in his pocket.

"It hurts," the punk moaned.

"I bet it does. Where are we?"

"Just past Mount Hood Village," he gasped. "Ajax said there was a logging trail he knew of. Please—the pain is bad. You have to help me."

"Oh, I'm going to help you all right."

"It wasn't me. It was Ajax. He's the one that sent us."

Braxton studied the punk's face. "I know you. You drove by my house."

The punk's face went white. "We didn't mean any harm."

"Yeah, right."

"Please don't kill me."

"You had no problem killing me."

"I won't tell anyone. We can both just leave. I don't want to die." The punk pissed his pants, the wet stain showing on his crotch.

"Who was in the car that ran my wife off the road? I know that Thompson was involved, but none of you do anything alone. Who was with him?"

The punk squirmed on the ground. "Ramrod was driving. Thompson just got the car and went along for the ride. Ajax told them to do it."

"And where were you?"

"I wasn't even there." The terror in his voice said otherwise.

"How do you know who was driving if you weren't there?"

The punk struggled to find the right words. "I—I—it was just that —I mean—"

Braxton lowered his stance and pointed the gun. "Save your breath. You were there. Even if you weren't, you didn't do anything to stop it. You knew what they were going to do and allowed it to happen. You want me to think that you weren't there, but we both know you were in that car too. You're as guilty as any of them."

"You promised—"

"No I didn't."

"Please," he began to cry.

"For Suzanna," Braxton pulled the trigger twice. The shots echoed off into the woods, devoured by the trees.

Braxton stared at the dead man. His sense of loss remained as it had before he had fired. There were others now, Ramrod, Ajax/Schumer, and Thompson. He cleared his weapon and tucked it into one of the plate holders on his tactical vest.

Braxton checked the punk's pockets. A bag of weed and a lighter. Looking down at the young man, Braxton shook his head. "This stuff is bad for you." He tossed the weed into the car and took the lighter. Straining, he pulled the young man back and stuffed him into the passenger seat, one leg dangling out the door.

Braxton recovered his knife from the trunk. Stooping, he found the gas tank. He jabbed it with case-hardened steel three times. Gasoline drizzled beneath the vehicle. He let it seep out for a few moments, then flicked the lighter and set it off.

The car flared as he climbed the embankment. He was halfway up the hill when the tank erupted in a brilliant orange ball, lighting up the sky. The car was so far down the steep slope, hidden by the trees and brush, he doubted that anyone would see the fire. Flames lapped the trees, setting the lower boughs on fire. They crackled and popped as the interior became an inferno. If anyone found it, they wouldn't look for gunshot wounds.

Every muscle aching, Braxton trudged downhill. With luck, no one would find the wreck for days.

Chapter 23

Internal Affairs

Special Agent Sonya Turner sat with two agents from Internal Affairs in the FBI's main conference room. Between them, the material she'd gathered on how the video of Angela Knox's death had been leaked to the media. The agents were impressed. She'd done their job for them. Their questions hadn't been about what she knew about the leak, but how she'd gathered the material and what her theory was.

Agent Brooks, in his sixties with short cropped gray hair, flipped through the report. "I like the videos you pulled up and the gaps in coverage you identified."

She caught a hint of his Obsession cologne. She knew it all too well from a former boyfriend. Just catching the light smell of it summoned unpleasant memories.

"Thank you."

"I think we should make a recommendation to put some cameras in the locker rooms," Agent Stockley added.

"You're likely to get pushback on that," Turner said. "People won't like being filmed in locker rooms."

"We're considering a warrant to surveil the reporter that pushed the video. If you're right though, that this was a blind drop, it's likely a waste of time," Brooks said.

"I tend to agree. Then again, I may be wrong."

Stockley sighed. "We're going to have to go over the video. There might be something that you missed. No offense."

"None taken."

"Agent Turner," Brooks said. "What do you think of the case against this Knox character?"

She could tell that Brooks was good. It was an open-ended question, designed to get her to reveal something she might not with a direct yes or no query. It was verbal bait dangled in front of her. She had to be careful.

"My opinion doesn't matter. My job is to protect the country and ensure the law is appropriately applied and that justice is done. I stand on the side of the Constitution... that's what I pledged to defend."

"That's a textbook answer. I didn't ask you that. I asked you how you felt about the case."

"I think it's a mistake to apply civil rights laws to the non-use of a personal pronoun."

Stockley leaned back in his seat. "Perhaps we should be taking a closer look at you." He was joking, but only slightly.

"Go ahead. You'd be wasting your time, but you're welcome to try."

"Agent Turner, why do you think it's a mistake?" Brooks said.

"It's a big stretch to say that Braxton Knox violated that person's civil rights. Look, he's going to court over this and claims that his speech is protected by the First Amendment. If you look at the laws, especially the Constitution, he's right. In fact, he's going to win."

Stockley weighed back in. "The US attorney feels differently."

"She's entitled to her opinion. I prefer to side with the law."

"Well," Brooks said, "she's the one with the law degree."

"She's not alone."

"What does that mean?" Books asked.

"If you check my personnel file, you'll find that I have a Juris Doctorate degree. That's a little more education than Ms. Rainsong has."

Brooks flipped through some of the files he brought to the meeting, looking for confirmation. "That's interesting. It's an impressive degree for someone who's a field agent. Why didn't you take the bar? Hell, you could have had Rainsong's job."

"I don't want her job. I like the side where I'm working. I like catching bad guys and helping innocent people."

"Isn't that what Ms. Rainsong is doing?" Stockley asked.

"Sometimes yes. In the case of Professor Knox, she is pushing a social agenda. It scores great points with the leadership of the DoJ. I don't think that's what that job is supposed to do. Her job is to administer justice."

"I don't need to remind you that a part of your role is supporting the US attorney in whatever prosecutions they seek. We don't set policy nor do we have the luxury of having opinions about what the prosecutors seek to pursue," Stockley said.

"I do my job. In fact, if you peruse my file, you see that I do it very well. I was there the night the two agents shot and killed Angela Knox. I am not your problem. And in terms of Ms. Rainsong, given my credentials, I am perfectly within my rights to question her. We are not supposed to be machines. The Bureau wants us to be thoughtful in our actions."

"This whole affair has damaged the reputation of the Bureau," Stockley bemoaned. For Turner, that was not a priority. She was in the minority in terms of that thinking. Much of the resources of the FBI were spent protecting the FBI's image.

"I can't speak to that."

"Surely you have an opinion on that matter," Stockley said.

"I wouldn't make that assumption. I like to think that I do my best to make sure that the reputation of the Bureau is seen as transparent and in the best possible light."

"No one is looking at you, Agent Turner," Brooks said. "You've done a remarkable job assembling this information. You've made our work easy. I, for one, thank you." From the way he was speaking, she got the feeling that Brooks wanted to leave.

Agent Stockley was another matter. He waved his hand in the air. "Not just yet, Aaron. Agent Turner, I'd like to know what you think about SAIC Durston."

"What exactly do you mean?"

"Do you think he might be the kind of person who would leak this information to the media?"

She hadn't seen it coming. She had to think of the right response. Durston was a good man. He fretted over the Bureau's reputation. "He means well. I have never heard him say or do anything that

135

might make me think he would be involved with the leak. In fact, he was the person who assigned me to get a leg-up on gathering the data once the media ran the Knox girl's story. He seemed quite upset about the entire matter."

"That's good to hear. Is there anyone else we should pay special attention to during our investigation?" Stockley asked.

She said nothing for a few moments. Agent Brooks spoke. "Look, I know it's difficult to even imply that one of your colleagues might be a bad apple. It's a standard question."

"It's not that," Turner said. "It's easier for me to say who I think it's *not*. I don't think it was Durston. If it was him, he would have personally taken the role of gathering all the security data. Instead, he assigned that to me. You can rule out Agents Forsyth and Hayden. They were on administrative leave at the time. Since they were responsible for the death of Ms. Knox, they had nothing to gain by releasing their bodycam footage to the media.

"I know the agents that were in on the Knox raid. They each had to know that when this went public, they would be dragged into court. You both are agents. You know we hate being put through an IA investigation and a court case. If I were looking, I would turn my attention to someone else, another agent that wasn't on the team that made the Knox arrest."

"Why not someone else in the building?" Stockley asked.

"If they did copy and smuggle the data out in the manner I suggested in my report, they had to know about how agents sync their bodycams and that the copies were stored in the cameras. An agent would know that, not some clerk."

Stockley and Brooks slid their chairs back and rose. Stockley extended his hand. They shook. "Thank you for your time, Agent Turner, and for pulling this information together." He started out the door.

Brooks walked around the end of the table and stood in front of her, offering his hand. "Thank you. You've given us a leg up."

"Do you think you'll find this person?"

He shrugged. "Leaks are part of government. Frankly, we rarely can pin down who did it. We can spend thousands of dollars polygraphing folks and end up at the same dead end. The whistleblower laws give them protection when we're lucky enough to find them. We're required to investigate these instances, but ultimately, it could easily turn into a dead end. A few hands will be slapped, some bureaucratic temper tantrums will occur, but in the end, the Bureau will move on."

"What a shame."

"In this case, it may all be moot. Between the two of us, Ms. Rainsong has all but conceded that she is going to have to rescind her indictment of Professor Knox. With his lawsuit looming and the media turned against her office and her personally, she's thinking of cutting her losses."

"That doesn't sound like her."

"She may decide to try and prosecute him sometime in the future, when the attention fades. Between you and me, I think she'd be happy if this goes away."

She probably knows this isn't good for her career aspirations.

"That's good," Turner said. "It will give everyone involved a chance to move on."

Agent Brooks left. She was more than happy that the entire matter might simply disappear. Braxton Knox didn't deserve what happened to him and she was ashamed by the Bureau's role in the affair.

Chapter 24

Mail Call

Braxton trudged downhill, half on, half off the shoulder. There wasn't much room on these mountain roads. A vehicle appeared behind him, headlights piercing the gloom. Braxton paused, half turned, and hung out his thumb. The car accelerated past, veering into the left lane to get as far away as possible. He didn't blame them. When he was a kid, you could hitchhike from town to town and not worry about being killed by some lunatic in a stolen car.

Occasionally, the lights of Mt. Hood City would twinkle through the trees but would disappear when he rounded a bend. Three vehicles passed him before an old man in a pickup truck, wearing a Cabela's hat, pulled over.

"Thanks," Braxton said, pulling the door shut.

"Where ya headed?" the driver said in a voice seasoned by nicotine.

"Portland."

"Getcha as far as Gresham. I don't go into Portland anymore."

"I don't blame you. I'm actually headed to Sunnyside."

"Used to love to go into Portland. Hear music, eat at a restaurant, visit Powell's. Now I wouldn't send a dog into Portland. Some fuckin' degenerate would try to eat it."

"I hear you."

"Whatchoo doin' up here anyway? You lost?"

"My car broke down and I couldn't get any cell service." His body still ached from the fight and the car crash. He was thankful that his hearing had come back.

The mountain road hooked up with Highway 26. The driver barely stopped at the stop sign before putting the pedal to the metal. The old truck accelerated with a rasp from the punctured muffler.

"You mind if I smoke?"

"It's your car."

The driver pulled a Marlboro from behind his ear and a Zippo from the center console and lit up. He cracked his window, admitting the smell of pine. Braxton cracked his window too.

"I'm Fred."

"I'm Roger," Braxton said. He had plenty of time on his walk to craft a backstory, should anyone ask why he was on a lonely road in the middle of the night.

"What do you do, Roger?"

"I sell Toyotas."

"You sell Priuses?"

"Not if I can help it."

Fred barked. "Why the hell not?"

"Well, don't tell anyone, but all this bullshit about saving the planet is just empty virtue signaling. We're nowhere near running out of fuel, and they never explain where the electricity for all these electric cars comes from."

"Yeah, but don't the electricity for the Prius come from its gas engine?"

"You see my point. And if that isn't bad enough, now they got all these all-electric vehicles they're trying to cram down the public's throat. It comes from coal-fueled power plants. Outta sight, outta mind."

Fred held out a fist. They bumped.

"What year is this truck?"

"This, my friend, is a 1977 Ford F-150, one of the finest trucks ever built. It has a three-hundred-inch inline six, and 220,000 miles on the clock. I change the oil every 3000 miles and keep it in shape."

"Did you buy it new?"

Fred laughed. "I ain't that old! I bought it when it only had 70,000 miles. Was that car that broke down, was that a Toyota?"

It was Braxton's turn to laugh. "How'd you guess?"

139

"What's wrong with it?"

"I have no idea. I'll send a tow truck in the morning."

"I'm thinking of moving to Idaho."

"You got family?"

"Got a wife, a son, and a daughter. Dan's a radiologist at Mercy Baptist in Portland, and Linda's a psychologist in San Francisco."

"You must be very proud."

"Well, yes and no. Dan's got his head screwed on straight. He's looking to move away too. Linda was a beautiful girl when we sent her away to college. After the first semester, she came back with half her skull shaved, the other half purple, a nose ring, and a tattoo that says 'eat the rich.' She makes six figures. Last time I saw her, she asked if I was still eating meat."

"Where'd she go to school?"

"Evergreen in Olympia. She's really proud of the fact that she was on the steering committee that voted to tear down a statue of George Washington."

"What's wrong with Washington?"

"Slaves, don'tcha know."

Braxton thought of the numerous cancelations he'd witnessed at Eastern State, including his own.

"You go to college?"

"No," Braxton lied. "I joined the Army right out of high school."

"See any action?"

"No. I was in Afghanistan. I did a lot of guard duty, but when they found out I could type seventy words a minute, they weren't about to take a chance on losing me. Priorities."

"Ain't that the truth. Seems like everything's fucked up these days."

As they approached the city, traffic increased. The lights of Portland showed in the distance.

"I'm only going as far as Gresham. After that you're on your own."

"I'll call an Uber."

Fred dropped him in front of a Popeye's Chicken. Braxton went inside and ordered a fried chicken sandwich and a coke. He slumped in a booth and ate. It hurt to chew. He called an Uber. It was a white Prius driven by a Pakistani immigrant. The plaque on the dash said *Singh*.

"Where to?"

Braxton gave him the address of his house. The driver peered at him in the rearview. "What happened to you?"

"Rough night."

"We are going by the hospital."

"That's all right, thanks."

"I don't understand it. When I first arrived, Portland was a beautiful city. I don't understand how your government has allowed it to turn into a war zone. I came here to get away from this kind of thing."

"How long have you been here?" Braxton asked.

"I arrived in 2019. It was my wish to open a restaurant."

"I didn't know Pakistani cuisine was a thing."

"I have trained in the finest Indian restaurants. It would have been an Indian restaurant."

"Why don't you move?"

"My wife's family is here."

"Well, I wish you luck, pal."

The driver dropped him off on his street. The yellow crime tape was gone. The lawn needed mowing. Braxton tipped the driver ten bucks and went up the steps to the house that was no longer a home. He'd left Monsieur at home. It was alright, he had a doggie door at the rear of the cabin. He'd be fine if he stayed away from bears. He let himself in, showered, and collapsed in bed. He woke at eleven and checked his phone. Ronin had texted him.

Call me at this number.

Braxton called.

"Yeah," Ronin said.

"What's up?"

"I'm tracking that phone in real time. Your friends are planning on destroying two businesses. Abe's Delicatessen and Park Korean BBQ, across the street from each other."

"I was at the meeting where they went over their plans. They didn't say when."

"Tonight. One in the morning."

"Should I phone the cops?"

Ronin barked mirthlessly. "What do you think?"

"Shit. All right. Thanks for the heads-up. I don't suppose you want to get involved."

"I'm already involved. Do I wish to don combat fatigues and run around with a gun? No. I operate behind the scenes."

"Where can we meet?"

"Do you know Happy Valley Nature Park?"

"Nope."

"It's about twenty miles southwest of here on SE Ridgecrest. Meet me there at five. I'll be at the dog park in the back. I'll be there with my border collie."

"Okay."

Braxton put on a pair of tan cargo pants and a khaki Carhartt hoodie. He went outside. Gorelick sat on his front porch in a rocker. Braxton waved. Gorelick waved back. Braxton walked over under a gray sky, par for Portland at this time of year. Braxton stopped at the base of Gorelick's stairs.

"How you doing?"

"Come on up. I got some mail for you."

Braxton climbed the steps. Gorelick heaved himself out of the rocker.

"You want coffee?"

"Sure."

"Follow me."

Braxton followed Gorelick into the old turn of the century bungalow, with its arched opening between the living room and the dining room, through to the kitchen, fitted with an ancient enamel stove and a Frigidaire that had to be twenty years old. Gorelick poured coffee into a Trailblazers mug.

"There's half-and-half in the fridge and sugar on the table."

Braxton fixed his mug and sat at the table.

Gorelick stepped out, returning a minute later with a cardboard box filled with letters. Costco. Northwest Window and Siding. The gas bill, the electric bill, the sewer bill, and twelve letters, some with return addresses, some not. Those without were addressed in block letters written with a ballpoint. Braxton held each one up to the ceiling light, trying to ascertain if they contained powder. He had no intention of opening them.

"Thanks, Albert."

"Soon you'll be getting letters from AARP and AAA."

"I'm not that old."

"They start early."

"You join?"

"Hell no. It's just another special interest lobby, only they ain't my interests. What the hell happened to you?"

"I was doing some work at my cabin and I fell off the ladder."

Gorelick reached into his sweater and pulled up a Life Alert button. "You oughta get one of these."

"Yeah, let me think about that."

Braxton pulled out a pocketknife and opened a letter that was addressed in elegant cursive with a return address that started with Ralph Sorensen.

Dear Professor Knox:

I am a Marine veteran who served in Desert Storm. Like many decent people, I am appalled by the treatment you have received by supposedly august institutions. I just want you to know you are not alone, and that if you were to start a GoFundMe to finance a suit against Eastern State, I would be happy to contribute and so would many others.

Yours sincerely,

Ralph Sorenson

There were several more in the same vein. The only letter with a business heading was from the *Daily Beat*, a conservative news organization popular on AM.

Dear Professor Knox:

Permit me to introduce myself. I am Faye Weldon, a reporter for the Daily Beat, *a news organization that strives for honest reporting without a leftwing bias. I have tried reaching you by phone, but I understand that you may have removed yourself from easy access. I am writing to ask if you would consent to an interview live on Daily Beat Radio sometime in the near future. We have an audience of over three million and have won numerous awards for our reporting.*

I encourage you to visit the Daily Beat *website, review our stories and credentials, and get back to me at your convenience.*

Yours most sincerely,

Faye Weldon

Braxton tucked that in his cargo pants next to Sorenson's letter. He stood.

"Well, I gotta get back up there and finish the roof. Thanks for the coffee and taking in the mail, Albert."

"Anytime. You musta got home late. Didn't hear you come in."

"I got home in the wee small hours of the morning and slept until eleven."

"I'll keep an eye out."

Chapter 25

Strategy Session

Braxton was surprised to learn Happy Valley Park was a private theme park with a castle, a swimming pool, water slides, and a Viking ship rising in a sandbox. At this time of year, there were few visitors, mostly enjoying the grounds or picnicking at one of the numerous kiosks.

He found a spot in the first parking lot, among a half dozen widely spaced cars. It was cool with a hint of moisture as he walked south, following the signs to the dog park. There were three dog parks, each with a handful of owners and twice as many dogs running around, pissing on the fence posts, sniffing each other's butts, and running in joyful abandon. Ronin wasn't hard to find. He sat at a picnic table, feet outward, wearing a Navy blue hoodie with a cartoon ghost on front, backpack at his side, border collie at his feet. Braxton sat at the opposite end of the bench.

"How are you, Ronin?"

"Fine. Contemplating life as a vigilante. Any trouble finding the place?"

"Hell no. I used a map."

"Good idea. As I already told you, the head of the ANTIFA cell that grabbed you is Joel Schumer. Goes by the name of Ajax. He's got his people all fired up. They have maps all drawn out, a timetable, the works."

"You seem to be able to pierce their security, despite their encryption."

Ronin waggled his fingers. "I should be working for the CIA. I've been doing some more digging into this guy. Schumer's thirty-eight, works part-time at DoorDash, and is living off an insurance settlement he got when he slipped on a patch of ice in front of Target. That store has since closed its doors."

"How much did he get?"

"Two fifty. He had a slick lawyer."

"Why would a guy with a nest egg like that waste his time running around setting fires?"

"You're asking me to explain the woke mind? He's a true believer. Attended Portland State for two years, and if you know anything about Portland State, you know how they operate. White, bad. All other races, good. Men bad. All other sexual permutations, good. America, bad. All other nations, good."

"What did he study?"

"I wish I could tell you he majored in the Problems of Whiteness, but no, he was studying psychology. In my experiences, those who major in psychology are most likely to be fucked up."

"What about this action tonight? Why don't we just drop a dime on them to the police?"

The dog sat up, wagging its tail, and laid its muzzle on Ronin's thigh.

"This is Binky. Binky hates communists."

"Good boy."

"The police ain't gonna do shit. They learned their lesson. They're going to lie low, try to get their twenty in, then retire and get the hell out of Portland. Besides, the local prosecutor won't actually file charges unless a gun is involved, and then only if a conservative is the one holding it. It's far easier to simply alert Korean BBQ about what's going on. Those Koreans aren't reluctant to use deadly force to protect their property. They understand that as Koreans, they have a right to victim status."

"How do they have that right? Aren't Asians supposed to have an unfair academic advantage?"

"Well, yes and no. I looked into that restaurant. It's owned by the Park family. That's like being owned by Jones or Smith. It's the most common name in Korea. But this particular Park, Yun-See, emigrated to the United States in 1980 and built the business up from nothing. Yun-Seo is now in his seventies and his two sons and a daughter run the restaurant. Son number one, Sang Mok, served two years in Afghanistan. In fact, he was over there at the same time as you. He won the Silver Star for courage under fire. Younger son Lim served two years in the Navy. Daughter Sun-Ah graduated cum laude from Stanford with a degree in marketing."

"ANTIFA isn't going to like that. Military veterans."

"There are two VFWs in Portland, and one American Legion with a combined membership of over 27,000. How do you think the lickspittle would react if several hundred veterans showed up on that street tonight?"

"Lickspittle?"

"My word for the press."

"I don't know. How would you do it?"

"I have screen caps of ANTIFA chapter Che Guevera, that's the group who attacked last time, telling their members to converge on Lake Oswego and to bring gasoline and Molotov cocktails. I could easily send those to every veterans chapter in the area and they wouldn't be able to trace it."

That can backfire on us, Braxton thought, and said, "I can see the headlines now. 'White Supremacists converge to stop peaceful anti-racism march.'"

Ronin grinned. "Now you've got it. What should we do? Just alert the Koreans? Or tell the whole damn world?"

"Wouldn't telling the whole damn world have the effect of short-circuiting the whole thing?"

"Of course it would. But they'd only regroup, be more careful, and plan something else. These are fanatics. They watched *Star Wars* and are convinced they are the rebels, when in reality, they are the Empire."

They are bringing violence on these innocent people. The only thing that they will understand is violence being brought on them.

"Well. I gotta tell ya, I'd prefer they show up and get shot," Braxton admitted.

"That's my inclination as well."

"How you gonna do it?"

"I'll send them the screen caps."

"May I see?"

Ronin pulled out his phone and poked. He turned the screen toward Braxton.

All eyes on the slants and kikes tonight. Teach them what it means to support white supremacy. Meet at George Floyd Park at eleven p.m. Dress dark and bring matches.

"Nobody likes them. You think the cops are gonna show up? You think if the Koreans drill a few of them, they'll show up in the morning with a murder warrant? No way. The few police that remain on the force aren't going to stick their necks out. I bet those Koreans have good trigger discipline. They're not going to start shooting randomly. But if someone heaves a Molotov cocktail through the front window, all bets are off."

"Do it."

Ronin poked and stroked. "Done."

"And they can't trace it?"

Ronin smiled, pried his phone open with a pocketknife, removed the battery and tossed it in a bowl of water someone had put out for the dogs. Ronin stood and stomped on the rest of the phone, grinding it hard with his heel. He sat. He pulled another phone out of his backpack.

"Now here's the deal. We don't want to miss this great event so I'm putting up a drone. I'll be on the roof of the Western States Bank by ten o'clock tonight. Join me. I'll put the fire ladder down in the alley."

"The roof of a bank? Are you trying to get us tossed in jail?"

"The bank's closed. They pulled up stakes a year ago. They were one of the first targets when George Floyd died. The owners had to seal their front window fourteen times with plywood before they got the message."

"Fourteen times?"

"It's hard for some people to believe that this entire part of the country has turned into a massive shithole."

"There are no homeless in Lake Oswego."

"Ha! You just haven't seen them yet. The mayor made a personal appeal for homeowners to take them in. You can imagine how that went over. You know they used to call Lake Oswego 'Lake No Negro.'"

"No."

"Yeah. Nobody says it anymore. Where'd you get the shiner?"

"They recognized me at the rally last night. I dressed like a thug, grew a beard, and they still recognized me. They beat the shit out of me, zip-tied me, put me in the trunk of a car, and drove into the woods."

"Holy shit. And?"

"And here I am."

"You're not gonna tell me what happened?"

A smile flashed across Braxton's face. "Much to my surprise, I find myself here today."

"I see. All right. You coming?"

"You drivin'?"

"Yeah. Want me to pick you up?"

Chapter 26

Rooftop Koreans

Braxton was on his porch when Ronin arrived at nine-thirty in a beige Hyundai sedan. Braxton hoisted a golf bag that had belonged to his father and skipped down the steps, wearing dark blue jeans and a black Carhartt hoodie. He slid the golf bag into the Hyundai's rear seat and sat in the shotgun seat.

"What's in the bag?" Ronin said.

"It's an Accuracy International AXSR rifle. One of the best sniper rifles on the planet."

Braxton examined Ronin. If he were going to bail, now was the time. Ronin put the car in gear and pulled out.

"These folks came at me and my brother. They tried to ruin my career and they did... *things* to my little brother. Stuff my family never recovered from." From the way he spoke, he wasn't ready to share the details, so Braxton didn't press the matter. He understood why Ronin was there. This was redemption. This was personal.

"I don't have to tell you the law."

"Nope. I know."

"You   packing?"

Ronin lifted the right side of his jean jacket to expose a .357 magnum in a leather holster.

"The thing is, the streets have become so chaotic and the police are so gun shy, these thugs take it for granted they can get away with murder."

"They'll have a hard time proving self-defense against a sniper's bullet."

150

"Just as they'll have a hard time requisitioning those Koreans' weapons."

Ronin pushed a button on the dash. A funk band wailed.

"Who   is   this?"

"The SOS band. Remember when soul and funk were a thing? And they played it on the radio?"

"Yeah, man. All I can find now is rap and Taylor Swift."

"What about Billie Eilish?"

"Who's he?"

Ronin chuckled. "Never mind."

A half hour later, Ronin pulled into an underground parking garage on Haskell Street, parking amid several other cars on the first level. Retail business had dropped off since the attack on the deli. Braxton shouldered his golf bag. Ronin shrugged into a backpack. They went out the back, down the alley, across the street, two blocks to the alley in back of Western States Bank. The alley was deserted, a faint gleam in puddles from sporadic rainfall. Ronin ran toward the fire escape ladder which ended seven feet off the ground, leaped, and snagged the lowest rung in his leather gloves. The ladder descended with an ear-wrenching shriek. They paused to see if anyone noticed.

Nada.

"You run pretty good for a fat boy," Braxton quipped.

"Watch it, gramps."

I'm not much older than you, I just look it. Ronin went first, followed by Braxton. It was four stories to the roof. The roof was covered with tar paper, with a kiosk for the roof stairs. Braxton tried the door. It was unlocked. He stepped inside, shut the door, and listened. The building was hollow. There was no sound, not even from Portland's ubiquitous rats. He stepped outside and closed the door.

They were southwest of the targeted businesses. They went to the northeast corner. Ronin pulled a pair of binocs from his backpack, Braxton from his golf bag. They looked down on the normally busy street, lined with restaurants and markets. It was nearly deserted. A car cruised by, pumping rap to the world.

"*I got to have booty. Don't carry no cootie. I like gangsta rap, don't listen to Hootie—*"

Braxton wondered if the driver had hearing damage.

The Korean BBQ was on their side of the street but they could see it because of the angle. The Jewish deli across the street was fronted by plywood.

"Looks like that deli has thrown in the towel."

"Yeah. Fucking shame. They made the best pastrami sandwiches. The Koreans didn't even have to replace their glass."

Ronin reached in his backpack and took out a silver flask, unscrewed the cap, swigged, passed it to Braxton. Braxton grinned and held up his hand.

"Not me, hoss. Somebody has to drive. Let me see that thing."

Ronin handed it over. The cap featured a bust of Lenin. On the side was a coat of arms featuring a sword with a five-pointed star marked with the hammer and sickle superimposed. The scroll said *KR6 CCCP*.

"Where the hell you get this?"

"I took it off a person of indeterminate gender who didn't like my Toby Keith shirt."

"What's wrong with Toby Keith?"

Ronin shrugged. "Too patriotic, I guess. Wish I could have seen him before he died."

"I saw Ted Nugent once."

"Really?"

Faint drumming and chanting emanated from down the street. They turned their binoculars the other way.

"Here they come," Ronin said under his breath.

Braxton pulled out the rifle, put it together, resting the rail on a shooting bag he placed on the parapet. He double-checked the Thunder Beast suppressor at the end of the barrel, making sure it was on tight. He pulled his Kestrel 5700X ballistics calculator and phone to check wind speed and barometric pressure. He used the laser range finder to approximate his range. He checked off a list of things he had to do, fairly certain that Rudy would be proud of him.

"I'm not gonna just start blasting. Can you point out Joel Schumer to me?"

Ronin pulled out his phone, scrolled through pictures. He handed it to Braxton. The picture showed the typical ANTIFA thug, black clothes, head to toe, black sweatshirt. The shirt had a message in white letters. "This machine kills fascists."

"Can't be more than one of those in this crowd. They don't even know where it comes from."

"Yeah, Schumer probably doesn't know. Just thinks it's cool."

The mob approached chanting, "Hey hey, ho ho, fascist stooges got to go!"

"Well, the Deli's unlikely to reopen so they must be referring to the Koreans."

Braxton scanned the mob through the sniper's scope. It reminded him of the Morlocks from H.G. Wells's *The Time Machine*. Most wore hoodies and scarves leaving only their eyes exposed, and every set of eyes Braxton saw was white. Persons of color were severely underrepresented. The mob was now a block away. They moved without fear because no one dared to cross them.

"You really gonna shoot someone?"

"I'm just browsing. Why? Are you going to run out on me?"

"Hell no. If they knew who I was, I'd be in prison for the rest of my life."

"I have always been a law-abiding citizen. Law enforcement and these people made me a criminal."

The mob was now almost directly beneath them, screaming so loud they gave up conversing. Braxton set down the stock, pulled out his binocs, and pivoted toward Korean BBQ. Three shadowy figures stood on the roof, each clutching what looked like an AR-15. Had Braxton brought one, and used it, the police would never know it hadn't been the Koreans. Who was he kidding? The police had little interest in chasing down any crime. The city had made that clear. Where other leftist hellholes had quietly restored their police budgets, most Oregon cities, at least those in the west, clung passionately to their dogma.

The mob stopped in front of the BBQ, taking up every bit of street and sidewalk all the way to the deli. On the other side of the street, ANTIFA goons pulled out spray cans and painted anti-Semitic slogans on the plywood, the brick, the front door, and the sidewalk. A caricature of a hook-nosed Jew. *Free Palestine. From the river to the sea!*

Streetlights provided enough illumination to read the slogans on their clothes. Braxton slowly swept the mob through his Nightforce 7-35 with a TREMOR3 reticle. And there he was. Front and center. Braxton kept his finger off the trigger. How could he be sure? What if there were two shirts like that in the mob? It wasn't inconceivable.

This Machine Kills Fascists pulled a Molotov cocktail from his kangaroo pocket, popped the cork, fished out the cloth wick, and lit it with a lighter. He stepped forward, leaving space between him and the crowd. It would only last a second. Aiming for his thigh, Braxton squeezed the trigger. Only Braxton and Ronin heard the shot, muffled by the flash suppressor. The Rooftop Koreans opened up, semi-auto. The staccato of fire raining down, ricochets off the pavement, people calling out in pain and fear, all of it filled the air.

Two more rioters fell. As one fell backward, her hood flopped off, revealing a half-shaven skull, the other half purple.

Braxton laughed. Ronin stared at him.

"What's so funny?"

The crowd panicked. No one had ever fought back before. They ran in both directions, climbing over each other to escape. The Molotov cocktail lay on the ground, several feet from the restaurant, still burning, then exploded, lighting up the street. An ugly black pyre of smoke rolled skyward. The flames spread to one of the downed thugs. In seconds, the street was deserted, save for three bodies, one of which was on fire. *This Machine Kills Fascists*, purple half-dome, and an emaciated figure of indeterminate sex dressed in black.

In the distance, a siren wailed. Ronin got up.

"Let's book it."

Braxton broke the rifle down and put it in the golf bag. He gathered the spent brass casings. They ran to the stairs, ripped open the door, and galloped down four flights to ground level. A door led to the alley. There was a red sign on the door. WARNING: ALARM WILL SOUND IF OPENED.

Ronin shoved the door open. No alarm. They ran down the alley, across the street, two more blocks through the alley to the parking garage. Neither spoke until they were a mile away from the restaurant.

"Nice shooting," Ronin said.

Chapter 27

Near Misses

It had taken hours for Braxton to fall asleep. He remembered taking the shot and the grim satisfaction when the bullet had found its mark. He awoke late morning. His body protested as he rolled out of bed. He got up and looked in the bathroom mirror. The bruises were purple, shading to a dull brown.

Braxton prided himself on his research. His Kindle had several textbooks on police forensics. He studied technologies and techniques that might be used against him. If law enforcement targeted him, he would give them little with which to work.

The night before, he had worn gloves. His clothing bore gunshot residue. He washed his gear, twice, in the tiny camping washer he had installed. He showered, scrubbing his aching body. He had discarded the brass casings out the car window on his way back to the cabin. He swapped out the barrel on his Accuracy International.

News offered scant coverage. He saw images that the thugs had painted on the Jewish bakery, but the reporters barely referred to them. Instead their focus was on the "young unarmed protesters."

The Koreans were arrested, marched out for the cameras. Braxton felt their pain. Memories of his own perp walk were still fresh. The NBC reporter put up pictures of the victims. They looked as if they were pulled from high school yearbooks, wholesome and innocent. When he looked at the photos, he didn't see what he wanted. When their names came up, his heart sank.

Joel Schumer was not among the dead.

He paused the newscast and stared at the screens. Braxton knew he had hit his target, so the issue had to be that the target wasn't

Schumer. It made sense to him. Schumer was the leader. He didn't want to get his own hands dirty. Schumer wanted plausible deniability if things went south. The shirt had misled him, tricked him into shooting someone that wasn't Schumer.

There should have been a moment of guilt at having killed the wrong person, but Braxton didn't feel it. In the case of ANTIFA, there were no innocents. At their meeting, they had referred to themselves as soldiers. The night before, they had brought war to the streets of Portland and people had fought back. Not just him, the Koreans too. They had showed up to firebomb two businesses. They didn't care if innocent people died. Braxton couldn't afford remorse. Suzanna would have understood, he was sure of it. He and Ronin had saved lives.

As he finished watching the newscast, he thought about Schumer. *Does he know that I killed his two thugs?* No one had found their car. By now, the ANTIFA leader would know something had gone wrong. Add in the disaster from the night before, he would likely realize that Braxton was still alive. If Schumer had half a brain, he might realize that he was the target. It was he who had arranged to have Braxton killed and his body dumped in the woods. That would make him more careful. Caution would factor into Schumer's thinking. His next steps would be more calculating, more measured.

Braxton turned his attention to his rifle. The big Accuracy International had been worth every dollar. It had originally been bright red, not exactly subtle. He had sprayed it gray, green, and brown. It needed something else. Looking at the weapon, the implement of his vengeance. It demanded a name.

He thought back to his teaching days. Themis, the Greek goddess of justice. The perfect name for a weapon that dealt justice. Themis was one of Zeus's wives. Her symbol appeared in almost every court in the US, blind justice holding a sword and unbalanced scales. On the rifle's flat side plate he sketched out an image of the scales of justice, then carefully painted it with white paint. His one change was that the scales were balanced. Suzanna was always better at drawing than he. Even so, he thought she would approve of his handiwork.

As he put the paint away, his satellite phone chirped, number blocked. He picked it up.

"Yeah?"

"How are you feeling today?" Ronin said.

"I've been worse."

"We missed our primary target. I ran a check of his phone and where it pinged. He was there for a few minutes, then left."

"He showed up to set things in motion, then left like a coward."

"That's what it looks like."

"What about the shirt?"

"Somebody else."

"Where is he now?"

"The stolen phone has gone dark. The last place it pinged was a bar called the Horse Brass."

"The guy with the phone is Tyler Thompson. He was in the car when my wife was killed."

"He's not the only one that went dark. So did Schumer."

Knox's mind went over the possibilities. "Do you think they're onto us?"

"It's possible. Unless Schumer is a moron, he has to know that someone tipped off the Koreans last night."

"And by now he has to know the two people he sent to kill me have gone missing."

"He's not ignorant, just vicious. For all he knows, something went wrong. He hasn't seen you surface, so he may assume that you're dead along with his homies. All of that makes me want to ask, what's our next step?"

He liked the "our" part. It was good to know he wasn't alone. "If he's onto us, he's worried. He probably warned Thompson too. ANTIFA is full of cowards, they only have strength in numbers. Schumer is a man who sends others to do his bidding. He talks big, but deep down he's going to be afraid. Paranoia is going to eat him up. That means he will go to ground."

"You going to hunt him down?"

"We'll see. There are a number of people who played a role in what happened to me. I'm going to focus on them for the time being.

Schumer will resurface when he thinks he's safe, then I'll go after him."

"You have a list, don't you?"

"Of course I do."

"How can I help?"

"For now, I need you to look for Schumer, Thompson, and some guy who goes by the tag Ramrod. They were responsible for my wife's death. I want them all, either together, or one at a time. Schumer... he's special. There's always a chance he will decide to go on the offensive, so I'd like him monitored."

"What are you gonna do?"

"Logistics, planning. A lot of people had a hand in taking me down. A few of them need to be dealt with. If I don't, they'll repeat their actions on some other poor soul." Braxton paused, then said, "Ronin—you don't have to do this."

"Yes I do. The same kind of people burned out my grandfather's business and did worse things to other members of my family. I owe these people."

"Why didn't you go after them sooner?"

Ronin hesitated. "I'm a geek. Granted, I'm an uber-geek, but I'm still a guy that does his best work sitting behind a PC. You're not the first guy to contact me about getting a piece of these guys, but everyone else only wanted to do half measures—you know, hacking their bank accounts or messing with their social media. Rookie-level shit.

"Until I met you, I only entertained revenge fantasies. When I met you, I saw that you were actually going to do what I only dreamed about. I wanted to be part of that."

Braxton understood. The world was full of people that talked about revenge against the woke trash that destroyed their lives. He had read a lot of online pieces about it. A few sued, but those warriors were a rarity. Others used the legal system to put a stop to their harassment. Knox was different. Harsh language or meddling in the courts would not bring justice for Angela and Suzanna. Only an eye for an eye would do.

"Find me those ANTIFA guys."

159

"Don't worry about me."

"Where can I get some fentanyl?"

"What?"

"It's not for me. It's for an old friend."

Ronin's forehead creased. "Try Mill Park. Horrible neighborhood. Lots of homeless and drug use. Very dangerous."

"I'll be careful."

"Watch your back down there. I had a friend die down there. Those people are dangerous and unpredictable."

"I appreciate the warning. I'll be a model of discretion."

"It's not just the drugs. These ANTIFA types are dangerous."

"You don't have to remind me. They killed my wife. They almost killed me."

"We set things in motion with people who are like spoiled children. They are prone to tantrums and actions based on their feelings. They just feel so vewy stwongwy."

"I'm counting on it." Braxton hung up. He needed to get to Planet Fitness, then secure some fentanyl for his next target.

Chapter 28

"Should auld acquaintance be forgot..."

There was surprisingly little on the internet about how to purchase illegal drugs. Braxton felt antiquated even searching. The internet was always strange. He had found ways to make IEDs, make and deploy booby traps, even install solar power at the cabin, but there was nothing useful about how to purchase drugs on the streets. John had warned him about the dark web. Perhaps there was an assumption that people who needed drugs already knew how to secure them. His entire understanding on how to buy drugs came from films and television shows.

How much fentanyl he needed was almost as confusing. There were different potency levels. More than one pill or tablet could be fatal. There were no standards as to the strength of pills, which made the exact amount he needed impossible to pin down.

Mill Park was the kind of place the media rarely covered. Every city had a place of broken people, shattered policies, and government failure. Mill Park was Portland's. The police didn't bother to patrol. Just driving through might make him a target for a carjacking, robbery, or worse. He wore his tactical vest and plates concealed by a flannel shirt. He took the Glock. He tucked the Mossberg beside the passenger seat.

He nervously turned his car off Southeast Stark Street onto Southeast 117th Avenue. The houses looked as if they belonged in the third world. Mangled chain-link fences, yards filled with garbage, abandoned cars. The kinds of homes he saw on *COPS*. The kinds of places where bad things happened. He hit the door lock.

A half block in, he slowed in front of a weathered ranch-style house. Two black guys sat on the hood of a car in the front yard, the car propped up on cement blocks. As he crawled to a stop, one of the youths came over to his window. Braxton lowered it halfway.

"What do you need, man?" the man asked. Rap boomed up and down the street. Not the same song. Dueling rappers.

"Fentanyl."

The twenty-something scrutinized him dubiously. "I can't help you, man."

"Come on. My money's good."

The youth's eyes narrowed. "I don't sell to no pigs."

"I'm not a cop."

"Yeah, right."

"I'm not."

"You're in the wrong neighborhood." The youth's friend approached the car's passenger door. "We're all law-abiding citizens."

"Look, I've never done this before. Give me a break."

The friend rested his arms on the roof. "This dude is either a narc or a fool."

The youth at his window sneered. "You really not a cop?"

"I'm just a guy."

"Well, 'just a guy,'" he said, reaching behind him, he pulled a gun. "Shut off your engine and hand me your keys."

The punk carelessly held a Smith & Wesson M&P .22, as if it were a toy. A .22 could be lethal. More people were killed by smaller caliber guns than any other. The car door hid Braxton's right hand as he drew the Glock, raising it to the window. His left hand reached across, pulled the Mossberg, and aimed it at the passenger window. He might miss with the Glock, but shotgun pellets had no friends and didn't require much aim. "Tell your buddy to step out in front of the car so I can see him."

The punk looked rattled. Gripping his weapon with determination he said, "Tyrone, move to the front of the gentleman's car."

"Lower your gun," Braxton said. "I'm here to buy some pills. That's all."

"I don't want no trouble," the punk said, lowering his gun. Braxton lowered the Glock. "Let's just do it."

"You sure as hell ain't a cop. No cop would have pulled a gun to force me to sell him some Dance Fever."

Braxton grinned. "Listen to the ground. There is movement all around. There is something goin' down…"

The kid stared at him.

"Man, haven't you ever seen *Saturday Night Fever?*"

"I never heard of it."

"Awright. A C-note for five pills."

The punk glanced at his friend. Tyrone shrugged. The punk slipped his pistol into his waist and dug in his pocket, pulling out a zip-lock baggie with white pills. "Show me the money."

Setting down the shotgun, Braxton held a C-note between his index and middle finger. The kid snatched it, unsealed the bag and dug around, handing Braxton five pills.

"Now you use these responsibly, hear?"

Braxton slipped them into his breast pocket. "Sho nuff. Thank you kindly." He raised the window and took off. Two hours later, he pulled up to the cabin.

Tomorrow was Saturday. Braxton knew his target would be at home. One thing about Alistair Grooper was that he was a creature of habit. His wife had left him eight years earlier, taking with her any hint of a social life. While he had been dean of his department, Braxton had gone out of his way to be supportive during his boss's ugly divorce. Grooper repaid him by siding with the disciplinary committee. Aside from heaping humiliation on him, Grooper had been a key player in the loss of his career.

Maybe Grooper didn't deserve to die. Donna had already filed a suit against the university. Letting Grooper live was not something he entertained. That was part of the problem with people. They bowed down to the woke crazies. They buckled rather than stand up to them. It was easier that way. They listened to anger and hate over logic and loyalty. Grooper and others had set things in motion that had taken his wife and daughter. He had to be dealt with. They all did.

The next morning, as a light drizzle fell, Braxton packed nitrate latex gloves and the Glock.

He drove down the mountain in silence, save for the swish of the windshield wipers and the thrum of his tires on the pavement. Local news was a drag. It wasn't that they lied, but their distortions and carefully chosen language angered him.

Braxton parked in a lot at a small park, now a sea of mud puddles, gun in a shoulder holster under his rain poncho. He put on the rubber gloves and got out. Even with his olive drab ball cap, the drizzle hit his cheeks. An ugly day for an ugly job.

Standing in front of Grooper's door, there was so much he wanted to say. *Just words. Ignore them. Do what you came to do.* He knocked on the door, forcing himself to relax.

Grooper opened the door. For an instant, panic rippled his face. He regained his composure "Brax? I hardly recognized you."

"Mind if I come in?"

Grooper hesitated. "I'm not sure we should be together. You are suing the university."

"I only need a few minutes of your time."

Grooper looked around. He saw no one. "Come in."

Braxton stepped into the tile-floored foyer. Grooper closed the door behind him. "You look different."

"The beard?

"You've lost some weight, too."

Braxton lifted the poncho off, keeping it between the two of them. As he lowered it with his left hand, he pulled the Glock.

"Having your family killed can change a person."

Grooper's eyes locked on the gun. He took a half step back. "I don't want any trouble."

"Neither did I. Why don't we go to your family room?" He gestured with the Glock.

"B-b-b-Braxton, please. None of this is necessary." The family room reflected Grooper's recent divorce. Mail and dirty dishes covered the coffee table, along with a half empty glass of Scotch. A sub shelf held a stack of magazines. Braxton lifted a copy of *Anal Antics* with two fingers, showing a woman with an enormous butt looking lasciviously over her shoulder. He raised his eyebrows. Grooper reddened and looked away.

Braxton gestured at the La-Z-Boy with the cracked vinyl seat. Grooper sat. Braxton stood before him, holding the gun. "None of this should have been necessary. You made it so."

"We're old friends."

"We were friends. Suzanna and I had you at our Christmas parties. We had you over for dinner when you and Judith broke up. I wasn't sucking up like some of the others at the university. I wanted to help you."

"And I appreciate that."

"Not enough to stand up for me with the Disciplinary Committee."

"That—that was a mistake. They threatened me too! If I didn't play ball, they would have come for me too."

"So you sold me out to save yourself. All you had to do was the right thing. That should have been easy. You should have told Driggs that in this country, I have the right to free speech. Her demands about pronoun use don't trump my rights under the law. It was so painfully simple, but instead you folded like a house of cards."

Grooper's face reddened. "I know. It was wrong."

"Have you heard of Marvin Heemeyer?"

Grooper's face wrinkled. "No."

"He lived in Granby, Colorado. All he wanted to do was run his business. The local government turned against him, leveling fees he couldn't pay. Why? Because a rival company wanted his property. The local paper covered up the actions of the government. They stomped on Marvin, they humiliated him.

"Marvin took a bulldozer and turned it into a tank, complete with armor and remote cameras for driving. He went after the businesses and people in town that did him wrong."

"That's the Killdozer thing," Grooper said, shifting uneasily.

"Exactly. An inaccurate tag that the media put on it. The only person killed that day was Marvin who shot himself."

Braxton took a step closer to his hostage. "You see, petty little people can take a normal person and push them too far. When they do, good men, normally reasonable people, will push back."

"Brax—please—"

He cut off his former friend. "Don't plead, Alistair. It demeans us both." Reaching into his pocket, he pulled out a ziplock bag. "Because of our past friendship, I decided against blowing your brains out. You will take three of these instead. Your overdose will be written off like so many opioid drug overdoses. From what I read, it is painless. Personally, think I'm being more than fair." Braxton held out the bag.

"I—I—I won't!"

"Defiance. I understand. It's your life. If you don't take this option, I will be forced to shoot you. Consider this. Like Marvin, I'm a man who has lost everything. Because of what the university did to me, Suzanna was murdered by ANTIFA thugs. And because the FBI got involved, I presume at the university's bidding, my daughter was killed. So, if you think I won't shoot you, you are mistaken."

Grooper sobbed. He wept and his nose began to run. He took the bag. His eyes went sad puppy-dog. Braxton was unmoved. "Swallow them. Use that Scotch."

He fumbled with the bag, finally opening it. Three pills fell into his trembling hand. Braxton wrapped both hands around the gun and aimed at Grooper. Grooper put them in his mouth. For a few moments, they were on his tongue as he sobbed.

"Swallow."

Grooper picked up the Scotch and swallowed.

Braxton put his Glock in its holster, leaning back on the sofa with crossed arms. Grooper's breathing accelerated. His eyes dilated. His body locked up. Braxton waved a hand in front of Grooper's face. No reaction. The overdose was in full session.

He stayed with Grooper until he died. Then he went to the front door, put on his poncho, and stepped out into the misting rain.

Chapter 29

The Long Arm of the Law

Joel Schumer was surprised when he opened his door and saw Multnomah County Sheriff, Marty Phelps. Phelps's paunch hung over his belt. The sheriff smiled when delivering bad news, a politician at heart. Joel had met with him many times and knew him for what he was, an ambitious man motivated by public opinion. Joel easily manipulated Phelps, discussing his organization. Phelps wanted what every elected official wanted, another term in office. Joel handed him a few token arrests, just enough to fool the public that the portly sheriff was doing his job. Disorderly conduct. Vandalism. As a result, ANTIFA had operated with the tacit approval of law enforcement.

"Sheriff, what brings you here?"

"Mind if I come in?"

Schumer ushered him in. "Is there a problem?"

"A couple actually."

"What can I do for you?"

"For starters, let's talk about what went down in Lake Oswego the other night. Three of your people dead and evidence on the scene that you were going to firebomb some of the businesses there."

"Sheriff, I had no idea that some fringe element was out there. I doubt they planned anything more than a peaceful protest. We were the victims the other night, not the antagonists."

"The Molotov cocktails say differently."

"I wasn't there, but I would suggest that those were planted on the scene by those Koreans."

Sheriff Phelps shook his head. "You and I know differently. What kind of protest is done after midnight? Yes, your people ended up being shot, but I doubt you were out there at that hour as a gesture of goodwill."

Schumer knew they'd pushed the envelope too far. "It wasn't anything I sanctioned."

"The district attorney has my people looking into this. He's inclined to not press charges against your people. His focus is on the Koreans. The last thing Portland needs is people playing vigilante."

"I hope the DA puts those Koreans away for a long time."

"That's his problem, not mine. All I know is we don't need people with guns on rooftops. It makes a lot of work for all of us and people get killed."

ANTIFA had operated under the legal radar. If the citizens started fighting back, it could cause problems. "I've been told that some of the people there filmed the event. I could arrange to get you that footage." Of course, it had been heavily edited to only show that his people came under fire. It was the kind of peace offering that the sheriff wanted.

"That would be helpful."

"I have always supported law enforcement."

"Another thing. Two of the victims were hit by the Koreans. Ballistics proved that. There was another shot though. The bullet we recovered was pretty mangled, but it didn't come from the Koreans. Did your folks say anything about another shooter?"

"No. They only mentioned the Koreans."

"I need them to come down for interviews."

"I will get word to them. Of course we want to cooperate."

"Damn puzzling. My people combed the area looking for a spent shell, but couldn't find a thing. No real evidence other than some disturbed gravel on the roof where they were positioned."

"Which roof?"

"From what we have gathered, given the trajectory, the shooter had to be on top of the Western States Bank down the block. At night, at that range, it was a pretty decent shot. We're talking an honest-to-God sniper."

Joel understood what the sheriff wasn't saying—someone had planted themselves to take out his people. "Have the Koreans said how they knew to be up there on their roof?"

Phelps nodded. "They said they got an anonymous tip. The working theory we have is that it was probably the same person that was on top of the bank."

Schumer's jaw set. No doubt it was some gun-loving fascist who'd made the call. Someone knew their plans and leaked them.

The sheriff poked at his phone and pulled up some of the crime scene photos. "You're going to have to rein in your people, Joel. Look at these pictures. People are dead, kids. I've always given you freedom of operating for the sake of public safety. Dead bodies in the streets make us all look bad. I'm telling you, for your own good, stand down for a while."

One of the images grabbed him. It was Markus York, sprawled out on the pavement in a pool of blood that was hard to see in the darkness. Markus wore a hoodie that read, *This Machine Kills Fascists*. Reaching out, he scrolled back on the image, zooming in on the dead body. Joel owned the same hoodie. Markus had looked up to him and was always trying to copy what he wore. Seeing the shirt made him cringe. It was a grim reminder that he could have been killed had he been there.

"Friend of yours?"

"Yes. Markus looked up to me."

"I'm sorry for your loss. There's another thing I need to talk to you about."

"And that is?"

"We've had a missing person's report filed on Kent Potter by his family. You wouldn't happen to know where he is, would you?"

The mention of Kent brought back the last time he saw him, when they loaded Braxton Knox in the trunk of Kent's car. "No, I haven't seen him since our last meeting. He's missing?"

"Yes. His mother is pretty worried. We had a ping from his cell phone just before Mount Hood Village. After that it went dead. We surmise he turned it off or got into some sort of accident."

"That's a pretty wild area, if I remember correctly."

"I've asked the Clackamas County Sheriff's department to look into it. So far, no luck."

Joel knew that Kent and Reed had not been seen since taking Knox out to be killed and dumped in the forest. Since they never reported back, he had been concerned that something had gone awry. Since he was unsure exactly where they had been heading, Joel had not tried to find them. The sheriff bringing up Kent was confirmation that something had gone wrong. "I wish I could help you, I really do. Kent was at our last meeting, but that was the last time I saw him."

"It's probably nothing. College kids go missing all the time. Ninety-nine percent of the time they're just out having fun and forgot to check in with parents," Phelps said. "He might have gone skiing or something else. I would appreciate it if you could reach out to your people and see if anyone has an idea of where he might be."

"I'll send out a text right after you leave."

"One more thing. There's a reporter that is starting to poke around. Wants to know why my department hasn't made more ANTIFA arrests."

"It can't be a local reporter. The papers and other media here always highlight us as enemies of fascists." Just bringing up the reporter made his jaw ache.

"Her name is Faye Weldon and she does shows and articles for something called *Daily Beat*. She has filed a Freedom of Information Act request for our correspondence and all police reports tied to ANTIFA. She showed up at the crime scene as we were finishing."

He knew of the *Daily Beat*. ANTIFA had labeled it an alt-right media site because it refused to follow the approved narrative. Why would a reporter be digging into his cell? The fact that she showed up at the crime scene was disturbing. The last thing he needed was a journalist, a *real* journalist, poking around. "I appreciate the heads-up."

Phelps shifted on his feet. "It's an election year for me. I don't have to tell you that neither of us wants the media digging around. You've benefited from my being in office. If someone replaces me, they might not be so understanding."

"Don't worry. I won't give her anything. I'll make sure she gets nothing."

"Good." The sheriff opened the door and left. Joel stood and watched him drive away. This Weldon woman would need to be addressed if she started digging in the wrong places.

His other target was Braxton Knox. He had been at the meeting when the attack on the Jews and Koreans had been planned. He was with Kent and Stew, stuffed in the trunk of the car. Somehow he must have gotten out and killed them. Was he the mystery sniper that had killed Markus? Without a dead body it was going to be impossible to know if he was alive or not.

If he was alive, Schumer would finish him.

Chapter 30

The Fourth Estate

"Honey," Suzanna spoke in a sing-song voice. "We should take Angela to the zoo today."

The memory tore at him in the early dawn, in that space between deep sleep and wakefulness. Braxton knew what they were, but he didn't want them to end. This was years ago, when Angela was seven or eight.

Looking into his wife's eyes, he felt warm, younger, almost giddy. "I've got a lot to do in the yard," his dream version replied.

"Forget that stuff. The yard will be there tomorrow. She wants to go today."

Braxton nodded, then jerked awake. *No!* The dream was gone. His wife was a memory, nothing more.

As he got up, the dream faded. It was a form of torture. He couldn't call them nightmares because he savored each one. After he shaved and trimmed his beard, he stood in front of the mirror. The bruises were fading, as was the pain. Working out helped, but he needed something more. An hour of searching identified a personal combat class that looked promising. Valhalla Academy was run by a former Special Forces soldier.

Braxton went to the post office in Mt. Hood City and set up a PO Box, then rerouted mail from his home. He went to Planet Fitness, stopping at Fred Meyer for groceries. His last stop was McKenzie Place, the assisted living facility where his father lived.

Walking down the hallways, he smelled disinfectant and urine. No matter how they made the place look, it still smelled like a geriatric ward. He knocked on his father's door and let himself in.

Grayson sat with a woman on the couch. She had short red hair and wore a jean skirt and denim jacket. She smiled.

Braxton hesitated at the door. "Sorry, Dad, I didn't know you had a visitor."

"This is Ms. Weldon," Grayson said. "She's a reporter. Wants to talk to you."

She rose and extended her hand. "It's nice to meet you. It wasn't my intention to surprise you. I sent you a letter."

"I got it," he replied, moving to the easy chair. "I've already given a lot of interviews."

"Nothing in-depth though," she said. "The local news ran two minutes with you. The local paper shuffled you to page eight and gave you two whopping paragraphs. The local media covered the story out of obligation, to create the appearance they were impartial and fair. Fox News gave you four minutes. You were there to make a political point about wokeness and the dangers of ANTIFA. I'm not like them. I'm a real journalist. I'm looking for something deeper. I want to tell your story, sans the spin or agenda."

They sat.

"Why?" Braxton asked. It was, in his mind, the most important question.

"You're skeptical. I don't blame you. I got hit by the cancellation bus too. I was working for the *Observer*. I wrote about a student protest at Eastern State that got violent. They didn't like that I called the protestors rioters. When I refused to change the article, they kicked me to the curb."

"That's not the same as losing your family."

"No, it's not. But it points to my integrity. I think what happened to you is important. You didn't do anything wrong, but you got painted with a big target on your back. The local ANTIFA chapter got involved. From what your neighbor told me, they were harassing you at your former residence too."

"I just don't think it's a good idea at this time, Ms. Weldon."

"Give me a chance," she said.

Braxton glanced at Grayson. "I'm not worthy of your attention."

"I have sources that say otherwise. One of my peeps at the US attorney's office says they're planning some sort of cash settlement over the death of your daughter."

That was news. He knew Donna had been in talks with them, but expected no progress.

"No amount of money will help. The FBI took my daughter's life for no reason."

"I'm sorry for your loss. It had to hurt knowing that the federal government was responsible for her death, especially given you are a veteran."

"For an alleged civil rights violation, they came in with a full tactical team. It was overkill from the get-go. If they wanted to arrest me, all they had to do is ask me to turn myself in. Instead, they brought violence into my home."

Weldon had broken the ice, whether he wanted to talk or not. They spoke for over two hours. She asked the right questions about Suzanna and Angela. He told her the theory that Schumer's people were behind the death of his wife, sharing with her the letter he had received about the stolen car and phone. Her queries about his former job at the university made him long once more for the classroom.

He didn't tell her about his attempt to infiltrate ANTIFA and how he had almost been killed. Confessing to a member of the press to killing two thugs was not a smart play.

He thought they were about to wrap up, when she said, "The ANTIFA group that came after you, what do you know of them?"

"Not much."

"I have a source in the sheriff's office. They apparently tried to burn out a couple of local businesses a few nights ago."

"From what I have seen over the last few years, it's my impression the sheriff's department is protecting them."

"It's a common mistake. Everyone assumes that all the police are on the take. In reality, a lot of them are good cops. They hate the DA and most dislike the sheriff. Most just want to do their jobs."

"Why don't they?"

"They're not stupid. They know they'll be punished for doing the right thing. Those that haven't quit are just hanging on until they can get their pension."

"I have no sympathy for them."

"Someone tipped the owners off that they were going to be attacked. They fought back. Three of their attackers were killed before they could throw their Molotov cocktails."

"I have always felt that ANTIFA was dangerous—a threat to our country. You look on their websites, you'll see."

"I have. My source says that there was someone else at the scene. There was a second shooter. The bullet was mangled, not enough for them to get ballistics. A deputy to whom I spoke said that whoever had tipped off the Koreans was there to make sure ANTIFA didn't pull it off."

"That sounds like a stretch," Grayson said.

"It might be," she said. "Then again, it makes sense. Someone knew their plan and took action."

"It's probably a traitor in their ranks."

She shook her head. "My experience with these people is that they are pretty tight-knit."

"It's almost as if they had something to hide," Grayson said.

"Exactly!"

"If there was a second shooter, the police will find him."

"That's doubtful. They are focusing on one of the ANTIFA kids gone missing."

"One's missing?"

"The parents of one of their little goon squad filed a missing person's report. My source says he was last seen at the last rally."

"College kids take off all the time."

"You're starting to sound like the sheriff. This kid simply vanished. These ANTIFA types often sever their family relationships. This kid didn't though. His name's Kent Potter."

"Gee. Too bad."

"You know, Mr. Knox, I'm pretty good at what I do. These things are connected."

"How so?"

"I've been monitoring the Hitler Youth for a while. Most of the time they fly under the radar. They target people, harass them. In some cases there's violence, but most of the time they keep it soft. Starting with you, they have become more aggressive."

"Go on."

"Now someone is striking back. No one has done that to date, but it seems that it's happening. This Potter kid goes AWOL... someone gives the Koreans a little cover fire. Someone is putting the squeeze on them."

"They've stepped on a lot of people's toes. Someone was bound to step back."

Faye tapped her chin, her brown eyes studying him speculatively. "A vigilante is a great story angle."

"I wouldn't know. I'm just an unemployed college professor."

She folded her notepad up and put it in her computer bag. "I'd like to start work on an article about this. I'll show it to you before I publish. I'll have some follow-up questions. How can I reach you?"

He gave her his satellite phone. She entered it into her iPhone. "I appreciate it. I think your story will resonate with a lot of people."

"I can't speak to that," Braxton replied. "I already have a bag or two of mail from people. Some of it is hateful. But the majority is from supporters or others that have been targeted by the mob."

"That might make an interesting add-on for my piece. We should connect again soon."

Braxton got up and held the door. He turned to his father. "Sorry she bothered you, Dad."

"No bother. Having an attractive woman drop in will make me the talk of the dinner hour. Besides, I think she's on the level."

"She's the media. I don't trust them."

"She raised a good point about these things being connected. Her vigilante scenario isn't hard to believe."

"I don't know. It seems a little far-fetched. People don't take the law into their own hands these days."

Hands on his belt, Grayson stared at him. "You never could get away with lying to me, son. Your mom fell for it, but I always saw right through you."

A part of him wanted to tell his father, but the small boy inside him hesitated. "You don't want to know."

Grayson rose and put his hand on Braxton's shoulder. "Suzanna was my daughter-in-law and I loved her. Angela..." Braxton had only seen his father cry once, during his mother's funeral. A tear rolled down his cheek. "I want to be read-in on everything. I want to help."

* * *

Grayson had been in law enforcement. He had been a good agent. A man who played by the rules. Grayson Knox was an advocate for law and order. Throughout Braxton's life, his father had told him the system was fair. Not perfect, but sound.

Now things were different. Grayson understood what his son had done and why. His father didn't say he had been wrong. In fact, the only thing he had done wrong was not letting his dad know sooner. Grayson's perspective of the system had changed when it led to the death of his only granddaughter.

When Braxton got back to the cabin, he contacted Ronin via encrypted text.

Please get me anything pertinent on a reporter named Faye Weldon with the Daily Beat.

Ronin replied a few minutes later: On it. I have a name for you, Lucas Cox. He was the other guy in the car that ran your wife off the road. Calls himself Ramrod. I've emailed you all the data I've dug up on him.

Now Ramrod was a target, like the others on his list.

Chapter 31

Injustice

Braxton sat between Donna and Marv Myer from the law firm. Grayson sat next to Donna. Grayson had insisted on attending. As Knox senior was former FBI, there was no disagreement. They had both suffered losses. The conference room they were in was big, the obsidian table exuding wealth. In a small tray in the center of the table were glasses and bottles of water. Their chairs were far nicer than his old office chair at the university.

He had gotten the call from Donna after confessing to his father. It confirmed what Weldon had told him. The Department of Justice wanted to talk about a settlement. Ms. Weldon's sources had been accurate. Braxton had dreaded going to the meeting. Even the word for it seemed wrong to him. Settlement—it settled nothing.

Looking around the room, Braxton thought, *My tax dollars paid for everything. I funded the forces that work against me. The Greeks would love such a tragedy.*

Donna leaned in and whispered, "I know this isn't easy for you. The offer is good. Remember, though, they can rescind it at any point before we sign off."

"You're telling me to control my temper," he muttered.

"Let me do my job. There will be a time after we're done for you to vent. Doing it here could backfire."

Braxton sighed. She was right. He wasn't worried about the charges that he had violated Debbie Driggs's civil rights by not using her personal pronoun. *This is still America—caught in a left-leaning shadow, but still America.* They couldn't make him say things he didn't believe. That the US attorney had filed the charges was an insult to reason he had been forced to endure. That wasn't the worst thing.

The FBI had killed his little girl.

The door to the conference room at the Portland District Office of the Department of Justice opened. The woman who led the procession was known to him, thanks to her TV interviews. Aurora Rainsong gave him an icy glance as she moved across the table from where his party sat. He knew her name and face from the TV, when she outlined the case against him. Another few people came in, their dark blue suits almost looking like uniforms.

The US attorney waited until the door closed and everyone was in their seats. "I am Aurora Rainsong." As if she were presenting the Queen of Sheba. "This is one of our internal counsels, Brantley Wilson." She gestured to one of the men, then turned to the other two. "This is FBI Special Agent in Charge Robert Durston and Special Agent Turner."

Braxton leaned forward with his arms on the table. Donna made the introductions from their side of the table. "I understand you wish to extend an offer to put this ugly affair behind us."

Rainsong couldn't help but correct her. "We are here to discuss the charges and your lawsuit, yes."

Donna leaned back. "Go ahead then."

"We are prepared to withdraw the civil rights charges against your client," she said, looking at Braxton. "We extend this in exchange for what the federal government believes is a generous settlement for the death of Angela Knox." She slid a piece of paper to Donna.

"This still gives you the right to refile those charges against my client at a future date."

"We concede that at this time, in light of the material leaked to the media, it would be unproductive to go to trial. That doesn't forego our option of reindicting him at a later date."

Myer, Donna's boss, spoke up. "You know no jury would convict a grieving father, not even one in this state. Not after that bodycam video was made public."

Rainsong's cheeks reddened. "I make no such admission."
Braxton experienced a frisson of loathing.

Donna spoke in hushed tones with her boss, Myer. She slid the paper in front of Braxton, tapping her crimson fingernail on the dollar figure. Nine million dollars.

Was it worth Angela's death? Braxton would never get to walk her down the aisle at her wedding. He would never have grandchildren. Was nine million dollars a fair amount? He didn't feel so. No amount of money was going to fill the gap in his life and soul. He fumed at what the government was doing—paying him money to make the death of his daughter go away.

Donna leaned in. "Are you alright?"

Braxton shook his head. "Continue."

"I take it you find this acceptable?" Rainsong asked, looking at him.

He fixed her in a laser gaze. "I have no idea if the money is enough. What I want is some respect from the Department of Justice and the FBI."

"I'm not sure I understand."

"How about an apology? How about an acknowledgement that they did something wrong, that they killed an innocent girl? You worked with the media to smear my name and reputation—so will there be a public announcement that you were wrong? What are you going to do to fix my life?"

"We are going to pay you," Rainsong replied.

Seeing the US attorney's mask of arrogance did nothing to diffuse the situation. *They think money is a solution... that it assuages their culpability.*

"I understand you are hurting as a result of what happened," SAIC Durston said, clearly sensing Braxton's frustration. "But I—"

"Who were the agents that shot my daughter?"

Durston fidgeted. "We are conducting an internal investigation. We will be changing our procedures going forward."

"Their names, Agent Durston. Surely you know who discharged their weapons into my little girl?"

"Of course we do. We just don't make that kind of information public."

"Why are you protecting them?"

"They have rights," the SAIC replied.

Killers have rights but victims don't.

Braxton slowly leaned forward, eroding the space between them. "What about the rights of a father whose daughter they killed?"

His words lingered in the air without a response.

"If we hear you correctly," Donna said, "you are saying that you will not apologize publicly for what happened."

Rainsong crossed her arms. "We have nothing to apologize for."

"So it's your policy to shoot unarmed little girls?" Braxton snapped.

Her cheeks turned red. "No, that is not our policy," she said stiffly.

"So, if I understand you correctly, you still believe I'm guilty of something, so you won't apologize. You won't admit that what you did was wrong or give me the names of who killed my little girl. You just want to shove some money in front of me and hope that will somehow make me go away?"

Donna spoke up. "If you don't mind, let's take a quick break. Can we have the room, please?"

The DoJ and FBI staff rose and left. When the door closed, Donna leaned over to Braxton. "I know you're hurting. But these people are never going to admit they were wrong. That isn't how the federal government works. Look at what happened on January 6th. It was years before we learned who shot Ashli Babbitt. The Capitol Police have never issued an apology. They promoted her killer. It isn't in the federal government's nature to admit wrongdoing. What we can do is make them pay more. While that won't ease your grief, it will hurt these people's careers. In the realm of justice, that might be the best that we can hope for. Let me go talk to them."

Donna's spoke directly and to the point. She was right. He nodded. Donna went into the hallway. He was left alone with his father. Grayson looked at his son. Braxton saw anger and helplessness in Grayson's face. "Son, you're doing the right thing. With that kind of money, you can restart your life."

"It's just money. Donna says a bid came in on the house. Along with the insurance, I have no need for more money."

"You can do something good with it, in Suzanna's and Angela's names."

That was something he hadn't considered. "Dad, I know you worked for them. I know they put food on the table. But I have to say it, the FBI is corrupt."

"This isn't my FBI. Back in the day, we weren't perfect either. But we didn't make mistakes like this. When we did, we owned up to it. And that US attorney—she's a piece of work."

"They don't have any regrets about what they did. All they have is rage and hate. I didn't break any of their precious civil rights laws and they know it. They just want to inflict pain on me, and so far, they've succeeded."

Donna and Meyer returned to the room. "We were able to get them to raise the amount to twelve million. They won't admit any wrongdoing. They don't plan on any public statement about this matter. They informed us that the Special Agent in Charge is being reassigned."

Marv Meyer cut in. "I know it's not what you want in terms of admission of guilt, but I think this is the best that we can do."

Braxton looked at his father, who nodded.

"Fine," Braxton muttered.

Donna ushered the government's party back in, sans the SAIC. Braxton didn't remember signing the documents. The smugness had faded from Rainsong's face. When they were done, no one spoke. The government party simply rose and left, except for Agent Turner, who lingered for a moment.

Turner walked around the conference table, extending her hand. "Our counsel said that if we apologized, it would be an admission of guilt. I was there during the raid. I'm ashamed of how this was handled."

He looked at her hand and realized that she was probably the only decent person in the government party. Braxton shook it, feeling something in her palm which she passed to him. He discreetly held onto it as Turner left the room.

The small piece of folded paper remained in his hand until he reached the car. He unfolded it. "Agents Rocky Forsyth and Frank Hayden." These were the names of the men who had shot and killed Angela.

Grayson took the passenger seat and looked at the piece of paper. "What's that, son?"

"Proof that the FBI isn't entirely a lost cause."

Chapter 32

Rivian

Professor Emeritus Sylvia Baskin-Kulberg lived in a lavish red brick Tudor fronted by white columns four blocks from campus. When she first came to the university, her specialty was History of Colonial Expansion, but she soon changed that to History of White Colonial Expansion, eliding Moslem expansion into Spain and throughout Africa, Japanese expansion into China and Korea, and the Aztec subjugation of countless other empires throughout Mesoamerica.

Braxton had parked his car at the University Flower Garden down the street and walked four blocks up Cooper Avenue wearing a Navy peacoat and carrying a briefcase. Just another assistant professor on his way to lunch at Vino Italiano. A new Rivian sat in Baskin-Kulberg's driveway. Seventy-five thousand dollars on the hoof. She'd probably paid cash. The "Kulberg" part of the equation was Professor of Journalism Jerome Kulberg, a frequent guest on CNN, mostly to provide a veneer of intellectual jargon over the message *du jour*.

With his beard, a watch cap pulled low on his forehead, and aviator shades, Braxton was unrecognizable. He'd only been to Vino a couple times when he joined the faculty, souring on the spot when he pegged it as a salon for groupthink. Most of the liberal arts department hung there Friday afternoons, soaking up wine, vodka, and dogma. Chilled by the damp spring weather, Braxton bought an overpriced latte. The pierced and inked barista asked for his name.

"Lothar."

The barista picked up a felt-tipped Sharpie. "How do you spell that?"

"L, o, t, h, a, r."

"Perfect."

Braxton sat at a table in the back and pulled out his laptop. At this hour, Vino smelled of wood and coffee. The drinking wouldn't start until four, when most of liberal arts stopped teaching. He booted up and went to Swisscows.com.

"Why do electric vehicles catch fire?" he typed.

"With EVs, there's no tank of explosive fuel and, compared to a gasoline or diesel engine, electric motors don't generate that much heat. So why then do they catch fire?

"In short, it's chemistry. The chemicals and elements that make up the individual cells inside an electric vehicle's battery pack are very sensitive. This is especially true with the lithium-ion chemistry that most modern EVs use. If an EV is in a serious crash and the battery pack is compromised, battery cells can rupture, and they will heat up until they hit a point called 'thermal runaway.'

"Thermal runaway occurs when a battery's cells get so hot that chemical reactions begin to occur, and the heat, in most cases, continues to increase uncontrollably. At this point, the cells can catch fire, which cascades throughout the pack until you have an EV burning to the ground. Battery cells that are improperly charged or balanced can also cause thermal runaway. Lithium-ion battery packs are very sensitive to how they are charged."

"Lothar!" the barista sang.

Braxton went to the counter and got his coffee, passing a handful of students, inked and pierced, walled off in the solitude of their iPhones and pads. He poured in three tiny containers of half-and-half, added two packets of sugar and returned to his table. Back to his search engine. Braxton typed "Rivian schematic." The Society of Automotive Engineers had an exhaustive breakdown. Braxton studied battery location and access. It wasn't the easiest vehicle to service, but the location of the battery, at the lowest level, offered opportunity.

First, he had to ascertain who drove what. He had no interest in causing the Kulberg half of the equation pain. He'd met Kulberg and was remarkably unimpressed. He was a stereotypical mousy liberal arts professor. Braxton had watched him once on *Good Morning America*, with Stephanopoulus pitching the fattest of softballs.

"What is the future of journalism in America?"

"Well, George, all signs point to a brilliant future, as journalists incorporate artificial intelligence into their analysis. Moreover, I am heartened by the consensus among so many respected sources that the country is on the right path."

Braxton sipped his coffee. The door opened admitting a gangly youth with a green mohawk wearing a surplus army jacket and the smell of marijuana. With his beard, watch cap, peacoat, and sunglasses, Braxton looked like any other aging hippie coasting in the groves of academe, insulated from life by the university. He got up, hunched his coat around his neck, grabbed his briefcase and left the cafe, slowly walking west, eyes fixed on the Rivian in the driveway. When he was a half block away, the front door opened and out streamed Sylvia Baskin-Kulberg wearing a thigh-length red wool coat, a white knit cap, and carrying a heavy leather barrister's case over her shoulder. She beeped the car open, got in, backed up and drove away, the only sound the soft susurrus of the tires on pavement.

Seconds later, the electric garage door opened and Kulberg backed out in his silver Porsche, straightened out in the street, chirped his tires, and *vroomed* in the direction of the university.

This one was complicated. He might be able to do it while it was parked in the driveway, if he approached after midnight. This was an upper middle-class enclave, but that didn't mean the residents were clueless. They could very well have front door cams. Braxton examined the eaves as he passed and there it was, a discreet dark gray globe fastened to the underside of the garage hangover like a wasp's nest.

Alternative: do it while she was parked at the university. He would have to scope that out. Faculty parking was adjacent to the buildings in which they taught, and the university did not have cameras in those lots, as far as he knew.

Maybe it was too risky. Perhaps he was overthinking. He didn't want to get caught, but these people had to pay. They had to be made to understand that they were evil. He wanted to do to them what communist regimes always did to their own people. Punish them for bad thought. Make them admit they were wrong. Force them to admit they had never read the Constitution or the Bill of Rights. That they were unsuited for any responsibility. That they couldn't run a lemonade stand. That they had gone into academia for the prestige and perks. That they had no deep understanding of the subjects in which they claimed expertise. That they were professional navel-gazers and ass-lickers.

Braxton went back to the park. He got in his RAV4 and headed for the cabin. He needed the solitude to work things out. He needed a fresh set of eyes on the project. Twenty miles outside of town, he pulled over at a QuikTrip and topped off his tank. It was only recently that the government had legalized consumers filling their own tank. A tiny victory against the state. He went inside, bought a hot dog and a Diet Mountain Dew. Eight ninety-five.

He moved the car to the side of the QuikTrip. He pulled out the burner Ronin had given him and called him.

"The number you have reached is not in service at this time."

Five minutes later, the phone rang.

"What?"

"Need to pick your brain."

"Regarding?"

"Stuff."

Beat.

"Where are you?"

"I'm on Twenty-Six headed for the hills."

"How 'bout I come up there?"

"That would be groovy. I'll text you the address."

Braxton texted and headed east. By the time he pulled into his yard, two hours later, Ronin was already there, sitting on the front porch, laptop open, a battered Camry parked in the dirt. Braxton got out.

"Been here long?"

"About fifteen minutes."

"Where were you coming from?"

187

"Gresham. It was getting too hot for me."

Braxton stepped up on the deck and unlocked the door. He checked the black thread he'd placed over the top. Still there. He'd placed threads on the back door too.

"Come on in."

They went into the living room. Cool and dark. Braxton went into the kitchen.

"Want a beer?"

"Sure."

"Scratch that. Do you drink bourbon?"

"You bet."

Braxton returned with two glasses and a bottle of Blanto's. He unscrewed it, poured a couple of fingers in each glass, and handed one to Ronin.

Ronin sipped. "What do you need?"

"Ronin, I'm not sure I'm going about this the right way. Let me tell you what I'm trying to do."

Chapter 33

Shaped Charge

Ronin took notes on a pad. When Braxton finished, Ronin looked up.

"That's quite a list."

"It's no more than they deserve."

Ronin reached for the bourbon, poured himself a couple fingers, did the same for Braxton. "I'm not disagreeing, but sooner or later someone is going to notice a pattern."

"Maybe. But if I stretch it out, make them look like accidents…"

"I getcha. And you want my help."

"I don't want to get you in trouble."

Ronin laughed mirthlessly. "Too late for that. What else I got to do? You know, this is the fate of every successful republic. 'A republic that is not governed according to reason is like a ship captained by a fool.'"

"I used to teach Plato, but no one was interested. They don't even know who he is."

"All right, so what we need to do is put together dossiers on each of these people and figure out when and where they are most vulnerable. The electric car thing is not a bad idea. Schumer and Thompson should be easy. These two agents are going to be a lot harder, and as soon as something happens to either one, the red flags go up. So let's save them for last."

"Is there anyone you feel particularly strongly about?"

"Most members of this administration, but let's not go there. There's only so much we can do."

"Got any ideas?"

Ronin grinned. "There's enough toxin in one puffer fish to kill thirty adult humans, and there is no known antidote."

"Great! Where do we get puffer fish?"

"Let's look at whether any of these people like seafood. It's called fugu in Japan, and it's considered a delicacy."

"Even if it can kill you?"

"You don't eat that part. You need an expert fugu chef." Ronin poked at his laptop. "Thrill seeking is not the only reason the puffer fish remain popular. Aside from its distinct, subtle flavor and unique chewy texture, fugu is low in fat and high in protein. The meat is very versatile."

"Even if we can get puffer fish, what are the chances Sylvia would order it?"

"If I can access her credit card history, I can ascertain whether she likes seafood, find out where she eats."

"That seems complicated."

"Yeah. The more complicated it gets, the greater the chance for discovery. Not to mention it would hang the chef out as the culprit. Let's think about something else. I like the car battery fire concept."

"Could you program her car long distance?"

"It would be better to plant an incendiary device beneath the battery, something that would pierce the polypropylene casing. A shaped charge."

"Where do we get one?"

"I think I can make one. That's the easy part. The hard part is triggering it at the right place. We don't want any collateral damage."

Braxton stretched his legs out in front, then his back. "I could follow her, wait until the vehicle is isolated."

"You could, but you don't want to risk being spotted."

They sat in silence. Ronin turned his hand palm up.

"I could do it."

"Ronin, no. It's not your fight."

"It is my fight. It's all our fight. Anyone who's ever studied history. What's happening here is the greatest crime in history. The deliberate destruction of the United States and for what? Fourth and fifth mansions? Because of malice, greed, and ignorant partisan zeal?"

"You know, Ro, it's a stroke of fate that we met. I was beginning to think I was the only one."

"That's what they want you to think. But believe me, if you got out of this cesspool and visited some other states, you'd get a different opinion. Not everybody wants government sticking its dick in everything we do."

"Why are you still here?"

Ronin shrugged. "I was born here. It's beautiful country. Up here, in the mountains, no one riding your ass, it's close to paradise."

"You're welcome to stay here as long as you want. I'll get you a key."

"'Preciate it. So are we decided? A shaped charge for Sylvia?"

"Whatever poses the least risk to us and bystanders."

"Alrighty then. I think I have everything I need. Here's what I want you to do." Ronin reached into his pocket and pulled out an Apple air tag. It looked like a dog tag. "Slap this on Sylvia's car."

Braxton took the tag. "What is it?"

"Apple air tag. Everyone uses them. A lot of people stick them on their cars in case they get stolen. Tells you where the car is. Twenty-four bucks apiece."

"Got any more?"

Ronin reached into the pocket of his peacoat and pulled out four more. "Go crazy. But you have to program them into your phone."

"I could just download them from the net."

Ronin shook his finger. He reached into his pocket and pulled out a black phone with no markings. "Here's a burner. It's already programmed to the air tag I gave you. Here's what you do."

Ronin explained.

"I get it. Even a child can do it."

Ronin smiled brightly. "And they are!"

Braxton threw some blankets on the living room sofa and went up to the loft. It took him a long time to fall asleep. If only he could turn off the jumble of emotions, but he couldn't. After they destroyed the United States, there was no place to run. He eventually fell into a restless sleep and dreamed he was driving his car, trying to get home, when he got a frantic message that Angela had been shot. Traffic was at a standstill. He saw flashing lights up ahead. Some kind of accident. He pulled onto the right shoulder and accelerated past fuming commuters, many of whom honked at him or flashed the finger. A police vehicle blocked his way, half in the ditch. A cop sat cross-legged on the roof, eating a sandwich. Braxton was forced to stop. He got out.

"Officer! I've got to get home! It's an emergency!"

Slowly chewing, the police officer tore his sandwich in two and offered Braxton half. Braxton threw it in the ditch. The cop came down off the roof and reached for his handcuffs.

"Littering's a felony."

He jerked himself awake. Pale gray light peeked through the blinds. He got up, took a shower, and went into the kitchen. Ronin was sacked out on the sofa. Braxton made a pot of coffee. The old cathode ray television in the corner stood inert. He had no cable, and his grandfather's jury-rigged antenna had fallen in a storm decades before. There was always the radio, but Braxton didn't feel that he needed an outside voice intruding. The morning was silent and peaceful.

Ronin sat up, put a hand to his head. "Man, I haven't had that much to drink since I was in college."

Braxton looked at the empty bottle on the living room table. "Holy shit."

"Yeah."

"You okay to drive?"

"Sure. I just have a splitting headache."

"You want some ibuprofen?"

"Yeah."

"It's in the medicine cabinet in the bathroom."

Ronin went in the bathroom and shut the door. Braxton heard the shower run. Fifteen minutes later Ronin came out wrapped in a towel, went out the front door barefoot, got a bag from his car, and returned. He put on fresh clothes in the living room. Tan cargo pants.

A gray sweatshirt. Argyle socks. The same hiking boots. He clapped his hands.

"All righty then."

"You want some breakfast?"

"What you got?"

"I could make pancakes."

"I'm down."

Braxton opened the fridge. He'd bought a six-pack of eggs. They were two weeks old. *What the hell. Eggs last forever, don't they?* He mixed the pancakes in a Tupperware container, with milk and olive oil, put a cast-iron skillet on the burner and threw in a little olive oil.

They sat at a small linoleum breakfast table, eating in silence.

Ronin belched. "You think you can slap that air tag on?"

"I'll get it done."

"Send me the code."

"I'll hand deliver. What are you going to do?"

"I'm going to make that shaped charge. We wait for rain. Shouldn't be long. Do it when it's raining. It will burn faster."

Chapter 34

The Usual Tulips

Braxton followed Ronin down the mountain. Ronin pulled off in Gresham. Braxton went to his house, parked in the garage, closed the garage door, and entered through the kitchen. Steady rain beat on the roof. Braxton was glad for the rain. He would wear a rain parka as he rode his bicycle to the campus. For him, that felt like a lifetime ago.

Like all universities, Eastern State catered to bicyclists with extensive pathways, racks everywhere. Braxton went in the garage and pulled his ten-speed Trek off the wall. He'd bought it as a teaching assistant seventeen years before and had been riding it ever since. Braxton pumped the tires up to eighty, grabbed his bicycle lock from his backpack and shoved it into the pocket of his cargo pants with the air tag, and put on his rain parka. He rolled out his bike and closed the door behind him. He looked across the street. Lights showed from Gorelick's house. It was ten thirty. No need to bother the man. He had scribbled down the address and phone number for Gorelick if any reason came up when they needed to talk.

Braxton slipped his feet into the toe traps and pedaled toward town. He crossed the river at Hawthorne and headed east toward Mt. Tabor Park. The trail wound through Tabor, one of the rides he enjoyed the most, although in the rain everything was gray. Forty-five minutes later, he pulled onto Eastern State's campus, following the bike path toward the Lawrence Clark History Building. He rode around to the faculty parking lot and there it was, Baskin-Kulberg's Rivian, pulled up to the red brick facade. Braxton circled around to the front where students, some with umbrellas, some with rain parkas, most getting soaked, crossed the commons or climbed the steps. The bike racks were half full this rainy day. Braxton pulled his nondescript bike into a slot and threaded the steel cable through the front wheel, the frame, and the rack.

Hunched into his rain parka like half the students on campus, he walked around the history building to the faculty parking lot. Glancing around, he saw that he was the only one there. He headed for the rear entrance and veered aside at the door, sticking like a lamprey to the brick wall as he stood in front of the Rivian. Kneeling, he slithered beneath the front bumper and secured the air tag to the underside of the massive battery with four inches of Gorilla tape. He slithered out, hunkering low beneath the massive front facade, on his knees scanning for legs. Zippo. He returned to his bike.

Fifty minutes later, he pulled into his driveway, entered the code, entered the garage, closed the garage door, and went into his kitchen, chilled to the bone. Pulling out his phone, he fingered the air tag app. It took two seconds to show the Rivian's location in the faculty parking lot. He pulled out the burner Ronin had given him.

"Yeah," Ronin said.

"You see it?"

"Yeah."

"You got the thing?"

"Yeah."

"You want me to do it?"

"Nah. I'll do it."

"You sure?"

"I'm sure. I'll show it to you. Where are you?"

Braxton gave him the address.

An hour later, Ronin pulled up in the driveway. It was pouring. He dashed to the front door and Braxton let him in. Ronin pulled off his rain parka in the foyer and handed Braxton a funnel shaped object, the top sealed with heavy wax. Braxton hefted it in his hand.

"Heavy. What's it made of?"

"It's part of a turbocharger from a Dodge dragster."

"Seriously?"

"I needed something small enough to fit under the chassis but strong enough to force the charge in one direction. Also, being a car part, it will probably be overlooked in the wreckage. That little gizmo attached to the bottom is the igniter."

Ronin reached into his pocket and handed Braxton what looked like a remote control key fob. "That's the trigger. No batteries because we don't want an accident." He reached back into his pocket and handed Braxton a disc-shaped battery. "Slip that in when you're ready to boogie. Once it's inserted, be careful. You don't want to push the button until you're ready."

"Why would you take this risk on?"

"We started this journey together. What am I gonna do, hire a bomb maker? I know just where to put it. If we do this right, nobody will suspect you. Timing is everything. We do it on a rainy day. People will think it's just another car battery that couldn't handle the weather. Hopefully, the conflagration will conceal the source of the ignition. It will blow the compressor off and the car will keep rolling until the whole thing goes *kablooey*. The other reason, of course, is that we're now living in a totalitarian shit-hole where all paths of legal redress have been blocked."

"I can't let you do that. You've done enough."

"Baby, I'm just getting started."

"I appreciate it, Ro. But I want to push the button."

"That's what I used to say whenever my parents took me on an elevator."

Braxton grinned. His cell phone buzzed.

"Shit! She's on the move. I gotta go."

"I'll go with you."

"You sure?"

"What the hell—it's raining cats and dogs, it's my handiwork, and I want to see if it works or not."

"You've never done this before?"

Ronin slipped into his parka. "Let's go. You keep your eyes on the road, and I'll tell you where to go."

Their target pulled into a Bison Coffeehouse. They parked right next to her as Baskin-Kulberg got out and joined the queue inside. Ronin took the charge, cracked open his door, then slid down to the wet pavement. Braxton watched as he seemed to work under her car for two minutes, then crawled back in. "Bang-bang is set." Braxton moved the car to a parking spot far from her vehicle, and waited for her to come out. It took almost twenty minutes for her to emerge with her large coffee.

Soon they were headed east through heavy rain, cars kicking up rooster tails. It was impossible to read license plates or see inside vehicles more than ten feet away. Ronin turned the radio on and tuned it to an all-news station in Portland.

"The rain will continue throughout the night, tapering off toward morning. Meteorologists estimate over an inch."

"Have you been in an accident, and the insurance company refused to pay you what you deserve?" a man bellowed. "Here at Watkiss Law, we only take on righteous injury cases, and you only pay us if you win!"

Braxton stabbed the radio to an FM jazz station. Vintage bebop boogied from the speakers.

"Art Blakey," Ronin said.

"You dig jazz?"

"Oh yeah."

"Me too. Love this jazz station. Except when PBS delivers the news."

"Our abused tax dollars at work. They are little more than an arm of the Democratic Party."

"Bitch bitch bitch."

Ronin laughed. "Everybody bitches about totalitarianism, but nobody does anything about it. You should be able to see her in a minute. She's about two hundred feet ahead."

They were on SE Division Street headed east, passing through Mill Park. Most of the cars had their lights on, including the massive SUV that appeared through sheets of rain.

"Give me the detonator," Ronin said.

"You sure?"

"You're driving. Keep your hands on the wheel. See if you can pass her. I want to be in front when it happens."

Braxton gently stepped on the accelerator and sped up to fifty-five. Most of the cars exercised caution, with the usual tulips creeping along in the right lane twenty miles under the limit. Braxton was careful not to pass fast enough to get noticed. A vehicle pulled in behind him, tailgating. It flashed its high beams. Ronin looked at the Rivian's driver as they passed.

"Fiftyish woman, red coat, white knit cap."

"Bingo."

The tailgater flashed his high beams and honked.

"Get ahead of her."

Braxton accelerated until he was a hundred yards ahead and got in the right-hand lane. Ronin twisted around in his seat, the detonator in his hand, watching the Rivian behind them. He waited until no other cars were visible and pressed the button.

Incandescence ballooned beneath the SUV. It leaped six inches and came down in a skid. First one way, then the other, each over-correction taking it closer to the guard rail until it finally smacked, went airborne, and fell on its roof, bursting into flames. Braxton watched in the rearview mirror.

"Eyes front!" Ronin snapped. Braxton barely had time to avoid rear-ending a semi. They rode in silence for a couple miles before Braxton pulled off into the parking lot of a 7-Eleven. They sat in silence for a minute.

"Holy shit," Ronin said.

"Yeah."

Braxton turned around and headed west. They were at his house in forty-five minutes, went in through the garage. Braxton put on some coffee. Ronin sat in the living room and turned on KGW, where a glamorous Asian woman addressed the camera.

"Four alleged Hoover gang members have been indicted in the 2020 shooting of a Portland Uber driver. The four were arrested on Wednesday. Uber driver Dhulfiqar Mseer was about to pick up a passenger when he was shot and killed in a hail of gunfire. Authorities are withholding the gang members' names for the time being, as they are all underage.

"I've just been informed that a vehicle burst into flames on SE Division Street near Eastern State University. Authorities are on the scene. Drivers are urged to take another route.

"In other news, the president has signed into law his executive order that fifty percent of all new vehicles sold in the United States must be electric, by 2030—"

Ronin switched it off. "Got any booze?"

Braxton went in the kitchen and returned a moment later with a bottle of Buffalo Trace and two red solo cups.

Chapter 35

Revelations

Joel Schumer didn't rise when Faye Weldon came to his table at the Starbucks. His grandmother would've been mad at his lack of gallantry. But she was dead. He'd agreed to meet with Weldon in hopes of spinning whatever story she might be crafting. She didn't bother with coffee. She stood in front of him holding a digital recorder. Joel liked her hair and figure. If she wasn't an alt-right reporter, he might have considered asking her out.

"Mind if I sit?" she said.

Joel shrugged and she sat. Weldon turned on her recorder.

"Aren't you going to ask if I want to be recorded?"

"No. You agreed to this interview. You should have assumed I'd be recording. If the recorder scares you, I will shut it off."

He wondered if she would be so assertive if she knew he could order her death. "What's your pronoun?"

"I don't have any. I have breasts and a vagina; it's pretty safe to assume I'm a woman."

Joel liked the fact that he got under her skin. "What a narrow view. That's not how that works."

"Actually, Mr. Schumer, that's exactly how it works. It has worked that way since the beginning of time. Just because a few people have suddenly decided that they can identify as a toaster, doesn't change biology."

"You don't believe that people can identify as whatever they wish?"

"When I was a kid, I used to pretend I was a nurse. My mom even made me a little nursing outfit and bought me a toy medical bag and stethoscope. It was a lot of fun. My mom called me Nurse Faye. Pretending I was a nurse didn't make me one."

"That's an incredibly insulting and narrow view."

"In your opinion, perhaps."

"What do you want to ask me?"

"Your little group is garnering a lot of attention."

"What do you mean?"

"Look at Lake Oswego. Your group showed up to burn down two businesses, and the result was three dead. Another one of your people has gone missing. Let's start with these."

Joel had expected her to be blunt, but had thought there might be a buildup. "I think someone has misled you, Ms. Weldon. My little social action team had nothing to do with that alleged attack at Lake Oswego."

"Little social action team? Your ANTIFA chapter is known for violence. The three people killed were part of your cell, weren't they?"

"ANTIFA is more of an idea than a formal organization. You should check the FBI's report on us. Sure, they attended some meetings. Personally, I don't remember them. That doesn't mean that their presence had anything to do with us. With any gathering of like minds, you're bound to have a few extremists."

"So you contend that these people, dressed in garb that your organization wears during its protests, were just bad apples acting on their own?"

"Maybe. I can't say for sure." Joel took a sip of coffee, studying her face. Her brow furrowed.

"And you had nothing to do with the Molotov cocktails? Or that they were in front of a building that your organization had targeted earlier?"

"Again, I wasn't there. I have no idea why they were there. It was an unsanctioned activity."

"So you admit you sanction protests."

"Well, of course." Joel knew he was being smug but didn't care.

"So your little hit squad isn't just an idea. You approve protests, which implies that you are indeed an organization."

Schumer hated her more as the conversation went on. "That is a matter of debate. I think we'd find ourselves on opposing sides of that contention."

"You sent your people to harass Braxton Knox at his home, didn't you?"

"I don't know what you're talking about."

"I spoke with his neighbor, and he gave me photos of a car cruising that neighborhood with known members of your group."

"Perhaps they were just driving through the neighborhood. It's a free country."

"Professor Knox confronted them."

"I have no knowledge of that."

"You don't seem to have a great deal of control over the group you allegedly lead."

He sipped his coffee. "Too bad no one has heard from him. There's no way to confirm what you're telling me." Joel had his people stake out Knox's house. It had gone on the market and sold in three days. One of his people said the professor had moved out. But, since Potter and Reed had gone missing, no one had seen the professor. Schumer presumed he had been killed and left in the wilderness as he had ordered. *My people know enough to lie low after such a crime.*

"I talked to him just three days ago. He confirmed that ANTIFA was harassing him."

In that instant, he knew that Reed and Potter were probably dead if Knox was still alive. *He must have killed them. Why didn't Knox tell the police? Where is he?* Fear gnawed at the back of Schumer's mind. He did his best to mask his emotions. "Whatever Mr. Knox has told you, he was probably lying."

"Why did your organization target him in the first place?"

"We didn't target him. Part of our mission is to highlight those individuals who are harmful to society. Our role is to make the public aware of them and the threat they represent."

"Who decides which individuals are harmful to society?"

"We do."

"What if someone decides you're harmful to society?"

Schumer shrugged. "I would question their judgment."

"What harm did he pose?"

"Professor Knox was the product of an old patriarchy. He got his position by leveraging his white privilege, something he flaunted. When he refused to use the student's desired pronoun, he was inflicting his will upon her. Knox was denying her identity and place in our community. He never apologized for what he did, demeaning her that way. Did he tell you that?"

"Why do you keep referring to her as her?"

"I meant to say that person."

She looked at him as one might examine a used condom. "The man lost his career over this. He was on the tenure track. All he did was not use a pronoun. He didn't owe anyone an apology for that."

"People like you don't understand the rules of the new world we are creating, Ms. Weldon. You think what we're talking about is meaningless words and phrases. We are forging a new culture. One based on equity and fairness. There's no room for old-school thinking in the future."

"And that's what gave you the right to harass Dr. Knox?"

"Is it harassment to call someone out for doing something wrong against society? What few things we did, we did for the good of all. You should be thanking me."

Weldon shook her head. "This was never ANTIFA's fight."

"You don't get to decide that."

"Were you responsible for the SWAT call that killed his daughter?"

"I have no idea what you're talking about."

"Knox's wife was run off the road and killed. I suppose ANTIFA had nothing to do with that either."

"I wasn't aware this had become a criminal investigation. From what I saw, she was involved in a hit-and-run. An accident."

"You didn't answer my question."

He took a long sip of coffee. "I have no knowledge of what happened to Mrs. Knox. But if you are going to ask me if I am going to grieve over her death, the answer is no. She bedded with a man that represented everything wrong in this country. Regardless of how that may tug at your heartstrings, her death was inconsequential."

Schumer remembered that night all too well. Running her car off the road was not an impulse. They had been waiting for her. On two previous trips, she wasn't in a position for them to make their move. Their patience had been paid off on that windy curvy road. Immense satisfaction had been the reward for ordering her death. The sound of the fender of the stolen car performing a classic police PIT maneuver, sending her car through the barricade and rolling onto the rocks some twenty feet below, was proof to his people that they could be bolder. That they could be more aggressive.

Weldon's words jarred him back to reality. "Don't you think it was cruel and excessive to harass him after his wife had died?"

"Her death was his problem, not ours."

"So you claim you had nothing to do with anything that befell him?"

"Correct. His abuse of the English language and refusal to accept social constructs cost him his job. The FBI killed his daughter, not us. His loss of his job, that's his fault. We were just there to make the public aware of his corruption. People need to know what will happen if they don't do what we expect of them."

"What you expect of them."

"That's right."

"How is it your duty to intimidate others?"

"It's not intimidation. It's a lesson in consequences. What Dr. Knox has gone through is all his doing, not ours."

"Kind of like saying the rape victim was asking for it."
Schumer colored. "That's not it. Not at all."

"Your view of the world is that you know what's right and what's wrong. That you and your Stormtroopers can force your will on people."

"We are not the Stormtroopers. We are against fascists, racists, homophobes, transphobes, and white male oppressors. ANTIFA literally means anti-fascist."

Weldon barked mirthlessly.

"ANTIFA is on the same side as the men that stormed the beaches on D-Day. You're the one sitting on the wrong side of history."

Weldon turned off the recorder and put it in her purse. "If you are so righteous, so just, why do you hide your faces? That's what cowards do, not patriots." Before Schumer could respond, she rose and walked away.

Watching her walk away, he sneered. She was dangerous. The press had always been neutral or favorable to ANTIFA. Part of it was their brilliant manipulation of social media. Weldon represented something corrupt, a free press.

His phone buzzed. "Yo, Ajax," Tyler Thompson said.

Schumer cupped his mouth. "We have a problem. Potter and Reed fucked up. Knox is still alive."

"Fuck me."

"It's safe to assume he knows we were behind what happened to his wife."

"What are we going to do?"

"We need to figure out where he is. I saw his father on TV a few times. We need to locate him too. There's this reporter, Faye Weldon, she knows about him. Squeeze her and we can get some good intel. We'll start by taking out everyone around him. We will get him so twisted up with anger, he can't think straight. Then we will kill him. That will send a message to anyone who thinks they can stand against us."

Chapter 36

Loose Ends

Grooper's and Baskin-Kulberg's deaths should have torn at Braxton's conscience. Instead, they brought him peace. He dreamed of them, but when he woke, he couldn't remember. He remembered his wife and daughter. For some, it would have been torture. For Braxton, it was like a balm. The only torture was when his dreams faded in the morning.

Donna called. The money had come in from the Department of Justice. Some would have been excited. To Braxton, it was blood money. When he arrived at the strip plaza law office, he was ushered into a small conference room with Donna.

"I know you aren't happy to be here, but I wanted to get this check to you." She handed him an envelope. He cracked it open and saw his name and the figure. His ears pounded with each beat of his heart as he stared at the amount. It was far more than he could have ever hoped to make as a tenured professor, yet was unsatisfying.

"Thank you," he said.

She rose and came around the table, putting her hand on his shoulder. "It won't bring Suzanna or Angela back," Donna said, fighting back tears, "but it may help you move on."

He folded the envelope as if it were nothing but a scrap of paper and put it in his pocket. "I'm going to pay you and Marv for your time."

"No," she said, slowly bringing her hand back. "This is pro bono. Suzanna was a part of our family at the firm. You weren't the only one hurt when she died. We want to do this."

"Professionals get paid for their work, and you are a professional."

"It doesn't feel right."

"I can afford it," he assured her. "I want an invoice for your time. Besides, I'm going to likely need legal representation in the future."

She nodded. "Have you had a chance to look at the offers on your house?" She had emailed him three offers two days before. "The realtors are champing at the bit."

Braxton told himself it was nothing more than a building. But for him it was filled with wonderful memories, and a single night of horror. "I saw them. They're all good. What do you think?"

"The one from RE/MAX is a cash offer. That means that we can wrap this up quickly, if that's something you want. Your realtor suggests getting them into a bidding war, seeing if we can get the price up."

"Tell the realtor to take the RE/MAX offer. The sooner this is behind me, the better."

"I'll handle it."

"Also, I want to take two million of this settlement and give it to Young Lives. It was Suzanna's favorite charity. They help young women with children. If you can arrange that, I would be appreciative."

"She would like that," Donna said, wiping a tear.

"I want to do something in Angela's name, but I haven't come up with anything yet."

"Maybe her school could use the money?"

"I pulled her out when this nightmare started. The school didn't do shit when it came to harassment."

"A lot of parents don't want their kids in public schools but struggle with getting tutors and materials. I seem to remember a Christian group, the OCEANetwork, that helps families struggling with homeschooling costs. We could do a donation in Angela's name."

Braxton smiled. "I like it. If you can set that up, let's put in two million. I want Angela's name on it, so she won't just be swept under the rug the way the FBI has done."

"It would be my pleasure," Donna said. "There's been no movement on your lawsuit with the university. They called to tell me that two of the people on our deposition list have died though."

"Really? Who?"

"Grooper and Baskin-Kulberg."

"What happened to them?"

"They're still autopsying Grooper, but from what their lawyer told me, it was a drug overdose."

"I know he had a hard time after his divorce. We had him over to our house several times. I had no idea that he'd turned to drugs."

"Baskin-Kulberg's vehicle caught fire. Right in the street. Those batteries apparently burn at several thousand degrees when they go up. She never had a chance."

"She was a real piece of shit, the way she tried to destroy my career. Does it affect our case?"

"It might. Those were key witnesses for the university. Now they have to rethink their strategy. I filed discovery motions on all of their email communications, just in case they try deleting them. I'm keeping the pressure up. If these deaths hurt their position, their counsel will reach out to me."

Braxton didn't care about the money as much as the financial hit on the university. He had no one in his corner because everyone either subscribed to the DEI cult, or were too afraid for their own careers. They were cowards and bullies, two things that Braxton couldn't tolerate.

Donna told him she would handle all the donation arrangements and the offer on the house. After she left, he swung by the bank and made a deposit that stunned the teller. When she asked him if he wanted to know about ways the money could be invested to get more interest than a paltry checking account, he said, "Yes." It was the first time in a bank when he was treated like royalty.

When he got back to the cabin, he received a call from Rudy. Rudy offered to come by to help test his night vision gear. His realtor left two voice mails, hoping to kick off a bidding war. Braxton sent her a text and said his mind was made up. She was angry. She would get less commission. He was on the verge of reminding her it wasn't about her when she acquiesced.

He took Monsieur into the yard. He'd sprayed all the traps with Dogmace. Monsieur wouldn't go near them. He'd bought enough to do it every day, due to the rain.

Dinner was fried chicken strips in the air fryer. It wasn't like the meals Suzanna used to make. Staring at the plate, alone at the small table, he found himself regretting not savoring the meals he had shared with his family when they were still alive. He ate the chicken and the serving of green beans he had warmed up, not tasting them at all. He gave half to Monsieur.

Rudy pulled up. Braxton met him in the yard.

"Stop right there, Rudy. I have to show you something."

Braxton knelt, carefully plucked a thatch of twigs revealing a foot-deep trench studded with sharpened metal tent stakes. "Don't step in this line. See it? It forms a kind of natural contour, but when I put the thatch down, it looks like solid ground. The stakes are coated with feces."

"Where'd you get that?"

"I made it myself." Braxton pointed to two trees perpendicular to the porch. "Look up there. That's a two-hundred-pound-log affixed to two chains. Anybody approaches the cabin on that trail, bam."

Rudy looked up. "Damn. If I were you, I'd put some wooden spikes in it. You don't want to bruise people coming at your cabin, you want them permanently incapacitated."

"Good idea. I've got some tent spikes left."

"I see your little stick holes back there."

"I thought I hid that stuff pretty well."

"I was in the service. Almost every place the Army sent me, someone was trying to kill me. I saw a lot of nasty shit. Mogadishu was the worst."

Once inside, Rudy pulled out the AN/PSQ-20B ENVG night vision gear. "These have thermal overlay with image intensifiers. Top-of-the-line stuff on the civilian market." He attached them to Braxton's tactical helmet.

"It's lighter than what I wore in the Army."

"A lot of the military-grade stuff isn't available commercially. Most guys buy the cheap-ass shit on Amazon. These came in at twenty-three thousand bucks."

"Assuming I'm using this to, let's say, defend the cabin, how will it work with my rifle?"

"Look, that AXSR is the prime weapon for long-range stuff. That doesn't mean it wouldn't be perfect for up close and personal killing. First off, put on the short barrel you purchased, the sixteen incher. You don't need the length for close-up shooting."

Braxton swapped barrels in less than a minute, putting the Thunder Beast suppressor back on. "Let's set up some targets and I'll show you how to use this beast."

The steel plated targets were shaped like men. Braxton and Rudy went back to the cabin and killed the lights. "Alright, you're gonna love this. Turn on your night vis."

Braxton complied, lowering it to his eyes. The world came alive in a wash of green. "It's been a while."

"Look," Rudy said, pulling the helmet off. "Set this to ENVG mode. That combines night vision and thermals."

"So I just aim and shoot?"

"Hell, son, it's easier than that. Look at that first target." He handed the helmet to Braxton. The target's heat signature stood out from that of the surrounding forest.

"Hit your range finder."

He toggled it on. The beam stabbed at the night. As Braxton shouldered the heavy rifle, he put the beam on the target. "You don't need the sights for close-up work. Put a round in the chamber, put the laser on target, and fire."

Braxton chambered a round, ignored the scope, and did as Rudy instructed. He squeezed the trigger gently. It stopped at the first stage. Just a little more pressure and the AXSR kicked into his shoulder, followed by a metallic ping. "Damn…"

"You can practically shoot from the hip like this. At this range, the AXSR is overkill. You might be better off with another weapon, but the principle is the same."

"No," Braxton said. "I like Themis."

"You named it? Good. I always named my weapons. It's good luck."

Braxton dinged one target after another. When he was done, he wrote a check to Rudy. They went inside and cracked open some beers.

"I don't aim to pry," Rudy said. "But you went from being a casual shooter to owning a state-of-the-art sniper rifle with all of the trimmings. Your yard has booby traps. This looks like someone preparing for war."

"I don't want it, but the bad guys came after me and my family. If they want a war, I'm more than willing to give it to them."

"The law isn't going to allow that. The goons on the internet will paint you as some sort of domestic terrorist. What's the label they like to use? Alt-right extremist, that's it. They'll come at you because people can't be vigilantes in this day and age. It undermines the authority of the state. Vigilantes hold individuals accountable. They feel they should be the only ones entitled to kill in the name of the law."

"What can they do to me? They took my career and my family from me. A handful of punks already tried to kill me."

"What happened to them?"

Braxton shrugged.

Rudy tipped his bottle to Braxton's. "Here's to that."

Braxton slugged beer. "We've wandered pretty far from the concepts of justice on which this nation was built. People are angry, frustrated, pissed off. The internet is poison. People know it's bad for them, but they think somehow they'll be spared. After the communists have killed everyone who doesn't agree with them, they'll turn on each other."

"The nail that sticks out gets pounded down."

Braxton drank his beer. "Most of my life I lived on the straight and narrow. One day all that changed. Just being a good person isn't enough. Talk is cheap."

Rudy slammed back the rest of his beer. "Good luck, my friend. If you need help, you've got my number."

Chapter 37

Hunting the Hunter

"Daddy," Angela's voice washed over him in the dark.

"Baby doll," he murmured. "I miss you so."

"I miss you too, Daddy. So does Mommy." He saw her, a blur in his mind, reaching out for him. Braxton reached for her, only to violently jerk himself awake. Throwing the bedspread off, he got up and stretched. After his morning protein drink, he went into town to Planet Fitness, where he worked out for an hour and a half. Braxton showered at the gym, and came back out to find Ronin leaning against his car, arms crossed.

"To what do I owe the honor?"

"Let's talk in the car."

Braxton unlocked the vehicle. Ronin took the passenger seat. "I've been monitoring our list."

"What's up?"

Ronin handed him a folder. "Special Agent Frank Hayden. He's still on administrative leave. Dude's paranoid. Lots of home security, managed by Apache. That's a contractor outfit started by an ex-Navy SEAL. They specialize in home security and fast response. Apache doesn't bother with the police. They get the signal, they head over."

"Any way in?"

Ronin shook his head. "I couldn't figure out a way. But there is an opportunity. Hayden's going hunting tomorrow, up at his father-in-law's property in the mountains. Just him and his son-in-law." Ronin pointed to a map and an aerial photograph. "Google Earth."

Braxton studied the map. "Going after an armed FBI agent seems a bit suicidal."

"He'll be exposed. He has no idea you're coming. This is recreational. He's leaving at five a.m. You can get out there in front of him."

"What about the son-in-law? What's his story?"

Ronin handed him a photograph of a clean-cut young white male arm in arm with an older Asian, both wearing karate gis. "He's in charge of TSA Portland."

"Every time I go there, they feel up my crack."

"If you pay them, you can skip the security lines."

"Doesn't that sound like a shakedown?"

"That's why I don't fly." Ronin shrugged. "It's all there, right down to the GPS coordinates of the stand."

"I didn't know it was hunting season."

"It's not. It's a private game reserve. It's the kind of place you need an invite to and lots of bucks."

"Thank you."

"There's more," Ronin continued. "His partner, Rocky Forsyth, will be easier. He's using his time off to get hammered every afternoon at Longchamps. At night he watches *Wheel of Fortune* home alone. He has a daughter, Roseanne, majoring in microbiology at Stanford. They haven't spoken in years. Judging from her campus involvement, she disapproves of her father. She thinks he's a dumb cop. I imagine this latest incident hasn't raised her estimation."

"I can use that. Any other family?"

"No. He divorced Roseanne's mother when she was ten. That might have something to do with it. As far as I can tell, he's had no long-term relationships since then. A couple of complaints alleging sexual harassment which the Bureau dutifully buried."

"Good."

"I've been looking into Faye Weldon. She's a straight shooter. Old-school reporter, so naturally there's a page up on X for haters to wail about. Now I like her even more. Her name has generated a burst of traffic starting yesterday. Your ANTIFA friends seem to have a heightened interest in her."

"That can't be good."

"I was able to get into Tyler Thompson's email. He used his Xbox ID for his password. Not exactly Mensa material. There's some traffic between him and Ajax. They're trying to find out what nursing facility your father's in. They've staked out your house."

"If they think my old man's a sitting duck, they've picked on the wrong geezer."

"They mean business from the emails."

"Sure they do. I killed two of them. They thought I was dead. The fact that they're staking out my house means they know I'm alive."

"You give these guys a raging hard-on."

"Not dying will do that. Ronin, do me a favor. Reach out to Faye. Tell her what you know. Warn her."

"What are you going to do?"

"I'm going to give my dad a heads-up. Then I'm going hunting."

* * *

Grayson lived at McCormick Place, a blond brick two-story in a campus-like setting in Hazelwood. The pert receptionist looked up from her computer behind the desk as Braxton entered carrying a leather gym bag.

"Why hello, Braxton. Welcome back."

"Thanks, Francine. How's Dad doing?"

"He wants to buy a motorcycle."

Braxton laughed. When he was little, his father had ridden a Harley. "I hope you told him that's not a good idea."

"He said he's prepared to ride a trike."

"Where is he?"

"Upstairs, far as I know. *Judge Judy*'s on."

Braxton took the stairs. Grayson's door was open. The old man sat in a Barcalounger, legs extended, watching a flat screen TV. Braxton paused in the doorway as *Judge Judy* fixed some hapless shmuck in her laser glare.

"Another outburst like that and I'll have Byrd take you out."

The gormless wonder, a puffy young man with a scraggly beard, glared but kept his mouth shut.

Braxton shut the door. Grayson turned.

"Hello, son. What brings you here today?"

"I brought you a few things I thought you might need."

Braxton sat on the sofa next to the Barcalounger. "Everything good? You feeling okay?"

"I'm feeling about as well as you'd expect. I have a little trouble sleeping. I'm worried about you." His voice dropped. "I'm hearing that the local brownshirts have you in their crosshairs. Sam Breckett fills me in at mealtimes. Sam's a retired FBI agent. Tells me the thugs are stirring like angry hornets and the FBI is curiously uninterested. They're only interested in pursuing phantom white supremacists. Like you."

"And you. That's why I came."

"I heard about that bitch who was your department head. Her vehicle blew up. What a shame."

"Terrible."

Grayson looked at him with cool gray eyes, a trait he shared with his son. "You have anything to do with that?"

"You know me, Pops. I'm a law-abiding citizen. I haven't even had a parking ticket. I'm hearing the same things, and since these thugs have nothing to fear from law enforcement, there's no telling what they might do. I brought you something."

Braxton got up and quietly locked the front door. It had a deadbolt. The staff had a master key, but it was only used in emergencies. Like if a resident hadn't been seen in twenty-four hours.

Grayson raised his eyebrows. Braxton sat with the satchel between his feet, unzipped it, and pulled out a fleece-lined pistol case and a box of .38 longs. "Here's your revolver, Dad."

Grayson took the case in his hands, unzipped it, and removed the blue steel gun with a three-inch barrel. "Very thoughtful, son. I was thinking of asking you to bring it."

Braxton pointed to his forehead. "Great minds think alike."

"What prompted your decision?"

"Rightly or wrongly, ANTIFA blames me for certain unfortunate incidents that have recently occurred. As you know, Nazis don't see individual human beings, only tribes. Oppressor tribes and victim tribes. You're an oppressor due to your connection with me. As such, you're deserving of a cruel death. Do I think they're going to storm this retirement home? Dubious. However, I wouldn't put it past them. I'd be on the lookout for new hires with neck tattoos and piercings. Goth types. They might be persuaded to put cyanide in your tea."

"Well, I can't exactly shoot them. Plus, how would I know?"

"You were in law enforcement. You know what to look for."

"Yeah, and I'm not the only one. There are four retired cops in here. Two city, one county, and one fed."

"Good to know. They solid?"

"Oh yeah. I see where two of the communists at Eastern State recently met untimely ends. Did you have anything to do with that?"

"I'm as baffled as you."

"What are the odds that two of the senior commissars who presided over your banishment should meet violent deaths within days of each other?"

Braxton shrugged. "Shit happens."

Grayson stared at him for a minute. He smiled. "I appreciate the visit. Can you stick around for dinner? We're having grilled pork roast."

"Dad, I'd love to, but there's something I have to do."

"Like what?"

"I have to meet my lawyer. Sign some documents. I sold the house."

"Does ANTIFA know you're not living there?"

"The sign out front says *SOLD*. Let's get together next week. We'll go get some barbecue."

"Sounds good. Come here and give your old man a hug."

Chapter 38

Stalking Prey

Just past midnight, Braxton headed west toward the private game preserve where Frank was hunting. It was one as Braxton drove by on Wilson River Highway. A fancy wood sign by the locked gate read Hunt Club. The facility was ringed with barbed wire to keep the game inside. Braxton drove a half mile past and pulled off onto an old logging trail not visible from the road. The Hunt Club's barbed wire perimeter was a mere twenty yards through the forest. Braxton slid under the fence.

He wore his ghillie suit, masking his appearance and heat signature. He found a good place to set up, the clubhouse dimly visible through the woods. The club was a deer slaughterhouse. A wooden hunting shed stood at the far end of a large clearing in the dense woods. The foliage had been cut in a triangle, starting at the shed, giving the "hunters" an unobstructed field of fire. At the far end of the range grew corn, bait for the deer. All sense of sport was lost. Braxton crouched in a dense patch of briar. He cut out a hollow where he could lie down with a crossing field of fire to the range.

He unpacked his AXSR, attaching the long barrel. He set up his Kestrel, feeding his phone app atmospherics and wind information. He lay on his stomach, the chill of the early morning making his joints ache.

Braxton had always enjoyed hunting. Real hunting, sitting in a tree stand, no bait, no defined field of fire. Hunting as it was meant to be. When he had married Suzanne, she'd gone with him. When Angela had been born, there was never enough time.

He dozed off, only to jerk his head up. Checking his watch, he saw he'd been out for almost an hour. Rubbing his eyes, he checked the scope and yawned. The forest spoke. Something dropped from a tree. Crunching and movement. Mourning doves. A squirrel cracking a nut.

Just after 0500 he spotted a flicker of light in the shed. Through his scope, he saw two men at the firing platform, silhouetted by ambient light at the firing platform. Zooming in, he saw the steaming coffee in a thermal mug next to one of the rifles.

At best, it was twelve hundred feet, relatively easy with the AXSR. With the dim lighting, it would be hard to make out which was Hayden. On top of that, it would look deliberate, drawing in the resources of the FBI. Shooting him in the field would look like a hunting accident.

The sun rose later than expected. Cloud cover obscured direct sunlight.

Two deer emerged right after sunrise. The buck, an eight-pointer, came first, followed by the lone doe. They were alert, timid. Walking daintily, they approached the dew covered cornstalks.

Braxton felt the cold still air and wiped his nose on his ghillie suit. Then it happened. A crack of gunfire from the stand. The doe bolted, but the buck reeled, its hind legs collapsing. It stumbled and fell, still alive.

A shout of joy from the stand as the buck, still alive and in agony, tried to run but could not stand. Panic set in. Braxton hated seeing an animal in pain. He was tempted to call off his assassination, to fire at the buck and put it out of its misery, but he couldn't. This was for Angela.

Frank Hayden emerged, followed by his son-in-law. "That was a hell of a shot, wasn't it?" the FBI agent said as he closed on the deer. Was it that much different when Hayden had shot his daughter?

Using his ranging laser, Braxton sighted in on the buck, punching the range into his iPhone as four hundred and sixteen yards. On his phone the ballistics computer app gave him the scope adjustments.

The two hunters approached their prey. The buck squealed, furiously trying to pull itself with its front legs, dragging its rear. For a moment, it looked like it might actually get up. It collapsed.

"That's how it's done!" Hayden said as he got within twenty feet of his prey. He raised his rifle, and took aim. Braxton did the same.

Hayden squeezed the trigger, and so did Braxton. Themis snugged his shoulder. Their shots were not quite in unison, but strung together.

Braxton's round hit Hayden above his left ear, blasting his brains and skull onto the dewy ground.

Braxton quickly gathered and stowed his gear. The voice of the son-in-law cried out. "Dad! Dad! Somebody, help!" The sound of panic, almost like the wail the buck had made.

Retracing his steps, Braxton quick-walked back to his vehicle. Folding the rifle stock and removing the suppressor, he stowed the weapon in a golf bag, shed his Nemesis suit, folding it into a small roller bag. With the ghillie suit off, the cold air hit sweat.

Driving away, he felt disappointment. Yes, Hayden was dead, but he died not knowing why.

I won't make the same mistake with his partner. He will know why he's dying. His last thoughts will be about the mistake he made and knowing that justice is being done.

Chapter 39

Priorities

After a late breakfast from Wendy's, Braxton went back to the cabin. He finished work on a doggy door large enough for Monsieur. Taking Rudy's advice, he drilled quarter-inch holes into the log deadfall in the pine boughs, fitting them with four twelve-inch rebars sharpened to a dull point in his garage back in Portland. A dull headache came over him, a nagging reminder he needed sleep. Braxton laid down on the couch and slept. When he woke, the sun was setting.

His phone chirped. It was Faye Weldon. Normally he wouldn't have answered, but he knew that Joel Schumer's people had her on their hit list.

"I got the message from your friend. Thanks for warning me," she said.

"These guys are serious."

"I met with this Schumer guy. What a piece of work."

"That explains their interest in you. What was he like?"

"He's a condescending prick. Arrogant... confident to the point of overconfidence."

"He's also dangerous."

"I know. I didn't tell him that you think he's responsible for the death of your wife."

"The sheriff's department doesn't seem too interested."

"That's an understatement. If they crack down on ANTIFA, they have a lot of explaining to do about the riots and looting back in 2020. It's easier for them to simply stick with the theory that they are just a social cause."

"I've warned you how dangerous they are. You met with him. You need to be careful."

"I'm packing, if that's what you mean."

"That's part of it. Remember, these guys are cowards. They're the kind of people that come at you in a mob, from behind. They're bullies who have never faced opposition."

"That sounds like the voice of experience."

"A couple of them tried to kill me. Schumer told them to, I'm sure of that."

"Shit. Did you take it to the police?"

"I handled it. The police weren't necessary."

"That sounds ominous. That explains the missing person's report. The Potter kid."

"I wouldn't know."

Braxton guessed Faye was attempting to wrap her head around what he'd said. "Are they dead?"

"How would I know?"

"Gotcha. I mentioned I had talked to you when I saw Schumer. He tried to hide his reaction. Now I understand why."

"So he knows I'm alive."

"Sorry."

The revelation didn't shake Braxton. He knew that Ajax's options were limited. He might run. Probably not. Schumer used violence to achieve his goals. It was his default setting. That meant Schumer would want to silence him. To do that, he would need to flush him out.

The people around me are in danger. He thought about his father. The senior Knox said he was aware, but he was old.

"I appreciate the heads-up," he replied. "Maybe you should stay with a friend or get a hotel room. ANTIFA is all about violence. Schumer believes might makes right."

"Forsyth's under review. Apparently, the FBI has some minimal standards for field agents, and Agent Forsyth's been cited four times for not following procedure. Two of the complaints were for excess brutality. Hopefully, five's a charm."

"You're saying they're fixing on letting him go?"

"They may even charge him with excessive force. Don't get your hopes up."

"What's to stop him from going after you?"

"Like I said, I'm prepared. Based on what you've said, maybe you should be the one that's worried."

"For the time being, I'm in a safe place. If he decides to bring the black-hooded Scooby Doo gang up here, they'll be in a world of hurt."

They hung up. Braxton assessed the situation. Killing Rocky Forsyth on the heels of taking out another agent might trigger a response from the feds. Braxton put Rocky on hold for the time being.

Debbie Driggs popped to the top of the list. She wasn't top priority. He wanted to confront her before ending her life. Let her know why she had to die. But this was Debbie Driggs. She would never own up to her role in his removal. Ideology always overrode logic with these people. She needed to die, but hearing her justify her action wasn't something he wanted to deal with.

Ramrod and Tyler Thompson needed to die too. They had run his wife off the road. He wanted to watch them die, but that didn't make them a priority. He wondered if he was a ghoul.

Ajax was number one. The others were targets. Joel Schumer was different. Taking him out before he could act was only logical. He was the brains behind ANTIFA. If he were dead, the others would scatter like rats. It would protect his father, Faye, and Ronin.

He called Ronin.

"What is it, chief?"

"I need to know where Schumer is."

"You planning on double-tapping him?"

"He's a loose cannon. He needs to be taken care of before he comes at me or the people around me."

"Well, you're in luck," Ronin said. "I've been tracking his phone, looking at his emails. He's got the group meeting at a warehouse tonight. They're planning something."

"Can you get me the address?"

"I'll meet you and take you there myself."

"You don't have to do this, Ronin."

"I do."

Braxton drew a deep breath. "You said the wokesters harassed you. That's not enough to get someone to do the things you've done."

"What are you saying?"

"Why are you helping me? Really?"

There was a long silence on the other end of the line.

"What I told you before was only part of it. I worked at a Big Tech company," he said softly. "On my private account, I liked a *Daily Wire* story. It wasn't a big deal, but I had some haters out there. They mined my social media for anything that might paint me in a bad light.

"They took perfectly innocent comments and reposted them with their own context, pictures and images designed to ruin me. I hung in there. They created posts I never made. They harassed my employer, demanding I be terminated.

"When that didn't work, they targeted my parents and my brother, Paul. He was autistic. Paul. He just wanted to meet other people. He didn't know what woke was, or right or left. They sent pictures, hounding every post he made. Calling him names.

"He took a bottle of oxy." Ronin stopped.

Braxton felt Ronin's pain as if it were his own. "I'm so sorry."

"The paramedics tried to save him, but it was too late."

"Jesus. Ronin, I'm sorry you and your family had to go through that."

"My employer understood. They had been going after him for years. They even posted where his private jet was and where it was going. He put me on a special project. To find people these cancel pigs were targeting and help them."

It wasn't coincidence that Ronin entered his life. It was serendipity. Ronin wasn't just a talented hacker; he was a kindred spirit. Like Braxton, he too had suffered loss at the hands of faceless cancel pigs. They'd injured both men. While Braxton was curious who Ronin's sponsor was, he knew better than to ask.

"Alright, we do this together. Get me what you can on this warehouse."

Chapter 40

Back and to the Left

The warehouse where ANTIFA met was on the Willamette River near the Port Terminal. A twentieth-century four-story red brick structure. From blocks away, it looked abandoned. Most of the windows were broken. The rest were filthy. Graffiti covered the first floor exterior. *Black Lives Matter. Whiteness Is A Disease. ANTIFA Rules!* Most of the doors were boarded up. One of the doors cracked open.

Braxton and Ronin stood on the rooftop of an abandoned gas station. With tall structures all around, the echo of the shot would be difficult to pinpoint.

As they settled behind the parapet, a light drizzle fell. Braxton had found his grandfather's old oilskin duster at the cabin. The dark brown leather smelled musty, but kept the cold and water out.

He ranged the door as his target. Looking through his scope, he watched people filter in. Ronin peered through binoculars.

"That's him, the one on the left in the dark gray windbreaker," Ronin said.

Squinting, Braxton got him in his sights. He knew the face. Memories of his infiltration flooded back. There were a few places, mostly on his ribs, where he was still sore from the beating. Payback time.

Looking at the lean face through his scope, he was tempted to squeeze one off before the thug entered the building. He and Ronin agreed to get him on the way out. Ronin had planted a recording device in the warehouse earlier. The seductive call to aim and fire was hard to resist.

Eighteen ANTIFA entered the old warehouse. Braxton rechecked his range and atmospherics. The misting rain was a problem. Wind was a problem. Randy had trained him to recognize the challenges and compensate for them.

"I hate this weather," Ronin muttered. "I took a job in computers so I wouldn't have to be outdoors."

Braxton checked his levels to make sure it was still balanced. "I haven't been outdoors this much since the Army."

"I looked at your record. You didn't see much action."

He got access to my Army records... impressive.

"One tour of service. Other guys have heroic stories of glorious battle. I sat in a room and typed."

"Did you have to fire your weapon at all?"

"Twice. I'd love to tell you I distinguished myself. In reality, the first time, I dove for cover. I laid down some suppressing fire for the guys that tracked down the shooter."

"And the second time?"

Braxton rolled his eyes. "I was in the shitter when someone sprayed the base with gunfire. I barely got my pants up. I didn't see where the shots came from, but one bullet went two feet over my head. The Army did me a favor by making me clerical staff."

"If you don't have any war stories, you've got to make some up." It was clear that Ronin wanted more than what Braxton had to offer.

"The movies and comics don't do the profession justice. They set unrealistic expectations. You and I both know there aren't a lot of people out there doing what we do. Those that run afoul of the law... they get branded as the bad guys or worse, lunatics—fanatics. It's page one of the government playbook. Those Davidians in Waco weren't bothering anyone until the ATF trained their sights on them. Randy Weaver was just a guy who sawed-off shotguns." His own mention of Waco made his forehead wrinkle and he paused, checking his scope again rather than talk any further about his feelings regarding the ATF.

"I was always a fan of guys like John Wick and I read *The Punisher* back when I was a kid."

"None of those guys got the shit kicked out of them by a handful of ANTIFA goons and were driven out to be killed."

"You didn't die."

"True. But my pride got injured. I learned my lesson. Don't let these bastards get the upper hand." Memories of being in the trunk, driving out to be shot, no longer made him angry. *I got better as a result of that experience.*

"So the Army didn't really prepare you for this?"

"Not true. One thing the Army does is teach you to learn. The smart people in the military, they learn something every day. I'm a good learner. When I left the service, I went to college and got my doctorate. I'm a lifelong learner. Now I'm learning how to deal revenge." He spoke with a sense of pride.

"I understand. These lessons are harder than most. And the stakes are higher."

"If I wasn't doing this, I'm not sure what I would be doing. I lost everything else."

"You got a settlement from the DoJ, right?"

Braxton nodded, adjusting his ball cap.

"So you could just leave Portland and put all this behind you. Take a cruise. You could go somewhere and start over."

"My wife and daughter mean too much for me to simply walk away. These people operate beyond the law. The entire justice system ignores what they do. Without me doing this, they would get away with murder. I can't let that pass. This is my life now."

"And when you succeed, the full might of the justice system will train its sights on you."

"Only if they find me."

They waited. Water trickled off of Braxton's cap and down the back of his neck. Braxton didn't cringe. The Army had trained him well. Weather was something you tolerated.

For a long time nothing happened. No new arrivals. Then they started to trickle out.

"Showtime," Ronin said.

Braxton looked through the scope and checked his ballistics computer. It was late afternoon and getting colder. The breeze picked up. He adjusted his scope. Each person who emerged loitered in his sights.

Ajax came out.

He stood next to two people talking, hood pulled up on his windbreaker. The person next to him pulled out a vape, puffing a light gray cloud of smoke.

"There's your boy," Ronin said.

"Got him."

Braxton felt his heart beat. He aimed for center mass. Schumer was turned at a slight angle towards him. Braxton waited between beats. He thought of Genghis Khan's hordes, who learned to release arrows when all four of the horse's hooves were off the ground. He squeezed the trigger.

The AXSR nudged his shoulder and chuffed.

"You missed."

"Shit."

ANTIFA scattered like cockroaches exposed to light. A man lay on the ground, clutching his shoulder. Ajax had vanished.

"Damn—I got the guy next to him."

"Let's get out of here."

Braxton broke down his weapon, angry with himself. They climbed down an iron stairway in the back and walked toward the car. As they drove away, there were no sirens. Ronin pulled out a Baofeng radio and put the earpiece in his ear.

"Why didn't they call the police?" Ronin asked when they were several miles away. "They didn't even call an ambulance."

"Think about it. They're all trespassing. They're all wearing black tactical gear. One thing nobody ever mentions, half these ANTIFA chapters are at war with the others. Mostly over who's the baddest."

"When they take that guy to the hospital, the police are going to get a call. I mean, the guy got shot."

"By then, they'll get their story together. They don't have to explain the building or the gear—they'll shed all of that before they take him in. Their story will be a drive-by shooting at some other location or some other stupid lie."

Ronin nodded. "That makes sense. How do you know that's the angle?"

"I taught at a university. You pick up how these kids think. They're basically vicious children."

"The police will investigate," Ronin said.

"Maybe. But they won't tell the cops the truth about location. The police will knock on doors, no one will have seen anything. There are no bullet casings because we were never there. That leaves Schumer and his pack of wolves able to carry out their plan. Plus, you've got to factor in the police are at fifty percent, while crime has exploded. They'll just go through the motions. They're resentful of these fucking black hats fucking everything up. Half the force will thank whoever hit that piece of shit."

"I'll go back tomorrow and pull the recording device."

They drove in silence except for the monotonous sound of the windshield wipers and the muffled sounds from the police scanner.

"What's the problem?" Ronin said.

"The reporter, Weldon, she tipped him off that I'm still alive and kicking. Schumer must know I killed his buddies. Now he's been shot at. Assuming he's not a moron, he'll guess that we're monitoring their plans. He'll assume I'm the one who pulled the trigger."

"Maybe not. These asshats have pissed off a lot of people."

"I took out two of them already. That bumps me pretty high on his list of suspects."

"They're not going to back off, are they?"

"No." The windshield was fogging up. Braxton hit the defrost control. "It's personal now. If he has half a brain, he'll figure it out."

"But he could run... move to another city."

"He's the big man on campus here. Ajax won't give up his power. He can't. He's an addict. Running makes him out to be a coward. His ego is his own worst enemy, and his addiction to power. He's a big man in ANTIFA in this city. Starting from scratch somewhere else would be next to impossible."

"So what does that mean?"

Braxton stopped for a light. "He'll have to up his game. He'll want to flush me out. Try and hit me with superior numbers. He'll look for pressure points, try and make me overreact."

"How?"

"I'm not sure yet. I suspect it will involve my dad or Faye Weldon. Those are the kinks in my armor. I told them."

"That may not be enough."

The light changed and he accelerated.

"Can you whip up some additional security for both of them?" Braxton said.

"Why not have them move out to the cabin?"

"Dad's stubborn. He's ex–law enforcement. He's not the kind who runs from a fight. If anything, he heads into it. And the cabin ain't that big."

"And Weldon?"

"She's tough. From what I have seen, she's not the kind of person who's willing to bend the knee when it comes to these thugs."

"So we have our work cut out for ourselves."

"I put a tracker under Agent Forsyth's electric Cadillac."

"How'd you do that without getting seen?"

"A little birdie told me he likes to hang out at Longchamps in Lake Oswego. In fact, he's there now."

Chapter 41

An Old Agent Leaves the Fold

Rocky Forsyth sat in a booth at the back of Longchamps, an upscale bar in Lake Oswego, watching the evening news on a flat screen above the bar. Because of the din, subtitles scrolled across the bottom. The White House had just declared the upcoming holiday of Easter Transexual Awareness Day, bringing it to three months and twenty-eight days set aside to celebrate the traditionally marginalized people. Rocky didn't give a shit, personally, but he'd learned to play the game, particularly since the Bureau had prioritized transsexuals in hiring.

With his movie star looks, he could have been a marquee idol. In fact, he'd been brought in as an advisor on two movies, one directed by Taika Waititi, the other by Sophia Coppola. He'd hired an agent and done a screen test. He was looking past the Bureau. Rocky knew that his odds of playing a hero as a straight white man were slim, but not if he played the villain. The field was wide open for straight white male villains. He was hoping to hear from his agent about Gavin Lurman's new film, *Transcontinental*, about a seemingly mild transsexual man taking a cross-country train ride to visit his wife John, when terrorists seize the train. That's when he reveals he's a former CIA assassin. Rocky was up for one of the terrorists.

Rocky was waiting for his date, a cute stenographer from the local office, who caught his eye when he'd given his deposition about the unfortunate shooting of the Knox girl. Rocky struck his lucky silver dollar on the oak tabletop, hoping for his agent to call. His days with the Bureau were limited. The shooting of the Knox girl was not the first blemish on his otherwise impressive career. He'd been involved in a collision with another vehicle three years ago on a winding mountain road, resulting in the death of an elderly couple who'd been heading toward Portland to see their granddaughter. Rocky had been three sheets to the wind, coming back from a bachelor party at the famous Timberline. He'd strayed into the opposite lane just as the elderly couple came round the bend in their Buick, clipping them, causing their vehicle to plunge through the barricade and fall two hundred feet into a stream.

Rocky had stopped his car and gotten out to look. They were all but invisible from the road. Just like that burn-out they'd found on Mt. Hood several days earlier. Rocky was smart enough to wait twenty-four hours before checking, knowing by then his blood alcohol level would be back to normal. When asked why he hadn't come forth immediately, Rocky explained he'd been overcome with remorse and spent the time praying.

He was so worried, that when he got home, he got down on his knees and prayed to the Almighty to forgive him for his sins, and that the elderly couple didn't suffer. But he knew, deep in his heart, it was all for show, and he didn't really believe in the Supreme. He just wanted to cover all the bases.

He caught the waitress's eye.

"What'll you have, big guy?"

"Another Jim Beam and a beer chaser. You're kinda cute. What's your name?"

The waitress pointed to the embroidered *Joy* patch on her shirt.

"What time do you get off?"

"I'm here until one, big guy. Think you're gonna last that long?"

"We'll see."

She brought him the drink. After that, he didn't remember too much except leaving the bar around midnight, stumbling to his car, and driving home on autopilot. He'd been stopped for DUI twice, and each time bluffed his way out via his credentials.

"I'm a Fed, baby!"

Home was an upscale condo on Hanover Street with trimmed juniper lining the entry. Rocky drove to the bottom level of the underground parking garage, parked his car at an angle preventing anyone from parking next to him, and took the elevator to his third-floor unit, with a porch overlooking the lake.

Rocky had to piss so bad, he almost whipped it out in the elevator. But the elevator had a camera. He hung on, fumbling with his keys at his door, finally banging open, slamming it shut behind him and racing to the half bath off the foyer. Some part of his limbic system warned him, *You can't go on like this, big guy. Someday you're gonna fuck up bad, and all the credentials in the world won't save you.*

He was home now. One more drink wouldn't kill him. He went into the kitchen, turned on the lights, and grabbed the bottle of Maker's Mark on the counter, pouring three fingers into a cut-glass decanter. Stumbling into the darkened living room, he collapsed into his two-thousand-dollar Ekornes recliner. Rocky sipped the drink, set it on the table next to the chair, and pushed back, elevating his legs. He sighed. He could fall asleep right there. Not for several minutes did he become aware of another presence in the room.

Holy shit. There was a man sitting on the sofa opposite him. Gradually, the man's contours came into view, dimly illuminated by the streetlamps circling the lake. Rocky automatically felt for his gun. He'd left it in the car. The man didn't bother to conceal himself, just sat there calmly, hands in his lap.

After what seemed like an eternity, the man said, "Hello, Rocky."

"Who the fuck are you?"

"I'm the guy whose little girl you killed."

Rocky sat there trying to digest the news. *Fuck fuck fuck.* The guy was a veteran, if Rocky remembered.

"Listen, I'm real sorry about that. It was a mistake. It was dark and we couldn't see who it was. It looked like she was going for a gun."

"I thought they trained you better than that."

"Listen, buddy, Mr. Knox, before you do anything stupid, remember that I'm a federal agent. I have the full might and support of the FBI behind me."

"That's not what I heard. I heard you were hanging on by your fingernails. That you were a loose cannon and a drunk. They want you gone."

"So what are you gonna do? Shoot me? I thought you were smarter than that. You think they won't figure that out?"

"Not at all. You're overcome with remorse. There's no coming back from this. Word of your character has spread at the speed of light throughout the entire federal system. They're drawing straws over who gets to give you the news. It's entirely understandable that after a life of failure, two failed marriages, three kids, none of whom will talk to you, you would consider ending it all."

"Hold on. Are you nuts? Nobody will believe that! People know me! They know I'm a sensible, responsible federal agent!"

The man chuckled. "Oh Rocky."

"How much? How much to make you go away?"

"How much have you got?"

"I'll get you a hundred thou in cash as soon as the banks open up."

"That's a lot of cash for a federal agent. You must be a wise investor. Or you're crooked."

"Listen. I know it won't bring your girl back, but you could do anything you like with that money! You could go on vacation! You could adopt a child!"

"Oh Rocky. I don't need your money. Didn't you hear about the settlement?"

"What settlement?"

"I guess you didn't get the memo. The feds settled. Of course, the money will never fill the hole you left in my life. Well, I've got to get going. I can't hang here jawing with you all night."

"Wait a minute!"

"You have a daughter. She's at Stanford. Microbiology."

Forsyth turned white. "What about her?"

"It would be a shame if something happened to her."

"You wouldn't dare."

"Look at me. I've lost everything that was important to me. My wife. My daughter. My career. Take a deep look. I am a person that has nothing to lose."

"Please, I'm begging you."

"I'll leave her alone if you'll write a note."

"You can't…"

"The hell I can't."

The man stood and approached holding a yellow legal pad and a ball-point pen. He was wearing nitrile gloves. "Take it."

Forsyth took the pad. His face went blank. "I know what you're thinking, Rocky. You're a trained FBI agent. This is your home turf. You are also six sheets to the wind. You're wondering if you can bound out of that lounger of yours and overpower me before I shoot you. I've run that math in my head already. You don't have a chance. The sooner you accept that, the better."

Hope and any thoughts of resistance drained from his face, he could feel his jowls sag. "What… do you want me to write?"

"My little girl hates me. And now I've taken someone else's little girl. I don't see a way forward. I apologize deeply for the pain I've caused others, including Maryanne. Maryanne, I love you."

For a long time Forsyth held the pad on his lap staring at nothing. The man reached behind him and produced a Glock with a suppressor.

"Found this in your closet. Write."

"May I have a glass of water?"

"No. Write. Write these words." Slowly, the man repeated the message while Forsyth wrote on the pad. When he finished, the man whipped the pad away and tossed it on the coffee table.

"Is this gun registered? Is this suppressor legal?"

Rocky leaned back and thrust out with his feet, but the man easily side-stepped, came around the back of the chair and put Rocky in a chokehold. He struggled and was strong, but Knox had the drop on him.

"Remember this? Every law enforcement officer knows it. But now they're not allowed to use it because it disproportionately impacts traditionally marginalized communities. Did I say that right?" Sarcasm tainted with rage spiked each word.

Rocky was aware that the man wore nitrile gloves. His vision tunneled with each passing moment and panic set in, but it came far too late. He blacked out.

* * *

Braxton placed Rocky's nine-millimeter Glock with suppressor in the FBI agent's right hand, carefully working his index finger into the trigger guard, held the pistol to Rocky's right temple and squeezed the trigger. *Choof.*

The smell of cordite filled the air. Braxton stepped back and shined a penlight. Rocky sat in the chair, eyes shut, mouth open, the left side of his head a bloody pit. Blood and brains seeped into Braxton's left elbow. He reached into his pocket, pulled out a pair of heavy canvas gloves and put them on over the nitriles. He picked up the grappling hook and rope he'd used to gain access to the third-floor deck. He went out on the deck softly closing the sliding door behind him. He lowered himself to the parking lot, hotfooted it to his car several blocks away, and drove to the cabin. Once there, he peeled off the gloves, his clothes, everything.

He set the discarded clothes in a fire circle he'd made in the backyard, doused it with lighter fluid, and watched it burn.

Chapter 42

Everybody's got Grandkids

Albert Gorelick sat on his front porch in his rocker reading Michener's *Centennial*. He had been reading it for six months. He hoped to finish it by the Fourth of July. The light was fading so Albert had turned on the porch light. He was almost to the point where the Denver Pacific started laying track when he heard a car coming down the street. It was a quiet residential neighborhood that rarely saw traffic, mostly on weekends when people held garage sales.

A lot more garage sales these days as folk sought to make an extra buck to keep up with the rising costs of everything. Gas was now six dollars a gallon, but at least the state legislature had finally overturned the rule that you couldn't pump your own gas. Albert picked up his notepad to write down the license plate. He'd started doing it a couple weeks before, right after the FBI raid. Some of these creeps were obvious. One in particular, a fourteen-year-old Toyota, its ass plastered with heavy metal bumper stickers. *Dokken, Poison, Megadeath*. To him it was more banging and booming than music. It wasn't a heavy metal neighborhood. It was an old hippy neighborhood. The car stopped across the street and revved its engine. Revved and revved, like it was trying to piss people off. Albert just wanted it to go.

He wasn't the excitable type who called the police whenever there was a disturbance. Even if he did, it would do no good. Everybody knew the cops were down to half-staff and were reluctant to engage in any law enforcement activity unless guns were in use. The mayor and the city council didn't have their back. It was a miracle any police remained on the force, mostly older guys hanging on to get their pensions.

Crosby, Stills, Nash & Young. Joni Mitchell. Those were bands. His mind went to Grateful Dead. Albert had seen Grateful Dead once, at the since defunct Bravo in downtown Portland. He'd been in college, studying urban planning. He had a girlfriend. Dolores was a beautiful Latina, but she was like emotional nitroglycerin. It was a miracle their relationship had lasted as long as it did. Six years later, he'd married Yvonne Palmer. They had two kids. The marriage lasted five years, but at least Yvonne didn't try to clean him out. Albert's son Warren had gone into insurance and was an account executive with BodyHealth in Los Angeles. Albert's daughter Janet was happily married to Austin Lake, an insurance executive with Home Life Car in Chicago. His kids really liked insurance.

They'd visited last Christmas with the four grandchildren and he was looking forward to their visit this year.

The Toyota burbled down the street. Albert knew the difference between a glass pack and a punctured muffler. This was a glass pack. Drivers who paid for more noise. The car lingered for a minute in front of Braxton's house across the street, chirped its front tires, and moved on. Albert wrote the license plate on his Mead Composition tablet, the same tablet he'd used in college.

Well, not exactly the same tablet. A new one. He kept all his old tablets in a box in the basement and was closing in on number forty-nine. The streetlights went on. Albert stretched and stood. Time to go inside and watch *The Last Kingdom* on Netflix. He'd be sad when it ended. But there was always something new to watch. When he was younger, he seldom went to bed before midnight. Now in his seventies, he looked forward to turning in by nine and enjoying a good night's sleep.

He went inside and turned on the living room light. Nothing happened. Had the bulb burned out? It was only a year old. He went into the kitchen and flipped the switch. Nothing happened. He had an adumbration of terror a split second before someone slammed a heavy canvas bag over his head and yanked him backwards off his feet. He landed on the linoleum floor and grunted, pain radiating through his back and neck. Albert reached for the bag, but before he could grab it, two sets of hands grabbed him by the wrist and dragged him backwards into the living room. Someone stomped him in the gut with a boot. He gasped for air.

"That's right, motherfucker," a voice whispered in his ear. "You mess with the bull, you get the horns."

On the other side a voice said, "You think we're stupid? You think we don't see you grabbing that Nazi's mail every day? And then he comes and visits you and you tell him who's been driving up and down the street. You're a good little Nazi too, aren't you?"

They flipped him over and used a zip tie to secure his wrists. They dragged him upright and threw him on the sofa. Fingers fumbled at his neck and the bag came off. It was still dark in the room and he couldn't make them out, but he could tell they were relatively young from their strength and their voices.

"Okay. Your buddy across the street. Knox. Where's he hiding?"

"I don't know. He doesn't tell me where he goes."

The talkative one kicked him savagely in the ribs. Albert almost blacked out.

"You think we're stupid? We know you're in cahoots with him. Tell us where he's at or we'll go after your daughter in Chicago. That's right, pig. We know where she lives. And guess what? There's a shitload of ANTIFA in Chicago."

"I'm just an old man. Is this how you build a new society? By attacking the weak and elderly?"

"We're not attacking anyone. We're fighting back. It was you and your generation that ruined it for everyone else with your racism and sexism and ableism—"

"Do you hear yourselves?" Albert barked.

One of them backhanded him across the mouth, drawing blood.

"We're the future, motherfucker. A future for everyone, not just white supremacists."

"What white supremacists?"

"Now who can't hear themselves? Who do you think? You and your people who have stood with your boot on the neck of the black man, the red man, women, the transgendered—"

"I've not oppressed anyone."

"Denial makes you the worst part of the oppressor class."

"You know, if you boys could just see individuals instead of tribes—"

Whack. The back of a hand.

"Pretty brave, beating up an old man with his hands tied," Albert spat.

"You think you can take me? How 'bout I untie your hands and you try?"

Albert laughed. "Go ahead."

"Ajax, don't be stupid."

"Shut the fuck up, man! You just said my name!"

"So what? Who's he gonna tell?"

"That's not why we came. Tell us where Knox is or we go after your granddaughter. Your boy's got two kids. Pauline and Kerry. Pauline's at UCLA and Kerry's in Berkeley, right?"

Albert felt his stomach knot. This was no longer about him; it was about his family. His jaw set as he stared in silence.

"Untie his hands."

"Don't be stupid."

"What? You don't think I can take this geezer."

"What are we gonna do if he beats you?"

"Ha! Listen to yourself. You've seen me in action. Don't be a fucking pussy. Untie his hands."

"Stand up."

Albert stood. In the ambient light through the window, he saw that they were dressed like the cowards they were. The traditional ANTIFA all-black with only the eyes showing. As soon as the dude sliced his wrists, Albert kicked the one called Ajax in the groin as hard as he could. Ajax howled and fell to the ground, shrimping. The other one threw his arm around Albert's neck and applied a choke hold. He knew what he was doing. In thirty seconds Albert passed out from lack of oxygen. When he awoke, his wrists were bound again and he lay on his belly on the floor.

Ajax got to his feet and kicked Albert in the head. The pain was excruciating. He saw stars. Ajax stomped him in the small of his back. Albert twisted, trying to get away from the onslaught but there was nowhere to go.

"One more chance. Tell us where Knox is holed up or your daughter, her husband, and the brats are dead. You think I'm kidding? You know how many people I've killed?"

Defeated, aching from every joint, Albert said, "He's got a cabin in the mountains. I don't know where. He didn't tell me."

"You got to do better than that."

"That's all I know! I swear! Think! Do you think he'd trust me with that knowledge? We barely know each other!"

"Quit jerking off, man," the non-Ajax said. "Let's do it. Ransack the place, and get the fuck out of here."

"Yeah. Okay. Hang on. Let me find a plastic bag in the kitchen."

Ajax used a penlight to rummage around in the drawers, returning with a four-gallon black plastic bag. He pulled it down over Albert's head and tied it tightly around his neck with a piece of rope. The last thing Albert heard was, "*Sic semper tyrannus*." He was surprised they knew any Latin.

Chapter 43

Robot Dog

Braxton and Ronin went up the mountain. The booby traps were undisturbed. The hairs Braxton left on the doors were there. He unlocked the door and they went inside. He thought about adding a booby trap for whoever broke in, but the only thing that came to mind was a shotgun mounted on a chair to blow the intruder's head off.

They went inside and Braxton came back with two ice-cold beers. Monsieur came over to Ronin, sniffed him, then went to the fireplace and curled up to sleep.

"You think I should rig a shotgun aimed at the front door for break-ins?"

"Nah. You've done plenty. They don't know about this place, do they?"

"I don't see how. It belonged to my grandfather. He left it to my dad, but it's not listed on any of his assets. They don't have the patience to sort through his shit. They have the attention span of fruit flies."

"Don't underestimate them. Some of their people are obviously tech savvy. They'll comb through your history to find anything they can to hang around your neck. They went after me, rooting through everything in my past and found I got my girlfriend pregnant."

"What happened?"

Ronin looked away. "It was a long time ago. I was a different person then. I offered to pay for an abortion."

"Did she get one?"

"No. She had the baby and put it up for adoption. That was the end of our relationship."

"Sorry to hear it."

"Don't be. We're not always our best selves."

"Would you do it again?"

"No. I've come to realize that when a woman becomes pregnant, it's really up to her how she wants to proceed. I'm against abortion, but it's not a hill I'd die on. And I don't think it's the federal government's business. If we're going to win that battle, it has to be woman by woman, not by government decree."

"That must have hurt."

"Oh hell yeah. Jackals howling for me to kill myself. I developed a program to scrub my name from the net. I'm thinking of marketing it, but I don't want to draw attention to myself."

"You could market it behind some kind of false front, like an offshore bank does."

"Yeah, it's just a matter of figuring it out. I've been too busy lately to do it."

"What do you do, besides help me?"

"Private security consulting. That and working for my benefactor."

"Could you scrub my name from the internet?"

"I could. There's also a company called Incogni that does it. There are several. However, since you have attracted the scrutiny of the mob, it will raise suspicions. It's like Sherlock Holmes—'The Adventure of Silver Blaze.' That's the one about the dog that doesn't bark. That's how Holmes found the killer. 'The Curious Incident of the Dog in the Night-Time.' When the killer murdered the jockey and took the horse, the dog didn't bark. So Holmes knew it was someone the dog knew."

"Hmmm."

"Up to you."

"Yeah, I think that's something I'd like to do. What do you charge?"

"Don't worry about it. Happy to do it. We're brothers-in-arms. I just need the time. I'm thinking of moving some equipment up here if that's all right with you."

"Sure. But I'm worried they'll find me."

"That's a legitimate concern, especially now as online detective agencies are incorporating artificial intelligence into their systems.

There's a company called Babel Street that's already using it. They specialize in threat intelligence and risk mitigation. In fact, it might not be a bad idea to contact them. They could inform us of any internet activity regarding your whereabouts. Who knows you're here?"

"No one, so far. This cabin belonged to my grandfather, Hayward Knox. He left it to my father, who's the deed owner."

"That's a problem. Babel Street could find that."

"What if we use Incogni to stop Babel Street?

Ronin smiled. "Now you're thinking. But I'd rather do it myself. What's your father's name and where does he live?"

"Grayson. McKenzie Place in Five Oaks."

Ronin whipped out a notepad and wrote it down.

"That's funny," Braxton said.

"What is?"

"You writing things down on a notepad."

"You can't wipe a notepad. Also, when you write something, it sticks in your brain longer."

"I should carry a notepad."

"Everybody should carry a notepad."

"How soon before you can wipe my grandfather from the internets?"

"I don't know. I don't feel comfortable using your equipment. I have to use my own. I'll get on it tomorrow. In the meantime, we have to expect that they're going to come after us here."

"They're coming after me, Ro. You've done enough. I can't ask you to risk your life too."

"Oh trust me. They're already coming after me. They probably know my name."

"What's your first name?"

"Seymour. Please call me Ro or Ronin."

"I see why you prefer the latter."

Ro chuckled. "I asked my parents, when they were alive, why they named me Seymour. They said they were inspired by *Mad* magazine."

Cans rattled in the backyard. Braxton and Ronin looked at one another. Braxton grabbed the Mossberg from its rack over the fireplace.

"You need a gun safe," Ronin said.

"You're right," Braxton said, softly going to the back door and peering out through the window. His posture went from tense to relaxed. "It's just a bear."

"The cameras I put in are working. You know, I can rig some external strobes. Super high intensity stuff. Hit a switch and the whole area lights up."

"That would overwhelm any night vision gear they might use."

"Yeah. These people are bargain basement warriors. They shop Temu and Wish for their gear. It's cheap Chinese shit. It looks good, but in reality, you get what you pay for."

"That's not a bad idea."

"I have a source locally. I can pick them up and do an install tomorrow."

"Save the receipts. Money is not a problem."

"What happened?"

"The Justice Department settled. Twelve million dollars."

Ronin whistled. "If I had that kind of money, I'd move to a red state and buy a house with a swimming pool."

"I don't anticipate that happening. I'm not the fleeing type. Besides, my dad is here and thanks to the FBI, we're all the family we have left."

"Man, I think you're an outstanding human being. I hate these motherfuckers as much as you do but I don't have that kind of money. Aren't you just tempted to say fuck it, take the money and run?"

"No. It's not just for myself. It's for every human being they've blacklisted, shamed, robbed of their livelihood, or driven to suicide. I took an oath. I do solemnly swear that I will support and defend the Constitution of the United States against all enemies, foreign and domestic."

"You always have your dog."

"Monsieur?" He glanced over at the sleeping bulldog. "I worry about him. ANTIFA would poison him as soon as they saw him. He's smart, but he's used to nice people. These people are not nice."

"You're right. Wait a minute. What about a robot dog?"

"Say what?"

Ronin pulled out his pad and poked. He turned the screen around. *Boston Dynamics' Spot Robot Dog Now Available for $74,500.*

"You can program them to alert you when there's an intruder."

"It's bright yellow."

"They come in whatever color you want, including camo."

"Do you know how I can buy one of these without it being traced back to me?"

"Let me look into that."

"Did you get anything from the recording devices in the warehouse where those asshats had their pow-wow?"

"Not much. The acoustics sucked in there. They're looking for you, that much I got. They mentioned your dad and that reporter. One of them, I presume it was Schumer, said he had an idea to get this address."

"Any specifics?"

"No."

Braxton's burner phone buzzed. He didn't recognize the number. "Yes?"

"Braxton, this is Faye Weldon. You gave me this number."

"I remember. What's up, Faye?"

"Someone hacked my bank account. The bank is working it, but it made me more, shall I say, situationally aware. Well, the same car keeps going by my place. The drivers are wearing black complete with face coverings."

"Hang on a minute, Faye."

Covering the phone, Braxton turned to Ronin. "It's Faye Weldon. They're closing in on her."

Ronin grinned. "Let's roll."

Chapter 44

Turning Point

Faye's place was a rented Victorian. Ronin handled the driving as they cruised by. A hybrid SUV sat in the driveway. It seemed out of place. Braxton used his thermal vision gear to see what he could see. Through the front window of the darkened house, he spied two figures in the front room. They looked male. No sign of Weldon.

Ronin rounded the corner and parked. "Did you spot anything?"

"It looked like two men."

"You think that's them?"

"Who else would be wandering around her place in the dark?" Braxton tightened his tactical vest. "If they're still there, she probably isn't dead yet."

"You have a plan?"

Braxton drew a deep breath. "In a perfect world, we'd go in together. The reality is, we haven't worked in close quarters before and I'm a little rusty. If you get their attention at the front door, I'll come in through the back through a basement window."

"Any ideas on getting their attention?"

"You can do it. You're a pretty creative guy."

"You sure you can handle them?"

It was a question he didn't want to answer, so he didn't. "Take a gun. When I call clear, come in. If they try to come out, make sure they don't get away." He adjusted his tactical helmet and opened the car door. "Be loud."

"Be accurate," Ronin replied.

Braxton gently closed the door behind him. He opened the gate to Weldon's neighbor's yard, using his thermal gear to see if there were any dogs. He climbed the short fence into Faye's backyard. It was sparse, a small single-car garage, probably built for a buggy or a Model T. Keeping low and moving carefully, he went up the four steps to the back door.

Weldon had it locked, but it was an old door and frame. Pulling out his knife, he worked slow and steady, prying the door away from the frame. The old wood on the frame gave way. He opened the door.

Stepping in, he winced as the floor groaned. Muffled voices echoed from the front. Braxton had brought his AR.

The doorbell rang, followed by loud banging on the front door. "DoorDash!" came Ronin's voice. "Your delivery is here!"

"What the fuck?" one of the voices said as Braxton made his way towards the front.

"What do we do?" a whispered voice asked. It was hard to tell if it was male or female.

Braxton crept the hallway as Ronin leaned on the doorbell.

"Just leave it outside!" a voice called out.

"What about a tip?" Ronin yelled.

A woman whimpered. Not one of fear, but anger.

That's three, counting Weldon.

"I gotta have you sign for this!" Ronin said.

"Just leave it."

"No tip?" Ronin cried. "That's bullshit!" His voice covered any creaking and groaning the old house made as Braxton moved down the hallway. He paused and switched to night vision. He reached the parlor, now a living room. A futon lay against the wall. Braxton saw two figures facing the front door. Weldon lay on the floor, hands behind her back, leaning against an upholstered chair.

Braxton planted the beam in the back of the person nearest the door. The man held a pistol in his right hand. Braxton squeezed the trigger.

Even with the suppressor, the crack was loud. He fired twice, so fast the noises blurred together. The man tumbled forward, hitting the front door face-first.

The second person wheeled with a long gun in her hands, searching for the source of the shot. The person fired wildly, hitting the wall three feet away. Momentarily blinded, Braxton shifted to the right, brought the laser on the person and fired as they hunched, scanning the darkness. The second intruder fell with a dull thud, wailing in agony.

Braxton shut off his night vision and hit the light switch. The man lay in a growing pool of gore on the hardwood floor. A woman, wearing ANTIFA black, held her right knee.

"Clear!" he barked. Ronin opened the door, hitting the body on the floor, and shoved. Braxton stepped over and grabbed the woman's AR-15. Her short cropped light blue hair had fooled him when he had driven by, mistaking her for a male.

"Check her for weapons and a phone." He turned to Faye. Duct tape around her face and the back of her head. Hands bound with nylon rope. Braxton pulled a knife and cut. It took some effort to get the tape off. He carefully released her mouth, leaving a swatch of tape on her hair.

"You okay?"

"You didn't call the police?"

"Nope."

"She's clean," Ronin said as the female moaned.

"My fucking knee! You shot my knee!"

"Gosh! We're sorry." Sarcasm dripped from his words.

"Call an ambulance. I'm in real pain here." Blood oozed between her fingers. Bits of fabric from the exit wound poked out.

"I bet," Braxton said, bending over. The shot had gone in the back of the knee and out the front without hitting a major blood vessel.

Faye got to her feet. "They came in here and tied me up. They said they were going to take me somewhere and finish me off." She rubbed her wrists where the rope had left a mark. She was mad as hell.

"Your friend there, he's a goner. You, you're a candidate for a knee replacement, if you are fortunate enough to survive."

"Please, call 9-1-1," she moaned.

Braxton squatted. "You came here to kill my friend."

"It hurts…"

"I need some information."

"I don't know anything!" Tears streamed down her cheeks. She had a nose ring now clogged with snot as she withered in agony.

"In my experience, sometimes people don't know what they know."

"What do you want to know?"

Braxton looked at Ronin, then back to the female on the floor. "See, she can be cooperative."

"Agony will do that," Ronin said.

"What's your name?"

"Loudon," she gasped. "Loudon Kelly."

"Your parents didn't like girl names?"

"I chose it. My pronouns are they/them."

Braxton laughed. "Alright, *Loudon*. What does Ajax have planned?"

"What do you mean?"

"Don't play stupid with me. You were at the meeting in the warehouse. What's he up to?"

"He said he had a way to find out where you were. He's sending a team to deal with your father. Those were his words, not mine. That's all I know, I swear it!"

"When is he going after my father?"

"Tomorrow night. He wanted us to take care of this reporter first." She looked fearfully at Weldon whose temper had not ebbed.

"How many are going after my father?"

"Two. Tommy-Thunderburst and Backblast. They're gonna try to catch him asleep."

Braxton gestured toward the dead body. "Your partner. Who was he?"

"Lucas Cox," she cried. "Please, mister, you have to call for help."

Ramrod.

Braxton said nothing. Ramrod was on his list, one of the people in the car that had murdered Suzanna. He walked across the wooden floor to Ramrod's body. Bending down, he rolled him over to look at his face.

A kid, in his late twenties, a single silver earring in his left ear. His hazel eyes were open and his mouth agape, as if he were preparing to scream. No sign of an exit wound.

Ramrod didn't suffer, which didn't seem fair. He died from two shots to the back. Braxton looked at Loudon. Fear and pain danced on her face.

"That leaves you," he said quietly.

"Just call an ambulance. I won't say anything, I swear it."

"Whatever lie serves the vicious child at that moment. Isn't that your creed? Your word means nothing."

She cried harder. Braxton aimed his gun at her. Faye pushed it down. "You can't just kill her."

"They were just a few minutes away from tossing you in the trunk of their car and driving you up the mountain to kill you. They never would have found your body. I know—they tried to do it with me."

Faye was stunned. "They did?"

"Yes. And they were going to do the same with you, take you into the woods and leave your body to rot."

The words hit her hard. Weldon was a good person; she was trying to stay in that space. His story eroded her resistance. "She's just a kid."

"Physically, yes. Emotionally, she's old enough to volunteer to kill you. She was a willing participant to kidnapping and murder— yours. Don't let the tears fool you. Those come from her pain, not from remorse."

"I won't ever do anything like this again—I swear!" Loudon said.

"Faye, if she lives, you will be dragged into court for years. Once she's wiped away her tears, she will create a story about the three of us conspiring to ambush them. Her kind loves to be the victim, and that makes you her oppressor. Her lawyers will strip away all of the black tactical gear and show her as an innocent girl of whom we took advantage. The left will paint you as the villain. Another crazed alt-right nutjob. There will be costly civil lawsuits because that's what Americans do, they sue. Your life will be hell as they parade you into court for weeks on end, and her friends… they will come at you for vengeance. You know what they did to my wife? Want them to do that to the people you love? She'll walk, but we'll all go to jail. If we're lucky. The legal system favors criminals, not victims."

"What are we then?" she asked.

"We are the only justice that matters."

Faye stared at him in silence. She closed her eyes and nodded.

She understands now. As a member of the press, she was not part of the story. Now she is.

Braxton turned and fired the kill shot.

Chapter 45

The Cleanup Crew

Braxton and Ronin helped Faye clean up. The wall had a bullet hole from Loudon's gun that was going to take some patching. Ronin checked the bodies and took their cell phones and a Baofeng radio off Loudon.

"What are you thinking, Ro?"

"The cell phones ping off cell towers. If they're reported missing, it could lead them here. We'll toss 'em someplace so no one traces them back to Ms. Weldon."

"And the radio?"

Ronin held it up. "People like to say that everything from China sucks. Not these. Baofeng makes good stuff. This points to a level of know-how when it comes to communications."

"Anything we can use to our advantage?"

"Oh, yeah. Now we know what channel they use. We can monitor their messages. We can also use this channel against them, jam it up, cripple their ability to coordinate."

Faye came back carrying four rolls of paper towels. "Won't they just switch to another channel?"

"They're using good gear, but that doesn't mean they're smart. Yes, they can switch to a backup channel, assuming that they have one. They're arrogant. We can use that against them."

Cutting the large throw rug in the living room, they rolled the bodies up. Ronin took the keys from Cox's corpse. They loaded their bodies in the vehicle.

Faye's hands trembled as they worked. For a long time, she didn't speak. Braxton understood. She was a writer, a reporter, a person who told stories. Now she was in the story, violently thrust there. He felt guilty. Weldon hadn't asked for any of this. The two ANTIFA thugs had planned on killing her, and almost got away with it.

They mopped the floor with bleach and wiped down the walls. Disinfectants stung their nostrils and burned their hands.

Faye drew a deep breath. "Now what?"

"I think you need to stay somewhere else. They know where you live, and it won't take them long to figure out that Cox and Kelly didn't come back."

"Should I get a hotel room? I can't put any of my friends in this kind of danger by staying with them."

"You can stay with me."

"Aren't they going to come after you?"

"Yes. But if you're there, we can protect you."

"What about the bodies?"

"We'll drive them and their car up in the forest, someplace isolated, and set the car on fire." Memories of the vehicle he'd burned with the two goons came flooding back. He could smell it.

"I need a few minutes to pack." Faye left the room.

"What about your dad?" Ronin asked, as he stared at the spot where the dead bodies had been on the floor.

"I'll talk to him first thing in the morning and let him know trouble is on the way. Having Faye at the cabin is the best way to keep her safe."

"It also puts her at risk."

"Well, golly gee."

Weldon carried a computer bag and a gym bag. The ANTIFA car was easy to spot. A hybrid Hyundai Kona. Street trash loved Hyundais because they were easy to steal. It had bumper stickers.

Be Kind
Stop Pretending Your Racism Is Patriotism
Destroy The Patriarchy, Not The Planet

Ronin followed Braxton and Faye. They passed the spot where Braxton's abductors remained undiscovered. As they drove, Ronin tossed the cell phones out, far apart. He tossed one at a bus stop. The forest was even darker in the early morning hours. Braxton led the way to an obscure logging trail. Pulling off, he motioned for Ronin to follow.

The muddy track twisted and turned. The car got stuck. Braxton and Faye got out and pushed. Ronin finally pulled the car to the side a quarter mile from the highway. He got out. "This is good."

"It should burn pretty hot when the batteries ignite," Braxton said. "Those bodies will turn to charcoal."

"To destroy human bones, you need just over one thousand four hundred degrees," Faye said.

Braxton and Ronin looked at her with raised eyebrows.

She shrugged. "I'm a writer. I know weird shit."

Braxton stuffed a rag soaked in lighter fluid into the gas tank and lit it with a Zippo. The rag flared. For a few minutes, it looked as if it was going to go out.

Whoomp!

The sudden heat forced them back as fire burned into the interior of the vehicle. The batteries ignited, intensifying the inferno. Within minutes, the tires were fully engulfed, adding black smoke to the funeral pyre.

They got in Braxton's car.

"Well, that was horrible," Faye said as they bumped and wallowed back to the highway.

"It was the right thing to do," Braxton assured her.

"It doesn't feel that way."

"It will," Ronin said from the back seat.

"That's what worries me," she said.

They headed back down the mountain to get some breakfast. Braxton pulled into a McDonald's just after five in the morning and they ordered meals to go. They ate silently in the parking lot. His body felt tired, but Braxton's mind was racing.

They are going to go after Dad. Somehow they know where I am. Once they go after him, they will come for us.

Ninety minutes later, he pulled up at the cabin and ushered Faye and Ronin in. Monsieur ran up to Weldon jumping up and down. She stooped to pet him and he licked her hand. Faye looked around, her eyes settling on the table that held the security camera monitors. "That's a lot of coverage."

"We're at war," Braxton said.

She eyed the guns on the dining table. "It looks it."

Knox nodded "You heard Loudon. They're bringing the war here."

"Still? They have to know those two scumbags are toast. Are they stupid?"

Braxton shrugged. "Their leader, Ajax, is probably in the dark. His people went out and he never heard back from them. He doesn't know if you're alive or dead and we need to keep it that way. He'll send someone by your house and they'll look in the windows and see nothing. He might think Loudon and Cox are simply taking their time disposing of your body. Without confirmation, he won't know for sure."

"You really think these things through, don't you?"

"This is a war. None of us asked for it, nor did we deserve it. Many people out there are targets of woke ideology. They don't fight back because it never dawns on them that this is war until they've already lost."

He walked over to the letters Albert had saved for him. "After my story was made public, I've been swamped with letters. Some of it is hate mail. I have a stack I call 'The Hitler Pile.' I'm 'literally Hitler.' But the vast majority of the letters are people offering support, or have been victims themselves. Some have lost their businesses; others have lost friends and family."

Faye eyed the stacks of mail. "You mind if I read some of these?"

Braxton yawned. "Go ahead."

Ronin stretched and yawned. "I need to run back to my place to grab some stuff, maybe get a few hours' sleep."

"I'm going to let my dad know what's heading his way," Braxton said. "Then I need to crash."

"Is there anything I can do?" Faye asked.

"Get some rest. It's been a hell of a night."

"You can say that again."

"Take the loft. I'll crash on the sofa. The next few days are going to be crazy."

Faye grabbed a pile of letters and went up the ladder. Braxton called his father. When he finished, he lay on the couch and slid into a deep sleep.

Chapter 46

Old Age and Experience Trumps Youth and Ignorance

Braxton arrived at McKenzie Place. Ruck sack over his shoulder, he entered the building. Andrew, the retired cop who handled security, smiled and waved.

"Mr. Knox. How you doin'?"

"Doing good, Andrew."

Weaving his way through the facility, Braxton ignored the smell of urine and disinfectant. For the better part of a year, he hadn't been allowed to visit his father due to COVID. They'd both ignored the mandate. As Grayson put it, "It's just a virus with sprinkles." His father never got COVID and didn't suffer like so many in the facility who were cut off from their loved ones. As memories oozed forward, Braxton wondered if it was worth it. *Did we do more damage to people in the name of protecting them?*

He rapped on Grayson's door.

Grayson opened the door. "Good to see you, boy," he said, patting him on the shoulder.

"You sure you don't want to come out to the cabin and wait this out with us?"

His father shook his head. "You don't win fights by running away. You think they're still coming?"

"No doubt about it. They killed my neighbor across the street to find out where I am. Our intel tells us you're on their list."

"Why won't they just go to the cabin?"

"They don't know where it is."

"Why waste time with me?"

"They went after a reporter friend and almost killed her. They murdered my neighbor across the street. You're on their list. They want to get me off my game. Killing you will do that. They think they can pick off my friends and family and isolate me."

"They killed Albert? Damn! Why would they go after him?"

"They thought he knew where the cabin is. He died because he was my friend."

"That isn't your fault, Brax. The kind of vermin that would kill an innocent old man don't need a motive."

"They're coming after another old man tonight. You."

"And these guys... they killed Suzanna and Angela?" Grayson struggled with the words.

"Yes."

"Then taking them alive is optional. I have some boys coming over to help."

"Dad, you think that's a good idea? I mean your old cop buddies, some of them are, well, past their prime."

Grayson grinned. "Never underestimate experience. We're a little rusty, but we all have guns and good eyesight. These punk-ass kids won't know what hit them."

"Okay. Shoot-out at the retirement home. Hope none of your neighbors get caught in the crossfire."

"We'll take pains that they don't."

Braxton went into the bedroom, took some pillows from the closet, put them between the sheets, and pulled the comforter up to create the illusion of a sleeping body.

Grayson watched. "Aha."

"These ANTIFA asshats are cowards. They'll find a way in. There's no way Andrew can prevent that. They'll try to shoot you in your sleep."

"Wouldn't it be easier to tighten protocols and not admit anyone that Andrew doesn't know?"

"That won't kill them. They'll just circle around and try something else."

Grayson nodded. "Mmhmm." He gestured to the closet with venetian slats covering the wall opposite the bed. "We set up in there and we'll have a bird's-eye view. One in the living room's even bigger."

Knock at the door. Braxton pulled his Glock. His father grabbed his Smith & Wesson from the nightstand drawer.

Braxton put a finger to his mouth and whispered, "We're not in position." He doused the lights. "Say something," he whispered, aiming at the door.

"Who's there?"

A muffled older voice responded. "Barney and the boys."

Grayson let them in and locked the door. There were three of them. Braxton had met Barney and David before. They looked ancient. They were the same age as his father. Barney was short and had a thick roll around his waist. David was slender to the point of frail. He pulled out a gun that seemed too large for his skeletal hands, a .44 Remington Magnum. *If he fires that thing, it might break his bones.* They'd been FBI agents when his father had served.

They hugged, slapping each other on the back. Grayson put a hand on Braxton's shoulder. "You remember my boy, Braxton. Braxton, this is Wally. You know these other guys."

"Wally was with the sheriff's department up in Seattle." The man smiled through his Coke-bottle glasses and three chins.

"Thanks for coming," Braxton said.

"Oh hell yeah," Barney said. "You're famous."

"Can't believe the shit you've had to go through," David said.

Grayson went into the kitchen. "You boys want coffee?"

"Yeah sure," David said.

Grayson filled five mugs from his brewer, put milk and sugar on the counter. They went into the living room and sat. "I suppose you're wondering why I've called you here."

"No," David said. "We know these commie fucks have declared war on Braxton, and like all good commie fucks, now they want to kill everyone he knows."

Grayson pointed. "You got it. They killed my boy's neighbor. They tried to kill him. That didn't work out so well."

"What happened?" Wally said.

David held his hand up. "We don't want to hear it. Keep it to yourself."

"Thing is," Braxton said, "they've demonstrated that nothing will stop them. They certainly don't fear the police. We think they're gonna come here next. Tonight. So here's the plan, boys…"

Braxton spent half an hour explaining the background and the plan. Their enthusiasm surprised him. This was probably the most exciting thing they'd been involved with in years.

"So we're staking out the bedroom?" Barney confirmed.

Braxton pointed to the louver closet in the living room. "The bedroom and the living room."

Barney grinned showing his yellowed teeth. "I hope your intelligence is right. I'm giving up *American Idol* for this. Marge is pissed."

Braxton laid out the tactical gear he'd brought in his ruck.

"You really think you need all of that?" David asked.

"They almost killed me once. I don't take chances."

David looked at Grayson. "These kids… all this tech and armor. We didn't have that shit when we were coming up, and we kicked some serious ass." The men all beamed.

"I only wear it because the bad guys do. Why give them the upper hand? Let's split up. Dad, you and David go in the bathroom. Wally, Barney, and I will take the living room closet. That way, if we both open up at once, we won't hit each other and we'll catch them in a crossfire."

"Back in the day, the only armor we had was our badges and a good suit," Barney said.

Grayson and David went into the bedroom. With the lights off, including a night-light, the only illumination was dim light from the window. The sky was overcast. Someone coming in from the brightly lit hall wouldn't be able to see into the bedroom.

Braxton waited while Wally and Barney got in the closet. He locked the door and shut off the lights. His father had a small night-light in the living room, giving them just enough visibility. They stood in the closet, shoulder to shoulder.

Braxton caught a whiff of Bengay and stale body odor. They were quiet for almost an hour.

"You got a timetable on these guys?" Wally said.

"No," Braxton whispered. "We just know they're coming tonight."

A half hour passed as they stood in the closet.

"I got to pee," Wally said.

"Seriously?" Barney said. "Come on, man."

"Wait," Wally said, then sighed. "I took care of it. Never mind."

The pungent scent of urine filled the closet.

Braxton rolled his eyes. "Wally, you don't need to announce your bodily functions. We can tell."

"We have means," Barney added.

Someone knocked lightly at the door.

"Alright," Braxton whispered as the men in the closet tensed. "Remember the plan. We want them in the bedroom and nobody moves until I give the word."

"This is great," whispered Wally.

God help us.

As he finished that thought, Braxton heard someone prying the doorframe.

Chapter 47

Gunfight at the McKenzie Place Corral

Braxton, Wally, and Barney watched through the louvers as the front door swung inward. Two figures slinked in, silhouetted by the hallway lights. They carried clubs.

The temptation to throw open the closet door and shoot was strong, but he stuck with his plan. They looked male, but he had already made that mistake with Loudon. They went to the bedroom. The night-light cast long shadows. The pair moved to either side of the bed and raised their clubs. One whispered, "Now!" The clubs rained down on pillows. Their blows fell fast and furious. Braxton wondered that they didn't stop, when they were obviously not striking flesh.

The bedroom lights went on, momentarily blinding the intruders.

"Freeze," Grayson said.

"Let's go," Braxton said. He, Barney, and Wally formed a semicircle facing the bedroom door.

The intruders were male, mid-twenties, decked out in black T-shirts and jeans. Their clubs were wooden baseball bats. They looked at the men holding guns with shock. Braxton felt a warm glow of satisfaction.

"Drop the weapons," Grayson said from the bedroom closet. "Hands on your heads."

One man threw his bat on the bed and put his hands on his head. He saw the pillows that he had been trying to beat to death. To add insult to injury, they were My Pillows. His partner held the bat, eyes darting to the door.

The youth bolted. David fired his revolver. Braxton's left ear popped. The hoodlum skidded onto the floor, alive, trying to crawl.

Braxton stepped forward. The shot had caught him in the ankle, leaving the foot nearly severed. Blood poured freely covering the thug's expensive Nike.

Acrid powder hung in the air as the old man looked surprised that he had fired. "I guess that trigger was more sensitive than I remember."

"Do we have to worry about anyone showing up?" Braxton asked as his ear popped.

"Are you kidding?" his father replied. "Most of these folks are deaf as a doorknob. I doubt we woke up anyone. Security here is a joke."

Grayson used one of his zip ties to secure the other thug's hands behind his back. The wounded youth continued to crawl towards the door. Braxton stood in front of him, aiming his Glock at the man's face. "You're not going to get there."

"My foot..." he wailed.

Braxton squatted and looked as blood oozed on the vinyl laminate floor. The shot had turned his ankle into human hamburger. "That foot's a goner."

Color drained from his face. "You need to call for help. I've got to get to a hospital."

"That depends."

"What do you mean?"

"What's Ajax planning next?"

The look of terror rippling across his face revealed he knew exactly what Braxton was talking about. "Ajax will kill me."

"Ajax is the least of your problems. I'm no combat medic, but based on the blood you've lost, you need help in minutes or you'll slip into shock."

"Please—you've got to help me."

"You came here to beat my father to death. Don't tell me what I've got to do. What has Ajax planned?"

"Okay," the punk said through clenched teeth. "He's coming with the rest of the chapter tomorrow."

"How many?"

"All of them. Like sixteen, maybe more. They're going to burn the place to the ground. Make an example of you."

"What time?"

"Midnight. I swear, that's all I know."

"I believe you."

Grayson stood next to Braxton. "How do you want to do this?"

Braxton pointed to the standing thug. "How were you going to tell Ajax that you'd succeeded?"

"We were supposed to text 'Geronimo' to him."

"Shut up!" His accomplice snapped from the floor. Wally clipped him in the head with the butt of his pistol.

Braxton held out his hand. "Phone and passcode."

The man fumbled with his pants pocket. "It's 420."

"Of course it is."

Braxton entered the code, found Ajax in the message list, and sent the text. `Geronimo—with some complications.` Braxton stuffed the phone in his pocket. "Get his buddy's phone out and smash it."

"The pain—" the youth groaned.

"Yeah, I bet." Braxton turned to Grayson. "I can't be here when the police show up. Too many questions and this *does* look like an ambush."

"The boys can handle this," Grayson assured him.

"What about David?" Braxton glanced over at the man who had fired the shot.

"Don't worry about him. Nobody is going to arrest us tonight. We're all former cops. David's got short-term memory issues. After he gets a good night's sleep, he won't remember any of this."

"Don't worry, kid," Barney said. "We'll give the cops statements. We were here having a party and these guys busted in with bats. They broke into the wrong room. They'll give us coffee and we'll swap stories."

"Ajax has to think you're dead," Braxton said. "I want him to think he's succeeded, that he's got me off-balance."

I can call Faye. She has connections. If she can leak the story that Dad's dead, it will take a day or so before the police get everything sorted and the truth comes out.

"I should go with them." Grayson nodded to his friends.

"Dad, I need you to come to the cabin."

A crease appeared on Grayson's forehead. "You have *never* asked me for help."

"That's because you taught me to solve my problems on my own. This is different. It doesn't take a mathematician to see the odds are against us. Having you would help level the playing field."

"Some people are too proud to ask for help."

"There's a first time for everything, Dad."

"Of course I'll come, son." He went to the closet, rooted around, and came back with a shotgun and a box of shells.

"Get me help," the thug on the floor groaned. "I'm getting lightheaded."

And pale. Braxton preferred to kill both assailants. Being in a room full of former police officers forced a level of mercy to which he was unaccustomed. Braxton turned to Barney. "Give us a few minutes to get out of here, then call for help. Take your time with the sheriff's department when they get here."

Barney turned to the youth near the bed holding his bleeding head gash. "Those two, they were never here, you got that?"

"Yeah, yeah, yeah," he muttered.

"You don't sound like it. How about we blow off one of your feet like your friend?" Barney said, jabbing his gun into the chest of the youth.

"Alright!" he snapped, clearly afraid of facing the same agony as his friend. "They were never here."

"Thank you. All of you," Braxton said.

"Are you kidding?" Wally replied, grinning broadly. "This was the most fun that I've had in years!"

"You two take care," Barney said. "We'll turn Wimpy and Limpy over to the authorities."

David was the only one who looked sad. "I'm sorry I fired like that."

Grayson beamed. "Don't worry about it, Dave. The kid will probably survive, which is more than he would've done if I'd fired." He took a shirt off a hanger and wrapped the shotgun up so as to avoid drawing attention.

The two of them, father and son, stepped over the wounded man and out into the hall. Braxton didn't remember the last time they did something together.

I wish I didn't have to draw him into all of this, but thank God he's here with me.

Chapter 48

Desperate Measures

Joel Schumer watched the morning news on KGW. There was a segment about a shooting at an assisted care facility in Five Oaks the night before. The early morning footage showed someone being taken out by ambulance. The reporter said that a source claimed the victim was Grayson Knox, and that someone was in custody. Made sense. They'd texted there were complications. After that, radio silence.

Schumer grinned.

He hadn't been able to reach Scroggy or Viper, but knew they'd succeeded. The news report confirmed it and that someone was in custody. ANTIFA had a bail and legal defense fund. Having his people arrested for murder was a minor inconvenience. Once out on bail, Scroggy and Viper would fail to appear. Other chapters of ANTIFA would help them craft new identities. The cops wouldn't do diddly. The city council had made it clear that ANTIFA was a protected class.

Still no word on the Faye Weldon broad. The pair that had gone after her never reported in, nor was there news about her death. They could be taking a long time to dump the body. He sent a drive-by to Weldon's house but there was no sign of his people, or reporters. If she were missing, it would be in the news. *The press loves to paint themselves as victims. Even though Weldon was conservative, they would be running with at least some coverage.* He assumed she was dead, and no one had discovered the body.

ANTIFA had always been about violence. Schumer didn't think they went far enough. Cracking the heads of counterprotesters was fun, but it was a half measure as far as he was concerned. If they were going to bring down the government, ANTIFA would have to up its game. It wasn't enough to destroy someone's life. *Once we show the other chapters that murder is the ultimate intimidator, they will adopt our tactics.* He anticipated a new level of terror. *Capitalism and the US government won't be able to resist us. Too many prosecutors and politicians support us. They find our terror useful. They can all hang. When they do, we'll be on top.*

The murder of Albert Gorelick had netted Schumer what he needed. The location of Braxton's hideout. They rooted through the old man's house for two hours before they found it. GoogleEarth showed a small cabin, miles from the nearest residence. His men would have free rein.

You chose a poor location, Dr. Knox. All those trees for cover. No one will even know you're in trouble, let alone come to your aid.

Tyler Thompson knocked on the door. He smelled of freshly smoked weed and his bloodshot eyes indicated stress. His man-bun was scraggly. Tyler knew that Knox wanted him dead for the death of his wife. He wanted to run, but Schumer assured him they would deal with Knox first.

"Did you get word out to everyone?" Schumer said.

"Yeah. Still no response from Cox and Kelly. It took me a while to track down Fister, but he's in."

"Good."

"What's the plan?"

"Pretty simple. He's up in the cabin," Schumer said, pulling up the images on his phone. "We go in at midnight. We cut the power, blind him if he's awake. We'll come in at every angle. We'll set the place on fire. When he comes out, we gun him down, and toss his body in the fire."

"Aren't you worried that the fire department will come?"

"No. It's isolated."

"What if he calls for help?"

"I checked with AT&T. I told them I was going to rent a cabin and needed connectivity and they were more than helpful. The good doctor has put up his own personal signal booster, his own cell tower essentially. They even showed me on a map where it was. We'll take out his tiny cell tower that services that mountain right off the bat. He won't be able to make any calls."

"I remember the news report from when the FBI raided his house, the one where his daughter was killed. He had a pretty big cache of weapons."

"It won't do him any good. We'll have his place surrounded. He's just one person. It doesn't matter how many guns he has. He'll either stay inside and shoot, and die in the fire, or come out and we'll cut him down."

"Everyone is pumped about this."

"What about you?"

Thompson didn't speak for a few moments. "I was pretty shaken when I found out that Knox had come to one of our meetings. I mean, he was right there. If he had wanted to, he could have opened up on us."

"You were in the car with me that night," Schumer reminded him. "If he wants any of us dead, it's you and me."

"That's been on my mind. I never understood why we had to go after his wife. I mean, our beef was with him. Running his wife off the road just served to piss him off."

"Knox needed to feel pain. He's ex-military. It's hard to make those Nazis feel pain. We had to hit him where he was weakest and that was his family. Remember us talking about that?"

"She didn't have anything to do with him not using the right pronoun though."

He's feeling guilt. That's probably why he's high all the time.

"Your problem is that you're thinking of Mrs. Knox as an innocent person. Let me assure you, she wasn't. She married him, didn't she? She knew the kind of person he was and wanted to spend the rest of her life with him. All we did is make that interval a lot shorter for her. She could have left him, or tried to educate him into thinking correctly, but she didn't. Well, after tonight, the two of them will be together again."

His words seemed to give Thompson some focus. "Yeah. It'll be a relief when he's dead. I'll be able to stop looking over my shoulder or dancing around when I'm pumping gas. I've had a hard time sleeping for weeks."

"Lay off the weed. You need to be on your game tonight. I need everyone sharp."

"Right. You sure this will all be behind us after tonight, right?"

Schumer held up his fist and Thompson bumped it. "Yeah. After tonight, we won't have to think about Braxton Knox ever again."

Chapter 49

New Sheriff in Town

Special Agent in Charge Sonya Turner winced at the smell of decaying flesh, so strong it made her eyes water despite the mask. An agent took a photo of Rocky Forsyth, focusing on the entry wound. Another agent marked a place on the wall where the bullet lay embedded.

Looking around Rocky's digs, Turner noted its opulence. Most FBI agents didn't come from money and didn't get paid a lot. The expensive furnishings made her wonder if Forsyth was on the take.

She remembered the night the Knox girl had been killed. Forsyth and Hayden had panicked. Hayden didn't say much but Rocky kept saying, "She was reaching for a weapon, right? You saw it, right?" Turner shook her head. "No. What I saw was you two firing at her."

Days had passed before anyone noticed Forsyth was missing. The local sheriff's department had done a welfare check and had broken down the door when they smelled the stench. Based on her experience, after the autopsy, they would only get a vague date of death.

"It looks to be open and shut," Agent McCreedie said. "Suicide note on the table next to him, bullet to the head, probably fired from the victim's gun. I know Rocky's handwriting, and that's it on the note. There are powder burns. It was fired at close range."

As far as the FBI was concerned, Agent McCreedie was right. An agent, on administrative leave for killing a young girl, a chronic drinker, overwhelmed with guilt, blew his brains out. An open and shut case.

Turner suspected something else.

Rocky Forsyth's partner, Frank Hayden, had died in a hunting accident—probably before Forsyth's so-called suicide. That was still open. The shot had come from a long distance. It looked as if someone else was hunting and had fired and accidentally hit Hayden. No one had confessed to it. Two hunters had been found two miles away, but they couldn't be linked to the random shot. It didn't make sense that they had been responsible. Most hunting accidents, the person that fired the gun steps forward. No one came forward, despite the press.

Their search found nothing. Ballistics didn't have much to go on. The question that she posed was simple, "Who wanted him dead?"

Braxton Knox came to mind. The investigation yielded nothing. There was nothing digitally or otherwise that placed Knox anywhere near Hayden when he died. An unsolved murder, destined for the cold file.

A cold case and a suicide of the two men that had killed Angela Knox. Coincidence? It appeared so. They would lift prints from Rocky's home, but she knew that Braxton Knox's fingerprints would not be found. He was smart enough not to leave any forensic evidence.

That was why she had given him the names of Hayden and Forsyth.

The Bureau had lost its way. Their focus had been a threat of domestic terrorism that didn't exist. They set up Americans who would never consider breaking the law. Then they arrested them. They, along with DHS and the US attorney, twisted and warped the law to fit a political agenda. It was beyond wrong for Sonya. It was against every reason for which had joined the FBI.

It would have been easy to quit. A lot of good agents did. They didn't want to be part of a corrupt organization that created the crimes it solved. That wouldn't make things right. Sonya knew the Bureau had to be reformed from inside out. That meant staying and fighting a covert war against the depravity she witnessed daily.

When the movie *Richard Jewell* came out, she had been amazed at how the FBI and the media had been portrayed as colluding against an innocent man. Back then, she had still been idealistic about working for the FBI. When she got in, she saw the agency's cancer up close. Despite everything that had been made public, people still had faith in the Bureau.

That will change at some point. They will need people like me in here when that happens to pick up the pieces.

Sonya knew people talked about her behind her back. People loved to complain about their superiors. Others thought it unfair she'd been promoted. She got her job because of diversity, inclusion, and equity. They never said it out loud, but she'd gotten Durston's job despite other agents having more experience and years of service. They suffered from being male and white.

Durston was the scapegoat for the Knox affair, shipped off to another city. Despite costing the government millions, Rainsong had been spared. Part of Turner's new role was working with the US attorney. It was part of her penance for giving Knox the names of two agents who were now dead.

Stepping outside, she pulled off her mask and let the cool air hit her face. The ambulance pulled up. She felt sorry for the job they had to do. Every dead body was hard to deal with, but one that had been fermenting for days was worse.

A mountain of reports needed to be filed. Suicides in the Bureau were rare. The Behavioral people would go over everything about Rocky's past performance in an attempt to determine why he had killed himself. In the end, they would claim it was inconclusive.

If it was Braxton Knox who had killed Rocky and Frank, he had done it right. Neither had suffered. Both got what they deserved.

Godspeed, Mr. Knox.

Chapter 50

The Alamo

Barney called Grayson in the morning. "Everything's going to be alright."

"Did he give you any details?" Braxton said.

"He didn't have to. If he says everything is fine, it's fine, son."

Faye and Ronin asked for a rundown. Grayson told them what happened. Faye took notes.

"What are those notes for?" Grayson said.

"My book."

Ronin nursed his coffee. "It could have been a lot worse."

"Tell me about it. No offense, Dad, but the geriatric brigade did end up shooting one of them in the foot."

"Something tells me that you would have done a lot more to both of them if me and my buddies hadn't been there."

"Can't argue."

After breakfast, Braxton walked them through the defenses he'd put around the cabin. Monsieur tagged along, tongue lolling.

"You've been a busy little beaver up here," Grayson said when they were done with the walk-through.

"I assumed they might track me down. I just wish we had more time."

"This is all so violent," Faye said.

"They were going to kill you, remember? All you did was interview Ajax. These people are monsters. They dream of violence. Most settle for destroying people's lives with slander and innuendo, but given the chance, they'll kill you in a heartbeat."

"Are we any better than they?"

"Ordinary people are consumed with making a living, taking care of their families, and kicking back on weekends. Maybe watch a little football. But there's a certain class of people who spend every waking second scheming how to gain power over others.

"They started this war. They had a problem with me. For using the wrong pronoun. They killed my wife. For using the wrong pronoun. The university got the FBI to come after me. For using the wrong pronoun. They said it was a civil rights issue. They murdered my daughter in her bed. For using the wrong pronoun.

"They never expected I'd fight back. They're used to people rolling over and playing dead."

Faye leaned on the ladder that led to the loft. "Part of my upbringing was in the church. The Bible talks about an eye for an eye, but when you're there, watching it happen, you question things. It helps to hear those words—to know that what I'm doing is right."

Grayson leaned on the porch rail. "I lived my entire life thinking the Bureau and the Department of Justice were beyond approach. They killed my granddaughter. They went after Brax. The whole damn system is corrupt."

It's got to be hard on him to find out that everything he worked so hard for in his life has rotted from within, Braxton thought.

Ronin nodded. "When they got my kid brother to kill himself because of the shit they posted online, I went after them financially. I ruined them. But it's not enough. I don't know if it will ever be enough."

Braxton opened the front door. "Let's go over the plan."

They gathered around the kitchen table. Braxton had drawn a map with the cabin in the center. "They're coming around midnight. We're self-sufficient in terms of power, but we're going to douse the lights."

Ronin pointed at the map. "The security cameras will pick them up along the perimeter."

"They'll have numbers on their side," Braxton said, "but not experience. This is a log cabin, so unless they get a lucky shot through the windows, the wood will absorb the shots. We'll open the windows to keep broken glass to a minimum."

"We recovered their radios," Ronin said. "If they use them, we should be able hear. They'll have some cheap-ass night vision gear too."

"Sounds formidable," Grayson said.

"We want them close, but not too close," Braxton said, poking his finger at the map. "The booby traps mark where we want to engage. We have some bear traps set, a log dead drop, and pits with spikes in them. That will throw them off. If they get too close, I've set up three buckets packed with Tannerite and nails." He pointed to the map.

Ronin held up a phone. "The explosives can be set off from these phones." The flip phones were marked "front," "boulder," and "rear." "All you have to do is hit send."

"Wow!" Faye said. "It's like going to war."

"Would you like a pistol?" Braxton said.

Faye blinked. "Me?"

"Yeah. Just in case."

She frowned, clearly thinking it over. "Better give me one."

Braxton reached in his pocket and pulled out a five-shot .38 caliber Taurus. "Okay. Real simple. You point and squeeze the trigger. There's no safety. It's got a pretty hard pull so it won't go off by itself."

Faye held it in her hand, turning it this way and that.

"Have you ever fired a gun?"

"At someone? No."

"Well, let's hope you won't have to."

"They tried to kill me once. It won't happen again."

"We'll jam their radios," Ronin said.

Faye's forehead wrinkled. "How does that work?"

"I've got a lot of tunes that we broadcast on their channel. They won't be able to communicate."

"What's the playlist?" Braxton said.

"Seriously?" Faye said.

"I want to scare them. Music blaring out of our speakers and their radios will rattle them. We'll lead off with 'House of the Rising Sun.' Then 'In-a-Gadda-da-Vida,' 'Hot Hot Hot,' 'Won't Get Fooled

Again,' 'Ballad of a Thin Man,' Buffalo Springfield, 'For What It's Worth,' and 'Street Fighting Man.'"

Braxton grinned. "Excellent. I'll be outside in my ghillie suit. We'll hit the strobes. They won't see shit."

"What about us?" Grayson asked.

"We'll need suppression fire. There're the guns, magazines are loaded, keep them pinned down. Avoid exposing yourself. Don't let them in the cabin."

"You're going out there by yourself?" Grayson asked. "I'll go with you."

Braxton shook his head. "No, Dad. I need you to defend the cabin. I have good thermal gear and a sniper rifle. They won't be expecting anyone on the perimeter. I can pick them off one at a time."

"Some are going to run," Grayson said. "Everybody's got a plan until they get punched in the mouth."

"Ronin will watch the cameras," Braxton said. "When the dust settles, I'll track down whoever's left."

"We'll need to park the cars somewhere," Faye said.

"Good point. There's a clearing back down the access road. It's not visible from the road, especially at night."

"That'll work," Grayson said.

"We need to be flexible. You probably know the old saying, no plan survives contact with the enemy. There's going to be a twist or two that we haven't planned. That means adapting to the situation."

"Davy Crockett at the Alamo," Ronin said.

"Everyone died at the Alamo," Faye said.

"Right... I forgot that part."

Grayson smiled. "More like the Battle of Rorke's Drift."

"What's that?" Ronin said.

"You've never seen the movie *Zulu*?"

"Is it good?" Ronin asked with genuine interest.

"When we are done with this, you and I are sitting down and watching *Zulu*."

"This is more like Helm's Deep," Braxton said.

Ronin smiled. "Hell, yeah!"

"It was from one of Angela's favorite books. We read *The Lord of the Rings* together. Desperate odds, valiant heroes. If I'm putting my life on the line, it's not against the Mexican Army or Zulu warriors. I'm going up against an orc horde."

"Never read the books or saw the movies," Grayson said. "It's your show. *Helm's Deep* it is."

Ronin looked at Grayson. "If I have to watch *Zulu*, you have to see the full director's cut of *The Lord of the Rings*."

"I'll bring the popcorn," Faye said. "Assuming, of course, we survive this."

Braxton smiled. "Don't think that way. Humans have a way of thinking about something and making it happen. We're gonna do more than survive. We're going to conquer."

"Because we're prepared?" Ronin asked.

"No. Because we must. Our opponents are vicious children. They will be completely unprepared for what we offer. I spent years teaching kids the epic sagas of good versus evil. Now I'm living one. It might not be worthy of Greek lore, but it's a good story."

Faye looked around. "So, what I heard was blah, blah, blah, popcorn, wine, and movies."

They laughed, knowing it would be the last of levity for a while.

Chapter 51

"The Calm Before the Storm"

Night came early in the mountains. Braxton offered the bedroom to Faye. He would sleep in the loft. The sofa converted into a sleeper, and the other sofa was longer than Ronin.

"Get some sleep," Braxton said, gripping the ladder. "Don't worry about a sneak attack. We'll have plenty of warning."

The loft had a skylight and a window looking out on the back, at the mountain. He lay in bed, staring at the stars. Someone flushed the toilet. Polite murmurs from below, then silence. Braxton wondered if the others were having trouble sleeping too. It was hard to sleep on the eve of battle. He'd learned that in Afghanistan. Not that he was on the front lines. The only time he saw combat had been wild shots into the shitters. The terrorists didn't care who they hit, they just wanted to hit someone. Now he was about to be in a war, protecting his homeland, killing bad guys. *This feels right.*

Braxton had repeatedly volunteered to go on missions. He'd been trained like every other soldier, but Major Halstead, who was in charge of their base in Fallujah, always said the same thing. "Sit your ass down. You're not going anywhere. Take a letter."

When he got home, Angela told him, "I'm glad you didn't go on any missions, Daddy."

A pang of grief pierced his heart and he found himself crying. He thought about what the night would bring and his sorrow turned to anger. Slow burn. They were coming. He could hardly wait. He knew he wasn't going to sleep, so he turned a bedside lamp on and picked up *The Two Towers.*

"War must be," said Faramir on the page Braxton read, "while we defend our lives against a destroyer who would devour all; but I do not love the bright sword for its sharpness, nor the arrow for its swiftness, nor the warrior for his glory. I love only that which they defend."

There was a poetry to Tolkien's prose that was hard to deny. He let the novel pull him in to the exclusion of all else. He was just on the cusp of the Battle of Helm's Deep when the sensor alert on the small table chirped.

Silently, he pulled on his trousers, wool socks, and combat boots and pulled out a burner phone to check the cameras. A blurry infrared image showed two people advancing from the south, up a deep slope. A quarter mile away. Braxton and his crew had plenty of time to prepare. He looked over the rail at the main floor where Grayson stood, pulling on a sweater. Ronin sat on the sofa checking his Ruger.

Braxton climbed down and picked up his AR. The lights were off. They worked by starlight. There was little point using the Accuracy International under these conditions. They would be fighting at close range. Ronin moved to the table where he'd set up two screens. He brought up images from the four cameras. Hostiles approached on all four cameras.

"I count nine," Ronin said softly. "No, make that ten."

"Let's get outside before they get here," Grayson said. "I'll set up in the buzzard's nest." That's what he'd dubbed a blind they'd put together out of boulders, a hundred feet from the cabin.

Braxton slipped into a dark blue hoodie, pockets heavy with ammo. "I'll go out the back and take up position behind the woodpile. That way we'll be out of each other's line of fire. Also, please hold your fire until I fire first. I want to take them out silently if I can."

"With what?" Grayson said.

"The deadfall for starters. Also, if they step on the punji sticks, they'll cry out, which will help us locate them."

Faye appeared in the bedroom door wearing a terry cloth robe. "What's going on?"

"They're here. They're approaching the cabin," Braxton said. "Go back in your room, turn off the lights, stay away from the windows, and lie low. You got your gun?"

She reached into a pocket and pulled out the gun.

"In terms of going to my room, that's not happening," she said. "My ass is on the line already. I'm fighting with you."

For a fleeting moment, Braxton heard his wife Suzanna speaking. *She is here with me, if only in spirit.* "Good girl. Okay. I got Cell Phone One. That's the Tannerite on the east side. Ronin, you've got Two. And Dad, you've got Three. That's the south side. You know where the bombs are. Wait until you see them at the bombs, okay?"

"Got it," Ronin said.

"Takes me back to 'Nam," Grayson said. "Only a hell of a lot drier."

Monsieur seemed to sense the excitement. Braxton bent down. "Stay." The bulldog looked disappointed.

"Let's go," Braxton said, slipping out the back door. He screwed in two hearing aids he'd bought for ninety-nine dollars. They amplified sound so that the forest clicked, rustled, and hooted. It was cold on the mountain. In the thirties. Braxton pulled the wool cap tight beneath his hood and went to the woodpile. The woodpile was covered with a tarp to keep it dry. He crouched behind the woodpile, peering through a saddle gap. It was possible the intruders could pick him out with infrared, but his shielded face was small enough they could easily mistake it for an owl. He set the phone on a tree stump and dialed in the camera he'd placed behind him, with a ninety-degree view of the approach to the southwest, including the cell tower.

The Tannerite bombs consisted of five-pound pouches packed with nails, each with a printed bull's-eye. Of course no one could see the bull's-eye in the dark, but it didn't matter. They knew exactly where each pouch lay because they'd marked each with a broad X of faintly luminescent paint. Not bright enough to attract attention, but bright enough to be sharply visible through UV lenses. Braxton's headset had both ultraviolet and infrared. Ultraviolet was mostly useless in the dark. But not in this case.

Braxton heard the creak of wood. He rotated the camera. Two interlopers scrambled up the cell tower they'd made a prefab fire lookout. They used wire cutters to detach the antenna and throw it to the ground. There went his remote control over the Tannerite. They'd have to detonate them with rifles.

Braxton switched to UV and scanned his field of fire. The intruders were a hundred feet from the nearest Tannerite bag, which they'd placed adjacent to a game trail that led to the cabin. Someone approaching in the dark would follow the same trail. They had no reason to expect a trap. As far as they knew, Braxton and company were clueless. None of these brave members of the proletariat had combat experience. What little they knew they had gleaned from *Red Dawn*. The remake, not the original.

Braxton switched to another camera. Three infiltrators advanced through the trees toward the clearing above which hung the deadfall. The infrared was sharp enough to reveal they carried AK 47s. *Of course they are carrying AKs. Good communist weapon.* Invented in 1947 by Mikhail Kalashnikov, Russian general and military engineer. His last words were, "The pain in my soul is unbearable." The junior revolutionaries had no idea. They just knew the gun was cool.

They approached the deadfall. Braxton had a split second of indecision. To end the life of promising young men and women or not?

Fuck it.

They weren't there to pursue higher education. The assassins stepped into the clearing.

Braxton waited, finger on the button. His signal would cause a solenoid to release the log. There they were, lined up one by one in the clearing. Braxton pressed the button. There was an all but inaudible click and then the 250-pound log swooped down, suspended by chains at either end, deadly spikes leading.

Chapter 52

Boyz in the Wood

A scream pierced the still of the forest. Braxton tried to make sense of what he saw on the screen. The massive log gyrated at the end of its chains, a body hanging from one of the outside spikes. A body writhed beneath the log, moaning in agony. The dull outline of a third invader froze, then leaped back.

Braxton wondered if he'd made a mistake not occupying the crow's nest in the cell tower. It would have raised him eight feet above the ground. But he would not have had access to the camera feed. The body at the end had stopped moving. Dead. The rebar must have pierced a vital organ. The survivor stooped to drag his, her, or its fallen comrade off to the side, pulled out a flashlight and turned it on.

"Put that out!" someone snapped. "Fucking idiot!"

Grayson texted, Two approaching Tannerite 2.

Braxton texted Grayson and Ronin. They took down the cell tower. We'll have to detonate with bullets.

No prob. Somehow, Ronin was keeping their texts functioning... probably using a boosted internet signal from the cabin.

Two more approaching Tannerite 3, Ronin texted.

Take the shot, Braxton replied.

All was quiet save for an owl bustling overhead in the branches. Grayson's rifle cracked the night, followed by a deafening report. Braxton knew it was his dad from the direction. A man screamed in agony. No shot came from Ronin.

Braxton came out from behind the blind, AR over his shoulder, holding the 1911 his father had given him when he'd shipped out thirty years before. He held the pistol in both hands, night vision on, as he approached the deadfall. He didn't want the survivor getting any ideas. The punji traps were marked with iridescent paint on nearby rocks. Each mark was no more than three feet from the trap. Thus far, none of the invaders had stepped on the spikes. They knew from the screaming and rifle crack that they'd been detected. Perhaps they would give up and retreat.

Of course not. They believed in their infallibility. They believed in their cause. They were the righteous ones striking back at the forces of darkness. He didn't want them to run; he wanted the fight. Braxton stepped carefully, avoiding downed branches and piles of leaves. He hadn't learned it in the Army. He'd learned it on this mountain, as a boy, when Grayson took him hunting pheasants. Braxton remembered the first time he'd killed one, leading it with his twenty gauge as it soared to the sky. *Blam!* A burst of feathers. The bird fell.

"Man, you nailed it!" Grayson had exclaimed.

Man, you nailed it. And here he was hunting humans. As he approached the deadfall, he heard voices.

"Jan, Jan, you've got to do something! The pain is unbearable."

"What am I supposed to do? Call nine one one? There's no cell service up here. Just stay put. We'll try to get this done as soon as possible. Then we'll carry you back to the car."

"What about Jonesey?"

"He's dead."

"Where's Ajax?"

"I don't know. Try your radio." Braxton fired at the source of the voice, lit up with his infrared gear, dropping him with a shot in his chest.

"Oh mannnn... they were waiting for us! We've got to get the fuck out!"

"No. You've got to shut the fuck up. It's just two guys. Three at most. There are ten of us."

Braxton did the math. Three down here. No word yet on how many Grayson took out with the Tannerite. Three if they were lucky. That left five active shooters. The odds were changing.

Shots plowed into the cabin with a *thunking* sound, erratic and deadly.

They got by me. Sorry, Ronin texted.

The invaders were now at the perimeter.

Turn off the night vision, Braxton texted. Here comes the light show.

He turned on the strobes and sound. "There is, a house, in New Orleans. They call, the Rising Sun..." the song's words echoed into the woods from massive speakers and blared from every radio that the attackers carried. The song echoed in the darkness, casting a creepy pall over the mountain. The night vanished in brilliant, pulsing light, stabbing out from the cabin. Someone screamed. Others cursed as their cheap night vision gear had been rendered useless along with their radios. Braxton smiled. *No wonder today's military was impotent.* Not that ANTIFA dreamed of joining up.

Braxton moved to grab the spiked punk and drag him back to the blind. As he headed toward the deadfall, shots rang out in a semicircle facing the cabin, penetrating the picture window in the living room, impotently embedding themselves in the thick logs. A shot took out the antenna on the roof. It skidded down metal. *Lucky shot.* He didn't believe they had any marksmen among them. Some of them had probably never fired a weapon. They had the hubris to assume they could take on ex-military with numbers alone.

Braxton moved through the trees outside the inner perimeter and came to the deadfall. The junior thug lay against a tree moaning, holding both hands to his chest. Braxton grabbed his rifle and hurled it into the woods. The man looked up. He appeared to be in his early twenties, shaved skull, nose ring, neck tat.

"Help me," he pleaded.

Braxton crouched. "Kind of ironic, don't you think? Didn't you come here to kill me?"

"Please. It was a terrible mistake. I'm gonna die."

"Did you have anything to do with the death of my wife and daughter?"

"No! That was all Ajax!"

"You weren't in the vehicle that ran my wife off the road?"

"No! I swear!"

"You didn't call the police and order a SWAT hit on my house?"

The young man started to cry. He was a boy, a child. Lights pulsed through the trees. Shots rang out. Braxton grabbed the man by his shoulders, hoisted him up, and threw him over his shoulders in a fireman's carry. Music drowned out the punk's groans. "In-a-Gadda-Da-Vida" morphed into "Hot Hot Hot." There were no neighbors to complain. There were no police to investigate. They might as well have been on the moon. Braxton effortlessly carried the fallen activist around the cabin and dumped him on the ground in the log blind. He couldn't have weighed more than a hundred and forty pounds.

Lights and sound cut out. Grayson shot twice. Braxton could tell by the sound of his rifle. He held a mini Maglite between his teeth while he unzipped the boy's hoodie and looked where the spike had gone. It had penetrated the punk's left abdomen. He pulled a bandanna from his hip pocket and placed it over the wound.

"Keep pressure here. You might survive."

"Thank you. Thank you. Please don't kill me."

"Is Ajax with you?"

"Yes. This was all his idea! He's with Salty. They were bringing up the rear."

"Of course they were."

"Please don't kill me! I swear I'll never talk about this! To anyone!"

"You have a come to Jesus moment?"

"What do you mean?"

"You think it's okay to kill people who disagree with your socialist utopia?"

"No! No! I didn't want to come. They pressured me into it."

Braxton thumbed through his wallet. "Nelson Broome. One four five Park Way, apartment two seventeen."

"Please, please don't kill me! I'll leave the state! I don't want to stay here. I want to start over somewhere fresh. I made a terrible mistake. I unequivocally condemn Ajax and his methods."

Braxton grinned. "Sure you do. Keep your yap shut. The jury's still out."

It was one thing to gun them down as they advanced shooting. It was another to kill them while they were helpless. He couldn't take time to deal with a wounded enemy while the attack was still hot. Kid might die anyway. Braxton didn't know what he'd do if he lived.

What's the kill count? Braxton texted.

Two confirmed dead, his father texted back. One more possible.

I have no idea, Ronin texted.

I'll recon, Braxton texted. Don't shoot me.

Braxton circled the perimeter, checking the punji spikes. The other three sites were undisturbed. "Approaching Tannerite One," he said softly into his phone. The bomb had gouged a hole in the forest, leaving a shallow depression surrounded by rock and root. Two black-garbed bodies lay in the hole. One's leg was blown off. The other's face was mutilated by nails. Braxton searched their pockets, taking two wallets and two pistols. The ubiquitous Glock 17 and a hilarious little Beretta .25 automatic. It came from the girl with the ripped open face.

Braxton spoke softly over his cell. "Ro, you and Dad meet me in the front yard. Move soft, move slow. Keep your eyes on."

Minutes later, the three of them converged in front of the porch.

"What's the body count?" Braxton said softly.

"I got three," Grayson said, "including the Tannerite."

"Maybe two," Ro said. "I think I hit one and he dragged himself into the forest."

"I got three, including the punji spike. I got one in the backyard. Says there were ten, including Ajax. He's gone. That's not bad. Eight out of ten. Ro, help me carry the wounded into the house. Got him with a spike from the deadfall. Looks bad. I ain't no doctor. I give him fifty-fifty odds on surviving."

Chapter 53

Ajax Gets Lucky

Ajax hotfooted it back to where he'd left the stolen Hyundai. It wasn't there. *I'll have to use a different car.* Randy "Salty" Jacobs had the keys for the backup vehicle. Thugs preferred to steal Hyundais because they were so easily hot-wired, but alas, those skills were beyond Ajax, who relied on others for the technical stuff.

He had been right next to Salty when a bullet shot hit him in the throat. Ajax wasn't ready for the gurgling and moaning.

This isn't at all how this was supposed to go down! That fucking professor is going to suffer for this!

Ajax had hoped for a little fight, but hadn't expected World War III. Some who had pledged to come didn't show. Still, the numbers were on his side. But Knox had been prepared. *What the hell were those explosions? We had the upper hand. This should have been a slaughter, Knox's slaughter!* The music blaring on their radios had made coordinating the attack almost impossible. *And that music, that old-school pre-rap shit!* He had been forced to shut off his radio just to avoid giving away his position. Joel wouldn't make that mistake again. How had they known he was coming? There had to be a rat in the organization. He would find him, her, or it, and make them pay.

At the car, he ditched his black balaclava and put on a bright white and red Portland Trailblazers jersey. His Glock disappeared into the kangaroo pocket. He hotfooted it back to the highway which, even at this hour of the night, had some traffic.

People who lived on the mountain were eccentric and did not keep city boy hours. Two cars passed him before an old F-150 pulled to the side of the road twenty feet down. A rear window decal said,

"Proud father of a US Marine." Country music played through the open window. Ajax ran to the side and climbed in.

"Thanks, man."

The driver wore a straw Stetson, had a white mustache, and chewed tobacco. "Hell you doing up here?"

"My car broke down."

"Well, I can take ya far as two twelve. I'm headed for Clackamas."

"That would be great. Thank you."

The driver reached for the radio, which had been lowered to a faint murmur, and turned it up. Toby Keith singing "Country Comes to Town." An in dash CD player. *Ugh.* Ajax discreetly examined the driver. Adam's apple the size of a cue ball. Plaid shirt, blue jeans, belt buckle the size of a dinner plate. Ajax was surprised there wasn't a gun rack on the back window.

"You a Trailblazer fan?"

"Well, they're the home team," Ajax said.

"Yup. Yup. I'm a football guy. I'm s'posed to root for the Seahawks, but I was born in Wisconsin so I gotta root for the Pack. It's the law. You born in Wisconsin, the Pack's your team."

Ajax knew nothing about football, except that Colin Kaepernick was a hero. Not wanting to be viewed as an intellectual, he said, "I gotta go with the Seahawks. They're the closest Portland's ever gonna come to a home team."

"Yup. Yup. I hear ya. You in school?"

"Yessir. Majoring in psychology at Eastern State."

"Psychology, huh?"

"Yup."

They rode in silence while Toby Keith sang. Ajax wondered how anybody could listen to that swill. After a while he said, "So your boy's in the Marines?"

"Yup. Doing a four-year stint. After he gets out, he's gonna open his own garage. They taught him how to be a mechanic."

"Can he fix electric vehicles?"

The driver barked. "No sir. They ain't gonna be around for long, that's for sure."

"Why do you say that?"

"Cuz the cost of replacing the battery is almost as much as a new car. Americans like to travel, and you can't go far in an EV. Try driving one across the country. You be better off with a Conestoga wagon. Besides, there ain't no shortage of petroleum. We just got a government that won't let us drill. Every decision they make seems planned to make the lives of ordinary citizens more difficult. They want our gas stoves. The morons want our gas cars. They want to take away our air conditioners. You got homeless vets living in lean-tos in downtown Portland while they're putting up illegal aliens in four-star hotels. Don't make no sense."

"I hear you," Ajax said, fingering the pistol in his pocket. *It's people like this that stand between us and the future we deserve.* They came up on a blind curve. The driver slowed to fifteen. When they rounded the curve, he stuck out his left hand. "My name's Earl, by the way."

Of course it is.

Ajax shook the man's hand. He had a grip like a stevedore. "I'm Ajax."

"You have any trouble getting to classes, what with all the demonstrations and such?"

"No sir. I just keep my head down and keep going."

"Good man. I never went to college. Went to a trade school. Learned how to be a carpenter. Thirty years ago I formed my own firm. Get 'er Done." Earl reached into the center console and handed Ajax a card showing a cartoon carpenter wearing a tool belt, hand on his cap, smiling, along with the contact info and the motto, "We exceed expectations."

Ajax tucked it in the pocket of his cargo pants. "Good to know. I hope to build my own house someday."

"How old are you?"

"Twenty-five," he lied. He was actually thirty-two, but looked young for his age.

"You wanna build here?"

"You mean in Portland? Why not? Portland's my home."

"Portland used to be a real nice town. Now look at it. Downtown's a ghost town. The city council has its head so far up its ass, it can see daylight. Homeless everywhere. It killed what tourist trade we had. I'll tell ya one thing. Those fuckin' homeless are dragging down property values so you could probably pick up a real nice place for ten cents on the dollar. Of course, then you'll be stuck in the middle of a third-world shithole, and you have to worry about squatters and thieves, and forget about callin' the cops. They made it so half the cops quit and the other half is afraid to do shit for fear of being labeled racist or sexist or some such shit."

"I don't look at it that way. I think a lot of these young people want to make things better. They see that the old way hasn't worked so they want to try something new."

"Like what? Decriminalizing shoplifting? Drug abuse? Place I used to live is now just a giant open-air drug market. I'm lucky I got out when I did. That was five years ago."

"You got family, Earl?"

"I'm divorced. Got two boys. The youngest is the Marine, the other's an oil roustabout up in Alaska. He's having trouble finding work since shit-for-brains took over the White House. Hey, I gotta make a pit stop. You just sit tight and I'll be right back."

Earl pulled off the road onto a gravel shoulder with a trash bin. Most of the road wound among trees or skirted the edge of canyons with no room for cars. Earl shut the engine off and pocketed the key. Ajax watched as he walked around the front of the truck, past the trash bin and entered the trees, where the land turned uphill. Quietly, stealthily, Ajax eased his door open, pushing the light button, then eased it shut with the same care. Pulling the pistol from his front pocket, he crept after the man who'd given him a drive, moving as he imagined a Native American might move, such as the Nez Perce or Walla Walla, whose culture he'd studied, flitting from tree to tree, shadow to shadow, until he saw his benefactor, pants unzipped, urinating on a cottonwood.

He jacked a cartridge into the chamber. Hearing the sound, Earl started to turn, zipping up his pants. Holding the pistol in both hands, Ajax fired twice, center mass, as he'd learned watching *The Unit* on television. Earl fell without a sound, his head landing on a rock. Ajax stooped and relieved Earl of his wallet, truck keys, and a folding knife. He stood, looking around for witnesses. He listened. Nothing but the sound of night, crawling over the dwindling impact of the shot.

Ajax hurried back to the truck and started the engine. Using the interior light, he examined the contents of the wallet. Five hundred and sixty bucks. All right. He put the truck in gear, pulled back onto the highway, and headed downhill.

Chapter 54

One Down, Two to Go

Braxton stalked his land, finding three bodies and trying to discern who he'd missed. The wounded had tried to flee, only to bleed out. As he moved through the pre-dawn darkness, he came across one survivor, a young man with a gut wound and a man bun. "Call me an ambulance," he growled as Braxton approached, pointing his ranging laser at the man's torso.

"What makes you think I'm going to do that?" Braxton said. He saw a Sig a foot from the intruder's right hand.

"Look, you Nazi-fuck," he muttered. "We came. We lost. Call me a fucking ambulance."

"I expected better than that from someone with a man bun."

"Screw you."

Braxton regarded the target in silence. "You people killed my wife. I didn't do a thing to you, but you tried to murder my friends, my family, and me."

"Spare me," man-bun moaned, trying to shift position. "When this is over, I'll sue your ass for whatever you have left."

Braxton laughed. "You try to kill me, get shot, and order me to get aid? Where's the logic?"

The man looked at his Sig Sauer.

Braxton could almost hear his thoughts. He smiled thinly. "I wouldn't try that if I were you. You make a grab for it and you're dead."

"It's dark as shit here. I'll take my chances. Fuck off!" He scrambled for the gun. His fingers found the barrel of the gun.

Braxton squeezed the trigger. A clap of thunder accompanied the sudden jolt of the man's body. He went limp. Braxton flipped up his night vision gear and took out a Maglite. Bending down, he checked the body and found a hemp wallet. Inside, he found a driver's license.

Tyler Thompson.

He'd been in the car that had killed Suzanna. Braxton's jaw set as he returned the wallet, then picked up the gun. The night had been brutal. But in the end, it had resulted in Thompson's death.

Where was Ajax?

He dragged the limp body towards the cabin, then combed the woods for signs of the ringleader. Ronin and his father checked Thompson's body. Ro told Grayson who it was.

The last trail was a blood spill leading down the mountain, fresh enough for him to follow. He never found the source. He found where ANTIFA parked their cars. On the way back, he found another dead body and dragged it up the hillside.

He made his way past the bodies in front and into the cabin. Gunfire had penetrated a few places, blowing through the chinking between logs. Inside, his friends and family looked weary. "Ajax got away," he said glumly.

"We still have that kid who's alive," Faye said. "He said his name is Nelson."

"He's a witness and that makes him a risk," Grayson said. Braxton was surprised. His father had dedicated his life to law enforcement.

"We're better than this," Faye said. "*You* are better than this."

Her words reminded Braxton of Suzanna. *That's something she'd say.* He was no longer sure that he *was* better than that. He didn't want to kill, but in most cases, it was the only conceivable justice. They started this. It began at the university and led to this standoff. Faye was right, there had to be a line somewhere. Maybe this kid was it?

Braxton stepped out to where Nelson lay. The blood had clotted but cracks of moisture oozed through. The boy was just a few years older than his daughter when she died.

"Where's Ajax?"

"I—I don't know where he is."

"You have all phone numbers and email addresses?"

Nelson nodded. "On my phone. The passcode is eight five zero zero." He fumbled with twitching fingers to pull out the iPhone. Braxton took it and handed it to Ronin.

"Would Ajax go to his parents?"

"I don't think so... no. He told me that he doesn't talk to them anymore. He's disowned them—said they were part of a corrupt capitalist upbringing. That's what he said. He told us when we joined that we needed to do the same with our parents."

"Did you?"

Nelson shook his head in shame. "I lied to him and the others. I love my parents. Just because they have different views on things doesn't mean I should abandon them. They're my family."

Perhaps there is something salvageable after all.

"My friend there," Braxton nodded at Faye, "thinks I should get you to a hospital. My concern is that you'll run to the police."

"I won't say anything to anyone! I swear."

"I think you would say anything right now to avoid me putting a bullet through your skull."

"I—well, I mean, no. I mean it. I won't tell anyone what happened here. I wish I hadn't come at all. The people I knew, they're all..."

"Dead. You can say it, Nelson."

"I was stupid to listen to Ajax and the others. They said you were evil. That killing you would send a message to anyone that crossed them."

"That didn't pan out for them, did it?"

"No."

"You seem like a nice enough kid. If you make me regret letting you go, I assure you, there will be no place that you can hide."

"Understood."

Braxton nodded to Faye. "Go get your car. We'll help you get him loaded. Take him in, drop him off. You don't want to get sucked

297

into filling out paperwork or having to talk to anyone about what happened."

"I can handle it," she said, heading for the door.

"What are we going to do?" Ronin asked.

"Dad and I will deal with the bodies. In the meantime, I need you to get on Nelson's phone and see if you can pin down where Ajax is."

Ronin nodded. Their long night wasn't over yet.

"I'm not sure I'm much help dragging bodies, son," Grayson said.

"I know. I need you to go to the car. Your buddy, the one with his own blacksmithing shop—go there."

"Why?"

"Coal."

"There should be a few bags of charcoal in the shed."

"We need real coal. While you're getting that, I'll set things up. We don't want to leave any DNA."

Grayson pointed at him. "Right."

* * *

Braxton was exhausted by the time he finished the in-ground oven. It was five feet wide and ten feet long. When his father returned, he packed in chunks of coal with firewood. Using chain drags, he pulled two of the dead into the oven, packed coal and wood around and beneath the bodies. "Make sure we pull their keys and fobs, just in case we need them. We gotta get rid of those cars too."

"This is messy work," Grayson said, hands covered with coal dust.

"We need it to be hot enough to turn the bones to ash. When we're done, we'll scoop up the ashes and dump them in the stream."

"It scares me that you know so much about how to evade the law," Grayson said as Braxton started the fire.

"Part of it is being the son of a law enforcement officer. I listened to you as a kid. Most criminals aren't smart—I learned that from you. I picked up some textbooks on forensic sciences, just to be sure."

"Well, *Professor*, this should work."

"The fire should burn well over the temperature we need. We can use the leaf blower to make it hotter. We'll drag in the other bodies when these are ash." He stepped away as the hole spewed smoke. It had the aroma of cooking meat, making his stomach pitch.

Braxton went inside to get a drink. Ronin worked on Nelson's phone with his PC that was jury-rigged into the satellite phone. The smell of fresh coffee drew him. He cradled the hot mug in his blackened hands. He took a sip and felt instantly better—more human. "You get anything yet?"

"That kid's contact lists were a gold mine. I've got queries running. So far nothing, but sooner or later, Ajax has got to surface."

"He can run, but he can't hide." Braxton's personal list of targets had dwindled to Ajax and Debbie Driggs. He closed his eyes and thought about his wife and daughter.

Angela, I made it through the siege of Helm's Deep. It's not over yet, but the end is in sight.

Chapter 55

Kamala

Braxton slept on the porch while the bodies burned. His father dozed on the couch. Ronin got a ladder, replaced the antenna on the roof and got his personal cell tower operating. Now he was crashed out in the loft.

The oven collapsed near the end. The leaf blower gave out two hours earlier. Rocks had cracked from the heat. Braxton felt the heat ten feet away. It would take a while for the coals to cool enough to scoop up the ashes. The odor from the fire, the burning of human fats and clothing, clung to the inside of his nostrils. Braxton dozed, his AR across his lap.

"Honey," Suzanna said. He saw her face in the dream. "Are you okay?"

"You bet, babe."

"You look like hell," she said with a smile.

"I'm fighting the good fight."

"Some of them were just kids."

"I know." Shame washed over the dream. "They brought the fight to us. I didn't have a choice."

"You always have a choice."

"I can't let them win. They took you from me."

Dream-Suzanna smiled brighter. "I know. I hate that they made you do this. You deserve some peace."

"I just want you and Angela."

"Don't worry, we are always with you."

The sound of Faye's car pulling in jarred Braxton awake. His body twitched as he was ripped from the dream. Faye looked tired.

Her usually vibrant pace looked as if she were forcing herself to walk. Wiping his mouth, he leaned forward in the chair on the porch. "How'd it go?"

"The kid told them he slipped and fell on a sharp stick. I got out before they could ask any questions."

"Not exactly your typical writing gig, eh?"

"You might be surprised. This isn't the first time some of these ANTIFA punks have come after me."

"Really?"

"A trio tried to jump me with baseball bats back in 2020. I had my head on a swivel... I saw them coming up behind me. Typical coward-shit. They were going to hit me from behind."

"What did you do?"

"Pulled my Ruger, spun, and took aim. One of the kids dropped the bat and ran. The other two told me there was some sort of mistake. I held them at gunpoint and called the cops."

Braxton nodded. He could feel the ache in his neck as he did so. "Did they end up in jail?"

Faye chuckled. "No. I got a citation for having a firearm in a no gun-zone. Can you believe that shit? Their parents and lawyers talked the prosecutor down to misdemeanors. A little fine and freedom. I wrote a story about it. At least it paid my fine and exposed those rat-bastards for what they are."

The front door opened. Ronin stumbled out. "I found Ajax."

"Where?"

"Kamala. Our friend Broome had Schumer's bank account information stored in a payment app. Ajax shook these kids down for dues and fees. He had quite a scam going."

"No surprise there," Braxton said.

"Well, the apps he used weren't PayPal or Venmo or anything that was trackable. It was written by some Albanians, lots of sloppy encryption, the kind of shit that terrorists use, only worse. Their code was crap. I backtracked it to get his account information. They cross-linked it to his credit card use."

There was an artistry in what Ronin did that intrigued Braxton, but there were more pressing matters. "So where in Kamala?"

"He checked in two hours ago at the Kamala Hotel, though it's really just a motel. It's a two-star place at best."

Energy shot through Braxton's body as he rose out of the chair and stood. "He's got to be stopped."

"Agreed."

Faye spoke up. "I'm going too."

"You should stay here, get some rest," Braxton said.

"This dickwad sent people to my home to kill me," she countered. "If you're going to take him out, I want to be a part of it."

Braxton looked to the smoldering ruins of the fire for a moment, then back to Faye. "Fine. He's not getting away this time."

* * *

Joel Schumer awoke in the hotel room and checked his phone. He had managed to get five hours' sleep. His joints protested as he moved. He went to the go-bag from his apartment and dug deep, finding a toothbrush and a small tube of paste. Brushing made him feel more human. Stripping off his clothing, he smelled the hint of spent gunpowder on them.

I'll have to throw these away.

After murdering Earl, he'd returned to his apartment, then headed north. Once out of the city, he felt safe. There was no way that Knox or his cronies could track him. He had paid cash for gas but the hotel had demanded a credit card, for incidentals. *What the hell could those be? This place is a dump.*

The hotel room was old. Near the bathroom, the carpet had a stain of unknown origin. He suspected that the room hadn't been rented in a long time. It smelled dusty. Joel showered. He felt better. The motel attracted hikers for the Blue Mountain Crossing Monument Trail. It was too cold now.

He had been cut from briar bushes outside of Knox's cabin during his flight into the darkness. He turned on the television. No mention about a massacre or shooting. Checking his phone, he found nothing. *Of course not. The professor would cover his trail. He would make sure that it never got into the news.*

Joel contemplated leaking the story himself. The pros: Knox would be arrested and Joel wouldn't have to flee. If he did it right, he could frame it so that he and his people were victims, lured into an ambush.

The cons were greater. There was no good explanation why almost a dozen had gone up to the cabin. There would be questions about their stolen vehicles and unlicensed guns. While the local sheriff was intimidated by ANTIFA, the same couldn't be said about Clackamas County. Giving the media a heads-up might just expose all his other activities.

No. For now, the professor can have his little secret.

His own plans were up in the air. He would head north to Seattle where there were other ANTIFA chapters. He could persuade them to help extract vengeance.

They will likely join in. The last thing any of them want is to be seen as vulnerable. It will take some time. If I can get enough people behind me, we'll run him down like a rabid dog.

Joel tossed his clothing into the wastebasket, stuffing them deep. Taking out his Berretta, he checked the magazine and saw that for all of the gunfire, he had only fired two shots. He smiled. *I could have sworn I fired more shots than this. Well, there are no witnesses to offer rebuttal. If asked, I'll say I emptied two magazines.*

It made him sound more heroic.

He stuffed his gear into his bag and slid the gun under his belt in the center of his back, throwing on a clean hoodie.

In just a little while I'll be in Seattle. Then I'll bring hell down on that fucking professor!

Chapter 56

The Sword of Hector

Braxton worried that Ajax might have left the motel before they got there. There were three cars and a truck in the parking lot. He knew he needed to confirm his target. Killing the guilty was easy. Killing innocents was something he wanted to avoid. Schumer had seen him face-to-face, as had Faye when he had interviewed him. Ronin checked if Ajax was still there while Braxton set up.

They'd dropped Grayson off at McKenzie Place. He'd wanted to come along, but the events of the last forty-eight hours had taken a toll. Reluctantly, Grayson returned to his room, dragging each step. "Tell me how it goes," he said, hugging Braxton.

Across the road from the motel was a pine-covered hill. Braxton used his range finder. The hotel was 732 meters away. Braxton used a pine log as a brace, placing the shot bag, and leveled the gun. A two-mile-an-hour breeze blew through.

Ronin went into the first floor office and came out minutes later. He trotted across the road and made his way up the hill.

"Any luck?" Knox said.

"Some. They did the usual 'We can't divulge the names of our guests' routine. It turns out she was more than willing to look the other way for a fifty-dollar bill. He's in room 105. That beat-up Ford truck is his."

"Not with that Marine sticker, it's not."

"Got to be stolen. You might want to send the plate to the cops. The owner is probably missing."

"Did the clerk get a good look at you?" Braxton asked.

"No. I wore a mask. Told her I had COVID. She backed away from the counter. I got a glimpse of their security cameras. One on the lobby, one on the vending machines, one on the lobby door. It's old hardware. All they got of me was a man-sized blur."

"Good call."

Braxton aimed the Accuracy International rifle at the door to 105 and rechecked the range, 741 meters, then double-checked the levels. Feeding new data into the Kestrel ballistics calculator, he made a series of minor adjustments to his scope.

"Faye," Braxton said in a low tone. "You watch for him. I want confirmation that it's him."

She put the binoculars on the door. "On it."

Braxton calculated. *If I shoot him as he comes out, there's a chance I'll only wound him and he'll retreat into his room.* Braxton had a good angle on the driver's side of the truck and reset his distance, adjusting the scope. *If I catch him at the truck but fail on a kill shot, I still have an opportunity to finish him off before he can get away.*

Distance was his ally. Even with the suppressor, there would be sound, but the surrounding trees would muffle the noise. The echo off the motel would bounce back to the forest, confusing anyone who might hear it. It was a typically overcast northwest day with a chance of rain.

They waited in silence, the faint aroma of pine in the air. He could feel the cool moisture bleeding through his camouflage pants from the bed of needles on which he lay. It was easy to ignore the strain on his neck and the wetness of the ground. Eliminating the man who'd caused the death of his wife and daughter filled him with anticipation.

Braxton tuned out the sounds and remembered his first date with Suzanna. They went dancing and she laughed at his clumsiness. When Angela was born and how frightened he was to hold her for the first time. The images swirled in his mind.

This isn't for me; it's for them.

He wiped the lone tear from the corner of his eye. Faye glanced at him and looked away.

Time oozed by. Braxton checked his Kestrel. The sun poked through a few times, only to disappear. Was it possible that Ajax had spotted them and had fled out the back? No. Ajax's room didn't have a rear access; it butted up against rooms on the other side.

The door to room 105 cracked open. A young man slid through the gap, letting the door close on its own. He held a black gym bag. It looked like Ajax through the TREMOR3 reticle.

"Faye, please confirm that's him," he said softly.

"Yes," Faye whispered. "That's Schumer."

Braxton drew a long breath and held it as he adjusted his aim. Ajax walked to the truck and opened the door, tossing his bag onto the passenger seat. He paused, casually looking around.

Knox let his breath out slowly. As much as he wanted to drill Ajax through the head, he aimed for center torso. He heard the pounding of his heart in his ears. Between beats of his heart, Braxton squeezed the trigger.

Themis kicked his arm. The bullet struck Ajax. A spray of blood misted the air, painting the truck's door.

* * *

An invisible force slammed Joel into the half-open door. His back throbbed, not from the bump, but something else. His legs went wobbly and his vision blurred. He tried to stand, but gravity pulled him down. He lost his grip on the truck and slid to the ground.

Joel saw blood splatter on the asphalt. He saw it on the truck.

He collapsed onto the pavement. He panicked. His chest felt on fire. Blood squirted from his chest. He struggled to inhale.

I've been shot! How could this have happened? I didn't even hear the shot. It had to have been Knox. How did he find me?

He saw the door to his room. *If I can get inside, I'll be safe.* He used his elbows and feet to crawl to the door. As a chill draped over him, there was a moment that he thought he might make it.

* * *

Braxton slid the bolt, chambering another round. He reacquired Ajax in the scope and saw that he had dropped to the ground. He wasn't dead, but from the blood, death loomed. He struggled to drag his wounded body across the cracked asphalt.

I will help him along.

Ajax pulled himself with arms, pushing with legs, trying to get back to the motel door.

He's a slippery bastard.

Aiming, he exhaled slowly, firing between the beats of his heart. The bullet hit Ajax's left buttock, sending a geyser of blood squirting upward. Schumer tensed, then slumped face down on the pavement.

Braxton stared through the scope, waiting to see if his body rose and fell. There was no motion.

He's got to be dead.

* * *

A boot kicked Joel in the spine. He went rigid. Darkness closed in. Agony. A pain unlike anything he'd ever felt, surged through him. Movement was impossible.

Mommy!

Blackness completed its journey.

* * *

"He's dead," Faye said, staring through her binoculars.

Braxton picked up the spent brass and put it in his breast pocket. Despite its weight, Themis felt light in his arms as he rose and grabbed his shot bag. He checked to see if he'd left any evidence he'd ever been there. "Let's get out of here." Walking briskly, he led his two comrades to where the Toyota was parked.

Braxton packed the rifle carefully, covering it with a moving blanket. There was a strange silence between the three of them as they set out for the cabin. Along the way, he turned his cell phone back on and called his father.

"It's done."

"I love you, boy," Grayson said.

The fire had finally died, leaving a thin wisp of smoke rising from the ashes. Braxton got out, secured his weapon, and headed for the door.

"So that's it? We're not going to talk about this?" Faye said.

Braxton wanted to talk, but didn't know what to say. Part of him was ashamed that he didn't feel worse about killing Ajax. The lack of guilt was strange. "What do you want me to say?"

"I don't know. It's not good for you to not say anything though."

"If you must know, I was thinking of the Ajax, the real Ajax, the Greek hero." They stopped on the front steps of the porch.

"Ajax fought for control of Achilles' armor with Odysseus. He lost. He went into a rage and eventually was driven mad by his failure. His shame was so great that he killed himself with the sword Hector had given him."

"I forget that you taught ancient history," Faye said.

"The empires of old are filled with tales of great heroes and gods. We could learn from them."

"You're not going to go mad and kill yourself, are you?" Ronin asked.

It was a fair question.

If you are insane, can you really tell?

"No. I'm not crazy yet and I have no desire to die. It just hit me that I am the sword of Hector. Our Ajax created the circumstances of his own death, much like his namesake. I was merely the instrument."

"Are you relieved?" Faye asked. "I mean, it's over, right?"

"Not quite. Debbie Driggs started it all. She was the first domino in this chain of events."

"And after that?" she asked.

"I'm not sure yet. I'm so focused on the next step, it's hard to see what the future looks like. I just know that I'm not done yet." He walked into the cabin for a much needed meal and rest.

Chapter 57

The Ashes of War

After a late breakfast, Grayson pulled up in his fifteen-year-old Lincoln. He helped gather the ashes of the dead in thirty-gallon plastic bags, taking them down to the stream at the foot of the mountain. Braxton felt uneasy. He hadn't set out to kill all those people, but they left him no choice. He watched the ash rush downstream with triumph mixed with regret.

Ronin worked on restoring communications and repairing damage to the security system. No one spoke. Braxton understood silence.

If we start talking, we'll talk about what happened here. We all feel guilty, whether it was earned or not.

He sat next to his father on the porch, looking out at the woods. Monsieur joined them. Braxton reached down and scratched the dog behind his ears. The bulldog grinned, tongue lolling. "You know, Dad, you said during the fight that it was like 'Nam. You never speak about your service. Even when I got back from the Middle East, you wouldn't talk about it. It was odd to hear you mention it."

Grayson's head hung low for a moment. He looked up and stared at the forest. "I'm not proud of what I did. I followed orders. Most of the time, those orders were justified. Not always though." His words came slowly.

"The Vietcong ambushed us, their usual hit-and-run shit. We got used to it. My squad chased them into a village. Hell, it wasn't even that… just a few huts. Damned place didn't even show up on the map or have a name. We didn't find a sign of the gooks that shot at us. My lieutenant and an interpreter went in, talked to the families.

309

They claimed they were innocent. My squad found a stash of weapons in one of the huts. They started cursing, lots of shouting. Someone fired, and when that happened, the LT told us to open up."

"Shit."

"I like to tell myself that they fired on us... that we were just protecting ourselves. You have to tell yourself those kinds of lies to get through life. We wiped them out, women, kids, everyone. Someone set fire to the village. Burned it to a cinder."

"Did Mom know?"

Grayson turned to face his son. "No. I never told her. She knew not to ask. I never told anyone."

"I appreciate you telling me, Dad."

Grayson nodded. "I guess it is time to say it out loud. We aren't that different, not after what went down here. In time, you're going to have to come to terms with all of this." He waved his hand where the battle had taken place. Silence stretched.

That afternoon they sat in the shade of the front porch. It was a rare warm day in late March. "We need to get rid of those cars," Braxton said.

"Whatcha got in mind?" Ronin said.

"Mill Park. We drive there, drop them off. The gangs and dealers will take 'em. If the police do stumble across them, they'll focus on the drug dealers, not us."

* * *

Mill Park was as ugly as Braxton remembered. A three-legged pit bull hobbled around a yard surrounded by a rusted chain-link fence barking as the cars cruised in. The dull gray Hyundai didn't need keys. Braxton had jammed a screwdriver in the ignition. Ronin tossed the ANTIFA phones on the floors of two of the cars before they left. They drove in a caravan, with Grayson bringing up the rear. Braxton stopped in front of the house where he had purchased the fentanyl.

The dealer who had sold him the drugs was on the porch and came down the steps. "I remember you."

"I'd prefer you didn't."

"You back for some more? Maybe a bag of bang bang?"

Braxton got out and closed the door. "Just parking cars."

The dealer got in his face. "You know, parking those things here isn't exactly the brightest thing. You leave 'em, here, those rides are toast."

"No prob."

"Just so we're clear. They aren't likely to last an hour. I don't want you showing up at my place with that sawed-off shotgun demanding answers. You park here, that's on you."

Braxton nodded. "I'm good with that."

The dealer cocked his head to the side. "You a strange dude, you know that?"

"So I've been told." He walked back to his father's car.

They pulled into traffic. "You've been down here before?" Faye said. "That's suicidal."

"It was risky, but worth it. My car was stolen, and I'm betting yours was too. The phones will tie the dealers to the kids, not us, as will the cars. If the police pick up on that, they'll assume that the missing ANTIFA kids came down here to buy drugs and the deals went wrong. No links to us or the cabin."

The drug dealers were scum. At least he left them doing business. He couldn't kill everyone.

"It's a little weird that you think through this shit so well," Faye said.

"Had to. I can't get Angela and Suzanna justice if I'm in jail."

"I understand. It's just so cold."

"I wasn't always this way. I was a history professor. All I wanted was a tenured position. I didn't kill anyone. I didn't break any windows. I refused to use a disturbed young woman's preferred pronoun. They made me like this."

They drove in silence for a minute.

"I don't know about anybody else," Ronin said, "but I could really go for a pizza."

"I know just the place," Grayson said.

* * *

The East Glisan Lounge was a hole in the wall, the kind of place that Braxton liked. Suzanna had always talked about them trying the pizza there, but they never got around to it. They'd assumed they'd have time. It was a lesson that Braxton had tattooed in his brain... *the future is far from certain. Live in the now.*

They got a booth in the corner. Grayson ordered a Detroit-style pizza. Faye and Ronin split a pepperoni with mushrooms. Braxton had a bottle of a Funeral Bock. The pizzas came and there was barely room on the table. They moved the plates to the next table, everyone eating off the pans.

The more they ate, the greater the sense of normalcy. Braxton only had one beer.

Ronin belched behind his napkin. "A man goes to the zoo," he said. "There's only one animal, a dog. It was a Shih-Tzu."

Grayson stared. Faye laughed, lighting up her face.

"That reminds me of my breakthrough story. I was a junior reporter for the *Boston Herald*. One day they were transferring a bear up from Rhode Island to the Franklin Park Zoo. The truck collided with some drunk and the bear escaped. Locals went crazy. The streets were empty except for this gang from Southie who thought they were in the Serengeti. They show up with their handguns. I interviewed them. One dude said he always wanted to go on safari. 'And now, safari has come to me.'"

"Did they get the bear?" Grayson said.

"Yeah. They found it in a tree in Harambee Park."

"Was that gorilla there too?"

Everyone laughed. For a few moments, Braxton forgot what had happened.

"What about Debbie?" Ronin said.

"The girl with the preferred pronouns?" Faye said.

"Yes. Him, her, it."

"Do you really need to go after her?"

Braxton looked around. No one was paying attention. "She set all this in motion. If it weren't for her, none of this would have happened. She could have just kept her mouth shut and realized she can't force the world to conform to her fantasies."

"But she didn't attack you," Faye said.

"She came at me on social media and the press. She posted the video, set the student body against me. Like some malignant party apparatchik. She went after my career with callous disregard for anything other than her wittle feewings. She started it all. She'll do it again. It's what they do. Given the chance, she'll destroy other people's lives. She gets a sense of power from it. I think it goes much deeper. With people like her, the terminally woke, they like it. No, they *love* it. Driggs will never see herself as an oppressor... her type have only one card in their deck, the victim card. This isn't just about justice for me and my family, it's about preventing this from happening to other people."

Faye leaned forward and said softly, "You're right."

Braxton turned to Ro. "When we get back, can you do a check on her, gather some intel?"

"I'll get you what I can."

Braxton glugged the bottle empty. "Groovy, baby. This one I do alone. The rest of you go about your business."

He waved his hand to get the waitress's attention and made a check motion in the air. The time was coming to bring this chapter of his life to a close.

Chapter 58

The Dog of War

Ronin called as Braxton was finishing breakfast. "Driggs will be in her place alone for the weekend."

Braxton sat upright at the small kitchen table. "How can you be sure?"

"She posted it on Facebook and Twitter. Her roommate is out of town for a wedding. She posted a picture on Instagram of a bottle of wine with the line, 'My Friday night is all set!'"

Ronin had given him her address and a Google street view of the small bungalow Driggs rented. In its day, it had been quaint and charming. That day had been in the late 1950s. For the last few decades, it had been a rental house for students. The paint was fading, the front porch rails falling apart. The yard was untended, scattered with garbage that the residents were too good to pick up. It was a corner lot. The house next door wasn't in use. Browning newspapers in plastic baggies were piled in front of the door.

Tomorrow was Friday. "Thank you, Ronin. One more thing. Does the house use gas or electricity?"

"I'll call you back." Ronin hung up.

Braxton patted Monsieur on the head. Monsieur looked up with devotion in his eyes. Suzanna used to have a similar expression. He missed that look in his life. "Monsieur, you and Dad are the only proof that I had a life before all of this."

The dog dropped to the floor and rolled on his side, resting his back against Braxton's chair. Reaching down, Braxton rubbed the dog's belly and watched as its bobbed tail wagged in response. It felt right. It felt normal, the kind of normal that was a rarity in his life. He didn't want it to end. Monsieur got up and went to his dog bed.

Braxton spent an hour digging bullets from the cabin walls, then drove down the mountain to Planet Fitness. He felt less pain than his last visit. He would increase his weights.

On his way home, he cruised by Driggs's place. The Google Street View image was a few years old. There peeling paint revealed gray, sun bleached wood. The pillar on the front porch had been replaced with a four-by-four that the owner had not bothered to paint. Hanging over the tiny porch was a fraying pride flag. No cars in the driveway.

As he entered the cabin, his phone chirped. It was Donna Craig, his attorney. "Hello, Donna," he said, sitting on the couch.

"I have some good news. The lead counsel for the university called. They would like to settle out of court."

I wonder if this has anything to do with two of their best witnesses being dead?

"I see. Is the offer good?"

"Six years' salary plus an additional hundred and fifty k."

He mulled it over. When it came to the university, it wasn't so much about the money, it was that they had buckled to Driggs. "Will they make a public statement?"

"No."

This wasn't like the negotiations with the FBI. The university couldn't go to trial without Kulberg and Grooper. "Then tell them I'll see them in court."

"I'll do that."

She knows not to question me on this point.

"Thank you."

"How are you holding up?"

"I'm getting by, day by day."

"I only ask because that ANTIFA leader, Joel Schumer, was found dead in a parking lot of some sleazy hotel."

"I hadn't heard that." Braxton had not watched the news.

"Someone shot him. He had a stolen truck."

"What a shame."

"My only reason for bringing it up, it might be interpreted as a pattern. Grooper kills himself. Kulberg's car catches on fire and kills her. Both of the FBI agents that were responsible for Angela's death are now dead. Now Schumer."

"I sense you wanting to ask a question."

"No," she snapped. "I might not want to hear the answer."

"Maybe it's just karma, Donna. That's how I see it."

She said nothing for a second. "I'm good at contract law and simple litigation. I'm not a criminal defense lawyer."

"No worries, I'm not a criminal."

"Keep on keepin' on," she said.

"Thanks, Donna. You too."

Ronin called. "I have that information you wanted."

"Fire at will."

"Debbie has a gas stove and furnace."

"Excellent. Thank you."

"Hey. Maybe I should come along."

"Not this time, Ro. You've done more than enough. I've got this."

"I've seen photos of this chick. Doesn't look like much of a threat, but you never know."

"I can handle it. Thanks again."

Braxton hung up and searched for local ether sources.

Chapter 59

Miss

Braxton parked three blocks away in front of an empty lot. His black backpack held duct tape, a bottle of ether, a screwdriver, rags, three spare magazines, a candle and lighter, and a pair of heavy duty pliers. He carried a mini Maglite and his Glock. He wore a Navy blue hoodie and black slacks. It was ten p.m. as he walked past her house. The lights were off in the living room, partially illuminated by the glow from her television. Somewhere in the distance, a bass thudded.

He checked the house behind her. No sign of activity. Either the people living there were gone, or were asleep. He learned from his father that the best way to observe was to not look like you were looking.

The evening air was cool, heavy with moisture. Braxton ambled the walk around the house, discreetly looking for cameras or police patrols. There were none. Two blocks away a student party blasted rap that flowed into the backyard of the house. Empty red Solo cups dotted the yard. The rap would mask whatever happened.

On his second orbit forty-five minutes later, he noticed that the TV was now off. Braxton hoped she'd enjoyed her wine.

He slipped into Debbie's backyard. There were two big bins near the back door, one for garbage, the other for recycling. From the aroma lingering in the air, he assumed it had been a while since the garbage bin had been rolled to the curb. He went up two concrete steps and tested the door. It was unlocked.

He slowly opened the door. Stepping into the back landing, he closed his right eye and flashed the Maglite. The stairs to the basement were in front of him, kitchen to the left. Braxton shut off the light and stepped onto the linoleum floor.

He shut one eye, allowing him to keep some night vision while the other eye adjusted. He waited. In the dim light of the kitchen, the kitchen was a mess. A stack of pizza boxes on the counter and dirty dishes filled the sink. The sink smelled as if the disposal was either broken or clogged.

He looked in the living room. The furniture was the kind students abandoned on the street when they moved. An empty wine bottle on the table, no glasses or cups. She drank from the bottle. *Classy.* Driggs lay on the sofa under a blanket tucked under her chins.

Braxton squatted and took off his backpack. He pulled the Glock out and held the Maglite. Shock and surprise were his allies. He wanted her to see it coming. He switched on the light and aimed it in her face.

Driggs held up a hand, attempting to block the beam. "Damn it, Trish, that's not funny."

"Trish isn't here," he said softly.

A flash of panic hit her face as she forced herself upright. "Who is that?"

He flashed his face. "Surprise."

Her eyes struggled to adjust. Shock distorted her face. "You."

"That's right, *Miss* Driggs."

"You fucking Nazi," she hissed, slurring her words. "You'd better get the hell out of here. I'll call the cops—I'll scream."

"If you do, I'll shoot you." Braxton showed her the Glock. Terror replaced panic.

"What—what do you want?"

"You ever see *Goldfinger*?"

"No! What does that have to do with anything?"

She would never appreciate the line anyway. "I'd like my life back. I'd like my wife and daughter back. I'd like to be in my old home, my old job, living the life for which I worked. Something tells me you can't give that to me. Am I right?"

"You can't just barge into my house like this."

"Evidence says otherwise."

Driggs comprehended her situation. "I don't want any trouble. There's no need for violence."

"How do you figure? What happened to my wife? What happened to my daughter? What happened to half the small businesses in town? I've lost everything. You gotta pay, *capiche*? First though, I want some answers."

"To what?"

"Why? Why did you do that to me? You knew I didn't deliberately misuse your pronouns. You filmed me, without my permission, and waged a campaign to destroy me online and with the media. Why did you do it, Miss Driggs?"

"People like you are the problem in our country," she fired back. "The only reason you had that job was because you're a white man. You wallow in your privilege then get all upset when people more deserving stand up to you. You needed to be taught a lesson. Highlighting your bigotry sends a message to anyone else who doesn't play by our rules."

Braxton cracked a thin smile and shook his head. "Don't lie to me, Debbie. I'm more than willing to shoot you."

"What do you mean?"

"Your rationale is bullshit. No one could be stupid enough to believe that, not even you."

"It's true!"

"You're a liar. Maybe the worst kind, the kind that lies to themselves. You want to know what I think? I believe you did this because you like attention. Maybe you have mommy or daddy issues, maybe you just have low self-esteem. I don't know. I don't care. You did what you did because it made you feel important. You like the power it gives you. People paid attention to you. You fed off of it. You love the limelight. Going after me was your moment in the spotlight.

"You think of yourself as a victim. You think being a victim somehow makes you heroic. It doesn't. Look at you, sitting here alone, chugging down a cheap bottle of wine and watching Netflix. I've seen your house. You have no dignity. When you look in the mirror, you hate how fat and unattractive you are, but don't assume

319

any responsibility for changing that. Instead, you eat pizza and go on social media attacking people who've done something with their lives.

"You embrace socialism because you want what other people have worked for. You think you're entitled to the kind of life people who work have. Socialism makes that possible without working for it. What separates us is that I own my shit. You want what I had in life without putting in any effort. It's worse than jealousy. It's ignorance devoid of personal responsibility."

Debbie said nothing. Tears rolled down her cheeks. "You don't know me," she said in a whiny tone.

Braxton snorted. "Oh, I assure you, I do. I taught you and hundreds of your so-called friends. I saw it all the time. You're so devoid of rational thought, you think that social media is the real world. It's your playground. I saw how you edited my speech so as to make me look far worse than I was. Social media was the only place you get any positive feedback. Your life is all about clicks and likes. Your online hoods pat you on the back for taking down a professor. You delude yourself that people who are your friends online are *actual* friends. Well, where are they, Debbie? Did any of them reach out to you to invite you over tonight? No. They left you here, by yourself with your wine and TV. You are so devoid of social skills, you won't even go to one of the local bars by yourself because you know you will be coming home alone and you can't face that.

"You curse your parents, blaming them for your shortcomings just like you did with me. In the end, when you have invested tens of thousands of dollars on a worthless degree and can't get a job, you'll slink on back home and demand they take you in. Tragically, they probably will."

She sobbed. "That's not going to happen."

"You lie to yourself so much you might actually believe that. Let me assure you, that was how things were going to play out for you."

Braxton let her cry for a moment, then she seemed to rally. Before she could respond, he said, "Tell me, Miss Driggs, did you call ANTIFA or did they pile on me and my family on their own?"

Her fingers were shaking as she wiped the tears from her face. "I attended a few of their meetings. I knew some of them, they were on campus. I called them."

"And they murdered my wife."

"I had nothing to do with that!"

"You set it all in motion. If not for you, none of this would have happened."

"You can't hold me responsible for that."

"Sure I can. You're going to experience personal responsibility tonight, for a change. Sadly for you, that lesson is coming in at the end."

Braxton bent his knees and reached for his backpack.

Chapter 60

The Quest for Calm

Braxton pulled the bottle of ether and two shop rags from his backpack. Debbie tensed up, despite the alcohol in her body. "What's that?"

"What's the passcode on your phone?"

"Why?"

"What is it?"

"One, nine, eight, four."

"Nineteen eighty-four." He shook his head in disbelief. "That's funny." He soaked the rag with ether. It felt cold on his hands.

"What is that stuff? It stinks!"

"Ether." He opened the bottle and soaked the rag. The smell made him wince. Setting the bottle down, he walked over to her. "Put this over your face and breathe deeply."

"I won't!" Her body squirmed on the couch, as if she could get away.

Braxton leveled the Glock. "I would like nothing more than to physically force you to do it. Having lost almost everything, I've gotten comfortable at taking risks, including shooting you in the hand or foot for persuasion."

More tears trickled down her cheeks. "I'm sorry—is that what you want me to say? I'm sorry! I'll never do anything like that again."

"We're far past the time for fake apologies." Braxton stuck the pistol in his belt. "Put the rag over your face, Miss Driggs. I promise you won't feel a thing."

She tried to fight, but she was weak and panicking. Braxton swatted her arms aside and used his open palm to force the ether-soaked rag over her nose and mouth. Driggs struggled, whining, trying to push him away. Braxton leaned in, grinding the rag into her face with his hand. She tried holding her breath. She gasped. The more she struggled, the more he leaned into her. She stopped, but Braxton didn't. He wanted to make sure she was unconscious and not faking. He enjoyed it. That realization made him stop.

He left the rag over her face as she slumped. Using his Maglite, he went to the musty basement and found the hot water heater. Gas, as Ronin promised. He removed the cover plate from the pilot light and saw the blue flame.

Braxton took the stairs two at a time. Driggs snored under the rag. In the kitchen Braxton rinsed off his hands. He turned his attention to the stove. It hadn't been cleaned in a long time. Pulling hard, he skidded it out on the floor.

He put out the pilot lights. The one in the oven wasn't working. Probably hadn't in years.

He rocked the stove side to side to get it to turn, to get to the gas line and electrical connections. He unplugged the stove, stomped his boot on the connection from the house gas line to the stove. It took three stomps to rupture. The line hissed with the nauseating aroma of gas.

Braxton returned to the living room where Driggs lay unconscious. He took her wine bottle and set it on the table. From his backpack, he pulled out the candle and jammed it into the bottle. While he was sure Debbie wouldn't wake before the gas reached the hot water heater, he wasn't taking any chances.

He found her phone on the coffee table. Entering her passcode, he went to X and posted, `The stupid stove isn't working. Now I have to fix it.` He closed the phone and set it on the table.

Gathering his gear, he put it in the backpack, making sure the ether was closed tight. No point removing the rag from Debbie's face. Ether was flammable. That evidence would never surface. He pulled out matches and lit the candle. The flame wavered, then burned steady.

Braxton went out the back door.

He walked to his car. Putting the backpack in the trunk, he got in the driver's seat. He adjusted the rearview mirror.

As much as he wanted to shoot her, there was a part of him that knew that no matter what, Driggs would never understand that what she had done was wrong. She was beyond reformation or even able to comprehend the results of her actions.

The minutes rolled by. *Maybe her roommate came back, or a neighbor smelled gas.* He didn't panic, but it made him tense. *If that were the case, I'd hear sirens.* The night was quiet. It was just taking longer than he expected.

The orange fireball appeared just before the massive boom that shook the RAV. Car alarms went off. In the rearview mirror, he saw a ball of orange and crimson flames rolling in on itself, rising into the night. A moment later, he heard the sound of wood rattling on the pavement behind him.

Braxton turned and saw flames roaring into the night. People stepped out of their homes, looking for the source of the explosion. Their eyes fixed on the ball of flames.

Braxton started the car and drove slowly. The distant echoes of sirens mixed with blaring car alarms.

As he drove toward the cabin, he was not remorseful. He was not the same person he'd been months earlier. He'd been a family man, a good employee, someone who enjoyed his job. Now his job was justice. Not only for himself, but for every innocent American who'd been destroyed by the mob.

The list of those that had crossed him was gone, burned and blasted into the night. *I should feel some sense of relief, but I don't. Why?* When he reached the cabin, he let Monsieur out and checked the security system.

He turned on the news and saw the news chopper footage of the explosion. There was nothing left. Burning bits of lumber landed on the neighbors' roofs. The fire department soaked the structure. The neighbors' windows were blown out. He felt bad about that. He never wanted the innocent to suffer. The banner at the bottom read, *Gas Explosion*.

Shutting it off, he rose and paced around the cabin. He felt as if he had slammed back several coffees. All wound up. It hadn't been this way with Ajax or the others. This was different. He took a deep breath and let it out in a controlled stream. Braxton felt his pulse slow. He did it again.

He thought about picking up *The Two Towers*, but his eyes fell on the stacks of letters sent to him. Albert had divided the letters into two stacks. Pro and con. Braxton went to the pro pile. One was from the family of a young girl that had tried to kill herself because of what her boyfriend had posted about her online—horrible pictures. The next was a Jewish student that was the target of anti-Semitic harassment on campus and had finally been forced to leave school because the administration had supported his harassers. All of them wished him luck, offered prayers, or simply wanted to tell their stories.

Somewhere after the tenth letter, Braxton slid into sleep.

Epilogue

What We Deserve

Three days passed in a blur. Sleep finally came. He had dreams of Faith and Suzanna, replayed memories from his life before it hit the wall. The rest did him wonders. He trimmed his beard to a goatee and mustache. The face he saw in the mirror was not familiar. He had lost weight and looked like he had when he'd been on deployment.

Braxton went to a jeweler in Portland to turn Angela's and Suzanna's ashes into titanium rings. He requested some special modifications. He didn't flinch at the cost or the long turnaround.

He kept busy cleaning up the cabin, going to the gym and starting his combat training. He repaired damage, extracting bullets from logs. He met up with Rudy and did some shooting. With no targets in mind, no list of those who needed his justice, he felt human for the first time since his nightmare began.

Donna called on the third day. Her negotiations with the university had come to an amicable resolution. They would issue a statement that his discharge had been in violation of his contract and settle for "an undisclosed amount." Braxton suspected that the untimely death of Debbie Driggs had been the final nail in the university's coffin. The money was nice, but the admission meant more. It was scheduled for the following week.

"No doubt the media will want interviews," she warned him. "If they ask, tell them to fuck off."

Faye told him that she had written an article about what had happened and wanted them to read it. She wanted his father and Ronin to see it as well. Braxton agreed. He invited everyone over and got steaks and shrimp for the grill.

There had been no sign of law enforcement after the death of Debbie Driggs. From what he read on the internet, it had all been chalked up to a home repair gone bad. Students held a campus memorial for her. He had almost been tempted to attend. Suzanna would have told him to move forward, not backward.

Schumer's death was still an active investigation. The sheriff's department said that in all likelihood, Schumer had killed the stolen truck's owner, driving it to the hotel where he had been shot. A trucker found Earl's body, and police connected him to Schumer through the pistol they found on Schumer. There were no suspects and law enforcement was asking anyone with information to come forward. To the casual observer, it sounded like so many other crime stories on the nightly news—bad people who had bad things happen to them. It would soon shuffle off to a cold case pile and be forgotten.

On a cool evening in early May, his guests arrived. His father was the last to pull in, driving his old Lincoln. Faye looked better than the last time he had seen her. Ronin looked good too, clean-shaven and wearing fresh clothing. They didn't talk about what happened. They laughed, drank, and joked. Braxton burned the shrimp. "I'm rusty when it comes to cooking for others."

As the sun set, they gathered on the cabin's porch. Monsieur sat next to him, huffing and puffing as Braxton rubbed the bulldog behind his ears. Faye went inside and came out with printed copies of her article. "This is just a rough cut, but I wanted you to see this first."

Looking at the page, Braxton drank in the words as if he were reading a paper for peer review:

"The Justice We Deserve"
Faye Weldon

A few nights ago, members of the local ANTIFA chapter broke into my home and attempted to kidnap me. Their intention was to take me from my home and murder me. When I saw them trolling by my house, I called a friend rather than the impotent county law enforcement. My friend had dealt with them before. They had tried the same stunt with him.

The same organization had tried to kill him and failed. They had murdered his wife. Law enforcement did nothing, much as they did during the 2020 riots. Indirectly, ANTIFA's injustices had led to the death of his daughter.

He came with his trusty sidekick, a modern-day Lone Ranger and Tonto. The thugs tried to shoot him. He killed them.

If you go looking for this story online beyond this article, you won't find it. The incident was not reported to the police. They would have arrested us for defending ourselves. The mainstream media didn't cover it. The story did not fit their narrative that ANTIFA was a peaceful student group. Yet I can assure you, it happened.

This wasn't the first time he had taken the law into his hands. He had been part of the effort that broke up the attempt to destroy Abe's Jewish Deli and the Korean BBQ in Lake Oswego.

Make no mistake, my savior and his colleague saved my life. ANTIFA tried to kill his father. A few nights later, almost a dozen of the same ANTIFA chapter members went after him. I was there. He wanted to make sure his father and I were safe. They came at midnight, with Molotov cocktails, guns, and a lust for our blood. This was no protest, no chanting, no professionally printed signs. This was an orchestrated plan to slaughter us.

They will never bother anyone again.

You may think this deplorable. This may rub your left-leaning morality the wrong way. Certainly the media will label it the work of a dangerous alt-right vigilante. They will craft their stories about him as examples of gun violence and paint him as a domestic terrorist. It couldn't be further from the truth. This is a good and honorable man. His actions were validation that when you push a good man too far, they move to protect themselves and the ones they care about.

Thanks to social justice warriors, this man lost his job, his family, his career, and perhaps his hopes of a future. He corralled his rage into action. Now he fights for those that cannot protect themselves. The measures he takes may be harsh in your eyes, criminal in the eyes of law enforcement, and heinous to the woke who fueled his wrath. Petty labels put on him by lesser people mean nothing to him. The contempt of those that have harmed him only makes him stronger and more dangerous.

As wrong as it may sound, we need this brand of justice. The laws we have protect the guilty and paint the criminals as victims. Law enforcement has become more interested in enforcing social measures than protecting those that need and deserve it.

You may think that vigilantism is wrong. I would contend it is the justice we need in these trying times. This is a man that fights

329

for those that cannot fight for themselves. Isn't that what we all want and deserve?

Many of you will scoff at this, write this off as the product of a fertile imagination. You have the freedom to do so. I know the truth behind these words because I was there.

I underwent a lot of soul-searching in the last few days. I faced death twice. Two times my life was saved by violence and conviction. It has forced me to examine my own core values. I had to put my definition of justice under a mental microscope and debate whether it was accurate.

My friend is not a comic book hero with a skull painted on his body armor. He's not the product of some elite military unit. In many ways, his armor is that he is every man, he blends in with the rest of society. A part of us all wish that there was a Jack Reacher or John Wick out there for us in our time of need.

All we need to know is that he is out there, doing what law enforcement and the shattered justice system cannot… delivering the only justice that really matters.

To those of you who have been attacked online and otherwise by the so-called social justice warriors, he is there for you. The only agenda he has is to protect those that cannot protect themselves.

And to the woke, the people who try to ruin the lives of others, know this. There are consequences to your activities. There will be no Miranda rights, no calling your mothers and fathers, no lawyer to arrange your bail. His

> justice is final. It is the only form of
> justice that ensures future tranquility. In
> times when freedoms are in jeopardy, his may
> be the only justice that counts... the justice
> we deserve.

Braxton lowered the article and looked at Faye. "You can't publish this. They'll come after you, then they'll come after me."

"I won't talk and they can't make me. Journalists don't have to give up their sources."

"You don't have to. They'll know."

"This will force the police to act," Grayson said. "And the Feds. They'll want to make an example out of us."

Braxton jumped back in. "You are practically advertising that I am out there playing vigilante."

"I've seen that stack of mail you got. Lot of people need help. Maybe we need a vigilante in the country right now."

Braxton shook his head. "Ix-nay. This would force the authorities to act, not that they need much persuasion. The only way you can publish this is to wait a couple years and pray that the situation changes. Put it in another city. Someplace on the east coast. People are sick of leftist bullshit. They're sick of being called racists. Work for regime change. That's the only way you can do it, and even then, you'd better think hard. The vicious left will never go away. They're drunk on power."

"Or put it in a novel," Ronin said. "Put it somewhere else, some other city. Make one up. Claim that it's a fantasy no different from all those movies about killing Republicans. *Death of a President*, remember that? How about *Vice*, the one about Cheney? You ever see a movie about a scumbag leftist? No. Because scumbags control Hollywood."

Faye made a face, her brow furrowed. "Are you just going to stop?"

"Why not?" Grayson said. "He doesn't need the money."

"There are people who need your help. You are in a unique position. There must be some way to reach those people."

"I can start with those letters. There are more. Lots more. People have been writing me for weeks. I haven't had time to go through them all. I want to help, but I can't do it alone."

"You're not alone," Grayson said. "I'll help you. My daughter-in-law and granddaughter demand it. It's got to be better than slowly rotting in assisted living."

"I'm in too," Ronin replied. "I'll have to clear it with my benefactor. I'm fairly sure he'll approve."

"Who is your benefactor?" Braxton asked.

Ro shook his head. "He likes his anonymity. Suffice to say, he's of a like mind on this."

"Someone has to chronicle this," Faye said. "Those letters are great stories. The best way to take down these woketards is to expose them to the public for what they are. Thugs, bullies, and worse."

Everyone looked at Braxton.

"For what it's worth, I had decided to go on without you," he admitted.

Faye put her hand on his shoulder. "And now you don't have to. We're in, all of us."

"I lost my first family, but I gained a new one." He finished his beer. The void that had been a part of his life had filled with purpose. "Let's proceed cautiously."

"Where do we begin?" Grayson said.

Braxton plucked an open white envelope, his name written in script, from the table. "This is from a family in Indianapolis…"

About the Authors

Blaine Pardoe is an award winning New York Times bestselling author who lives in Spotsylvania, Virginia. He is the author of numerous science fiction, military history, true crime, horror, and business leadership books. He is considered one of America's best writers about the Great War. His books have been published in six languages and he has been a featured speaker at the U.S. National Archives, the United States Navy Museum, and has appeared on numerous television and radio programs.

Mike Baron is the author of Helmet Head, Whack Job, Biker and Skorpio, four mind blowing novels that will change the way you feel about horror fiction. In 2018, Liberty Island will release six Josh Pratt novels in The Bad Road Rising series. Josh Pratt is a reformed motorcycle hoodlum who found God in Jail, got out, and became a private investigator. The stories are bleak, brutal, and harrowing, and often very funny.

Mike broke into comics with Nexus, his groundbreaking science fiction title co-created with illustrator Steve Rude. He has written for Creem, The Boston Globe, Isthmus, AARP Magazine, Oui, Madison, Fusion, Poudre Magazine, Argosy and many others. Nexus is currently being published in hardcover by Dark Horse. Baron has won two Eisners and an Inkpot for his work on Nexus, now being published in five languages including French, Italian, Portuguese, and Spanish.

He lives with his wife Ann and some dogs in Colorado.

Printed in Great Britain
by Amazon

56367112R00188